THE BELL FORGING CYCLE, BOOK III

Red Litten World

K. M. Alexander

THE BELL FORGING CYCLE, BOOK III
Red Litten World

Print Edition ISBN: 978-0-9896022-6-6
eBook Edition ISBN: 978-0-9896022-5-9

Published by K. M. Alexander
Seattle, WA

First Edition: October 6, 2015

Cover Design by: K. M. Alexander
Cover Lettering by: Jon Contino
HTTP://JONCONTINO.COM

Did you enjoy this book? I love to hear from my readers.
Please email me at: hello@kmalexander.com

BELLFORGINGCYCLE.COM
REDLITTENWORLD.COM
KMALEXANDER.COM

1.0.6

For Jake

...it had come from a mysterious inner realm beneath the red-litten world — a black realm of peculiar-sensed beings which had no light at all, but which had had great civilisations and mighty gods...

— H. P. Lovecraft & Zealia Bishop,
The Mound

RED
LITTEN
WORLD

PROLOGUE

His finger rasped along the rough texture of the plaster wall as the tip ran dry. His heavy breath caught, his flawless teeth—now smeared with red—locked into a tight smile. Perfect, yes, but there was a long way to go. It had been a while and he had forgotten how quickly blood could dry. With the finesse of a master painter, he gently dipped his finger in the liquid and continued his work.

The letters weren't the curls of Cephan or the straight-backed lines of Strutten, they were something much greater. He didn't know the letters, he never did. Like most Lovatines he spoke only Strutten, and could understand only a little Cephan. He had learned the latter so he could deal with his servants, hire the occasional rickshaw, or buy a meal from a food cart. But he knew the shapes were correct once he saw their perfect forms. He could feel it—a hum along the edge of perception. He could recognize their patterns and see similarities in the lines.

Muffled laughter—the sound of Auseil revelers—drifted in from somewhere behind the walls. The winter holiday was nearing its end, the scraps of paper that had been sealed against doorways at its start now fluttered down the streets like snow. As the poor struggled in the cold below, the elevated, the wealthiest of Lovat's citizens, competed with one another through ostentatious parties and vulgar displays of abundance. The hum of the party added a smidgen of gravitas to this glorious ending: the final sacrifice accompanied by the music of a jazz band.

He ignored the dead stares from the plush animals that lined the wall and covered the small bed. It was strange that this all ended in a child's room. It was the noblest of work and it should have ended in a more sacred space: some temple or sanctuary. In his imagination this last sacrifice took place in a hidden tabernacle with rising stone pillars and a glorious altar to Ashton. It was almost obscene for the writing of the Founders to sit alongside posters for monochrome stars and jazz musicians.

Pushing the decor out of his mind, he squinted at the shapes, adjusting the edge of one, rubbing away a drip from another. Feeling that vibration with the completion of each glyph. He scratched his chin and pondered the next one as his eyes grew heavy. Exhaustion was creeping in, darkening the edges of his vision. He took a moment to catch his breath, allowing himself time to lean against the wall.

How long had it been? Over a year, surely; this had all started before the blockade, before the rationing, before the Breakers had marched in the streets. Yes, the first pharos had been laid years earlier, even before the collapse of the Humes Tunnel and the death of that damn Peter Black.

The first had happened in the Sunk, below the waters—the

perfect place. The first had been a cephel, a young cephel. He could barely remember her now. He never collected trophies, never had the desire to file away a scrapbook of clippings like some shamble-touched. What was her name? The memories were a fog.

Memories were funny that way, like idols in the corners of homes—unless visited regularly, they are forgotten. Dust and cobwebs build upon them, obscuring their shape. He could remember a few things. She had been frightened, of course, but it hadn't lessened how special she was.

He had taken her quietly and even that had been more difficult than he'd imagined. He, a creature of dry ground and she, a creature of water. Finding a chamber of air in that sunken level of the city had proven to be a challenge, especially there, where it needed to be. The placement had to be perfect.

Her eyes, with those hourglass-shaped irises, had been wide and terrified. Her beak had clacked sharply in the dark space as the life drained out of her.

She was young, scarcely out of adolescence. If she had been a larger one, say a fully mature female, would things have ended differently? He wondered this often. It could have been him lying in that pocket of air beneath Lovat.

But things hadn't been different. She had died, and he had painted the symbols with his hands. His hands, red with her dark blood. He had completed the pharos. Like he was doing now.

They never found her body.

Feeling energized, he pushed off the wall and resumed his work. Dipping a finger in his ink and working to make sure everything was perfect. Everything had to be perfect. This was it, the epilogue. His legacy.

He paused again. Studied his work. Took another breath. Sweat dripped down his brow, soaked into his collar. He was in a mad rush this time. Had only precious moments to complete his life's work. At any moment someone could burst in, one of the merrymakers could stumble through the door and catch him. Worse, they could try and stop him.

It reminded him of the second pharos. It had happened on Level Two. Which warren had it been? Some northern one, near the end of the Sunk. She was older, human, a pitchfork addict. The marks on her arms were already festering and the smell of death hung about her. She was worthless. A tick suckling off the flesh of the city, spending her days moldering in some forgotten corner. In life she might have been worthless, but in death she became something great.

The process still scared him then. As he built the second pharos he had to make sure the line from the first was perfect, and so she had to be sacrificed in a public space. He chose an alley. He was certain that someone would catch him. Certain the LPD would round the corner and drag him away. She had been so doped out of her mind she never even noticed the blade as it cut into her. One second she was in the mortal realm, the next her bright blood was staining the walls of a wonton joint. No one had caught him. The few Lovatines who passed by looked away quickly and hurried about their business. He had slipped away.

A cough rolled up from somewhere in his belly, shaking him out of his reminiscence. His insides flipped. The smell of vomit was pungent and he wondered if his knife had nicked the stomach. He'd done it before, and even now, at number nine—glorious number nine—the smell sent shudders of revulsion through him. He swallowed thickly and resumed his work.

The sound from the band swelled from behind the closed door. A crescendo to his work. He finished one line and started on the second. It might not be a cathedral, but it would do nicely for the great rebirth. The sun would touch the final pharos, the link would pass down and signal to him. The next time he was called...

The thought made him giddy. Camalote would be pleased. The Herald would resume his march forward. The purification would come yet again.

He hummed along with the muffled music as his mind drifted to the third pharos. That one had been a male maero. How difficult that one had been—such a struggle. The fellow had to have been a construction worker or an engineer. He found him working on the superstructure of the city, tied to a line as he clambered outside a lift shaft. This one happened on Level Three. The words. The marks. The pattern on the floor. All of it.

Killing a maero isn't easy. He still bore the scars from the fight. Ragged marks ran across his back from the nails of a seven-fingered hand, the ghost of a bite still visible on his shoulder. The maero had fought his hardest, but like those before him he had succumbed to his destiny.

The memories came easier now. Moving from the murky past toward the present. Towards this, his final sacrifice.

Unlike the junkie, the police identified the maero immediately.

He remembered the monochrome news report. The slack-faced, shocked friends and family. He felt guilt, he always did, but these acts served a great purpose.

He wondered if the police had ever found a connection to him. He had never been called. Never been so much as mentioned. Rumors of serial killers occasionally drifted through Lovat like the morning fog, but no one spoke his name. No one mentioned the words. His face never appeared on the monochromes. There were no posters. He had somehow remained hidden.

It made sense that no one had ever found number four. She was beautiful and so young, not quite a woman grown. She was bright-eyed, with a wide smile and shining black hair. It was clear why Ashton had wanted her. The ancient words flowed in her veins just as they had in the maero's, and the human's, and the cephel's. It was his duty. His calling was to release them. Free the Herald. He was his evangelist, handpicked from among the converted to spread Ashton's message upward.

His finger ran dry again and he paused.

He gulped another deep breath. His chest lifted and fell. He was tired. So tired.

He would miss the planning, the hunt, the chase, and yet... he was also glad it was coming to an end. While he never shied away from his duty he would spend the long months after each death struggling with the method. But the parchments were specific. Life flowed from blood, it lived in blood. If life wasn't ended in the host then it couldn't continue in words. Ashton would remain forever trapped in the black realm. That made him susceptible to enslavement. He couldn't have that.

He continued his scrawling. He was getting close. Dipping his finger in the ink and making another character and then another. A smile flickered across his lips as more memories surfaced: number five. A dauger. Base-born, Iron or Lead, he couldn't remember and it didn't matter. He was a janitor. A worker drone in some mid-level tower, arriving, doing his duty and returning home to a beer and a jai alai match on the radio. He had been easy. Weak. But it was worth it.

He had peeked.

It was his most delicious secret. He had looked under the mask. Seen what lay beneath the dauger's faceplate. What he had seen beneath that base metal mask was surprising. He'd felt shocked… yet strangely empowered. Even the Precious Families could hold nothing from him, fools like that smug Janus. He knew their most sacred secret and, grinning, he kept it tucked away.

Muffled footsteps echoed behind him and he turned as he heard someone move to the door and stop. A pair of shadows blocked a part of the light that eked from under the door and into the child's room. He froze, eyes fixated on the door. What if they caught him? What if they stopped him? He was near the end now and so close.

He mouthed a prayer to Ashton. Time stretched out as it slowed. The figure on the other side of the door said something, and then another responded. A second pair of shadows joined the first, four feet. There was muffled laughter. Then a quick exchange of words. Then they drifted away, leaving an unbroken line of light.

The evangelist breathed. He returned to his work.

Six had soured the ritual for a time. They had been related. Simon, the eldest son of his cousin Annalise. A strapping lad with broad shoulders and pale blue eyes. He'd lived in a room much like the one he was in now. He also had stuffed animals that occupied the corners of his room. Similar posters adorned his walls. They had a similar look, sharp features, bright blue eyes, skin paler than most humans. Simon's long neck had reminded him of his mother's. Cutting it was unbearable.

"But you ask," he rasped at the wall. "You ask, Master, and I obey. No matter the cost."

Simon had stared at him as his life drained away, blubbering soft whispers. His soft hands clutching at his jacket. He had taken his time, drawing the swashes of the words through stinging tears. Adding his own elegant touch to the characters. His small way to honor Simon's sacrifice.

He still missed him, but he had served such a purpose. He had been the perfect stanza in Ashton's song. Those that followed were nothing compared to him. Important, yes, vital to the completion, yes, but he had been perfect. With his perfection everything else was soured.

Seven had been Madam Bonheur—a society matron, elegant, wealthy. She ran the Bonheur Seafood Company out of Demetrios and was rumored to be one of the members of Camalote. He knew her well as she had been a client of his for some time. She was a dimanian with small horns that curved upwards like corkscrews and two smaller spurs that broke forward from her cheeks like stubby tusks.

That hadn't been so long ago. Right at the beginning of the Syringan blockade. She had died on Level Seven and when was the last time someone was killed on Level Seven? Her death caused a stir. The family demanded justice. The mayor promised protection, patrols were increased. They had dragged some liquor-sodden kresh into the spotlight. Claimed he was the killer and naturally, the elevated demanded his death. The mayor—hiding behind that wide cocksure smile of his—obliged. After all, their demands were of the utmost importance. If they didn't feel safe... how could anyone?

The family would recover. Her loss was unfortunate, but she was survived by her three sons and the eldest was well equipped to take her place at the head of the company.

Madam Bonheur had been the easiest, though. She seemed to understand. She had smiled, gripped his hand in her boney ones and seemed to help him cut along her belly. As she bled out, she mumbled something. Words he couldn't make out. But he knew they were his words. Words she set free.

Eight was a male kresh, a servant. There was nothing special about him. He was old, quiet, but chosen. Odd he was selected. He had always considered the kresh a vile race. Something about those black eyes and fleshy beaks. He never accepted them as clients, and refused to hire them. Why the words resided in the veins of a kresh he'd never understand.

"I just follow, Master. I follow and I obey," he said to the lifeless room.

He sighed. That was all of them. All except this one: number nine.

Tracing his hand along the wall, he finished the spine of the last character and then cut it with the final swash. There.

That was it. The final pharos was complete. His job was complete. He looked around at the stoic audience of stuffed beasts that lined the room. They made him shiver. Their empty gazes gave the place an eerie quality when it should feel wondrous and hallowed. The signals were now set. The barrier would slip. The gothi would make a mistake. Ashton would be free once again!

He wanted to sign his name. Leave some mark indicating that he was the one, him all along! What would those elevated fools think now? What would LPD say? Nine sacrifices up the nine levels, each one a step in setting the signal. Pharos to pharos, from the blackest of shadows into the brightest red sunlight of the spires.

With a weak breath he collapsed, and the world went black for a time. When his eyes reopened, he looked down the length of his body. His gray suit was ruined, the jacket open, and his shirt was stained and torn. He eyed the ragged gash he had carved into his own stomach. His knife lay in a pool of blood an arm's length away. He felt light.

Outside the room the band quieted and the voices of Auseil partygoers could be heard.

His name was being called. His name…

He poked his finger into the wound and pulled it out again, studying his blood, his paint. It glistened delicately in the light of the setting sun. A dark stain against his tan skin. The room around him glowed red. He squinted at his hand, it almost seemed like it belonged to someone else. So many times it had drawn the words along walls of stone, brick, plaster, iron, and even steel. Now, like him, it was finished.

He wondered if Ashton would visit him. He hoped he'd see him again, one last time.

The world grew fuzzy and warm. He shivered.

Pain welled from inside. Sharp angry pain that sprouted from his stomach, crawled up his back, and slithered along his throat. It was tremendous. Suffocating. He wanted to scream. Cry out. The enraptured feeling that had blocked out so much was fading as his world darkened.

Outside the band began playing a new lively number. It warbled in the background, a strange accompaniment to the gore-covered room.

He heard his name again.

The pain clenched onto the back of his eyes and squeezed. He tried to scream but no sound came. He heard voices now, growing louder. They'd find him in here, laying in this altar of his own blood. They wouldn't be able to do anything. Lovat would be reborn.

The door swung open and music spilled in. There was a beat, he heard laughter, and then a scream filled the room. A man's. He turned his head and smiled, seeing an umbra in a tux, mouth hanging open, and next to him a maero in an evening gown gasped and dropped a full glass of shimmer.

The umbra ran in, shouting something, sliding onto his knees through the blood. He leaned over the evangelist, his face a pool of shadow that drew him in.

"No, no, no, no, no," the umbra said.

"Is that—"

"By the Firsts!"

"Someone call the police!"

Voices rattled. The music halted. More people rushed in, their faces blurring on the edge of his vision. People he recognized: friends, servants, but where did that damned caravan master go off to? He should see this. He needed to see this! Hadn't he been here not too long ago? Hadn't he traded words with the others?

"No! Please. Someone help him!" yelled the umbra's voice.

He heard another gasp—his own, his last—but it was too late.

It was over.

It had begun.

ONE

Ihaunt this city; I drift through its emptying streets like a cold wind. I'm the forgettable face in the crowd, the brief reflection in the frosted storefront. I linger around the food stalls, prop up its cheap bars, and slump in the seats of its monochrome picture houses. I'm not alone. In this city of millions, packed into nine levels, you're bound to find others just like me.

A swarm of people clustered around the coffee cart in a thicker crowd than I had expected. The vendor worked quickly to keep the hot, black brew fresh. Hot cups of overpriced coffee replaced the crumpled lira held in outstretched hands, claws, and tentacles. Was this to be the way of it? More and more my trips to the carts were becoming a small battle, the shove of shoulders, the press of populace. Eating from carts, usually convenient, was becoming an annoyance.

I had been back for a few months now. Settled into a routine. With a job gone bad and work so dried up it'd take a monsoon to revive it, money had become difficult. I found myself living in a small tick-infested flophouse in the Terraces and working the odd shift along the wharf to make ends meet.

I shoved my folded bill forward and watched the cart owner snatch it away quickly, replacing it with a warm paper cup.

Lovat hadn't seen a fresh caravan in six months. The Big Ninety, the main road leading east, was still closed. The military forces of Syringa and the constabulary of Lovat stared at one another across the Rediviva at the Grovedare span. Hunkered in their bunkers, pissing down frozen latrines, they kept their rifles trained at one another as they shivered against the wind.

Shortly after the hostilities between Syringa and Lovat erupted, the road south to Bridgetown had been blockaded by the Purity Movement. The bastards. Conrad O'Conner's church operated out of West Lovat. He preached a message of human dominance and intolerance towards other races and species. Non-humans were sub-human. Their demands were simple, and impossible: no non-human caravans could enter the city until the city was free of non-humans. The lunatics never think small. I sighed, sipping the black coffee. It was weak.

All-human caravans weren't common in the territories. You'd be hard-pressed to find a company running without a mix of human, maero, and dimanian at a minimum. You get further out it'd be rare to find a company without a bufo'anur or a lengish or two. You'd think an entrepreneurial sort would be able to work around their request, but the scumbags who kept the road closed made sure to keep out the food, too. It was a smart move on their part. You don't bring about change, good or ill, by keeping people comfortable. With no steady supply of food Lovat was growing hungry... and quite uncomfortable.

The occasional ship still came into port, rusted, barnacle-encrusted, and loaded with cargo. But they weren't reliable and what fodder they did bring never reached those that needed it most. Wharfingers unloaded goods for cash and the food wound up on porcelain plates in the upper reaches of the city.

Most restaurants were empty and shuttered. Lines formed for even the smallest promise of food. Yet still the mayor droned on. Urged calm. Promised that things would get better. No one believed it. After months of hearing the same speeches and reading the same op-eds in the paper folks had little faith in their elected officials. Lovat was up against an edge and it was peering over the precipice.

The clamor around the coffee cart added to the noise of the street. I shouldered my way through the crowd, hobbling away, heading south on Pontius Avenue on Level Four. The cold played havoc with my knee, and it throbbed with each step. I was glad to be on a slight downslope. The buildings here were about four or five stories tall and butted up against the roof. Pale yellow light leaked out from behind apartment blinds and cast strange shadows on the ground. Glowing neon signs dueled one another as they dangled off the facades of buildings. They blazed messages for cigarettes, liquor, cafes, and cheap loans. The words were spelled out in various Strutten and Cephan styles; the two most common languages spoken in the city. Warm steam billowed from grates and sputtered from open pipes in great opaque clouds.

My own breath traced my trail behind me in a cloud that dissipated slowly in the icy air. The paper cup of coffee worked hard to warm my hand. I stared down at the black liquid. I hadn't had coffee in a month. You were lucky to get a cup of chicory, and you might still find tea, but coffee was growing rare. I slurped it, feeling the warmth and tasting the roasted beans as the liquid trickled down my throat and settled in my belly. The coffee was burnt, bitter, and piping hot.

Hot. That's what I had really paid two lira for, not the taste, but the warmth it would provide. Exactly what I needed this afternoon. It did its job. Feeling warmer, I straightened, my back popping. I hadn't realized how hunched over I was getting.

Winter had set in a month or so after I got back. The coldest winter Lovat had seen in decades—generations, a few old timers claimed. Street mystics insisted it was a warning, a sign from the prophecies of the coming re-Aligning. Tales were spoken of walls of ice, taller than any building, emerging from the north and crushing everything in its path. Stories from the elevated on the sun-litten levels claimed they had seen snow. All we had down here was wind—wind and ice. Snow doesn't make it down into the scrape and the span.

Ice was everywhere. The cold air froze the trickles of water that continually dripped from the higher levels, creating columns along pipes and icicles that hung from the narrow gaps between street and sidewalk. The ice reflected the yellow glow of the sodium lamps and the garish light of neon and gave parts of the city the feeling of a twisted fantasy land.

I hadn't been lower than Level Three since my return, but there were stories from below of whole apartment blocks encased in ice. People who had to hack their way out of their homes with axes and knives. I wondered how cold it got inside. Would the ice freeze the inhabitants or would it work as an insulator?

As I hobbled along I pulled my heavy coat tight around me, flipping the collar up. I was glad I hadn't shaved. My beard had gotten long, and my hair longer, making me look like some mountain man, but in this weather my shagginess was working to my advantage.

The rattle of holiday decorations added to the din. It was Auseil, sometimes called Bresh in the inner Territories. The month-long winter holiday, a time of feasting, drinking, celebration, and remembrance. Decorated five-limbed branches hung from ceilings or were mounted above doorways festooned with twinkling lights. Families wrote the lyrics of the traditional Zann hymns—ancient accounts of the Aligning—on long strips of paper and sealed them around doorframes with brightly colored wax. They were said to bring fortune and good luck, something Lovat could use these days. The strips of colorful paper moved and twisted in the breeze, giving the whole city a strange quavering appearance. They tore from their seals and danced down the street, creating a constant rain of inadvertent confetti.

I wasn't in the mood to celebrate much. My stomach rumbled. I had skipped lunch and I regretted it. Hunger sharpened the smells from the street vendors: the spices and pepper of the dimanian grills tickled my nose, the richer, more muted scents of the anur and cephel carts made my belly ache. Crowds huddled around what carts were open, shouting, complaining, and rushing off when they had procured what caught their eye.

I paused and watched a throng bustle over a Cephel's jalky cart. The whitefish rolls were common in the lower levels, and generally to be avoided, but even the fish supply had dwindled, propelling jalky to the rank of delicacy.

A tall figure passed the throng. It was clad in black, its head topped with a tall sharp pointed hood. It drifted silent and unnoticed through the crowd, like a lingering shadow. Dark robes floated about its form like an ebony fog. Where a face should have been was… nothing. No eyeholes were cut into its hood, no outline of a nose pressed at the back of the fabric.

I suppressed a shudder, slurped my coffee, and watched it pass. I had been seeing them here for a while. Months, actually. I've tried tailing a few, but that got me nowhere. On the Broken Road we had given them the name "gargoyles," and it had stuck. Seeing those things brought back bad memories. An uneasy feeling rose and lodged itself in my guts. I tried to ignore it.

"Wal!" shouted a voice, snapping me from the figure. "Wait up! Carter's cross. Would you hold up?" It was Hannah Clay, my business partner and scout. Her echoing call snapped me from the figure. I turned and saw her push from the crowd huddled around the coffee cart. A steaming cup of coffee was clutched in her right hand. Carter's cross, I had forgotten to wait for her. She stomped towards me wrapped in a thick black jacket that hung mid-thigh and with a knit beanie pulled low over her auburn hair, a sour look plastered on her face.

"Thanks for just leaving me! You might have got your coffee, but I still had to pay the guy," she paused and narrowed her eyes. "You know, for a fella with a bum leg you move pretty quick."

I scowled. Hannah and I had worked a lot of runs together and she had become a good friend. She was the kind of woman everyone underestimated. Big bright-green eyes, heart-shaped face, a playful smile. But those looks hid a sharp edge—an edge that over the last few months had been further sharpened. For a while—after Methow—I hardly saw her. Then she telegraphed me. Wanted to get a bite to eat. See what was available. Since then we had been spending more time together. Two veterans of the road, tired of drinking alone. I was happy to see some of her sardonic humor had returned, but she was more reserved than before, quicker to anger, always ready for a fight.

"Just saying. You could have waited," she said, annoyance in her voice.

"Lost in thought," I admitted. "I didn't think it'd take you so long. I—I didn't think. Sorry."

Now it was Hannah's turn to frown. She absently shoved her wooden left hand in her jacket pocket. She had been doing that a lot, hiding it. She'd lost the hand recently, while on our last job—long story. It's amazing what you don't realize will be affected by something like that. Minor things like pulling out a billfold to pay for a cup of coffee had to become a new skill and she still fumbled. I wasn't used to considering how long it took her. I probably should have offered to help.

"Look, let me make it up to you. You want to get something to eat?" I asked, trying to change the subject. The smells of the carts had worked their magic and it was hard to get my mind off food.

"My treat," I smiled.

Hannah's frown turned into a chuckle and she nodded, then shivered as a blast of cold wind whipped through the street. "Let's find someplace warm. Get out of this damn cold." She narrowed her eyes at me and smiled. "Cedric's?"

"Cedric's," I agreed.

In the entresol between Levels Three and Four sits Cedric's Eatery. It's not a place visited by tourists or non-residents of the cafe's warren: Denny Lake. It's also buried.

The long-dead engineers who designed Lovat's superstructure made its massive floors and ceilings hollow. A lot of these hollows are crammed with the things that make a city livable: sewer pipes, air ducts, electrical lines, generators. Others are empty intermediate spaces. Some are occupied with shanty towns packed cheek by jowl, some are filled with trash, some harbor narrow mushroom gardens, and a small number have become storefronts. Cedric's operates in the latter. An in-between place for in-between folks.

We found the stairs leading to the entresol in the alleyway between a laundry and a rundown automat. A glowing yellow arrow that read "Cedric's" in bright cursive Strutten lit the alley and pointed down. It was only one story, but my knee popped as we descended into the low space between levels and kept aching as we made our way to the floor of the entresol.

We passed piles of garbage, ignored a pair of giant centipedes fighting over a dead rat, and finally made our way to the narrow storefront that is Cedric's diner. From the outside it looks like any street diner: big windows line the outer walls, the same cursive Strutten hanging from the ceiling spelling out "Cedric's" in glowing yellow letters. Instead of facing a street, Cedric's faces a wall of disabled vents that once billowed exhaust from the energy plants buried somewhere in the bowels of the city. A few drunks were passed out and leaning against the opposite wall. Their outstretched legs lay across the entrance, an annoying barrier for my stiff knee.

A dauger patron in a copper mask was leaning by the entrance and smoking a hand-rolled cigarette. He nodded to us as we pushed through the door and into the warm diner. Long unfurled scrolls decorated the doorframe and waggled in the soft breeze, tickling my head as I passed beneath them. I never liked the holidays much. Even ones that were celebrated with feasting. Seemed like a waste of time in a gray world like Lovat.

The inside of Cedric's looked like something out of a monochrome. A row of high-backed, lacquered wooden booths ran the length of the long window that looked out at the wall of vents. They're tall enough to give each table a bit of privacy.

Opposite of the booths sat a long counter with a row of wooden stools half-occupied by regulars. An open space in the wall behind the counter allowed customers to peer into the kitchen where the eight-limbed Cedric worked his magic as fry cook.

The place slung typical lowbrow human fare: breakfast all day, burgers, scrapple sandwiches, tamales, deep-fried fish, and piles of salty golden fries. These days, the menu was more limited. Things came and went. Cedric worked with whatever he could get and his work was cut out for him.

We settled into our regular booth and waited for the server.

"Heard from Wensem?" Hannah asked. She tapped her wooden hand against the tabletop absently.

I shook my head and tried to swallow the worry that welled up. Wensem dal Ibble is my closest friend and also my partner in Bell Caravans. I hadn't seen him in weeks. Last time we had talked he'd said he was thinking of going south with the Blockade Breakers, the group of civic-minded citizens in red armbands who were determined to open up the road to Bridgetown or end the Big Ninety Blockade.

I hadn't been too surprised. He had been worked up for a while. It's hard to understand why the Purity Movement is tolerated by the mayor's office and Lovat PD. When the Blockade Breakers began to organize, Wensem was enthralled. The end to the blockade was just one of their goals, sending the Purity Movement packing was another. Human support in the city was welcome but their participation in the campaign to the south wasn't. The whole concept behind the Blockade Breakers was to show the Purity Movement that a group of non-human protesters could come together and stand against them.

Being maero, Wensem had gladly signed on.

About a month ago, he packed up his family and left to face O'Conner's brutes on the road to Bridgetown. I hadn't heard much from them since and it was difficult not to worry.

"No," I said. "Who knows what's happening? There's reports of a siege, clashes, but nothing solid. Most folks are saying it's like Grovedare, two forces staring at each other, waiting. The papers aren't saying much. No eyewitness accounts or anything.

I tried to wire Kitasha but I got no answer. Maybe the telegraph lines are down?"

Hannah frowned.

"I'm sure he's okay. Maero are hard to kill," I said, repeating the old adage. It rang hollow inside my chest. I didn't want to think about it.

"Yeah, I suppose," said Hannah, smiling slightly. "It's just... I don't know. I don't like not knowing what's happening with him. I like knowing where you two are..." She let her voice drift off for a moment. "Ever since the Broken Road, I just...," she sighed. "Nevermind."

"You two again?" said a voice.

I looked up and into the brightly smiling face of our server. Her name badge read "Esther" but she always insisted on "Essie." She wore the official Cedric's blue apron over a pair of dark trousers, and an untucked chambray shirt.

"Hey, road boy," she smiled down at me, resting a hand on my shoulder and letting it linger. "Hi, Hannah. It's good to see you, hun. Happy Auseil."

We both echoed the holiday greeting.

"We can't stay away," I said with a smile. She gave my shoulder a squeeze and pulled out a well-worn notepad.

"Food here's too good," said Hannah, looking at me across the table with an inscrutable expression.

"I'll be sure to tell Cedric," said Essie, glancing at me again and flashing a small smile.

Essie was human, like we were. She had shoulder-length hair the color of burnt wood, dark umber eyes that were almost black, and a small button nose. She always painted her lips in a bright red that made them pop against her dusky skin. She looked like something from another time.

"He likes seeing you two come in here, likes seeing roaders in his place. Says you *legitimize* what he's doing," she said, drawing out the word. Lowering her voice for the affectation, she impersonated Cedric. "They're good folk, honest folk."

I was about to chuckle when Hannah said, "So we've become mascots?" Her smile was warm but there was a hint of annoyance there, too. She looked from Essie to me and then back again, her lips pursed and eyebrows knitted.

"What's on the menu today?" I asked, changing the subject.

"The main is vegetable stew with a side of homemade crackers. There's not many of them, though. Ced found a small bag of flour and put it to good use. Oh!" She looked down at her notepad. "We got our hands on some fresh salmon as well, it's just bits and pieces, and it's pretty expensive. It's available in a scramble. Couple of eggs, some greens, onions, mushrooms, and the fish."

She stopped talking and looked at the two of us.

"Is that it?" asked Hannah.

"Afraid so," said Essie. "We have oatmeal and the like, but supplies are tight. Every time we go to the market more stalls are shuttered. I hear it's worse down below, especially on Two."

"Well, here's to the Breakers," I said, lifting my paper cup. "May they actually do some good." I drained the cup. Lovat was growing desperate.

"The stew and crackers are fine. It's my treat, don't let this one pay," I said, pointing at Hannah. I didn't feel like fish, and anyway, I didn't have the money to pay for it. I hoped Hannah's order would be as light. "Coffee too, if you have it."

"No coffee now. It's under ration for Denny Lake as of yesterday." Now I understood why the cart was swamped. "We're on the docket to get a fresh bag next week but the best we have now is chicory or black tea."

I shook my head. "Right. How about vermouth, then?"

Essie cocked an eyebrow. A smile played on her ruby-red lips. "We have a little. Your usual?"

I nodded.

"Okay," she said. "What about you, Hannah?"

Hannah ran the fingers of her right hand over the table and chewed on the inside of her cheek before making up her mind. "Does Cedric have any of that sugar-kelp pie from yesterday?"

"There's a few slices left, I think."

"I'll take one of those, and a cup of chicory."

"It'll be right out."

Essie paused again and smiled at me, lingering by our table for a brief moment before she rushed off towards the kitchen. I watched her go, followed her legs as she moved toward the counter. Before she disappeared, she paused again and looked over her shoulder, caught me watching and gave me a small wave and a wink. A slight smile graced those bright red lips. It made me want to grin. This had been going on a while. I should really ask her to dinner.

"Hey," Hannah snapped fingers in front of me. "Hey, boss? You hear me?" She slapped the table.

I jumped and turned back to face her. "Oh... sorry. I was—"

"Staring at Essie like a slack-jawed teenager," said Hannah. She studied me for a few moments, her lips twisted in a frown.

"Oh, come on," I said. "She's fun. I think she's into me. She's pretty. Can you blame me?"

Hannah huffed and cast a glance in Essie's direction. "Not my type."

I rolled my eyes. "What about that wain driver?"

"We're not talking about this."

"Dark hair, dark eyes…"

"I said, we're *not* discussing this," Hannah snapped, but her tone wasn't angry. "I asked what time it was, not how pretty Essie is. Then I asked if you had given any more thought to Kiver dal Renna's request. It's good money."

I sighed. I looked at my watch. "Well, it's nearly four. And as for Renna: I thought about it. I did. I just don't know about those elevated CEOs and bureaucrat types. I'm certainly no investigator..."

"His uncle gave you high praise. Really talked you up. He sought you out. Thinks the world of you after hearing about what you did at Methow."

"What we *all* did at Methow, you included."

Hannah looked down at her wooden hand, and then pulled it below the table, her mood sobered for a moment. "Yeah? Well, I'm not the damn Guardian."

That again. *Guardian*. It was a title given to me nearly a year and a half ago. It followed me around like a specter. It always dredged up bad memories. I had a hard enough time sleeping. The Firsts. Creatures of legend. Titanic creatures from beyond with incredible powers that were said to destroy all in their path. I had faced two now, somehow, and emerged on the other side. That's not supposed to be the outcome. That's not how the stories go.

According to the myths they had appeared once in ages past. They destroyed cities, leveled mountains, and ruined the seas. It was said that in their rage they brought about the Aligning and changed everything forever. But then, inexplicably, they left, and the earth was left in shambles. Humanity was no longer alone. Other species and new races roamed the wastes that were left behind. We rebuilt. From the ashes of the previous world, our strange new society formed. So it was said.

Few believe in that anymore, most folk think of the Firsts as boogeymen and tall tales. To most, they're the villains in monochrome pictures, the antagonists in the fantasy rags. There's a few who still hold to the old stories and who believe in the ancient prophecies spoken by prognosticators from long-dead empires. They're supposed to come back. The legends say when the stars are right they will once again return to our realm and wreak their havoc. A re-Aligning, as it were.

I used to laugh at those stories. But now I see things differently.

Hannah looked at me. I rolled the empty paper cup in my hands.

"Who cares if it's elevated folk?" she said. "So what if it happened on Level Eight? A kresh servant was found dead in a broom closet. Murdered. His blood used to write strange symbols that covered the walls. Esoteric bullshit. We *know* what that means."

Aklo.

I tried to suppress a shudder. Of course it was Aklo. It couldn't be anything else. I had seen the gargoyle out on the street. I had been seeing them for a while. I knew what they meant.

Somewhere, something stirred.

I didn't want to be dealing with this again. I was trying to pull my life together. Establish myself before the city went to hell.

"What? What does it mean?" I snapped.

Hannah raised her hands. "Sheesh, boss. Bite my head off, why don't you? I just figured you'd be willing to look. He said the police aren't helping, he wants help."

I just want a quiet life. It had only been a few months.

"What about real private investigators? Why me? There's got to be a bloodhound who'd be willing to look into it."

"He's tried. You don't find a lot of elevated bloodhounds and this guy seems wary of scrapes in general. You were recommended."

Scrapes. The word was slang for those of us not fortunate enough to live under the open expanse of the sky. Scrapes lived in the span, the covered levels of the city that stretch off in all directions.

"Well, I'm as sub as you can get."

"Yeah, but you have a reputation with this stuff now. Others don't."

I sighed and leaned back against the hard booth. "If you ask me, it sounds like another one of the gilded murders."

Hannah raised an eyebrow and scowled at me.

Murder happens all the time in a city of ninety-eight million people, especially in the lower levels. A pitch addict rides a bad load and, next thing you know, four people wind up dead. That sort of thing happens so often that papers like the illustrious *Lovat Ledger* barely give space to the reports. Instead, the editorial staff worked up a murder section, right there between the classifieds and the obits. It's crammed full every morning. Jane and John Does are listed next to factory workers and spouses. With one exception. If you happen to have a wad of lira and a view for miles then you're something different. Your murder is dubbed "gilded" and the papers stop at nothing to make sure justice is served. I'm sure it drives Lovat PD nuts.

For whatever reason, gilded murders were on the rise. Every other day, big bold headlines spelled out the latest sun-dweller to get iced. Big, thick lettering across the top of the page, as if anyone in the subs cared. Crack reporters asking questions about the deceased, looking into their pasts, what enemies they might have had. As if the rich don't build empires on the backs of their enemies and the have-nots. Carter's cross, I know outfit goons with less trouble on their tails. Might as well be a different world up there.

"Hear me out," I said. "Rich guy finds a stiff left in some corner of his flat. Strange markings on the walls add to the scene. It scares him. Now, could be anything. It could be a rival, a jilted lover, hell, could be the Outfit looking to collect.

You know how close the crime syndicates are with the wealthy. Yet you jump right to Aklo."

Hannah screwed up her face like she had just sucked on a brakendale.

I raised a hand. "I understand what it looks like. All I'm saying is that there's a million other things it could be."

"Gilded murders are all high profile: business folk, monochrome stars, writers, singers, CEOs—not servants. This guy was a kresh servant."

"Kresh, huh?"

I don't know many kresh, personally. They aren't anything like the humanoid races. Nor are they truly aquatic like the cephel or anur. They exist in a halfway state between the water species and the humanoids. They are squat, four feet tall at the most, with wide bodies and narrow, vaguely birdlike heads. Two eyes sit on either side and look like hearts laying on their side. If they have a nose, I hadn't yet distinguished it. Their mouth is a sort of fleshy V-shaped beak. They have short legs, and small arms that end in boney claw-like hands.

"Maybe things uptop are as bleak as things down here. Carter's cross," I sighed. "Maybe it's just a squabble between two servants."

"And the writing?"

I breathed out slowly. "Look, the police are on it. He's in the queue."

"Yeah? Well, they're moving pretty slow."

"I don't meddle in police affairs."

"Ah yes, the *glory* of Lovat's finest, better not get in *their* way. Tell me, when have they been anything more than a nuisance? Especially these days?"

I thought about Detective Bouchard. It had been almost six months since I had thought of the dimanian homicide detective. Big as a house, with swooping horns and the pallor of someone deep in the drink. I remember him chasing me, gun drawn. He had thought I was the Collector Killer—an actual serial killer—and wanted to lock me up. I have him to thank for the knee. That damn leap from Level Seven to a roof on Six. Later, I was cleared of all charges and the blame was laid at the feet of Peter Black and his Children of Pan cult. I gave the knee a rub.

"No, Hannah," I said.

"What will it hurt, boss? Just hear the guy out?"

"What's in it for you?" I asked, narrowing my eyes.

She grinned and I saw hints of the woman that had been, her laughter, her joviality. "Well, I'm hoping you'll drag me along! At the very least, I'll get to wear a dress, do my hair, eat my fill of some elevated food. Maybe drink me some shimmer." Her eyes twinkled and I let out a laugh, shaking my head.

A distraction would be nice. I am no detective, but it wouldn't hurt to poke around a rich guy's flat and take his lira. Hannah was right, I could make a lot more in a few days with consultant work than I ever could working the wharfs and hauling barrels.

"Okay. I'll need a suit."

She grinned. "I asked him to meet us here in half an hour."

TWO

He was right on time. A tall maero, with a narrow clean-shaven face, sharp nose, high cheekbones, and piercing gray eyes that took in the diner with long sweeps. His thin black hair was striped with gray and pulled back severely in a stubby ponytail at his nape.

Two humans in simple suits slipped in behind the maero as the door closed. They looked clean-cut and dull, like moneymen at a mid-level firm. Dark hair. Dark skin. Dark eyes. Dark suits. On the more elevated levels they'd be perfect hired protection, able to blend into a crowd, disappear.

A gust of cold air followed them in from outside, along with the pitter-patter of fluttering Auseil pages pulling against their wax seals. The maero shivered and rubbed his seven-fingered hands together before removing his heavy black coat and handing it to one of the men at his side. Below his coat he wore a smart gray suit and a crisp white shirt with bright blue tie and matching pocket square. He reeked of sandalwood, juniper, and bergamot.

A smell that meant money and power. He instantly stuck out among the Cedric's crowd.

I like maero. They're an honest and straightforward people. They look a lot like humans but they have pale gray skin, long features, and seven digits on their hands and feet. They're usually quite tall and they're tough as nails. The adage goes that "maero are hard to kill" and—from what I've seen—it's true.

This had to be my client. Mister Kiver dal Renna of Renna Monochromes. One of the richest maero in the city.

I pushed the remnants of the stew away from me and leaned back in the booth as I studied him. He looked around calmly and caught sight of me watching him. Recognition dawned on his face and he broke from his escorts to walk down the narrow lane towards our booth. His glistening shoes clipped along the tile floor, each step a punctuation mark.

The two bodyguards didn't follow, and instead took up residence along the counter. Near our booth, but just out of eavesdropping distance. The bulges of shoulder holsters could be seen beneath the fabric of their jackets, and they made no effort to settle in, just perched on the stools, watching. Their awkwardness drew glances from an old dauger in a bronze mask that sat a few stools down.

He stopped by my table and looked down his nose at me. "Happy Auseil. Are you Bell?"

I nodded and slowly rose. He was taller than me, but shorter than Wensem. The top of my head came to about his chin so I had to tilt my head up slightly to meet his gray eyes with my brown ones.

"Happy Auseil to you as well. Yes, I'm Waldo Bell. Call me Wal."

We shook hands. He had the handshake of a maero who was in business: solid, firm, trustworthy. My old man always said you could tell a lot about someone by the way they shake hands. Kiver's handshake told of confidence and ease with power.

"Pleased to meet you. I'm Kiver dal Renna. Thanks for taking the time to meet. I understand you're a busy man."

I nearly laughed.

"Have a seat," I said, motioning to the space across from me and next to Hannah as I sat back down on the hardwood of the booth. Hannah barely moved, just raised a hand in greeting and sipped her chicory, watching Kiver carefully.

There was a tension in her shoulders I recognized only because of our time working together. I also knew that she was watching the two bodyguards out of the corners of her eyes.

"This is Hannah Clay. My business partner," I said. She gave Kiver a curt nod.

Kiver smiled wanly and settled, pulling on his lapels to straighten his coat. A small pin in the left lapel sparkled. A tiny sun with seven bolts emanating from its core. A corporate symbol I recognized: Renna Monochromes.

"It's freezing outside. You must be very concerned to come yourself. Especially during Auseil. Aren't most elevated focused on their midnight holiday parties?"

"They are," he said, looking around Cedric's with a slight frown. "I need help. You seem to know what brings me here."

"Hannah has filled me in a bit, told me about your servant. I'm sorry to hear it."

"Not as sorry as I was," he said curtly.

"Your uncle recommended me, is that correct? He was one of the Methow refugees?"

He leaned back. "Yes, he was one of them. I am sure you remember him: Mika dal Borhev. He's an uncle, yes. From my mother's side. Let me be frank, my side of the family and his are estranged. We don't speak. We don't attend joining together. We don't celebrate holidays. However, he heard the report on the radio and took it upon himself to send me a telegram. Told me a little more about Methow than what I read in the *Ledger*. He suggested I seek you out."

I tried to remain impassive. I didn't recognize the uncle's name but there had been a lot of people in that town. I wasn't sure I wanted to remember, anyway. Only a few months had passed and I still found myself occasionally waking in a cold sweat.

"Mighty trusting, taking the word of an estranged uncle," I said.

"These are bizarre times," he said with a spreading of his hand.

"You're the son of Renna," I said. "Renna Monochromes, correct?"

He nodded. Renna Monochromes was the chief producer of the black and white tubescreens that brought us cop serials, variety shows, local news, and the occasional reformatted film. It was an enormous company, operating an immense factory south of the city. Before monochromes the company had been the biggest supplier of radios. Probably half of the radios in the city were Renna products. These days it's difficult enough to justify lira on a cup of coffee, let alone for entertainment.

"Indeed. My father inherited the business from his father, also a Renna. He retired about ten years ago."

Old money.

I tried not to mentally calculate his net worth. It had to be in the millions. "I see. So, as I said, Hannah filled me in on your problem—"

I was interrupted by Essie, who appeared suddenly at our table.

"Welcome to Cedric's. Can I get you anything?" she asked Kiver, glancing at me with raised eyebrows and then flashing a bright smile at the maero.

"Tea, if you have it."

"We only have black."

"That's fine."

"Anything else? Something to eat? Hannah, you need a refill? Road boy?" She looked around the table.

I had hardly touched my vermouth. We all shook our heads and she disappeared. I kept my focus on Kiver, despite wanting to see if she'd give me another one of those smiles.

"I told him what your uncle told me," Hannah said.

"Estranged uncle," Kiver corrected.

"Right, well, Wal knows about the death of the servant. And you weren't able to get any help from Lovat PD?"

He nodded and leaned forward, his voice dropping an octave. "Yes, yes. That's right. Last week one of my housekeepers found the body of Hokioi Taaka—a kresh servant of mine—in one of our closets. It was terrible, heartbreaking. He had worked for my family for years, always a solid and reliable employee." He swallowed and cleared his throat. "The way he died..." His voice trailed off and he stared at the table for a few moments. I waited. Eventually he shook himself from his memories. "I contacted the police immediately, they sent a coroner, collected the body, snapped a few photos, and that's it. I haven't heard from them since. Here..." He pulled out a few pieces of folded paper from his jacket pocket and pushed them across the table to me. "After they took the body I tried copying down the symbols on the walls. It was tough. The closet smelled awful and I just kept imagining Hokioi laying there.

"I moved my family out immediately. Locked the place up and left. Went to the Shangdi. We couldn't bear staying there. That whole tower feels oppressive to me, dangerous. I don't think we could move back to the Commoriom, even if we wanted to." He looked away and grew silent.

"Commoriom? Is that your old building?"

He nodded. I slid the paper in front of me but didn't unfold it, not yet. I was worried what was waiting for me inside. "Did you contact LPD again?"

"Yes. Many times. I spoke with a desk sergeant. She said with the action at Grovedare they were short staffed. All the detectives were working double overtime. Said I would have to wait. I called the papers after that. They said they'd list it in the Murders section, but they couldn't spare a reporter."

I nodded. Lovat is a city-state, and one of the most powerful political and economic forces in the Territories. It holds a large swath of land along the coast, stretching from the Victory wall in the north to the Rediviva in the south. It's protected by ocean on one side and a massive mountain range on the other. It's a natural fortress. As a result it's never had a use for a standing army. The constabulary has been protection enough. But in times of unrest, it left Lovat not only unprotected but growing more and more lawless.

"How long ago did Mr. Taaka die?" I asked.

"About a week," Kiver said, then paused, thinking. "Eight days."

"Did you clean up the scene?"

He shook his head. "No. Not at all! I've watched the monochromes. I've read crime novels. I know how it goes. *Never* disturb the scene. I copied the markings and then had the doors padlocked. No one in or out. I placed one of my security detail outside the flat."

"Good," I said, trying to ignore the sense of dread growing in my chest.

I looked at the paper on the table in front of me. The softened corners looked harmless enough but they seemed to hold an edge of menace and I still didn't want to open it. I thought of the gargoyles I'd seen wandering the city. Dark shadowy figures, messengers for the Firsts. If they were here... Well, I'd eventually be involved.

I swallowed, and then realized both Hannah and Kiver were staring at me. Come on, Wal. I unfolded the paper.

For a moment I felt a separation. A rift. Like one part of me was being tugged somewhere else. I was sitting in Cedric's, yet there also seemed to be an endless wasteland that stretched across the horizon. Around me were the ruins of a city. Strange leering yellow faces peered out from behind crumbled walls, watching me. A broken sun burned above me in the colorless sky.

It was shattered like a broken looking glass, jagged black lines split its glowing face. It cast my shadow out in strange, unnatural angles. In the distance the ragged remains of a once great city smoldered, its towers shattered, the levels flattened, and in the distance, beyond the ruins, something terrible moved. A huge presence on the horizon. I felt both the hot, stinging sensation of dust blowing across my skin, and the hard booth pressing into my backside. As soon as I had that realization, it all disappeared. I was back in the booth. Back under the yellow lights.

My breath rolled out and I realized I had been holding it. I blinked.

I felt Hannah's hand on my own. Looking at her I caught a flash of concern in her eyes. I gave her a small smile and an even smaller nod.

"You all right, Mister Bell?" asked Kiver. I could hear the uncertainty in his voice.

I nodded, trying to slow my breathing. That hellish nightmare.

"I'm fine... I'll be fine," I stammered, my heart pounding in my chest. I took a drink of vermouth and noticed my hands were trembling as I lifted the glass. I glanced at Hannah, and saw fear etched on her features. I smiled at her, and turned to the paper before me.

Jagged letterforms ran along the paper in wavery lines. They stared up at me as if alive. Hannah had been right; it was Aklo, the language of the Firsts. I had seen it enough over the last year and a half to recognize it. I couldn't read it, but I knew a few people who could. If history was any guide, whoever killed that poor kresh was doing it for some deeper reason. Aklo wasn't a language to be trifled with. Each letter, each word, held power. The connections seemed clear. Gargoyles roaming the streets, Aklo-stained murders. Something was up in the city and it always led to the same thing: death.

I couldn't do this. Let someone else stand up and oppose these creatures. It seemed like yesterday that I had faced Curwen, but all these signs pointed to another First. Another threat. The thought made me sick. I was just now getting my feet under me. I wanted to scream.

The vision though, the city...

"You seen anyone strange around your place?" Hannah asked, breaking the silence. She shifted, and placed her wooden hand on the table. Seeing it again, I couldn't help but think how lucky she was.

"No, no one strange. But my house is quite busy. We have people coming and going all the time, staff, business associates. I reviewed the doorman's logbook. No one stood out, it was just friends of the family, business associates, employees…"

"You sure you can trust your employees?" Hannah said.

"I have everyone vetted. My children play in my house. I don't want anyone I can't trust around my children. Obviously, now there are doubts. This is why I need an outsider. I want to trust my security but what if they've been compromised?" He looked directly at me. "You come recommended."

I tilted my head. "Wait, you had me vetted?"

He smiled. "I do thorough research on all my employees. *Especially* contractors."

The thought of someone rooting around in my past didn't sit right with me. I looked down at my hands as anger, worry, a strange unsettling nervousness all moved through me. It made sense he'd look into me. He wasn't sure who to trust. Would I have acted any differently?

"So can you help me? I'll pay. I have money." I looked up and met his eyes.

"Hmm..." I said. The words "how much" were on the tip of my tongue but I bit them back.

"Please, Mister Bell." The word seemed awkward in his mouth. I wondered if he'd ever used it before. "I don't like the idea of someone accessing my home and killing someone not far from where my children sleep. I haven't rested well for eight days. I toss and turn. If we can't figure out who did this... I'm not sure what I'll do."

He breathed out and stared at his hands.

I looked across the table at him. When he had entered, he had seemed so confident and in control. Now I saw the lines of worry around his lips, the creases near the corners of his eyes. I saw the haggard exhaustion in his face. But I needed time. This was too soon.

"This writing," I explained, clearing my throat to hide my nerves. "It's Aklo, a long dead language. I've run into it before. It's usually favored by fringe faiths or found in antique books from the pre-Aligning. It's usually associated with nasty business."

I left out the Firsts and the hooded gargoyles. Aklo was complicated enough to explain.

"That's why I need help!" Kiver said, frustrated.

"I'm *not* an investigator and I'm no bloodhound. Best I can do is confirm that someone with access to your home is messing with something dark. Beyond that I can't help you." My words were choppy and forced. As I spoke them a feeling of guilt came upon on me. I took a deep breath but it clung to me like an angry carbuncle and refused to let go. There was something very wrong about that kresh's death, and it was probably putting Kiver and his family in danger. An old thought echoed from somewhere in my mind: *You're the Guardian. This is why you're here.* Over, and over, and over and... No. I didn't want this. I couldn't do this. I wouldn't allow myself to be dragged back into this a third time.

I was tired. I needed peace. I looked at Kiver, my eyes meeting his. "I can point you in the direction of a good—"

He didn't let me finish. He leaned forward and slapped both of his hands down with a loud bang. Hannah started and I looked around, slightly embarrassed.

"You *have* to help me! I'll pay!"

My nostrils flared. Lira would be nice right now, but no. I couldn't get involved. Stay strong, Wal. "Look, I appreciate the offer, but I can't. Wait for Lovat PD. Keep your security on alert."

"What would it take? I have the means. Set your price!"

I wavered. *That* was tempting. My finances as of late were bleak. The recent failures and deaths associated with Bell Caravans had placed us severely in the red. Anything I could raise would go much further towards keeping Shaler Ranch off our backs and keeping me fed—well, as long as Lovat's food supply held out. But... Aklo, the potential of a First. The fear rose once again, like a bubble from the deep sea. I swallowed hard. Money wasn't worth it. It wasn't.

My emotions must have flashed across my face because Kiver leaned toward me, pressing his offer. He looked at Hannah and then back to me. "I'll pay you both, hundreds a day if I have to."

Hundreds a day.

I shuddered and hoped he didn't see it. I could use it. But... I looked down at the Aklo with its twisted swirls, strange diamond shapes, its jutting forms. It danced on the paper, swirling into a writhing mass. My eyes blurred. Tentacles. Flames. My hands went to the glass of vermouth. My heart hammered. My neck felt prickly with sweat. The memory of the vision returned. The wasteland. The ruined city. The... thing that moved... beyond. That vast endless *creature*. Impossible in size.

I took a swig of vermouth. I was already operating on a knife's edge. The swirling chaos I had faced in the mining tower above Methow still terrified me. I still saw that eye. Could still hear that laughter shattering the sky.

Once had been lucky, twice had been impossible, three times... ? Could I tempt death a third time? Eventually luck runs out.

"No," I said, not looking at Hannah. I could feel her eyes on me. "I can't help you."

Kiver leaned back, exhaling a long slow breath. He looked deflated. He arched his back and studied me from across his tea for a long moment, chin buried in his chest. I frowned, sipping the last of my vermouth. Watching as the red liquid pooled thinly around the remaining cubes as I sat the glass down.

"Let me make one last offer," said Kiver. "Just come up once. I'll pay you for your time. You can look in the closet, see the scene, and then decide."

I tightened my mouth, considering my words.

"Please. Consider it. My wife is throwing a small party tomorrow evening. A distraction from this..." he paused. Frowned. "...occurrence. There will be food. Drink. You're welcome to attend. Both of you. Here." He reached into a pocket and withdrew two small cards. He slid one to Hannah and one to me. "Here's my card. It'll get you past security. Just consider one visit."

I looked at the pale blue card with Strutten letters pressed neatly into its surface and finally plucked it from his hand. I wasn't going to call on him. Let the professionals handle it.

Kiver said goodbye, rose and, leaving the diner, let in another gust of cold wind and a flutter of small Zann scrolls.

We watched him go, his two bodyguards following closely behind. He had left the Aklo reproductions on the table. The edges of the paper were bent, the creases cutting a few forms in half. I didn't want to touch it again. It was more than the nightmarish vision. I felt that if I touched them again I'd become wrapped up in this whole mystery.

When I looked up, I found myself under Hannah's green glare.

"You idiot," she said. She threw a balled up napkin at my face and it bounced off my nose.

"Agh!" I said.

"He offered to pay you *hundreds* a day for a little help. *Hundreds*. That's more than we'd make on the Big Ninety in a week!"

"Yeah, I was sitting here the whole time, Hannah. I heard him."

"You turned him down."

I nodded. "Yup."

"Why? Work for him for a few days and Bell Caravans would be back in the black! You could hire a full crew, get new gear. We could get off the Big Ninety even, move onto the King's Highway down to Ohlone. Maybe even bid against Merck."

It had tempted me as well. She had to know that. But promises weren't cash in hand, and where Aklo went trouble followed.

"It sounds fantastic," I said. "But it wouldn't be. There's a fair chance this will end up the way Methow did, or at the feet of another madman like Black. I can't do it Hannah, not right now. I need time." I stared at her, trying to will her to understand.

"Maybe the Guardian doesn't get time," she snapped.

I let out a long slow breath.

Hannah frowned, then gave me a pitying look. "Look, I'm sorry. I shouldn't have... maybe you can—"

I raised my hand, cutting her off. "I made up my mind."

She nodded. "Fine, but consider this my formal complaint."

"Duly noted," I said, catching her glaring from the corner of my eye.

The thought of that vision surfaced again, the flat expanse, the emptiness, and Lovat smoking on the horizon. I felt my heart flutter.

I flipped Kiver's card around in my fingers. "Renna Monochromes" was written on the back in plain modern letters. The symbol from his lapel sat above it: the sun with seven bolts.

On the back was Kiver's name, a telephone number. The old address had been crossed out and replaced by a handwritten new one: Level Eight, Shangdi Tower, Floor Sixty-Two. There wasn't a flat number, which meant it was *all* of floor sixty-two. Ritzy.

Lovat is all levels. Nine to be specific. They're all built roughly level, but years of construction has made this a city of holes. No roof or floor is truly complete. There are spaces in central Lovat where you can see down through the city and other locations where it cramps in like large corridors. Many of the biggest buildings start low, their structure passing upwards through the floors until they pass even Level Nine, serving as both building and superstructure as they reach for the sky. Others rest on the backs of structures below. A haphazard jungle of steel, brick, cement, and iron.

At the bottom of Lovat is the Sunk. It was said that it was once a great city itself but it flooded generations ago, during the Aligning. It's now home to the aquatic races: the eight-limbed Cephels, the amphibian anur, the kresh, and the rarely seen bok. Near the top, on Levels Seven, Eight, and Nine is where the wealthiest citizens live. Anyone can visit—the lifts run from the Sunk to the upper reaches—but most don't. The poor are harassed by the private security officers and the whole place is lacking in color.

It also lacks the bustle of the lower levels. The vying for space. The adaptation. The culture. Up there, it's clean and neat, everything in its place. But life thrives in chaos. Hell, life *is* chaos. I was a man for the subs, clearly.

I'm not sure why I pocketed the card. Maybe it was the allure of a paycheck. Perhaps. Perhaps part of me knew I really had no choice. I left the Aklo scrawl on the table. I didn't want to touch it again. The wasteland still moldered, hot in my memory. Better to let those words end up in a landfill.

We paid for our meal and I said goodbye to Essie. We braced ourselves for the blast of cold, pulling our garments tight as we stepped out of Cedric's. We made our way up from the entresol, our reflections warping and twisting in the frozen neon glow.

It was good I kept Kiver's card. I'd be needing it soon.

THREE

We passed beneath decorated tree branches that hung from the ceiling on gossamer strands of wire. Each was wrapped with strings of brightly colored lights and paper banners that read "Happy Auseil!"

We walked south on Third Avenue heading towards Pergola Square. A crowd of pedestrians moved around us like a river of life flowing through the city. The lights from the shops and terraces painted their faces in shifting and sliding hues of gold. The buzz of a thousand conversations in a myriad of languages filled the air.

The corner apartment I called home was situated in the Terraces and about an hour's walk from Cedric's. I wasn't overly fond of the place. It was a single room, with a shared bathroom down the hall. When I moved in, it bore the unmistakable odor of wet dog. Now it smelled more like a sweaty caravan master. All my ten spot had bought me was a double bed with a thin mattress and a dirty old sink that ran brown. The heat barely worked and these days it was usually freezing. But it was home, at least for now.

"I'm exhausted," I said, rolling my neck and feeling it crack. "I have a shift first thing in the morning. I should hit the sack."

"How's things at the wharf?" Hannah asked.

I dreaded answering. I was glad to have work but it felt odd to be back at the docks. I was still sorting out my feelings about it. It felt like a step down and, with the knee as it was, I wasn't exactly in peak hauling condition. The healthier stevedores ran circles around me and didn't take a day and a half to recover. The harbormaster was a dimanian I had worked with years earlier, so we were friendly enough but I knew that I hobbled a dangerous line. Eventually I was going to get cut. I ached for the Big Ninety to reopen.

"Slow," I said. "Real slow. We haven't seen the *Gamble* in months. Other boats aren't coming as often as they should. When they do, we barely get them unloaded before everything's snatched up. Hell, there's enough folks lurking around waiting for food that we could probably just have them unload the boats for free."

Hannah gave a sad chuckle, frowned, then sighed.

"Any protests?"

"No, most folk are scrapes like us. They know we don't have much control over the wharf-masters' deals."

She nodded and her frown deepened.

"You want to meet up day after tomorrow?" I asked her. We paused to let a vendor push an empty cart across the street in front of us. Sold Out signs were plastered all over the interior of the cart's glass. Nearby an old fourgon rumbled, belching black smoke into the air. Its driver yawned in the cab while a man in a pair of gray coveralls unloaded slabs of graying meat from the back and hauled them into a butcher shop. A pair of armed men in matching gray coats stood to one side, clubs in hand.

Motorized vehicles were rare in Lovat. The city doesn't have a refinery of its own, so vehicles were always scarce, but fuel shipments had become increasingly rare in recent decades. Occasionally an old oil ship will pull into the port but in the in-between times most vehicles sit idle.

"I can't," said Hannah. "I have another date."

I raised an eyebrow. "Yeah? Anyone I know?"

"No, and it's none of your business." She gave me a friendly sock in the shoulder.

"I'm up a level," she said, pointing down a side street towards one of the massive lifts that carried pedestrians up and down Lovat's levels. I still had a way to go myself.

"Well, send me a 'gram when you have some time to get a drink or catch a show. I'll be quicker now. I found a telegraph office near my flat."

"Yeah, I will. Take care, boss."

We hugged and she walked away towards the lift as I continued on to the Terraces. The city used to run a mono-rail going there, but budget restraints forced them to close the line. I passed under more Auseil branches and banners, and street-level window displays peppered with the Zann hymns of jubilant holiday revelers. As I walked, the lamps mounted in the ceiling above began to dim. Dusk in Lovat.

When the engineers built this place they designed the lighting in the ceilings to mimic the cycles of light outside. Artificial night was beginning to fall and with it the temperature. My breath came out in thick huffs of vapor.

In the dimming light, the neon signs cast the street in a gaudy glow. Liquor stores, pharmacies, shoes. It was all there, crammed behind narrow doorways. Vendors lined the streets selling secondhand clothes next to street mystics who entertained crowds with tricks prominently featuring fire. It was late enough now that the occasional pitch addict would wander through the thinning crowd. Faces hanging limp as they stumbled, lost in a world beyond. I stopped to rest my knee near a busker who was working an old saxophone in long, sad notes. The sound intermixed with the noises of the street, a perfect fit in this part of lower Lovat. I recognized the tune. An old song my mother liked to sing. A sad tune about lost love. I could still remember the lyrics and I could still hear my mother's contralto as she sang:

I strolled down to St. Angell's infirmary, I saw my baby there
She was laid out on a long white table,
So sweet, so cold, and so fair...

It was a dark song. I'm not sure how long I stayed there, listening, watching the crowd, shivering in the cold. There were so many things I did not want to think about. I longed for a lazy afternoon, a comfortable place of my own. Hell, how long had it been since I enjoyed an afternoon inside with a six-pack and a jai alai match?

My stomach growled. I looked around and bought the last of some overpriced shrimp-stuffed dumplings from a dauger vendor with a bronze mask, and ate them as I continued towards home, and my bed.

I was nearly there when I spotted it.

Another solitary hooded figure. It passed like a ghost, moving among the crowds. Its dark robe billowed around it, graceful like the winter mist that settled in the nooks of the city. The figure moved with purpose, passing shoppers and addicts, buskers and laborers. My thoughts returned to the vision I'd had when I touched the copied Aklo script. The figure paused and I held my breath. It turned its blank, featureless face in my direction. Was it watching me?

We stood there, facing one another across the crowd. The folk clustered near it either didn't see the figure or couldn't be bothered.

Gargoyles in the streets and Aklo now appearing above a stiff. If they were here then there was something big coming and Carter's cross, Kiver was trying to pull me into it.

The gargoyle broke first. With a small tilt of its head, it gave me a slight nod before continuing on its way. It moved with a lyrical bob, like it was half-walking and half-floating. I watched it go until it disappeared around a corner.

I kept walking south, and tried to clear my head. To keep it clear. I only made it a few blocks.

"Mister Bell." A voice echoed from behind me.

I jumped. The tension tightened in my shoulders. There was a slight accent but the vowels were perfectly enunciated. It was the voice of someone educated, someone from the elevated levels. I turned and saw a tall, well-dressed dauger standing a few feet away.

"Who are you?" I said, hearing the wariness in my voice.

He tilted his head slightly. A movement that reminded me of the gargoyle. He was as tall as a maero, and quite thin, with long arms and long fingers on perfectly shaped hands. His mask was simple, unadorned, and of a soft white color polished to a high, almost mirror-perfect, sheen. The mask lacked a nose, and two narrow slits for eyes stared out from under a heavy brow. The single, thin slit for a mouth gave his mask a stoic expression. His hair was tidy, jet black, and slicked back away from the edges of his mask. He had the air of a financier, a barrister, or a broker. It was the way he held himself: back straight, shoulders square, chest puffed out. He was immaculately dressed in an ash gray suit with thin stripes, under which he wore a darker gray shirt and a black tie with matching pocket square. He and Kiver could have traded style tips.

Dauger are hominids like us humans. They look a lot like us as well: two arms, two legs, ten fingers, and ten toes. They'd pass as human except for one thing: their masks. Full face and specific to the dauger wearing it.

The masks have a deep significance to all dauger. They are never removed in the presence of non-dauger. I've yet to meet anyone who can describe what's underneath. It seems that being allowed to see a dauger without mask is a purely intimate experience. It's rarely done even among family. Never among friends or strangers.

They mix well within Lovat, but their own society is caste-based. Families display rank with the metal of their masks. The hierarchy is simple enough to follow: the more precious the metal is considered, the more powerful the family. That's what made this dauger different from the others I knew. Most of my dauger friends were of the lowest caste, the base or noble families: Inox, Tin, Nickel, Zhelezo. This one was wearing a *silver* mask.

"My name is Rulon Argentum. I've been trying to reach you for months. You and me, Mr. Bell, we have business to discuss."

We found seats in a small alehouse that squatted below a closed restaurant that claimed to serve dimanian comfort food. The scents of the spices from above had embedded themselves in the walls of the tavern, making my mouth water. The place was packed with a mass of noisy patrons, many of whom were singing Auseil hymns in loud drunken voices and spilling ale all over themselves.

If food was in short supply, alcohol seemed to be abundant. Every bar in the city, from lowly two-seat alley jobs and popular warren taverns to the expansive dance clubs on the elevated levels that served thousands, all were crammed with Lovatines. Everyone trying their damnedest to make merry and drink away their hunger.

"So, Mister Argentum. What can I do for you?"

Argentum. *Silver.*

It struck me as funny that a roadman like me, bearded and shaggy, wearing a weathered old jacket, blue jeans, and trail boots, had recently sat across a table from not one but two elevated. On the same day and less than an hour apart. Lucky me.

Argentum said nothing, just studied me, turning his head this way and that. The slits in his mask were so narrow it was impossible to see his eyes. I half-wondered if he wasn't blind. Most dauger masks had larger eye slits, allowing others to see more expression. Argentum's narrow eye slits gave him a permanent air of suspicion. His posture and silence made me uneasy.

He traced a circle on the cheek of his mask with the nail on one of his littlest fingers. It took me a moment to realize that the nail was nearly double the length of the others, and coated in the same silver as his mask. It made a tinny ringing sound as the metals scraped against one another.

I shifted in my seat. The hairs on the back of my neck tingled.

"Well?" I asked. "What can I do for you?"

Argentum jerked slightly, as if I had roused him from a deep reverie, but then he settled back into his routine. Staring, scratching, and skeeving me out.

"Okay, I'm not going to play this game," I said. "I have a shift tomorrow morning. So if you just want to sit here and stare, do it on your own."

His shoulders bounced a few times as if he was laughing, but no laughter sounded from behind the mask.

"I apologize for my silence," he said finally. "These first meetings are always a bit strange and I like to ruminate on what I am going to say before I say it."

"First meetings? Will we be doing this again? I'm not exactly looking forward to another awkward stare session." I moved to leave.

"Oh yes, we will be doing this a few times. Until your debt is paid."

I paused, and turned to give him a long look. "My debt?"

I slid back into the chair.

"Mister Bell, what exactly happened to Margaret Shaler?"

My words immediately clogged my throat and I felt my cheeks warm. Shaler had been my employer on the Broken Road. She had been taken by a creature. Tortured. Killed. We buried her near Methow, next to a member of my own company, a greenhorn named Ivari Tin who was killed in a similar fashion. Outside of my crew and the family no one should have known about Margaret Shaler. Especially not some dandy dauger from the upper reaches. I searched my thoughts for something to say.

The revelers around the bar started in on a new tune and for a while it was too loud in the bar to know if Argentum was saying something. We sat there looking at one another. Finally, when the song died down and the singers moved to refill their ale cups, I answered. "She was killed. Killed along the Broken Road." He made no indication of having heard me. "A few weeks into our trip, she disappeared. We found her dead outside of Methow, along with most of the town's citizens."

"Ah, yes. My clients know that much. They want to know *how*. How did she die?"

His clients? Who was this guy? Upon our return to Lovat I had wired her family, explained the situation and offered to do what I could. There was no reply. The response from the Shalers had been silence.

I stuck to the official story. "She was murdered. Some loon had been terrorizing the town. A fellow named Cur—er... Boden was responsible. He had been killing people for years."

"Yes, the article written about you in the *Ledger* said as much, but it was as light on the details as you are right now. I want details, Mister Bell. *Specific* details."

I narrowed my eyes. "Why exactly are you here? If you wanted to ask me questions about Shaler you could've wired me. A personal trip..."

I didn't finish the sentence.

"I'm working for William Shaler." A clammy moisture crept into my palms. The bar had been chilly when we entered but now it felt hot and oppressive. The revelers' songs, so full of joy when we walked in now seemed dark and sinister. I wanted to leave. "He contacted the Society, filed an official petition for recompense and received no response. After the allotted time they contacted their local chapterhouse and placed a writ of collection. The price was set. I have been assigned as the collector."

A damned *collector*. Carter's cross.

The Society of Collectors work in large part with banks and brokers. They assume the role of repo men, making sure debtors pay what they owe. It gets darker when they can't. Collectors have been known to take the debt any way they deem necessary. Even with flesh. Aboveground organ sales are legal and common in Lovat but they fetch incredible prices on the black market. If a collector was assigned to the Shaler case, then it had been approved. It was all above-board. That wasn't good.

"What does the Society want with me?" I asked. A dribble of sweat trickled down my back.

"The Society wants nothing with you, truly. It's William Shaler you wronged. You owe him recompense for what happened."

"I don't understand. Bell Caravans sent a formal apology. We refunded the full amount paid and we're planning to garnish profits for the predetermined amount. The contract has been followed to the letter. Legally, we should be settled." I could hear the waver in my voice.

Argentum nodded slowly and ran his long fingers through his hair. "Recompense has been set. You still owe a sum of twenty-five thousand lira. While this won't adequately cover the life lost, Mister Shaler believes it will be a suitable punishment for your... er, *mishandling* of the situation."

"Mishandling?" I paused. "Wait... did you say *twenty-five thousand?*"

He nodded his head again.

"We all know the value of a life, Mr. Bell. Mister Shaler's demands are, well... quite fair."

Carter's cross! I tried to come up with words to spit. I wanted to reach across the table and throttle him but I also felt my own throat tightening. Twenty-five thousand? I hadn't ever seen ten thousand, let alone twenty-five. It was an impossible sum. Argentum's posture seemed to imply he knew that. I knew what was coming next.

"As with all Societal contracts, failure to pay on time will result in the process moving forward. Something I know neither of us wants. It's messy work, organ extraction."

So, that was it. William Shaler wanted me dead. This was no fair request. This was a revenge-collection. Usually debtors approach the creditor and work out a payment strategy before calling in the Society. He hadn't done that. He'd bypassed dialog and went directly to them. This sum was chosen precisely so I would end up under a bonesaw. My insides squirmed at the thought.

"When?" I breathed, my word a rasp that was drowned out by the revelers at the bar behind me.

Argentum bowed his head forward ever so slightly. "Well, as mentioned, I have been trying to contact you for months. It is a shame we are only now running into one another."

"How long?" I braced myself.

"You have one week."

I sat back, speechless. My breath fluttered out of me.

One week. I nearly laughed.

It was a death sentence. William Shaler had figured out a way to kill me, legally have my body cut up. My organs would be divvied up among the upper levels to keep some elevated bastard alive.

I needed a drink.

I needed a lot of drinks.

I ran my hands through my hair.

Argentum folded his hands and laid them on the table. The sharp silver nail on his pinky finger caught the light and glowed like an Auseil decoration. "Please do us both a favor and do not try to run. I have seen it before and it only delays the inevitable. I will always find you, Mister Bell."

A promise.

I said nothing. Stared into nothing as the crowd around me laughed and sang and celebrated.

Argentum stood and straightened his jacket.

"I will see you in a week. As far as payment is concerned, the client has requested it be provided in cash, if you please."

I blinked.

Argentum bowed his head towards me ever so slightly, then turned, and disappeared out the front door.

FOUR

The rowdy crowd was gone and most of the lights dimmed by the time the bartender appeared at the table and asked me to leave. It had to be well past midnight. My shift at the wharf would start in a few hours. I pulled myself off the chair and slipped outside, ignoring the sour expression on the bartender. A blast of freezing night air slapped my face and froze my lungs. Most of the shops along Third Avenue were dark now, proprietors gone home for the evening, windows barred by accordion security gates. Only a few late night food carts and street vendors remained, and even they were closing down. Shuttering sides and pulling their carts away for the night. A few left their carts where they stood, chained down what they could, and hoped for the best.

The lights in the ceiling were dim. The thin crowd was lit only by humming neon signs, glowing Auseil branches, and the occasional pools of light that dribbled out of apartment windows.

Clouds of vapor rose from vents in the street making the whole scene look familiar, like a detective serial from the monochrome. A low trumpet sounded a primal call from somewhere, resonating through the avenue and narrow alleys. It seemed a sad old song, a tune by Pops himself: *West End Blues* or something similar. I thought of my mother, swaying to the radio on a cold morning.

Head down against the cold, hands buried in my jacket pockets, I walked north. Mindless north. In some warrens, not watching where I was going would have put me at risk of stumbling through an open floor, ending up in a different level. At this moment I wouldn't have minded. Some adrenaline might be nice. Warm. Something to spice up this heavy dead feeling that currently resided in my chest.

What mattered to me anymore? I was stuck. I could wish for all the time in the world, but I didn't have it. This threat was very real. The money was more than I could come up with and I only had a week. What could I do in that time?

I considered liquidating my portion of Bell Caravans, but even that wasn't much. A small gearwain, some supplies, a few weapons. My half would be a couple thousand, three at the most. Banks wouldn't consider me. I could go to my parents but they were just as broke and the last thing I wanted was to drag them into this mess. Most of my friends were dead or also struggling. There was the Usurer Guild, but they were out of the question for a sum that large. Few thousand maybe, but twenty-five? Not a chance. I knew what I had to do, but I didn't want to consider it. Not now.

Twenty-five thousand lira. It was the kind of money entire warrens dreamt of. If I had that sort of cash I wouldn't even be here.

I changed course, heading west to the edge of the city. Tried to lose myself in the views of the ocean and the archipelago.

From far above, Lovat is shaped like a fat fish hook. It crawls south, rising across hundreds of small islands, and sitting atop the remains of a flooded ruin of a city far more ancient. That has always been the way of things—the young building upon the backs of the old, the old eventually forgotten. Lost beneath the waves of memory.

The majority of the city occupies the hook's stem, while a portion arches out west where the barb would be. From where I stood I could see the gap of the hook's bend. See the lights from West Lovat twinkling across the narrow bay that invaded the interior of the city.

Beyond West Lovat's small towers I could see the Rosalia Mountains, black shadows against a starry sky. Somewhere north of the mountainous islands lay Empress, the only open port of Victory; the hermit nation to Lovat's north. Beyond all of that was the open ocean, unknowable and immense.

The fresh air along the open side of the city felt good. It brought clarity to my foggy mind. I settled on a bench to watch a freighter with massive sails disappear below the floor of Level Three into the wharf district in the bend of the fat hook, the space between the warren of South Dome and West Lovat.

Somewhere beneath Level Three's floor were the massive gantry cranes used for moving rusty containers from boats and settling them gently onto cargowains. I imagined their engines roaring to life, belching black smoke as the docks burned precious fuel to aid in the quick unloading of cargo. Their smaller cousins sprang from the side of the city, held in place by thick cabling. The cranes were helpful for lifting all manner of goods up and down the city's edge. The waters far below were dangerous and generally avoided.

The blasts of wind that howled down streets and burrowed their way into the city behind me kept me focused. I stood and moved to the edge, pulling out the card Kiver had handed me and staring at it again.

The offer he had made *might* be able to keep me afloat. I doubted he'd pay twenty-five thousand for my help, but maybe there were deals that could be made with the collectors—with interest of course. Make sure it was more than they'd get from cutting me up. I had heard stories of people who'd tried to work out deals with the collectors. They hadn't been exactly successful. The Society didn't want to bother with payments and bills. They were quick, efficient, and had a lot of sharp objects. However... if I could make the offer tempting enough. Maybe there was a chance.

Maybe.

I sighed. I rubbed my thumb over the thick card. I knew what taking Kiver's job meant. The thought blackened my mood. Damn the Firsts. Damn their plotting and scheming and their unholy terror. I slipped the card back into my pocket.

"Didn't expect to run into you out here."

I started at the voice, standing up straighter. I whipped my head around in its direction. Essie. She stood there, wearing a thick knitted hat over her dark hair and a heavy coat that hung down to mid-calf. A cigarette jutted from her fingers, the wind too strong to let the smoke linger. The end glowed a hot orange that reminded me of an umbra's eye.

"Essie. Hi. Er... I didn't expect to see anyone out here." It had to be nearly three in the morning.

"It's pretty late, Wal... or early. Depends on how you look at it, I suppose. Didn't you say you had a shift this morning?"

I turned from her and leaned against the railing. I looked at the wharf. The dull blue glow of the lights that guided ships into the mouth reflected icily on the rolling black water. I was supposed to be there in a couple of hours, but what did it matter? A few extra lira means little to a dead man.

"I quit."

"Really?" She sounded surprised. "I thought it was your gig until the roads opened back up. Something to do before you could get back to caravanning."

Was that all it was? That's what I had told her, yes, but I wondered if it wasn't a bit of a lie. My knee was still a problem, and with my last run such a failure and showing up in the papers I doubted many exporters would be interested in retaining Bell Caravans anytime soon. Having deaths on the shoulders of your company did little to encourage business. I let out a long breath. Maybe Wensem had the right of it. Maybe I should have looked for a new battle to fight instead of scrambling backwards to some dead-end job I loathed.

For him it had been the Blockade Breakers. For me... I guess Kiver's job was my new battle to fight.

Essie drew up next to me. I could smell the kitchen grease that clung to her and the sharp scent of cannabis tobacco from her cigarettes but I didn't turn to look at her. I was too lost in my troubles.

"You come out here often?" she eventually asked. I heard the pop of a match as she lit another cigarette.

"Not really. No," I said. "Just a lot on my mind."

"I come out here all the time. Usually after work," she said, inhaling deeply from the cigarette. She offered it to me. I looked at it. Normally I'm not a smoker but what did it matter when you only have a week to live? Plus, it was freezing. I took it and put it to my lips.

She went on. "If it's early enough—and the sky isn't too hazy—I can get a good view of the Rosalias. Make sure West Lovat is still there. Be certain it hasn't been swept away or something," she laughed. A pleasant sound, warm and friendly.

"Why do you check up on West Lovat?" I asked, handing the cigarette back to her.

"I was raised over there, went to school there, hell, almost got married there. I got out before it swallowed me up. I haven't been back in years."

"Why not?" I said. I watched a small fishing boat chug its way toward the wharf. From this height it looked like a tiny little beetle. I imagined the hungry people that waited for its arrival. And the shady, besuited figures that slipped in and walked away with crates before they could get to them.

Essie let out a breath of smoke and handed the cigarette to me. "Just wanted a quieter life," she said. "Wanted something simple. Things back home... they weren't simple. I guess I just grew in a different direction. It's not my Lovat. Not anymore."

Her voice was wistful and sad. Her words sounded a lot like mine. I thought about the starving city surrounding us and understood. In a lot of ways this didn't feel like my Lovat, either.

"Yeah?" I said, letting the word out with a cloud of smoke. "I know the feeling."

"Oh yeah?" Essie asked, accepting the cigarette. The smoke had begun to warm my chest. "What do you mean?"

"Well—" I blinked, realized I had almost started to explain. I reeled myself back in. Essie was a hardworking woman with a decent job. I was a regular who tipped well and smiled at her. She didn't need to hear my problems.

"It's nothing," I said, expecting her to drop it.

"Bullshit."

I gave her a sad smile and sighed, then turned back to the water. Everything in my head churned. The words didn't come. Up until this moment most of our conversation had been small talk, but this was something else. Essie stood there silently. Just being. It was nice. She didn't prod. She just stood there, passing the cigarette and leaning on the railing next to me, staring out over the water.

"You want to grab a drink and talk, road boy?" she said after some time had passed.

The nickname made me smile. I pushed back from the railing and looked at her. Her skin changed from a blue hue to a soft yellow as a sign near us flashed through its cycle. Her dark eyes studied me and her red lips were turned up at the corner in a playful smile.

I looked back towards the water. The fishing boat had disappeared, swallowed up by Lovat's superstructure. I still had a few lira in my pocket. Maybe a drink wouldn't hurt. Help me relax. It'd be great company, a new friend, and I could dull my thoughts a bit. Allow me to start fresh tomorrow.

Yeah.

It'd be real nice to have some company.

"Sure. I could go for a drink," I said.

She flicked the cigarette butt over the edge, let out a warm laugh, and smiled. "I know a great place just down the street. Come on."

FIVE

In that moment between sleeping and waking I heard things. They were subtle at first, but they pulled me towards the waking world. In the distance a bass thrummed a beat. Somewhere above a mother yelled at her children. Old pipes gurgled away as air and liquid was forced through them. It was the buzz of Lovat, the endless cacophony of life. I yawned. I stretched. My eyes popped open.

I woke staring at a drawing of a tropical island taped to the ceiling. It looked old. The words that once covered a corner of the poster were faded beyond legibility and in a strange and unfamiliar kind of Strutten. I could make out only a few of the characters. I looked at the poster. Where did such things exist?

I pushed myself into a sitting position and dropped my feet off the edge of the bed and onto the carpet. I wiggled my toes, feeling the thick piles scrunch between them. My head throbbed behind my eyes and my throat felt raw. Something had changed. My mood from the night before had shifted.

I turned and looked at Essie. Her dark eyes were closed. Her breathing was steady and calm. Her brown shoulders rose and fell with each breath. Her small apartment was cool, and I readjusted the blanket so a chill wouldn't rouse her. I turned, rubbing my eyes with the heels of my palms and trying to clear away the headache. It had been a good night.

We had gone to a small bar on the second story of a building on Level Three. An all-night tiki joint. We talked. Drank strong fruity drinks. Mentioned our families only fleetingly. Talked about our mutual desire for a simple, quiet life. We talked about politics only once—joint laughter over the ineptitude of the mayor. One drink turned into two, and two into three, and any inhibitions I had about getting close to Essie disappeared. When we exhausted the tiki bar we hit up another all-night dive. Then another.

I could barely remember stumbling back to her apartment. There was kissing. The clothes came off. A blur of skin on skin, mouth on mouth, her legs wrapped around mine. I felt the smile on my face as I tried to dredge up more memories from beneath my hangover.

I wanted more. Craved a deeper connection. I didn't want this to be just a throw between two lonely people looking for some companionship. Walking the trails between towns, struggling against obstacles, fighting so many fights. It had begun to wear on me. I could see the lines forming in my brow, crinkling in the corners of my eyes. My sleep as of late had become more and more restless. Being a drifter wasn't the life I wanted. Not anymore. I needed a refuge. I ached for a place to call home. I wondered if I could find that with Essie.

She was different. There was a familiarity there, something I hadn't really felt before. An equal footing. The way we had laughed together last night, the flashes in her eyes as she looked at me. She understood me. She understood why I was tired of the road. Maybe it's this place, maybe it's the temporary nature of this city. She wanted stability too. A home. Somewhere to hang up your boots. It was refreshing. Uplifting, even.

A bright beam of light cut in from behind thick curtains and told me it was early afternoon. I rose and poked my head behind them, squinting at the bright light coming in from outside. Essie's apartment was on the top floor of a Level Three block. The view was minimal. Another building sat across a narrow alley. Huge sodium lamps hung from the ceiling and blazed on their afternoon setting. Above them a tangle of wires hung down from the roof, dripping sparks that burned themselves out before hitting the alley below. Massive ducts crisscrossed one another, running this way and that, like the roots of some enormous tree. Big circulators slowly spun in their housings.

Across the alley, atop the building opposite, stood a gargoyle. My heart jerked. The thing didn't move. Just stood there, head tilted so it could look downward. Its blank face—inseparable from the tall hood—seemed to face in my direction. Watching.

"Bastard," I growled, pulling my head back inside. I readjusted the curtains to keep the interior dark and I gently settled back on the bed, trying to wipe the thing from my mind. I looked down at my hands, rough from weeks of dock work, the nails dirty. I could use a shower.

More of the previous evening shifted into clarity. I remembered the face of the dauger—Argentum—staring at me across the table. The way his words felt like a verdict. A feeling of being cornered. This morning it was different. Maybe it was Essie. Maybe it was my throbbing head. Maybe it was just a good sleep in a real bed. Regardless, the path was clear. I was going to help Kiver. Maybe enlist the help of some friends along the way. I was better with friends. Better with people beside me. I couldn't go at this kind of stuff alone. I had tried that before and it always fouled itself up.

If I negotiated properly I could collect a hefty sum. It'd be the first step towards salvation. The Society of Collectors are first and foremost a business. I could probably negotiate a payment plan. If I couldn't… well, I would run. I could head south. Join up with Wensem and his Blockade Breakers or lose myself in the Giffords, the mountains south of the city. The wilds held nothing fearsome for me anymore.

Quietly, I rose again and padded across the carpet to Essie's tiny bathroom and closed the narrow door behind me. I could barely turn around inside. A shower was crammed into a corner, a toilet squatted beside it, a small sink beside that. It was clean but messy: bottles lined the small shelves and little notes were stuck up on the mirror with plastic tape reminding Essie to "Pick up mail" and "Return books to Raul." A few old copies of the *Lovat Ledger* were piled in a corner. A towel was draped over a steel curtain rod, dark eye-makeup stains staring up from the terry cloth.

Pulling the towel free, I stepped inside the shower and closed the curtain. The initial burst of cold water jerked me out of the last vestiges of sleepiness. Now fully awake, I luxuriated in the water pouring over my shoulders. I let the increasing heat soak into my back and ease the dull ache in my knee. It had been a long time since I had felt anything other than cold.

After a solid sleep and a hot shower, I found myself wishing I had a razor and some clippers to clean myself up and ditch the vagrant look.

I had to be presentable. No one would take me seriously in the upper levels if I showed up in my ragged coat, dirty boots, and worn jeans. I needed a suit.

When I came out of the shower I felt cleaner than I had in days. Essie was stirring under the blankets. She rolled over to face me, the blankets falling away. Her eyes sparkling, her red lips turned up at the corners. I couldn't help myself from looking. She was beautiful.

I wondered what she thought now of the ragged roader before her, still clammy from a shower and wrapped in a makeup-stained towel. My arms, chest, and back are scarred. My right knee has an odd lump to it. My body softened from these months in the city. My beard was long, my hair even longer. I had to be a sight.

"Morning, road boy," she said, giving me a languid smile.

"Good morning. Hope I didn't wake you."

"I had fun last night."

"Yeah. Me too," I said.

There was something about her face. Her eyes. The shape of her lips. It was hard not to compare her to Samantha. There had never been a chance with her. I should be enjoying whatever this was, not lingering over missed opportunities. I pushed the priestess from my mind and focused on Essie.

I looked down at the towel and back up at her, smiling sheepishly. "I should have asked…"

"About what? Using my shower?" She threw a pair of her underwear at my head and laughed as it bounced off and landed in the pile of dirty laundry at my feet. "Do I look like the kind of girl who cares?"

She didn't, and I said so.

Her laughter filled the room as I dropped the towel and climbed back into the bed.

When we were dressing Essie asked if I wanted to get some food.

"I have some business a little later, but I'm always up for some food," I said.

She smiled at me as she slipped on a sweater.

"You think we can find a real breakfast still?" I asked.

She ruffled her hair, then rose to pull on a pair of jeans. "There's always a diner somewhere. Where you going?"

I yawned and stretched. "Some maero offered me a job yesterday. It's not my typical work, but the pay is good so I figured I'd explore it a bit more."

"That elevated from Cedric's? The one with the nice suit and the muscle?"

There was no sense in lying about it so I nodded.

"What's that about, anyway?" Essie asked.

"One of his employees was murdered at his apartment. He wants me to look into it."

"Oh, yeah?" She seemed surprised. "Why does he come to a mangy road boy like you instead of going to the police?"

I heard her light a cigarette and turned to look at her. She was bent over and pulling on a pair of mid-calf boots, her hair hanging in a curtain around her face. Her dark eyes sparkled behind it. There was so much I could have told her. My history with the Firsts. How many times I'd nearly died alongside my friends. I held my tongue. Not yet. We had just begun to know one another. Perhaps sometime soon.

"I have some history in helping with stuff like that. With Syringa drawing so many officers from the city and the police spread so thin, help can be hard to find."

"You good at it?"

I gave a weak laugh as I pulled on my jacket. "I'm available. He's willing to pay and his lira goes a lot farther than the wharfs."

"Good," Essie said, drawing close to me and lifting her lips to mine. She had that warm diner smell: grease, butter, and sweet syrup. When she pulled away there was a light in her eyes. "After you get paid you can take me to a real dinner."

I left Essie about an hour later after a meager breakfast of rice stewed with beans we found at some half-open dive near her place. The meal had cost nearly twenty lira apiece. Robbery. Six months ago, that would have been a couple of lira, tops.

I was still hungry and the cold only heightened the empty feeling in my stomach. Head down, hands shoved in my pockets, I headed towards King Station to enlist my help. The city rose and fell around me. Catwalks crossed above my head, rickshaws rolled by, and the occasional bicycle whipped past.

I needed to talk to Hagen. That meant I needed to visit his shop, Saint Olmstead. It sat in King Station, a crumpled little warren to the southeast of Pergola Square. It's a tight space with narrow streets and a maze of alleyways with low ceilings. It's stuffed with restaurants, small shops, a handful of antique stores, tiny manufactories, and, in warmer times, the occasional garden. In some sections walking through King Station feels like wandering the hallways of some enormous building.

Maynard Avenue was largely devoid of life when I arrived. A small noodle stand I had visited in times past now stood empty. A large sign hung off its makeshift counter reading: "No Ingredients. Thank Syringa and those racist bastards. Come back another time."

I passed the storefront once occupied by Thad's shop. In the narrow confines once lined with spectacles and cubbies there now stood a small forge. A lone kresh gripped a hammer in its clawed hand and pounded away on a piece of iron with loud clangs. Clouds of billowing steam carried the scent of hot metal. A year ago Thad had been killed by a bloodthirsty cult calling themselves The Children. They were stopped, but Thad's brood had been too young to continue his business. None of his brothers or sisters were keen on keeping Russel & Sons Optics operating, so the shop was closed. I was glad to see life in the narrow space again. Despite the hardship, despite the cold, despite everything, the city rolled on. Life rolled on.

I left the kresh to his work and moved up the street towards my destination passing a small gathering of dimanians in yellow robes and a pair of cephels clacking at one another over a folding table covered with used instruments.

At the end of the block sat Saint Olmstead, the shop owned by my friend Hagen Dubois. A simple sign hung above the leaded glass door, and a small Auseil display was set up in the shop's window. I pushed my way in, the ring of a bell above me signaling my arrival. Hagen is Samantha's brother. He's primarily focused on religious antiques but he also dabbles in some history of the arcane. If he was willing, I was sure he and I could easily get to the bottom of the kresh murder.

The shop had much the same feeling as a library. It was warm inside and I rubbed some feeling back into my hands before proceeding further. Somewhere a soft bebop tune was playing and I noticed Hagen had replaced the oil lamps on the walls with new electric lamps that buzzed a subtly flickering yellow light. The space smelled of leather, oil, cleaning alcohol, and peppery incense.

"I'll be with you in a minute," Hagen's voice called out from somewhere among the shelves.

I moved through the haphazard maze of aisles that made up the shop.

Saint Olm is tall and narrow. Shelves occupy the front. A loft extends from the rear and halts about halfway out. Upstairs is where Hagen keeps his book collection. Barring some religious institutions there are few places in the city with a more expansive collection. A twisted iron staircase sits along one wall and leads upstairs. Dominating the space below the loft is the counter. It's an immense thing that arcs outward into the shop like the prow of a ship and it separates the shop proper from Hagen's office, small bathroom, and living quarters in the back.

The register was located at the rear of the shop and it was always an adventure getting back there. The inventory at Saint Olmstead constantly changes. Every time I visit the rows have been readjusted to make room for a portable altar, some sort of statuary, or a crate of Hasturian knickknacks.

As it was impossible to see the counter it was surprising that items weren't nicked from time to time. Whenever I mentioned it Hagen would smile and say, "The benefit of a religious customer base is they all feel guilty about stealing. Especially when it comes to objects centered on their faith."

It made sense.

Robes, statuary, idols, and icons lined the shelves. Prayer coins, blessed instruments, and wooden basins covered others. I passed by a stack of Yiggo religious tomes. Gold-leafed glyphs of snakes decorated the leather spines. A sign hung below them offering fifty percent off ornate reliquaries.

Hagen Dubois stood behind the counter. He's dimanian. They look a lot like humans. Two arms, two legs, two eyes and ears. Where they differ is in the boney spurs sprouting from their knuckles, elbows, knees, and most often as horns along the head. Anywhere that bone comes close to the skin. Dimanian and humans have interacted for thousands of years, at least as far back as the Aligning, and for the most part our people get along.

Hagen's nest of dark curls were still tangled atop his narrow face. The single horn that sprouted from his forehead had grown back, though he had trimmed it and was obviously allowing a dimanian barber to shape it. His sister was probably pleased with that. When I first met him it was growing wild, sticking up and out, but now it curved through his hair slightly, following the shape of his skull. He looked up and smiled as he saw me coming.

"Wal! I didn't know you were coming over this morning. I thought we were getting lunch next week?"

Next to him, leaning over the counter studying a tome was his sister, Reunified Priestess Samantha Dubois. My heart jumped and my mouth went dry. My hands felt a bit clammy. I hadn't seen her in months. She looked fantastic. She was leaning over the counter wearing a loose sweater and dark jeans over lace-up road boots, a style she had picked up over the last year. When I first met her she had dressed in a style more in line with to her occupation as priestess—slacks, robes, and the like. Today she looked like any other shabby roader. You'd have no idea she was in line for a cardinalship.

She looked up as she saw me approach, her umber eyes flicking up from a book. She pulled a thin pair of spectacles from her nose and dropped them onto the counter. Her thick curly hair was cut around the length of her chin where two small spurs jutted, and the horns that grew near her temples had been freshly trimmed back to subtle nubs.

It was strange seeing her after being with Essie. Essie is beautiful but Samantha is… well, she's something else. She had a presence in the room. Her words carried weight.

"Hi," I said, trying to sound natural.

"Good to see you!" Hagen said, coming around the counter and giving me an enthusiastic shake of the hand and slap on the shoulder. "Oh! Remember those prayer drums I was telling you about? The ones that street mystic ordered for his congregation? They came in last week, you need to see them. They're downright *obscene*!"

He gave a bawdy laugh and fluttered behind the counter and began shuffling boxes and small crates aside, looking for the drums.

"Hey Wal," Samantha said. She smiled, but it seemed forced. She stood but didn't come around to give me a hug or shake my hand. These were the first words she had said to me in a long time. Any closeness we had once shared had frozen along with the city. Sucked away into the ether. I understood. Samantha had once said that she worried for my safety, that I was impetuous, that my brashness made me dangerous. She was right. I put myself at risk, and in doing so put her feelings for me at risk. So when she had pulled away, I let her go.

"It's good to see you," I said, trying to establish a mote of confidence. "Been a while."

"Yeah," she said. It was better we didn't talk about it.

She looked down at my hand, her eyebrows lifting slightly. I had gotten new ink done a few weeks after we returned from Methow to go with the black wagon wheels on each of my forearms. On the back of my left hand I had gotten a simple tattoo of a rose. It was black against my brown skin, a reminder of what Hannah had lost. On the inside of my left wrist was an apple for Margaret Shaler. I had hated the woman, but she did not deserve to die, and she should not be forgotten. On the inside of my right wrist was now an ox skull, an old roader symbol and a mark I had chosen in memory of Ivari Tin. Both Shaler and Tin had been lost to us in Methow, and both were now buried outside the ruins of that cursed town. The tattoos were small tributes and reminders I wanted to carry with me, remembrances of what had been sacrificed.

"New tattoos?"

I nodded. "Reminders. Hannah's hand. Shaler. And Tin," I said. Pointing to each in turn. "Didn't want to forget."

She touched her chin and stared at the ink, but didn't say anything.

"What brings you here?" I asked, changing the subject. I came to Hagen's shop a few times a week. Usually to see how he's doing, sometimes to play cards in the back office, sometimes just to drink and talk. He had mentioned his sister once or twice but we hadn't really talked about her. He knew it was a tender subject.

She lifted the tome she had been reading. The title, *The Natural History of Tsath*, was spelled out on its cover in curving Strutten and below was the image of a robed and bearded human man, his arms outstretched to the heavens.

"Research," she smiled. "You'd never guess this, but I was asked by Lovat PD to look into some pre-Aligning history for them."

"Bouchard?" I blinked.

"One and the same. He says he heard about it on some case

of his, some witness babbling about a gilded murder. He tried the library, but got nowhere. Asked if I had anything."

"No shit," I said, a little surprised. Bouchard was an old foe. A dimanian detective with a drinking problem and a superiority complex. After my name was cleared he had begrudgingly apologized, but we weren't exactly friends. Samantha helping him gave me a mixed bag of feelings.

"What's Tsath?" I asked, trying to keep emotion from my voice.

"A great underground city built in a massive cave system. Some suggest it's beneath the Plateau of Leng, others think it could be deep below Thamadon or Lovat. No one has been able to find any architectural evidence of it, mind you."

"What's Bouchard's interest?"

"He wouldn't tell me anything more than what the witness said. He hoped I had information on it. He's going to be disappointed. Honestly, outside of this book there isn't—"

"A-ha!" Hagen yelled, interrupting her. He rose up behind the counter holding a small box. "Here they are. Wait till you see these." He reached a hand into the box. "I'd mentioned these were for a fertility dance or ritual… whatever. I had to go through all these hoops to find them. They don't even *make* these in the Territories. I had to send word with a sailor and he brought them from Leng or Catheria, it doesn't matter. You need to see them. The drums depict a woman laying on her back and her leg—"

"Can you wait before you pull out those things again?" Samantha said. "At least until I leave."

Hagen rolled his eyes. "Fine. I can wait." He pushed the

box aside and changed the subject. "So how's things? Aren't you supposed to be at work?"

"I quit."

"Oh yeah?" Hagen said, raising an eyebrow. "Why?"

Samantha quietly shut *Tsath's* cover and set it gently back into a worn box with frayed edges.

"Something new came up. Yesterday, a distant cousin of one of the Methow refugees came to see me." Samantha tensed visibly. Her brow furrowed. I went on. "He can't get help from LPD and he wants me to look into a death on his property."

"What does he expect you to do?" asked Samantha.

I rubbed my neck. "No idea, honestly. Outside of pointing him in the right direction, the pay is good and I could use it."

"Everything okay?" Samantha asked, her lips drawing tight.

I debated telling them about the collector and decided better of it.

"Everything's fine. I just want to make sure the caravan is back in the black by the time Wensem returns," I lied, then turned to Hagen. "The guy invited me to some party in the upper spires. I was hoping I could borrow a suit from you."

Hagen is a bit taller than me and slightly thinner but I could probably make it work. I didn't own a lick of decent clothing. Even on my best days I looked like an unemployed drifter. Dress for the job you want, I guess.

"I have a spare suit somewhere."

"You're telling me some elevated found you and offered you a job as a private investigator?" asked Samantha.

"That's the whole of it. Yes."

"And you just went along with it?" she said, her eyes narrowing slightly.

"Well, I thought it over, but yeah. As I said, I need the money."

Samantha frowned but didn't press further. She went to work tying a bit of twine around the tome and then tucking it into her bag.

"There's something else," I finally blurted. It would have been easier to do this without Samantha here. She was already suspicious and asking Hagen about Aklo would only raise her suspicion further.

Hagen raised an eyebrow. "Oh yeah?"

"Whoever killed the employee wrote some messages on the wall in the deceased's blood."

"Oh, Carter's cross," Samantha swore. "Why does this sort of stuff always happen to you?"

I gave a weak smile. "Just lucky, I guess."

"This isn't one of the recent gilded murders, is it?" Hagen asked.

I shook my head. "Doesn't look like it. The guy was a kresh servant. Outside of scaring his former boss, his death isn't going to change the business landscape of the upper reaches. He was just an old kresh, killed in a rich guy's flat. But... the killer left a message."

"What was the message?" asked Hagen, leaning forward slightly.

"Well, that's just it, I can't read it."

Now both Hagen and Samantha's eyebrows raised. I rubbed my neck and let out a deep breath. "Yeah, you see... it's in Aklo."

SIX

Standing stiffly in Hagen's old suit, I watched the levels of Lovat slowly drift past. The suit was tight across the chest, long in the legs, and short in the sleeves. I hoped it didn't show. The jacket worked if I didn't try to button it, and the pants would be bearable if I kept myself from eating too much.

I had pulled my hair back into a loose bun and combed my beard in an effort to look presentable. Truth be told, I should have seen a barber. In my mind I looked less like a down-in-the-subs drifter and more like a mid-level broker. I doubt I pulled it off very well. The tattoos, of course, didn't help. Plus, I lacked that upper-level attitude. A certain lira-laden snobbery that lurked in the uppers. Trying to wear that attitude was about as comfortable for me as the suit.

"So what exactly are we looking for?"

I turned and glanced at Hagen. The suit he wore was nicer than mine, newer, with the high collar and brass buttons currently in favor among Lovat's elite. A thick aiguillette wrapped around his left shoulder. While it wasn't specifically fashionable it was common among dimanians. One could likely do an entire study on dimanian formal wear, but my own knowledge was limited. The thickness and style of the braiding apparently denoted the wearer's name, occupation, and status. Not unlike a coat of arms from the old legends of the Penitent Queen. Samantha probably had one, too.

I had filled him in on the meeting with Kiver but hadn't covered all the particulars. "The body was removed by the coroner's office a few weeks ago, but he said the scene was untouched. Sealed off."

"Why didn't he just bring you a copy of the text? It would have made this all a bit quicker, and you wouldn't have had to borrow a suit."

"Well..."

"Yeah?"

"He did," I said. "I just left it at Cedric's. As I told Hannah, I didn't expect to be taking the job."

"She didn't take it?" Hagen scratched his chin.

I stared at him blankly, and then slowly winced.

"She going to be upset that we're taking this job together?" Hagen asked.

I hadn't thought about that. I'd been so wrapped up with Essie and Argentum that I had completely forgotten about Hannah. A weight slumped in my stomach. I felt awful. I should have telegraphed, I should left a message at her building. Something.

"Yeah, she probably will," I admitted. "I'll cut her in."

Our lift slowed to a halt.

"Level Five!" called out the conductor, a hefty dauger with a brass mask in the pine-green uniform of Lovat Public Transportation.

Lifts rise and fall through Lovat's superstructure constantly. Because of their size they're pretty slow, but it beats climbing the stairs between levels. Hundreds of them whir, hum, and clack their way along, passing between floors, carrying passengers and cargo up and down. The public city lines usually run inside the massive pillars that hold the levels aloft, though those aren't the only hoists in the city. Lifts of all shapes and sizes owned by all sorts of interests run day and night. There are express lines and extravagant lifts for the rich. There are lifts for cargo, and for school children.

The lifts themselves are usually multi-leveled and lined with seats. A few have small bars on their top floor and can be quite lively at night. At full capacity a lift can carry a few hundred people but it's rare to see one that full.

A huddle of passengers disembarked on Level Five and then a fresh line of arrivals were allowed to file in, the conductor counting on a mechanical tally machine. A few climbed the stairs to the floor above, while others filled empty seats. Some followed our lead and stood near the windows, looking out at the city.

"Well, I'm not going to complain about rubbing elbows with elevateds. The last time I was on one of the upper levels I was with my father. Let me tell you, there is no better buzzkill for a glamorous evening than a Reunified Cardinal.

"*Old* Reunified Cardinal," Hagen corrected. "It was a few years ago. At the time he had some wild hair up his ass about abstaining from the pleasures of the wealthy. He wanted to show how humility and poverty can lead to happiness. Didn't think it was right for a cardinal to be seen enjoying the extravagant entertainment of the elevated."

"I doubt Sam would be much of a buzzkill," I said, thinking of Samantha's future ascendancy to the rank of cardinal.

I thought about that kind of a gig. What kind of belief did that take? A few years ago, I would have told you the legends of the Firsts were a load of crap. It had taken two of them to set me straight, and they weren't even the strangest thing I had seen. Now my own thoughts surrounding God, the old legends, and the Firsts were... well, complicated.

"I wanted to see the glass waterfalls and he didn't," Hagen continued. "So I suggested we catch the Vipond Orchestra—they were playing a suite of W. J. Bassy arrangements at the time—but no, we couldn't even listen to music. Even the old songs! 'I am a man of the people. I serve them.' *Priests.*" Hagen sighed dramatically and then chuckled. "You see why I chose the glamorous life of a trinket dealer."

"All the music and sightseeing you could want," I said, feeling the lift shudder into motion again as it started rising. The crowd on this lift were white collar types, probably heading home from a day at the office.

"If only I had known," he said wistfully. "It's all bookkeeping and cleaning. I can't remember the last time I got out from behind that desk."

I could. It was when we'd met. Hagen had been connected to me by that cult, the Children of Pan. I had hired him to do some research for me. By assisting me, he had drawn their ire. We'd barely escaped, that first time. Samantha had sheltered us in the seminary at Saint Mark's. It was more for him than me, but I was grateful.

I didn't respond. I looked out the window and leaned my forehead against the cold glass. Those memories felt like another life. Emotions clung to their sides like barnacles. They were probably better left buried.

Dozens of stories above our last stop, the lift passed from Level Five, traveled through the entresol, and emerged through the floor of Level Six, where it slowed to a stop and belched warm air, releasing another huddle of passengers.

"So, how much we making off this?" Hagen asked.

I did the math in my head. "You know your normal rate?"

"Yeah?" Hagen said, his voice rising an octave along with his eyebrows.

"Triple it."

"Carter's cross," he whispered. "You're kidding!"

I shook my head, wondered why I had turned the job down in the first place. *Hundreds* a day. It was more than I could make in months of trail work. Shame it was now all going to pay a collector bounty.

"I don't know how much we'll be able to do for him outside of looking at the scribbles, translating them, and taking the cash. But he's eager for some movement. He's scared."

"Can you blame him?" Hagen said, "Imagine having one of your servants killed, and then having the scene of the murder remain in your house."

"Well, first I'd need to imagine having servants..."

Hagen rolled his eyes. "The point stands."

"He's not living there now. He's moved to some other apartment until this gets sorted out. LPD haven't even been around to take a statement."

Hagen's face went serious, but his tone was not. "Maybe the butler did it."

I laughed. "You're an asshole."

Lovat is a funny place. Levels aren't one solid floor but instead a maze of them—a connection of floors. They rise and fall and start and stop all over the city. It's an ever-changing haphazard jungle of steel and concrete.

Level Nine wasn't nearly as finished as Eight. It wasn't complete like the levels below. It was a proper level, but hardly complete enough to be called a roof, let alone a ceiling. At most it was a series of raised plazas and gardens twenty or thirty stories above the floor of Eight. Lifts didn't go there yet.

A gray sky greeted our lift and a bitter wind kissed our cheeks as we stepped off onto Eight and looked around for the Shangdi Tower. A light snow blew around us, lifted on the wind.

"By the Firsts!" swore Hagen. "It's cold as hell up here."

Enormous buildings forty and fifty stories tall rose around us. Minimal glowing letters above glass doorways displayed their names: The Hallmark, Daedalus, Fallowshire. They blocked any direct view of the Rosalias and the ocean to the west and they did a wonderful job working as funnels for the icy wind that howled this high up.

Simple Auseil decorations rocked in the wind and the soft voices of street singers floated from somewhere down the wide lanes.

The elevated city had an odd antiseptic quality to it. No strange smells to greet my nose. No graffiti to draw the eye. No abrasive calls of vendors to fill the air. No gaudy neon splashing its color about.

Small manicured parks shuddered in the breeze, twinkling with frost. Naked deciduous trees planted in pleasing patterns swayed down the centers of divided streets. Topiaries cut in animal shapes whispered to one another as the cold blew through tightly tangled sprigs. I recognized a centipede, a fish, an ox, and even a shambler among the shapes.

Everything on Level Eight was tasteful. And unsettling.

"The Hale. Daedalus. Hmm, where's the Shangdi?" Hagen asked, pulling his thick coat tighter and turning up his collar. I had considered bringing my own jacket, but the canvas roader coat clashed outrageously with the suit. I already looked strange enough up here, no sense calling it out further. I would just have to deal with the cold. Besides, the inside of the Shangdi should be warm enough. As soon as we found it.

I shoved my hands into my pants pockets. The cold cut through the thin material and sent chills down to my bones. A numbness spread throughout my body. Fortunately, it also numbed the constant pain in my right knee and allowed me to walk a little straighter and with less of a limp.

"Come on," I said through my chattering teeth as we tromped northward towards some of the taller towers on Level Eight. A few of the buildings around us originated somewhere below, their foundations built on the superstructure of Levels Six or Seven, their sky lobbies opening on Level Eight's street level.

There were few people out and about. Most were pulled along in enclosed and heated rickshaws with mirrored windows and small chimneys that billowed smoke. Their windows were darkened leaving only shadows inside. Those we could see, who couldn't afford tinted glass, were festooned in strange fashions. Women in dark veils. Men in corded turbans. Everyone was wearing heavy cowls fringed with gold and silver, pulled up and around their faces making them look like fancy road bandits.

The servants who pulled the rickshaws varied in race. I saw a maero, an umbra, and even a cephel. In the cold weather it was rare to see cephel folk outside of their watery homes and this far from the Sunk, but a few moved past, outfitted in heavy robes that gave them an appearance of ghosts gliding among an oddly manufactured forest of slumbering trees. I wondered what it was like up here in the summer. I thought of the breeze as it might be then. Inviting and warm. Folks could waltz around on the plazas and take in the sun. Lie in the gardens.

"Okay, I'm freezing. Can we just find the damn place and get warm?" Hagan said. He wrapped his arms around himself, shivering.

"Let's ask that security guard," I said, nodding toward the guard.

A human security officer in a thick ankle-length black wool coat, smoking a fat cigar, stood near a crossroad. He was watching a traffic officer and holding a rifle in the crook of his arm. A big patch blazed on the arm of the dark coat. In large Strutten letters it read: "Shangdi Security." Excellent.

We approached him. "Excuse us…"

He waved a hand, shooing us away. "I'm not buying. Move along."

"We just need some quick directions," Hagen said.

He blew out a cloud of blue smoke that was snatched away by the wind and turned to look us up and down. "Well, aren't you two an adorable pair. A human and a dimanian in their church-day finest. Sorry, boys, there's no churches near here. No proper ones, anyway."

Ignoring his comment, I went on. "We're looking for Shangdi Tower. We just arrived."

A bitter wind whipped around us.

He blinked, then snorted, then grinned. "Are you, now? Look at how fancy you look! You planning on waltzing into Shangdi and being whisked into its uppers? Looking for a pad of your own? A little *love nest* away from the scrape? Well, I'm sorry to say it's completely full. No rooms at the Shangdi. No, sir." He took another drag from the cigar and chuckled.

"We're not looking for a *love nest*," said Hagen, annoyed. "We're actually here—"

"It's tough times," the guard interrupted, smirking. "Based on that suit, it's obvious this is not your scene. Unless you're going to a costume party?"

Hagen frowned slightly and bowed his head, rubbing a hand on the breast of his jacket. His cheeks flushed, and not from the cold.

The security guard didn't let up. He turned to me. "What are you, a vagrant? Junkie? Hoping someone inside will take pity on you and feed you, fill your belly, buy you a suit that fits?" He chuckled and turned away, ready to ignore us.

Even through the cold I could feel my nails digging into the palms of my hand. "I'm here at the request of an occupant," I said. He was lucky that was all I did.

"Oh?" He grinned, amused. He took a long pull from the cigar and blew the blue smoke in my face. "And who would request a *scrape* like you?"

I imagined slamming my fist into his rows of white teeth. The sound of it. The perfect little pearls flying off, being taken by the wind and mixing with the snow. Instead, I pulled Kiver's card from my pocket and held it a few inches from his face. I waited a beat so he could comprehend what he was reading.

"Kiver dal Renna, of Renna Monochromes," I said coolly, trying not to let my teeth chatter and hoping there was a tinge of menace in my voice.

The guard's eyes widened slightly. Hagen gave a snort. I was sure I could feel him smiling behind me.

"Way I see it: the quicker you help us out, the better your chances of keeping your job."

The Shangdi was only a few blocks from where we found the security guard. With the guy now humbled, we had a direct escort to the building.

He walked briskly, mumbling to himself as we made our way down Terence Avenue. We passed a few more building entrances—Woolford Tower, The Brass—a public fronton, and crossed the wide Paramount Plaza. A bitter wind whipped at us across the vast open space.

Near one end of the plaza sat City Hall, the mayor's office. It was a low-slung building whose roots rested several floors below. These upper reaches, still sun-touched, served as its formal entrance. Two big doors bearing the Seal of Lovat sat in the center of a swath of wide, mirrored windows that stared out into the cold. Its handful of stories and low, flat roof looked out of place among the rising towers around it. A few protesters wearing red armbands gathered near the front stoop. They were chanting something lost to the wind, holding signs I couldn't make out.

At the opposite end rose Waite Tower, headquarters to The Camalote Group, one of Lovat's private organizations. It was a thick building, dull and lifeless save for the flower logo of The Camalote Group at its crown. I remembered the billboards they had scattered around the city. Pictures of smiling Lovatine families staring out from underneath text that read: "EMPOWERING PEOPLE. CHANGING LIVES."

The plaza itself was huge. The sheer space in the elevated levels never ceased to amaze me. Down below, in the mids or lower, there was no space like this. Open, unused. Every square foot was precious, every corner a kingdom. It seemed to me that half the city could gather here.

Once we crossed the plaza we turned onto Howell Street, finally finding ourselves standing before the Shangdi's entrance.

Residents and visitors milled about the front doors, clad in heavy hoods and thick collars. A few smoked. A couple sipped off bottles of beer. Laughter rose among them as they moved in and out, nodding to a porter who seemed to keep a keen eye on everyone. The guard led us to the door without a word. We followed close behind.

"Binger, you still have ten minutes left on your lunch," the porter said, checking his watch. He was a dark-suited dimanian with dusky skin and thick curving horns like a ram. "Who are these two?"

"I didn't get their names. They're guests of Kiver dal Renna."

I flashed the powder blue card to the porter.

The porter hummed and said, "You're the third visitors today without an invitation. You attending the party?"

"Third visitors?"

"Yes indeed."

I looked at Hagen for a moment, worry flashing in my eyes, before I turned back to the porter.

He went on. "Go on in and talk to the front desk. They'll put a call in to Kiver and then direct you. Just around the corner. Follow the green carpet."

"Thanks," said Hagen as we left the security guard outside with the porter and pushed into the warm lobby.

I still felt numb inside, but no longer from the cold.

SEVEN

You could feel it in the air: a tension, lurking beneath the surface. It waited, like water just about to boil over. This might have been a holiday party but it wasn't a real joyous occasion. The laughter of the guests sounded forced, a little too loud. Conversations were short, topics tossed around rapidly. The liquor was flying.

They were living in fear. Discussion of the recent murders, gilded or otherwise, crept into every conversation. I couldn't really blame them—hell, I could sympathize. I had my own killer after me. That edge is hard to shake. Even as I stood here in my borrowed suit. Drink in hand, Argentum's threats played through the back of my mind. One week. Well... six days now.

"These people are scared," Hagen said, biting into a fat, deep-fried prawn.

"You see it, too?"

"It's obvious. The few conversations I've had around the buffet have all been about the recent murders and LPD's glacial response." Hagen looked at his plate, piled high with steamed dumplings, fresh salads, and fat pink shrimp. "I realize there's been a few murders but this feels... off. To be this nervous at an Auseil party? With the kind of security here?" He nodded towards a pair of burly, heavily armed dauger with steel masks standing by the doorways. They were dressed in black, with large rifles slung across their backs and sidearms hanging at their hips. The perfect complement to a holiday party.

I took a sip from my drink. The ice had cooled the vermouth, removing a lot of its inherit bitterness. The bartender had looked at me with a puzzled expression when I had ordered it. I've grown accustomed to puzzled glances.

"Look, keep poking around. Kiver's servant was drained, most of his blood used to paint inscriptions on the wall. When I last checked, the cops weren't sure how the elevated victims were killed. To me, it all seems too..."

"Intentional?" Hagen asked.

"Something like that. I don't think it's related."

Hagen swore, and shook his head. "Poor Lovat. Seems like it's always something. The gilded murders. Now this thing with the kresh. Before this we had Black and his Children."

He sighed.

I nodded. There was always something. The city was already volatile.

I plucked a piece of har gow from Hagen's plate and popped it into my mouth. I knew the shrimp dumpling was hot and delicious, but I couldn't enjoy it. The flavor in the dumpling disappeared, leaving me with an empty pit in my stomach.

"Kiver said he wanted us to mingle and he'd come find us a bit later."

"He seemed surprised to see you."

"Yeah, like I said, I wasn't going to take the job initially. Look, I'm going to get back to the party," I said. "Keep an ear out."

Hagen smiled and nodded and contented himself with his plate of food and the expansive view. I moved across the apartment towards another corner. Since being rushed into the party I hadn't had much time to look around. I had no idea who those other visitors had been. I had hardly seen Hagen, just been thrust from one conversation to another by some drunk guest.

Kiver's small get-together had somehow exploded into a full-on Auseil party. Strings of subtly twinkling yellow lights hung from the ceiling like golden spider-webs, their motion making the room shimmer in the fluctuating light. Branches dipped in chrome hung among them looking like the venation of a dragonfly's gossamer wings. They reflected the light, causing tiny golden motes to play out on the floors and walls. Everything seemed to be dancing.

Somewhere in the large hall a band played an old Auseil tune: "Body and Soul." Near the band a few intoxicated guests danced in pairs while others watched.

Kiver's apartment, like most maero homes, was sparely furnished. The walls were bare—no million-lira tapestries hung against them, no luxurious furniture covered the floors. What furniture did exist was maero design. Simple shapes. Usually cubed. Nothing overly assuming, nothing ostentatious.

It was the view that was the real gem.

The flat occupied one whole floor of the Shangdi Tower. Its outer walls were made up of huge panes of glass that offered expansive views of Paramount Plaza, the newly forming streets of Level Nine, as well as the scrape and span of the lower levels that extended out across the archipelago, rising and falling like frozen waves. The lights of millions upon millions of souls crammed atop one another into small apartments, offices, and hovels twinkled from below. A small bit of sanctuary on the edge of the vast wilds of the Territories.

Partygoers—Hagen among them—stuffed themselves along a table festooned with dim sum dumplings, thick red cheeses, platters of cubed bacon topped with ginger and spicy peppers, and piles of fresh salads. On one hand, it was not at all what I expected, but on the other hand, there were no surprises. With the rationing in full effect and supplies so scarce, a party like this was excessive. It seemed strange that the papers would leave this alone, but knowing the *Ledger* they were probably so deep in elevated pockets they wouldn't touch it. Their reporters were probably even here, stuffing their cheeks along with everyone else.

Didn't Kiver understand how many people were going hungry? Was he really so callous to the lives suffering in the warrens below? He had been down there. He'd met me in Cedric's. He had to have seen the people clamoring for overpriced scraps.

I found the group in a corner, speaking softly as the ice in their drinks tinkled. Kiver had made quick introductions and left me standing with them earlier. I had already tried to probe about the kresh servant and that had gone nowhere. There had been some discussion of the gilded murders, but the topic had been quickly changed. The market and tariffs were much more pleasant topics. I had wandered off then. Now I hoped the topic had finally changed. Luckily, it had.

"Ah, Mr. Bell, welcome back," said an older human woman. I hadn't caught her name yet.

"Yes, welcome back. I meant to ask earlier: What sort of business are you in?" asked a maero named Caleth dal Dunnel. He was big, thicker than Wensem, and taller. He wore a tuxedo that hung loosely about him. His dark eyes were glistening above liquor-flushed cheeks. It was tough to place how old he was. Maero tend be difficult to judge when it comes to age, they don't wrinkle like we do, and it takes a long time before their locks go gray. Even so, I was confident Caleth was on the young side.

"Caravans. I'm one of the owners of Bell Caravans," I said.

"Rough time for you lot," said Caleth. "Sorry about that."

I nodded. "It is what it is. What do you all do?"

I looked around at the gathered group.

Caleth laughed. "Personally, I do a little of this and little of that. Frank here's a doc. Joy works the boardrooms for Camalote. Cora here's in fish—Lawton Island Fish, specifically. Janus is—"

"Please, do we need to blather on about work?" interrupted the doc—Doctor Frank Adderley. He was tall and rail-thin with sharp chiseled cheekbones and handsome features. His immaculate chin-length hair hung limply around his face. He had bright piercing eyes that glinted in the cascade of lights.

He was also pale. It was odd. Humans are usually swarthy, with dark skin, dark hair, and dark eyes. It varies slightly, but it's rare to see humans as pale as Doctor Adderley. It's said that before the Aligning—when the Firsts wreaked havoc—humans were once as variously colored as all the species of earth. We came in all shapes and sizes and colors. Then something had changed. Now we're more or less constant: dark hair, dark eyes, dark skin. This man was peculiar, an anomaly.

"Alright," I said. "What were you all talking about before I stepped in?"

"The recent jai alai rankings," Adderley said.

"You been following?" asked Caleth.

I shook my head. I didn't go much for sports. Never had time.

"Not particularly. Nothing against it, but it's been years since I watched a full match."

"Too much time on the road," said Adderley.

"Something like that," I said. "What have I missed?"

I looked around the group.

A middle-aged human woman named Joyce Pickett-Derby answered first. She had kind green eyes and a wide smile. She wore a simple suit with a skirt. The logo of The Camalote Group was embroidered on a breast pocket. "We're coming up on the Northern Semi-Finals. Me, I like the Fausti brothers. Aggressive play. Nice defense. I think they have a great chance."

Drunken laughter rose from Caleth and he shook his head. I turned to him. "You disagree?"

"Carter's cross, Joyce! You know shit all about jai alai if you think the Faustis will clinch the semis!" said Caleth. He cleared his throat and chopped a hand in her direction. "Let me tell you why you're wrong. You ask anyone and they'll tell you the same thing: Reddick and Monty have the best chance at taking the trophy this year. Like the year before. Monty's chula is second to none and Reddick can catch like nobody's business. They've won twelve out of their last fifteen matches. Twelve out of fifteen! No one else in the damned league can come close to that. And you pick a pair of quims like the Faustis? They don't have a chance! And before you say anything, Shain..." He smirked at an umbra standing nearby. "...neither do that pair of demons: Denaiud and Roux."

Demon, a slur for dimanians. I shifted my weight and buried my darkening cheeks in an awkward sip from my drink. Caleth went on, holding up a forefinger and pinky together and slapping them to his wide forehead. A crude imitation of a dimanian's horns. He belched and laughed, throwing a wide fleshy grin at the group.

I was glad Hagen had stayed by the food. For years the slang term "demon" had been thrown around, despite the fact that dimanian horns were cutaneous. Nothing like the ancient stories of red devils and whatnot.

"Hey, let's not—" I said, intending to cut this short.

The old human woman standing to my left huffed in disgust and rolled her eyes, cutting in. "I wish you wouldn't be so churlish, Caleth. Really. It's below a maero of your standing to use such slurs. You know they're just drummed up and spread by the Purity Movement."

"Hah!" Caleth laughed. "It's all in good fun. Everyone knows I'm kidding."

He looked around the group for accomplices but found none. Miss Pickett-Derby folded her arms and frowned.

"At the very least, don't do it in front of Kiver's guest," said the old woman. There was a tone of authority in her voice.

I looked from her to the maero as I took a sip of vermouth. It was very good, sweet and sharp, rich with spicy botanicals, perfect for washing away offensive comments. I hoped I had enough.

If Caleth was embarrassed he certainly didn't show it. Instead he took another swig from his wine glass and grinned at the old lady. Then he reached out and slapped me on the shoulder. "You don't mind, do ya, pal?"

"Actually, I do mi—" I began.

Caleth ignored me. "Cora, you forget, some of my best friends are dims... d–demons... dimanians." He grinned a set of huge white teeth. She took a sharp intake of breath and set her jaw. His reaction had clearly been a mistake.

"Careful now, Cal," warned Adderley.

"Indeed," said Pickett-Derby.

"I'm fine," said Caleth. "Cora knows I'm just fooling."

Did she? A fellow who had been introduced to me as Janus Ambrose Gold chuckled. As his name suggested he was a dauger with a simple but glittering mask of bright gold. He wore a dark blue suit trimmed in a similar color that did much to hide the wide paunch of his belly. It was clear he was the most wealthy of the gathered throng and with his sweeping statements he wielded his power like a scythe. There was something in the way he held himself. Absolutely upright, but relaxed. And the way the others never directed questions at him. They perked up and stopped speaking when he spoke.

What an odd lot.

"He may be a bigot and without class, Miss Dirch, but I can assure you that Caleth's jai alai predictions are not to be discarded. He's successfully predicted the last six championship teams." Gold looked at me. "You'd do well to take his advice and back Reddick and Monty, Mister Bell."

Caleth nodded smartly, as if Gold's comment was the perfect testimonial.

"I'll keep that in mind," I said.

"Keep it in mind only if you want to find yourself broke," said the umbra. I cringed. I get uncomfortable around the umbra. The shadow people are usually a rare sight in Lovat. Seeing one as elevated as this was even more rare. He had warmly introduced himself as Charles Shain, a human name that had left me perplexed. I had always thought of umbra as cold but his hand had been warm, pleasant even. And I had always thought, because of their form, that umbra were soft but his grip had been shockingly firm when we shook hands. His eyes glowed a friendly yellow.

But then, my experience with umbra was limited. A little over a year earlier I had a run-in with one. That's a nice way of saying she had killed some of my friends, both close and distant, as she carried out orders for The Children of Pan. The dark cult that dragged me to my first encounter with a First. Cybill— the kindler. That umbra had died with Cybill, in a tunnel far below, somewhere beneath the bedrock of the Sunk, killed by Samantha and buried with her god.

Shain seemed the absolute opposite of her. A tailored pale gray suit draped his form and he wore a bright yellow tie that matched his eyes. Tight gloves covered his hands. He also wore a silken keff—a roader's headscarf—wrapped around his head, covering all but his face. You could hear the smile in his voice as he corrected Caleth. "Denaiud and Roux are younger and faster than Reddick and Monty. Injuries have plagued those two all season. I think you'll be surprised who's standing on the podium in the end."

Pickett-Derby took a sip of sparkling wine and nodded. "Cal, you've picked Reddick and Monty every damn year. Every damn year! Like clockwork. We all stand around, eating dim sum, drinking, you have a few too many, and we end up talking about who'll win the championship. Every year: Reddick and Monty. As if they never aged. As if there weren't another forty pairs out there as eager as they are to win."

Gold seemed amused by this. He rocked on his heels and gave a chuckle.

"One would think Lovat's Jai Alai League is rigged," said Dirch, the old woman, with a wicked smile. She was human, and older than the others. She wore a rose-colored dress with a matching jacket. Glittering jewelry adorned her neck and clattered on her wrists, clear gems and gold. A small matching stickpin graced her lapel. She had coppery skin and dark hair that was fading to white near her ears. Above her sharp features sat keen eyes that studied everything and missed nothing. She seemed a force to reckon with.

Shain launched into another anecdote on Caleth's behavior when Gold interrupted him. The umbra went immediately silent, his eyes dimming slightly. "How about you, Mister Bell?"

"Er..." I stammered.

I don't know much about elevated culture. That includes how status is determined. It's not a caste system like the dauger society, but it's also not a hierarchy based on wealth. It's also not based on experience, which is how we roaders weigh a person. Power here is hard to judge. If someone higher on the ladder of power talks over you, asks a question, or even looks in your direction you're supposed to respond in some manner. A respectful bow of the head. A glance away. Just shutting the hell up. But as an outsider, these rules are beyond me. I didn't know how to navigate it. The only thing I did know was that out of everyone at Kiver dal Renna's Auseil party, I was at the bottom. Hell, the servers and bartenders probably ranked higher than me.

Gold inclined his head as if to indicate for me to go on.

An old mantra welled up. *Trust no one but your company.* One of my rules. I didn't know these people. They weren't trail-worn. They were the soft-palmed aristocrats of a city on the verge of crumbling. Playing their games, maneuvering with words and bankrolls and in some occasions murder, instead of hard work and honesty.

"As I said... jai alai isn't really my game," I said, meeting Gold's blue-white eyes. His mask was different from Argentum's. The eyes were wider, the mouth slit large enough to show teeth. Two brown ears peeked out from either side.

"More of an ausca fan?"

I paid even less attention to the small field gridiron. I doubted discussing the sports I attended would be welcome in this group. When in Lovat I usually caught a few cock fights, or the occasional boxing match in the Level Two rings, and many games of alley bones. Never professional sports. Professional sports are for the more elevated. I preferred the games of the scrubs and subs.

"Not really, professional sports have never really interested me. My work is exciting enough."

"Hah. Well, following a team is more than a good way to relax or wile away an afternoon. It's even more than a way to make money like our friend Caleth here does."

He paused and nodded at me as if waiting for a response.

"Is that so?" I said, waiting to see where this was going.

"It's a path to immortality," he said. "We're a part of something larger than ourselves. You become part of history. The team is a way to put yourself into something that is beyond you, bigger than you, something out of your control." He gave a chuckle. "In a less esoteric sense, it's a fine way to be part of your community, and cheer for a local team. Builds warren spirit, too."

The others gave polite laughs and nodded in agreement.

"Maybe," I said. "I guess I never felt like a local anywhere." I must have spoken a little too quickly. Gold's eyes narrowed slightly behind his mask and Dr. Adderley visibly tensed. I glanced at him and his eyes looked apologetic.

"What sort of business are you in now, Mister Bell?" the dauger asked. His voice had changed ever so slightly.

Good question. I was trying to figure that out myself. It was hard to be a caravan master without a company. I also wasn't here in any official capacity, just a roader trying to make some money off an elevated maero with the help of a much smarter friend. I went with something simple. "I'm a consultant. Kiver asked for my input on a project."

"A consultant."

"Second tonight," said Cora, bemused.

"Ah!" said Kiver dal Renna, walking up and draping a hand over mine and Gold's shoulders. If it bothered the dauger, he didn't show it. Kiver must rank higher than Gold. "How are my friends treating you, Mister Bell?"

"I'm enjoying myself," I lied.

"It's been a pleasure," said Shain warmly, his yellow eyes twinkling. "Don't listen to all the scra... er... lower-level rumors about us up on Seven, Eight, and Nine. We're good hardworking people as much as any other Lovatine."

Yeah? I thought, looking first at Gold, then Dirch, then Pickett-Derby who all seemed oddly quiet. Caleth laughed and shook his head. "Just like a scrape."

"Caleth," said Kiver, as firm and cold as I ever heard him. The other maero went immediately quiet. "I will not have that word or any other slur used in my house. Is that clear? *Especially* at Auseil. This is a time of unity."

Caleth didn't understand. "What? All I did was call him a scrape?"

Kiver bristled at the slur and snapped his fingers. A pair of big servers appeared behind him. One, a large maero with thick threaded muscles, the other a grim bufo'anur. I didn't expect to see one of the anur's big cousins outside of the high desert, and certainly not in the house of one of Lovat's elevated. They were fierce warriors and did not work cheap.

"Yes, sir?" the two asked, almost in unison.

"Mister Caleth is done for the evening. Please take his drink and see him out."

"Ah, Kiv. I'm just celebrating. Just wanted to let off a little steam. I was named chairman of Styer & Sons' board yesterday."

Kiver blinked, his face draining of emotion. It was gone in a flash. Replaced by the impassive graciousness that he had worn much of the night.

"His drink," he said to the servers.

Caleth's expression darkened. His eyes narrowed, his mouth turned to a scowl. For a moment the drunk maero didn't look willing to hand over his tumbler, but under Kiver's cool stare he capitulated. He handed his drink to the maero and looked up at the big toad-like creature who remained. His bulbous eyes blinked once, and his anurian expression turned dour. After a breath, Caleth shrank.

"Go get yourself some coffee," ordered Kiver, all smiles now. "Sober up." Then he turned to the two servers. "Keep him away from the liquor."

Caleth frowned and then drifted off, followed closely by the pair.

"I'm sorry about all of that," Kiver said.

"Wouldn't be a party if Caleth didn't make a fool of himself," Dirch said. "He just gets out of control. Easier to talk about the leagues as opposed to everything else going on. We're all just 'blowing off steam' these days."

"Yes. Well, I'd expect one of you to chastise him sooner."

They all shrank at Kiver's words.

"If you all will excuse me," said Dr. Adderley. "I have a telegram to send. It might be the holidays but the practice never slows down and I need to check up on some of my patients."

"I have a teleprinter in my office. Just down the hall. You're welcome to it."

"Th–thank you," Dr. Adderley stammered. A look of surprise on his face. He tilted his head at the maero. "I appreciate that, Kiver. Happy Auseil."

"And you, Frank. Make sure you get some of the fen guo this evening. I acquired some of the ingredients earlier this year *especially* for this occasion. I know it's a favorite."

The doctor smiled and nodded, backing away from the group. "I will. Thank you. It was nice to meet you, Mister Bell."

Kiver turned to those that remained. "Janus, Cora, Joyce, Charlie, if you'll excuse Mister Bell and me, we have some business to discuss. I hope you don't mind."

The four of them nodded, and Kiver guided me away, towards an unoccupied corner of his flat. I looked around for Hagen and saw my dimanian friend stuffing his face. He looked up from a plate of dumplings and raised an eyebrow. I nodded, calling him over.

"I'm sorry it took so long for me to pull away from my guests.

Auseil is a busy time for me. Lots of hands to shake, and frankly, I'm surprised you're here."

"Yeah? Well… I gave it some thought. You were very convincing," I said. I hoped he'd forget our last discussion.

It seemed to work. His eyes narrowed as we walked and frowned in confusion. "Well, you certainly have a funny way of showing it. I thought you were leaving me high and dry by sending another of your crew."

"Hagen is good people. I trust his expertise in these matters."

"Hagen?"

"My bookish friend over there." I pointed.

"No, I don't mean your dimanian friend," he said.

I blinked.

The crowds around us thinned as we passed into the corner where Kiver was leading me.

"Ah, here we go."

There was someone standing in the corner looking out over the view of Level Nine. Human. A woman. On the shorter side. Her dark brown hair was curled and swept into a neat pile on her head, a silky blouse draped low on the back, exposing dark smooth skin. A tight skirt clung to a pair of muscular thighs. One of the large hoods now in fashion among elevated citizens was elegantly slung over her shoulders. Tight gilded gloves and leather-laced ankle boots completed the outfit.

"Hannah?" I said as she turned, my eyes wide. She looked as surprised to see me as I did her.

"Boss?" she asked, at once drawing her shoulders up. She blushed, a mix of confusion and embarrassment crossing her features. Her dark makeup was perfectly applied. I had to admit, she was one of the more stylishly dressed of the attendees.

Hagen walked up and seemed as confused as I was. "Hannah?"

A weird mix of emotions brewed in my chest. I was angry she had tried to snipe the job, but I also admired the moxie. She was obviously more tenacious than I'd thought.

"You look lovely," Hagen said, swallowing a mouthful of dumpling and extending a hand. Hannah let him take it and kiss it lightly, but her eyes didn't leave mine.

"Sorry about the confusion," I said, recovering and turning to look at Kiver. "Just some miscommunication on our part."

"It's all right. I'm just glad you're all here. This is a better showing than LPD made. Honestly, when I left I thought I was lost. I was at my wits' end."

"So, you've met Hannah. Let me introduce Hagen Dubois, occult and religious expert."

"Nice to meet you," Kiver said, shaking Hagen's hand.

Hagen adjusted his glasses. "I'd like to take a look at the scene, if you don't mind. See if I can't get to translating the message."

"I trust Mister Bell has filled you in on all the details."

Hagen nodded.

"I moved out of that flat after it all happened, but the Commoriom's not far. Follow me."

The lift opened onto a cold and dark apartment that occupied the thirty-sixth floor of the Commoriom. The lights were off, and the heat had been turned down. Cold leaked into the place through the massive walls of windows.

The space had an odd feel to it. It hadn't been cleaned, and the carpets hadn't been vacuumed. Square footprints from the heavy but simple maero furniture could still be seen in the thick carpeting.

The four of us entered the flat, lights in hand. The dull yellow glow of the lanterns cast long shadows against the blank walls.

Kiver shivered. "I haven't been here in weeks."

His voice echoed off the walls. It was fascinating that no matter how small the space, all empty rooms still sound the same. The echoes might grow larger but the emptiness is no less heavy.

"Show us the room," I said, holding my lantern high.

Kiver and Hagen took the lead, moving through the large open area toward the far side of the building. Hannah and I followed behind. Close but out of earshot so we could talk.

"I thought you turned him down," she hissed at me.

"I did," I said.

"So?"

I scratched my beard and looked at her from the corner of my eye. Argentum's threat, that's what happened. I considered telling her but then thought better of it. Better to keep my cards close to my chest on this one. "Something came up. I need the money."

"Something came up?" she said. "You could have told me."

I smiled weakly. "But then I wouldn't have seen you in a dress."

She frowned, but not unkindly. "Oh come on. If I was on your other side, I'd knock the shit out of you for saying that."

"Well, I'm glad you're on my left," I said with a smile.

Silence fell between us.

"Sorry," I said after we rounded a corner and made our way down a small hall. Hagen and Kiver were well ahead of us now and we could talk with less of a hush. "I did want you here. Something came up and I decided to take the job. I should have contacted you. I'm sorry."

Hannah paused, noticing the edge in my voice. "What's going on, Waldo?"

"I got it handled," I said, trying to move the conversation forward. "As long as Kiver is good on his payment we'll cut this three ways."

"Sounds good to me."

We plodded along through the empty space.

"Hagen's not wrong though," I said.

"What do you mean?" she asked.

"You do look good."

I smiled and Hannah rolled her eyes. A wooden hand slapped my shoulder.

EIGHT

It was what I had expected. A bloody stain had been left where the kresh had fallen. Its green blood had stained the floor of the closet leaving a faint outline of its stocky body. The walls and cabinets were covered with letters. Strange shapes rose around us, twisted jagged lines all emanating from the massive stain on the floor. It didn't matter how many times I had seen it written out, Aklo always chilled me.

I slid under the police tape and stepped inside the closet, careful not to tread on the blood. The stains were long dry, the bright green blood had darkened as it dried to the color of the ocean. A deep soulless green.

"By the Firsts..." Hagen swore, his words trailing off.

"He was drained," said Hannah.

I turned and looked at Kiver. The maero's jaw was clenched, his eyes wide as he stared at the spot on the floor where the kresh had lain. The security detail that had been standing outside the flat leaned against the wall behind him, looking bored. Two women, maero and human, both in dark generic suits.

"This hasn't gotten any easier," Kiver said in a melancholic tone. "Hokioi worked for me for ages. I liked him, he was a hard worker. I like all my employees. To know something so violent could happen to a member of my household—"

I interrupted. "You said one of the housekeepers found him?"

I felt out of my element. It had been Samantha and Hagen who helped us pin Black, and Methow had been significantly more straightforward. I had no idea how to investigate a murder. I imagined Argentum standing in a corner, his shoulders shaking in that silent chuckle. I closed my eyes and inhaled deeply, trying to shake the looming black cloud. I tried to remember what I had seen on the cop serials, how the lantern-jawed detectives had gone about their questioning.

My eyes opened as Kiver spoke. "Yes. Spratt—he's an old human fellow. Was badly shaken after he found the body. I gave him a few days off."

I turned to Hagen and gestured to the walls. "Can you read it?"

Hagen hummed and studied the walls, spinning slowly in place like a dancer in a music box. His eyes squinted through his spectacles at the writing.

"Actually, yes. It's crude, given the writing instrument and the, er, ink but it's simple enough. If anything, it's too simple. Almost childlike. Whoever wrote this had a limited understanding of the language."

"How do you mean?"

"Well, Aklo is complex. Tense and tone, subtle marks in a letter can change an entire word. This doesn't have any of that.

It's like having a conversation with a four-year-old. Simple words. Simplistic sentence structures. It's—"

"What are these?" asked Hannah, pointing to what I had assumed were long spatters of blood that traced the larger spot on the floor.

"Oh?" Hagen furrowed his brow. "You know, I'm not sure."

Hannah was more prepared than I was. She pulled a small notebook from her handbag and began to draw the lines.

"It looks like a symbol." She crouched down, her muscles tight. You can dress up a roader in as much finery as you want—dresses, suits, fancy hats—but it won't change them at their core. She still looked ready to spring forward.

"There are some more complex sentences here. Words I don't understand. I think we'll need to go back to my shop and do some research."

I turned to Kiver, who was talking with his security people. "You have guests, feel free to return to your party. We'll lock up after ourselves and come find you when you're done."

Kiver breathed a sigh of relief. "Carter's cross, thank you. I hate this place. This whole floor. Not even sure how I feel about this buildi—"

"Sir!" a panicked voice echoed from down the hallway. "Sir, are you here?"

The security detail tensed, each reaching a hand into their jackets.

"That's Landel," Kiver said, holding up a hand to calm the guards. "It's just Landel." He called out. "We're down the hall. Where we found Hokioi."

A tuxedoed servant came around the corner. He was dauger, his mask simple and made of brass. The eyes behind the slits were wide and he appeared jittery. He stopped, doubled over, breathing heavily.

"I came as—" A gasp. "—fast as I could."

"Take a breath. What is it?" asked Kiver, a hint of trepidation leaking into his question.

Hannah and Hagen paused and looked up.

"Sir," the servant said. "There's been an incident. Someone else has been killed."

"W–what!" Kiver shouted. He blinked and stumbled back. "Where? W–when?"

"In Shangdi Tower. In your apartment."

"Who!" Kiver bellowed.

"Sir, it's D–doctor Adderley. Doctor Adderley has been killed."

A handful of Lovat's finest were already at Kiver's apartment by the time we arrived back at Shangdi Tower. We had run the few blocks between the two towers, scaring what few elevated pedestrians had braved the cold air. We didn't stop when we entered the Shangdi's lobby. Kiver signaled for us to follow and despite the protests of the watchman at the front desk we pushed into a lift and rapidly ascended.

When the lift opened into the secure vestibule, we surprised a pair of uniformed officers with stoic faces and heavy bags under their eyes outside the flat's door. They both started and their hands immediately gripped their clubs.

"Wh—" one said, his words sputtering to a stop when he recognized Kiver storming towards him. "Sorry, sir."

Kiver ignored him and pushed past. The rest of us followed.

The strained party scene we had left had changed significantly. News of the death had quickly spread through the crowd and the holiday spirit had evaporated. A man in a white tuxedo jacket and a maero woman in a sparkling evening dress were arguing with one of Kiver's security team. They clearly hadn't let anyone leave. Partygoers clustered in groups near the entrance.

The flashing lights that hung from the ceiling now played across the faces of the crowd. Turning each face into a terrified pantomime. Frightened guests whispered loudly to one another, a few crying out and shouting when Kiver entered.

He ignored them, too.

"What a mess," mumbled Hannah behind me.

The orchestra had stopped playing and now meandered together near the buffet table. The servants in their tuxedos looked distraught. A couple were smoking near a staircase to the upper floor. I couldn't imagine what was playing in their heads.

Kiver's security detail looked aghast, and along with that was a clear expression of shame. Someone had been killed under their noses.

"Where?" Kiver demanded from one of his security team, a dauger with a steel mask who was built like a brick.

"Back here, sir. Follow me," the dauger said.

We all did.

The scene was nearly identical to the one we had just left in the other tower. Only this blood was red, and the body was still in the center. A couple of cops tried to stop us from entering but Kiver pushed his way inside.

Doctor Frank Adderley was still in his smartly cut gray suit. Except now his chest and stomach were cut open, and it seemed he had tried in vain to stop the bleeding. His arms were soaked in blood up to the elbows. Some had even spattered his sharp chin and chiseled cheekbones and there was a smear across his forehead. His green eyes were open but clearly empty. Seeing nothing. He stared at the blank ceiling of Kiver's loft. A disturbing, enraptured smile on his face.

The smell was awful. The bowels or stomach had clearly been nicked. I had to turn away and take a few deep breaths.

The room was large, with floor-to-ceiling windows that looked onto the construction of Level Nine. It was obviously used as a child's room, most likely a teen's. In very un-maero fashion, posters of monochrome stars and jazz musicians decorated the walls. Near the door lay a maero bed-mat, piled high with stuffed animals. Besides that sat a small stool. The rest of the room was largely empty.

I turned and reevaluated the scene.

It was nearly identical to the previous one. An odd pattern like the one Hannah had spotted was traced around the body and partially obscured by a growing pool of blood. Rising along the wall below the body was more Aklo.

Out of the corner of my eye I could see Hagen was taking notes, immediately working on copying and translating the Aklo.

Hannah had also started sketching portions of the scene that caught her eye, the notepad pressed against her fake hand as her real one worked a pencil. I watched her circle the room, sketching out the symbols on the floor, observing and then taking notes about the position of the body.

"I was just with Frank," said Kiver to one of the officers. "He was fine! What happened?"

I was wondering the same thing.

The umbra, Charles Shain, stood in one corner, wiping his shadowy nose and giving a statement to an officer. Blood smeared the front of his suit, obscuring most of his yellow tie. He broke away when he saw Kiver enter.

"Chuck, what happened?" Kiver declared as he took in the umbra's appearance.

"He was still alive, Kiv. He was still alive when I found him here," said Shain. The umbra collapsed and Kiver rushed to hold him up. He eased him onto the stool. The umbra's shoulders shook. The color of his eyes had faded to a dull yellow. Tendrils of smoke drifted from his face where his cheeks would be.

We waited a few moments as Shain took a deep breath and began to speak. "After you two left, I got engaged in another conversation. I realized half an hour had passed and it doesn't take that long to use a teleprinter. So I went to look for him."

He stopped, taking another few breaths before continuing.

"I found him here, b–bleeding out. All this bloody writing on the wall. He turned to look when I came in. I called for help, rushed to him... he smiled when he saw me. Smiled! He tried to say something but his voice... it was so weak."

"By the Firsts…" Kiver said, his voice trailing off to nothing. "He d–died a few moments later."

Kiver's voice was so low it was almost a whisper. "Who? Who attacked him?" Shain gave a weak shrug and shook his head. Kiver whipped his head around to the beat cops. "Who!" he shouted.

"We don't know, sir. All we can do for now is secure the scene. Ask questions. We were down below when the call went out. The central office is sending an investigator."

I tried to take mental pictures of what I was seeing. Frank Adderley was dead. His chest and stomach gashed open. The writing was the same as the other scene, the symbols similar. But I was missing something. There was something about this scene that I was missing.

I stood there, looking down, going over what I knew when the scent of cigarette smoke and cheap whiskey wafted into the room from behind me. I felt his presence before he even spoke.

"Bloody shitting Firsts…" a familiar voice said.

I turned, knowing the source. My spine felt electric, and I shoved my hands into the pockets of my borrowed suit to keep them from shaking. Filling the doorway in a cheap suit stood Detective Carl Bouchard. He grinned a wicked grin at me and scratched behind one of the two heavy horns that curled up from his bald pate.

"Waldo Bell and a murder scene," he said with an exhausted chuckle. Then he leaned back to his partner. "I'm feeling a heavy sense of déjà vu. How about you, Muffie?"

NINE

Bouchard is tough as nails, stubborn as an ox, and big as a house. The kind of classic detective they write cop serials about. We do not get along. You don't just forget about being thrown in jail. Thankfully a puking drunk had given me an opportunity to escape. It hadn't stopped Bouchard, who had hunted me all over the city. It took the collapse of a tunnel and a handful of half-drowned cultists to clear my name. Even then, Bouchard had been begrudging. He made his apologies in my hospital room as I recovered. It seemed genuine at the time. I only recently discovered that he had been forced into it by his superiors. That his hat-in-hand game was all show. Just another corrupt cop trying to keep his neck out of the noose. A real class act: Detective Carl Bouchard.

He's a dimanian, but not rail-thin like Hagen. No, he's big. Thick barrel chest, expansive gut, wide shoulders, and legs like tree trunks. Heavy jowls that seem to hang from his round nose and small dark eyes that peer from beneath the shadow of his sizable brow. A short horn jutted from his chin like a frozen goatee, and two swooping horns rose from the apex of his forehead and then curved back to run along his bald head. Looking at him then, I felt dumbfounded. He grinned darkly. All white teeth and black promises.

"You want to tell me why I keep finding you at my scenes, Bell?" He spat the words, and his partner chuckled next to him.

Muffie was the opposite of Bouchard in almost every way. He's human, with a long narrow face, sharp cheeks, and hollow eyes. He looks emaciated. He doesn't say much, seems to be the type of guy who rides coattails. His nose sits crookedly on his face—a old souvenir from me.

Bouchard crossed his sizable arms and waited for a response. I could feel the hair on the back of my neck stand on end. I didn't want to give him another chance to get me in cuffs. I already had one maniac after my neck, I didn't need two.

"I was hired," I said. I scratched at my neck nervously and then worried about how it made me look.

"Hired, huh?" Bouchard said. "You realize how odd this looks. A previous suspect, known to police, at the scene of my DB? Not something you see every day. Most fellas in your position stay as far from police as possible."

I looked to Hagen and Hannah. Hagen had met Bouchard, but had Hannah? I couldn't remember. Hagen's eyes twitched from Bouchard to Muffie and then to me. He scratched behind a horn.

Bouchard followed my eyes. "Friends of yours?" He turned to Hagen. "You own that religious knick-knack store, right?" He didn't wait for Hagen to respond. "I'm working with your sister on another case." He turned to Hannah. "Who's the broad?"

"Name's Hannah," she said coolly. Bouchard let his eyes linger on her for a long moment. A smile twisted up on his face. She stared back, her expression cold.

"Wal," Hagen said, putting a hand on my shoulder. "Maybe we should go. Leave this to the authorities."

Bouchard laughed. "So, you moonlighting as a bloodhound now?"

"Ain't everybody?" Muffie said and then laughed.

I stood my ground. Felt my teeth tighten. Bouchard leaned towards me. I could smell his coffee breath, cheap aftershave, and body odor. He stopped, his nose nearly touching mine.

"Look, I can't have you here. I'm sorry." His voice was low, nearly a whisper. He looked down at his shoes and then back up at me. "There's too much heat on you. The papers would eat this shit up."

I blinked. Bouchard's tone had shifted but his expression hadn't changed. The wide grin still split his face. He spoke from behind a line of white teeth.

"I was asked—" I said, keeping my own voice low. Over Bouchard's shoulder I could see Muffie's eyes narrow. The thin cop took a step towards us.

Bouchard held out a hand, waving him off.

"I know. But look... we're stretched thin. There's enough problems with the gilded murders. I can't have you here."

I stared at him. Who was this Bouchard, appealing to me? The wide grin was still plastered to his face, but his eyes... his eyes were different. But how could I walk away from this? The Kiver job was going to save my life.

"I can't," I said. I cleared my throat and then spoke louder. "I can't."

Bouchard's smile faltered. I saw a bit of pity in his eyes. "Shame," he whispered.

The false grin wavered, and he stepped back. Seemed to size me up. I saw his expression tighten. Was that anger in his eyes? "You got a private investigator license?"

I didn't and he knew it. I glared at him. I knew where this was going.

"We're consultants," said Hagen. "I'm an expert on esoteric and religious findings. These writings—"

"—aren't your business," said Bouchard with a heavy finality. Pity and anger mixed in his eyes. He had given me a chance to walk away and I didn't. I couldn't. Walking away was a death sentence. I had to help Kiver and get paid or I'd be facing dismemberment or worse from Argentum.

"We're invited guests," said Hannah. She glared daggers at Bouchard and Muffie.

"Let me be clear: I don't care why you're here. This is now my scene. My DB. This is LPD jurisdiction. I don't need three civilians sticking their noses into my investigation."

"It's nice to see the police finally giving a shit," said Kiver coolly.

Bouchard spun, ready to abuse whoever interrupted him. When he saw Kiver, he caught himself. "Ah, Mister Renna. I'm sorry. Didn't realize you were—"

"I invited them, detective," said Kiver. "I was told about Bell's involvement with the Methow refugees. I sought him out. He has my personal invitation to be here. He was looking at the other scene when this happened." He motioned to Adderley's body.

"Other scene?"

Kiver's expression broke. His gray skin darkened. His eyes narrowed. "Excuse me? I've called LPD! Hokioi Taaka, a kresh, one of my servants, was killed at my last apartment. You sent the coroner. I was told a detective would come. I waited and waited. Nothing!"

Bouchard frowned.

"And you *still* don't know what's going on," Kiver continued. "Hence Mister Bell."

Bouchard glanced over at me and then back to Kiver.

"What?" asked Kiver, his voice thin and stretched. I couldn't tell if he wanted to throttle the detective or cry. He was a hard man to read.

"LPD is here now. Until we get to the bottom of this, the scene is closed. No outsiders."

Kiver set his jaw and stared down at the detective. "I have rights."

"Look, Mister Renna, a body was discovered in your home tonight. An *elevated's* body. We are under *strict* orders from the mayor to focus on elevated-area crimes until the border issue is sorted and we are back to full force. The death of a servant, while tragic—and I don't discount the loss, believe me—doesn't raise the attention it once would." He grimaced and lit a cigarette, taking a long draw and blowing blue smoke in the air before him.

Kiver glowered.

Bouchard's frown deepened into a sour scowl, the cigarette clenched in his teeth. "I don't make the rules. Now... clear the scene."

"This is my house!" Kiver shouted.

Bouchard nodded, pointing the smoldering end of the cigarette at me and then at Hagen and Hannah. "You three. Out. Now. Before I'm forced to throw you in jail." He stared at me as he spoke. His eyes were a strange mix of emotions.

His words, while curt, were not harsh. Missing was the abrasive edge I was used to, but I didn't care. My stomach felt like it was full of lead. I could only think of the lost paycheck and the doom it would bring.

As we walked away from the Shangdi, all I could envision was Argentum's placid mask, smiling at me.

TEN

"This is more generous than I expected," said Hagen, taking his stack of lira and counting it. Satisfied, he slid the bills into the cash register. I watched the money disappear, trying to push the negative thoughts out of my mind. I needed to focus on the present. To find a way to get myself out of this.

I tallied the days I had remaining. I had met Argentum the previous evening, so that left six days to get the money. The Kiver dal Renna case was now lost to me, along with its hefty payout. Kiver had handed us what he had in his pocket and pushed us out the door with his apologies.

I looked at my own stack of lira on the counter in front of me. It was a pittance. Before we divvied it up it had been just under three thousand lira. That meant we each walked away with about a thousand. Not even ten percent of what I needed to save my neck.

My stomach gurgled. The last time I had eaten was hours ago at Kiver's Auseil party, before we examined the Taaka murder scene. It felt like days ago. The whole incident, Adderley's death,

Bouchard. Any other detective might have tolerated our presence. But Bouchard... I breathed out slowly and tried to forget my empty stomach. What I wouldn't give for a bowl of noodles or a heap of sour dumplings right now.

Hannah seemed just as pleased as Hagen. She slipped her small wad into an inner pocket of her elegant jacket and then smiled sadly at me.

"I wish you had told me you wanted the gig."

I ran my fingertips over Saint Olmstead's old wooden counter. The place had begun to feel more and more like a home to me. The smell of incense and oiled wood. The sounds of bells and chimes. It had a peaceful quality about it. I turned and watched a shopper examine a shelf of small crosses before frowning and disappearing out the front door.

"I was glad to have you along," I said. It wasn't a lie. Even if it did cost me a third of the payout. "You noticed things Hagen and I skipped right over."

Hagen rolled his eyes and hummed at this.

"A lot of good that does us now," Hannah said. "It's LPD's case and with everything tied to Kiver they'll undoubtedly start looking into Taaka's murder as well."

"Yeah," I agreed. I stared at the bills, thinking.

There were two connected deaths. Two messages written on the walls in their blood. There were gargoyles wandering the streets. We had two probable signs and one definite sign of First involvement. I couldn't sit idly by. Argentum's threat was a problem, but I'd have to figure out a solution for that while I worked on this... whatever it was. I was the Guardian. It seemed time I acted like it.

"Boss?" said Hannah.

"Hmm," I said.

"You got that look in your eye."

"Oh?" I asked. "What look is that?"

"The one you get when you're about to raise hell," she smiled.

I grinned. I had the best scout in the Territories in front of me. An expert historian next to me, and his sister had more ancient religious knowledge than most libraries. And me... well, I could be one hell of a battering ram. We were a formidable team. Who cares about Bouchard? Who cares about the LPD and their jurisdiction? Kiver hired me to solve this, and I'd do my damnedest.

"Yeah," I said to Hannah. "Suppose I am."

"Count me in," said Hagen.

"Me too," said Hannah. "When do we start?"

"Tonight?" suggested Hagen. "I wired Sam and asked her to come over to help with translation."

At the mention of his sister's name my hands immediately went clammy.

"I'll stick around," said Hannah. "It'll be nice to see Sam." She draped her jacket over a stool seat and perched on top.

Saint Olm had been a tavern in a former life. Its well maintained counter had been a bar and Hagen had liked the idea of keeping a few stools for clients to ruminate upon as they discussed antiques, trades, or acquisitions.

"Great!" Hagen was visibly excited. "She was supposed to be here by now, but with this cold, who knows how long she could be? You guys want a drink?"

It was hard to focus on what Hagen and Hannah were saying. Thoughts of Essie fluttered through my mind. She was grounded. Smart. Quick. A comfort. It made me feel guilty. Somewhere inside me there was still a stir for Samantha. All of the last year was spent pining over her. Memories of our fateful trip to Syringa and down the Broken Road. We had come so close. There was a moment and then it had crumbled. I had pushed away.

I swallowed the lump in my throat, tried to clear my mind.

"Well?" asked Hagen, looking at me. "Drink? I actually have some of that rusty vermouth you like."

"Th–that'd be great," I managed to stammer out. Maybe a drink would do me good. Calm my nerves.

Hagen didn't move for the drinks right away. He just looked at me, a look of concern on his face. Finally he nodded and disappeared behind a door, emerging with two bottles and three glasses with ice. He poured my drink and two whiskeys, nudging one over to Hannah.

"You know how hard it is to find this stuff these days?" I said absently, looking at the ruby liquid sloshing against the cracking ice cubes.

"Mhm," Hagen mumbled around a sip of whiskey. "Near impossible. I heard the banks are beginning to horde it, doling it out on the side."

"Ugh," I said. We had seen it on our descent from the elevated levels. Streets growing ever dirtier as we moved down. People looking weaker and thinner and angrier. I knew what they'd think if they had heard Bouchard's words. The mayor's orders to look out for the elevated citizens first.

"They're going to get much worse," said Hagen. "You see the spread Kiver had at that party?"

"I haven't seen that much food in all my life," said Hannah. "Even in the good days."

Hagen took another sip. "Kiver's a maero. They're known to be simple and frugal people, even at their parties. Can you imagine some of the soirees dimanian households are throwing?"

"Or the humans," added Hannah.

"It'll leak eventually. Someone will tell, word'll spread," I said.

The bell above the front door rang and in a few moments Samantha emerged from the maze of shelves that occupied the front of the shop. She wore a heavy coat, leather and hooded, over her priestess garb. It was something you'd expect to find on the back of a road priest, not an urban priestess.

She smiled at me and embraced Hannah before moving around the counter and giving her brother a peck on the forehead below his single horn.

"Hi all, sorry I'm late. Some trouble broke out in the Terraces and it took forever to get around it."

"Uh oh," said Hannah.

"Carter's cross, that's where my apartment is," I said.

Samantha frowned. "I'm sure it'll be okay. Someone said it was related to an assault on a cargo lift."

The Terraces was the warren directly north of King's Station, where St. Olmstead sat. The neighborhood occupied most of the Levels from Three through Six and was a collection of businesses stuffed between a maze of apartments built for the lower working classes. Stairwells moved people up and down, crossing between levels and half-levels where shops were built onto the sides of brick apartments. It was decent but not the sort of place you'd want to raise a kid.

"What happened?" I asked.

"You have another glass?" Samantha asked Hagen.

"Sorry, I should've offered," he said.

"I'll have some of that vile vermouth," she said as Hagen fetched another glass. Samantha continued. "Anyway, apparently a cargo lift was loaded with a bunch of food heading to the upper levels and some locals seized it."

Hagen reappeared and poured her a glass of vermouth. The ice tinkled like the bell above the shop's door.

"You can imagine what happened next. LPD shows up, they go at one another. Parts are on fire, and the brigades are struggling to put it all out. They have streets blocked off and are directing folks downtown. I don't know much more than that."

"Carter's cross," said Hagen, draining his glass and pouring himself another.

I swore. "I hope my place is okay."

"You do?" Hannah asked me, an eyebrow raised.

I chuckled. "Well, not the flat. Just some of the stuff."

"I'm sure it's fine. Aren't you on the south side?" Samantha asked.

I nodded.

"Yeah, this is closer to Broadway Hill. The lowest level there is Three, and I couldn't drop down farther to avoid the mess. I would've canceled, but I know how important this is." She looked at me, her dark eyes fixating on mine for a brief moment before she looked away.

"Well, not sure how much use this translation will all be, anyway," I said.

"Why?" asked Samantha. "Is the Aklo fake or something?"

"While we were looking at the crime scene there was another murder and everything got mucked up," said Hannah.

Samantha blinked. "Another murder? Where?"

"Kiver's new apartment," I said. "In the Shangdi Building. Level... Nine." I remembered the construction of Level Nine's floor. Hokioi Taaka had been killed on Level Eight. Adderley on Nine. I scratched my cheek and mulled that over.

"Who?" asked Samantha.

"One of the elevated. A doctor named Frank Adderley," said Hannah.

Samantha set her glass down and stared at us.

Hannah continued. "We followed Kiver there. Found a similar scene as the previous murder. But this one still had a body."

"It looked like the work of the same killer," I said. Hagen nodded.

"So? That doesn't explain why translating the message won't be useful," said Samantha.

"The LPD showed up real fast," I said. "Carl Bouchard."

Samantha blinked and lifted her glass, taking a long sip then staring off into the air in front of her. "Millions upon millions of souls in this city and you run into him again."

"Yeah," I said. "He gets around."

"Why isn't he on the front lines?" asked Hagen.

"Good question," I said.

"Why is he up your ass?" said Hannah. "What did you do to piss him off?"

I had forgotten Hannah wasn't around during my run-in with Bouchard. I quickly filled her in. When I had finished she let out a slow breath and said simply: "Damn."

I nodded then stretched, feeling my lower back pop. "Sam makes a good point. Let's take a look at those translations. There could be something there. People are dying and more could still die. I'd like to prevent that if possible. The city is already fighting itself. Murder, especially murders concerning Firsts, adds an extra complication to an already complicated situation. The sooner we can help wrap up the case, the better."

"Think Kiver will still pay us? I mean, if we figure it out?" asked Hannah.

I had a thin hope that if we helped solve this there would be a reward, but did that matter any more? A Guardian's job is to guard. To put others' lives ahead of your own. I looked at my friends sitting around the counter. None of them realized how dangerous things had become for me. Losing the Kiver job had put me on the fast track to a collection. A week from now I could be lying in a Level Two gutter with gaping holes in my guts.

Still, I hesitated to tell them.

I thought back to what Samantha had said on the Broken Road. About trust, about how silence is not a form of protection. What were her words? "This isn't Wal versus the world"? Something like that. She was right: I needed to rely on my friends.

Right then I almost told them everything. The collection on my head. The twenty-five thousand lira due by the end of the week. But the words were heavy in my throat. They lodged there, impossible to get out and hard to swallow. I looked from Samantha to Hagen to Hannah.

They smiled, joked, sipped their drinks.

Not right now, I thought. It'd take Samantha and Hagen some time to get the text translated. While they worked I'd go see the Society. Explain the situation. Then I'd tell them. The city was already on the verge of collapse. Stealing a happy moment seemed wrong somehow.

Samantha's smile faltered as Hagen did his best impression of Bouchard. His cheeks flared, his chest puffed out. Her eyes, those pools of infinity, cut right through me. She read me like the dumb book I was. Her smile wavered slightly and one of her eyebrows ticked up. I wondered if she saw Argentum.

Then Hagen said something funny and she snapped out of her gaze and laughed.

Somehow I laughed along. It rang hollow.

ELEVEN

A cold wind cut through the streets and made the lights above my head sway. The shadows around me grew and shrank in the swaying light.

The Society of Collectors operates chapterhouses all over Lovat. I hadn't been inside many but they seemed to style themselves after a typical office or upscale bank. The larger ones in more elevated sections of the city are grandiose. The floors are marble, the hallways are lined with pillars. The desks are massive and made of a wood that no longer grows in the Territories. Smaller offices, in the lower warrens of the city, have more humble trappings. Three of four desks with typewriters, cork boards, filing cabinets, and coffee pots. Wood paneling covers the walls, dotted with old wanted signs and faded inspirational posters featuring rivers, mountains, and soaring birds with words like, "teamwork," "courage," and "persistence" written below them. They all have their own teletypes. A few even have telephones. Usually they're operated by a single employee sitting idly, puffing blue smoke in a worn suit, waiting for contracts to come over the wire. When a job comes in the employee dutifully takes down the assignment and then pastes it up on the wall alongside its case number. If a collector wants the job they inform the employee who then telegraphs the other offices and lets everyone know who has volunteered and the job is carried out.

My dealings with the collectors have been limited. I didn't know where to find a chapterhouse. That meant I had to check with a directory agent near Saint Olm's who told me the nearest was in a warren to the south named New Holly. The chapterhouse was on Level Five. To get there I needed to take a lift up to Level Six then catch a monorail to the warren and then find the place.

I had left Hannah, Samantha, and Hagen back at shop. I offered to go find some food and figured I could stop in at the chapterhouse. I was no good to them until I could square this, anyway. The food run gave me the opportunity to get my troubles with the Society ironed out. I felt like a man at the gallows, bag over my head, noose around my neck, just waiting for the floor to drop out.

What was that? Out of the corner of my eye I swore I saw movement. The flurry of robes, the tilt of a pointed hood. A gargoyle. I snapped my head left, peering down an alley. I wished I had my gun. Those things were really starting to get under my skin.

I felt uneasy. Exposed. I could use some protection. My gun—a hefty five-shot revolver called a Judge—and I had been in more than a few scrapes together and its weight at my side would have been welcome, especially walking into a Society chapterhouse. But it could also land me in jail. Lovatine law restricted citizens from carrying weapons. I had skirted the law before but when I got back after Methow I had vowed to keep my nose clean. But this was before Aklo showed up at murder scenes, the gargoyles started appearing, and a Society contract was placed on my head.

The alley was empty, but I couldn't shake the nagging feeling that I was being watched. I knew what that meant, of course. The faceless things were the ancient servants of the Firsts. We had faced them a number of times now. They aren't any species I recognize. Hell, I'm not even sure if they are mortal. I've seen them shrug off gunshot wounds and disappear into clouds of smoke. Umbra might look like living shadows but at least when you shot them they left a body. Gargoyles didn't.

I decided to talk with Hannah and Samantha about them when I got back to Saint Olm. They would want to know.

I found a lift east of Hagen's shop. I stood shivering at the stop in the cold, pulling my jacket close around my chest, burying my hands in my pockets, and watching the people of King's Station move past. It was late. The streets were pretty clear. A dimanian and a maero youth dressed all in black with red armbands ran past, whooping and shouting, and chanting something I couldn't make out. The Breakers, it seemed, were getting more and more bold. Behind the youths came a crowd of kresh in winter robes. In their clawed hands they carried signs that read, "WE NEED FOOD" and "END THE BLOCKADES" in thick block Strutten. Protestors. Things in the city were heating up.

A bell dinged and I turned to watch the lift slowly rise from the shaft below me and come to a stop. I boarded the empty lift and the bored cephel conductor nodded at me, clucking a half-hearted greeting in Cephan. I smiled and returned his greeting. I moved to sit in a chair near one of the heaters. I had three levels to go and I appreciated the warmth near the back of the lift.

I leaned back in my chair and settled in, watching the girders pass as the lift began to rise.

We were halfway to Level Four when a voice over my shoulder said, "Fancy meeting you here."

I started, then turned, and saw Rulon Argentum sitting in the chair behind me. My heart jumped. He stood and slipped around the line of seats to stand before me, motionless. He was wearing a heavy coat—expensive from the look of it—with wide black wool lapels that matched his hair. His hands were in his pockets, his white-metal face was frozen in that stoic expression. The narrow eye slits seemed to regard me suspiciously.

Was he looking for me? I couldn't be sure.

"I'm working on your money," I said, my voice cracking and betraying any feigned confidence. Argentum, however, oozed it. A sleek threat of a dauger, wearing his self-assurance as easily as his coat.

"I hope so, for your sake," he said. "You have five days remaining."

I ran my hands through my hair and chuckled awkwardly. "Yeah, I know. Funny, I'm actually on my way to talk to your bosses. See if I can't—"

"You are what?" Argentum snapped. He stepped closer, gripped the front of my jacket, and pulled me to my feet. We now stood face-to-face at the back of the lift. He was so close I could feel the warmth emanating from behind his mask and hear the words whistle as they escaped from the narrow mouth slit. "You were going to talk to whom?"

I narrowed my eyes slightly.

"Your bosses. See if I can't work out a payment plan."

"They won't talk to you," he said. He released his grip with a small shove.

"Sure they will. They do—"

"No," he interrupted me again. His composure had fallen away. There was venom in his voice. "I am your point of contact with the Society. Me alone. We discussed that."

I took a step back, trying to put a bit of distance between us. I didn't want to be standing too close to an angry collector.

"I don't think we did," I said carefully. "Besides, what does it matter? If I can get on a payment plan, then—"

"Well, we have discussed it now. If you have something to say to the Society, it goes through me." He tapped his chest.

Fine. I could play this game.

"I want to work out a deal," I said.

He laughed, the sound hollow. "No. No deal."

"The Society has done it before."

"On some contracts, yes. This is not one of them. There will be no deal. The money or your life. You have five days."

The bell at the front of the lift dinged. The cephel conductor yawned and clucked out our arrival at Level Four. No one boarded. I was alone with an increasingly angry collector and a half-asleep conductor.

"Look, I got a gig and it promises to pay well, but it might take longer than a week. If I'm dead I can't get your money. So I figure we set up a payment plan. It's better business and I don't have to be dead."

Argentum thought on this for a moment and then shook his head. "No."

The doors at the front of the lift closed and we began to rise once again.

The fear and nervousness that had leapt to the surface when I saw him now drained out of me. Anger replaced it. The Society worked with contracts. I knew this to be true. It was partly why they were able to make so much money. The interest rates are incredible but it's amazing what folks will agree to when their life is on the line.

"Yeah? Well, then I'll need to go to the Society directly," I said, forcing the words out and trying to keep calm. I really missed the Judge.

"I said no," Argentum said, stepping forward to give me a harder shove. I was slammed backward into the wall of the lift and my head bounced against the hard glass. I blinked away bright flashes.

"Hey," I said dumbly, but Argentum wasn't stopping. A fist caught me in the jaw before I had a chance to duck.

Stars exploded behind my eyes and my ears rang. I slipped down to my knees, a hand gripping my jaw and the other keeping me from rolling over.

"Look, why don—"

Argentum kicked out but I was able to see that coming. I

grabbed at his foot with my free hand and caught it. Twisted. He grunted and I gave the leg a jerk, pulling him off balance for a moment. He wavered but didn't go down.

I rose quickly, feeling a popping in my knee that shot waves of pain up my leg. Another punch came my way but I blocked it with a forearm and sent a punch of my own at his gut. I missed as he stepped back and regarded me.

I breathed out in gusts, trying to catch my breath before the next assault.

The conductor clucked angrily at us, waving an arm.

Argentum drew a long fillet knife from inside his coat and whipped it around in the air before him. My mouth went dry. In the reflected lights of the lift the blade glowed white.

"Hey," I said, pressing myself against a windowed wall. "Hey. You said I had five days."

I thought of the Judge. It was back at my flat. Sitting useless in a nightstand drawer.

"I think the terms will need to be readjusted," he said as he stalked towards me. I scrambled away from the wall and to a center row of the lift.

"Hurry up!" I shouted at the conductor. "He's crazy! He's going to kill me!"

The conductor had stopped working the lift. We slowed to a stop. He stood there, his enormous eyes staring at me and then flicking to the tall dauger now stalking around the row of seats, blade in hand.

Argentum lunged at me and the blade caught the side of my jacket. It sliced leather but didn't hit the skin beneath. I moved away, careful not to trip over the chairs bolted to the floor.

"Look, five days. I won't talk to your bosses. Fine," I shouted, breathless.

Argentum said nothing. I considered going to the cephel, knowing the octopoid creature could be helpful in a fight, but I didn't want to endanger anyone else. I needed to get out of here.

I glanced at the windows. Outside I could see the shaft's superstructure, a latticework of girders and beams. I knew service ladders ran up and down the shafts but I didn't see one outside the lift. But there had to be one.

The doors moaned open and a blast of cold air swept through. We were still mid-trip, not near a station. I stared in shock as the cephel disappeared out the front doors, pulling itself up and outside the lift with its many arms. Escaping.

Now I was alone with this maniac.

Argentum took a quick look around the lift and then lunged at me. Carter's cross, he was fast. This time I didn't have a chance. The knife hit one of my ribs and then deflected upward. I managed to pull away before it got too deep or too far. Hot pain flared and I let out a curse.

The hasty lunge had placed the dauger's arm under my armpit. I ignored the pain coming from my side and dropped my arm, locking Argentum in place. We were now face-to-face.

"You're going to die, Bell," he said. This guy was clearly no collector. So... who was he? Why was he after me?

I flashed him a pained smile as I brought my left knee up into his crotch. He deflated and howled, collapsing to the floor. Why do thugs like him always forget about that? Ridiculous.

A bolt of pain shot through me. I remembered what I had to do. *Get out!*

I moved to the open door of the lift. The cephel was long gone. In the distance I could hear the wail of sirens. The law wouldn't be on my side. Argentum—whoever he was—was posing as a collector. He was from one of the Precious Families. No cop would believe my word over his. No cop would stop a supposed Society member performing a collection. I needed to lose him and then lay low.

I leaned out the door. Gusts of cold air blew through my hair and beard. The gash was a sharp pain in my side, and I touched it gingerly. It was bleeding badly, and the fillet knife had cut deep. Argentum would recover quickly, and I was wounded. I had to go.

I looked up the way the cephel had gone. We were near Level Five. The entresol between Levels Four and Five was directly above. I could see the lights through a narrow space between the lift and the shaft. If I could get up there…

Behind me, Argentum stirred.

"Don't think you can escape, Bell," he shouted. I turned and saw him moving towards me on his long legs. His coat flared behind him. I had only moments. I slammed the lift's lever into action and with a groan it began to rise. I leapt out, pushing myself into the open girders of the shaft and away from the rising lift. Wind whipped around me and the cold of the metal bit into my fingers.

I turned, saw legs appear in the open doorway. Argentum cursed and his shiny shoes disappeared as the lift slipped past the roof of Level Four and up into Level Five.

I breathed out. That bought me some time. I looked for a way down. I gripped the steel beam and looked for a way off the lattice. Birds and bats fluttered from their perches and chirped and squawked at me. I was invading their space.

Stairwells run next to most lifts. They're rarely used in the more elevated levels, and closer to the Sunk you're more likely to find them occupied by addicts shooting pitch into their rotting veins, but they're always there. I began to look for one, moving along the girders and making sure not to look down. At this location Level Four was roughly ten stories high. Slipping and falling would not be pleasant.

If I was right, there should be a stairwell just around the corner. I moved for it.

Above me, I heard the lift stop.

I turned in horror and saw that it was slowly beginning to descend. Now I had only seconds.

I quickened my pace, finding an enclosed stairwell on the east side. Between the girders and the tall narrow box that held the stairs was a service ladder. The entrance would be near the lift's stop.

I wrapped my hands around the ladder, ignoring the pain from my side, and gripped it tightly with my thighs. I pulled my jacket over my palms to protect them and slid down the ladder to the first platform. I looked up and saw a shape exiting the lift, climbing out onto the girders where I had been. Argentum was coming after me and he was faster. I repeated the process, not looking up, but sliding down the three remaining ladders to Level Four.

Never stop moving, I told myself. I was getting pretty good at running through Lovat.

Argentum's words played through my head as I did. The promise he had made as we sat in that tavern a few days earlier: "I will always find you, Mister Bell." Let's see how true that was.

I slipped inside the stairwell and began to descend. He was clearly capable. Leading him back to Saint Olm was a bad idea without warning my friends first, and Essie's place wasn't an option. I was sure he knew where my apartment was. I needed to lose him.

Level Two would be my destination. A maze of haphazard buildings and shanty towns, it sat right above the flooded Sunk. It was a great place to get lost.

He clearly did not want me to visit the chapterhouse. What was he afraid I'd find? Was my hunch correct? Was it all a ruse? The Society wouldn't be happy to discover some knife-happy thug was posing as one of their own.

Behind me his footfalls echoed off the walls of the stairwell. I kept moving, the cut in my chest growing more and more uncomfortable with each step.

I passed Level Three. My whole left side was slick with blood. My shirt was clinging to my chest. Pain flared in my right knee, the old wound feeling like it would seize up at any moment.

Argentum was above me, descending. I imagined those shiny shoes slapping down onto each stair. The knife gripped in his hand.

Never stop moving.

Level Two.

I slipped out the open doorway and blinked back a gust of cold fetid air that slapped at my face.

"By the Firsts!" said a voice.

A stunned anur slipped off a box he had been sitting on, scrambled backwards, and stared at me eyes wide with surprise. He took one quick glance at me, saw my harried expression, saw the stain of blood on my chest, and he took off. Ran away screaming for help.

I looked around frantically.

The street I stood on ran east-west and a pair of buildings extended away to my left and right. I might be able to find an alley down there, but with Argentum so close I didn't have a lot of time. I didn't have much room to run. The street ran along an open hole that wound its way through Level Two. The waters of the Sunk lapped against the edge. Trash and an oily film floated on the surface. I could see shapes moving under that water, most likely cephels, kresh, or anur.

He was so close now, I knew. I whipped my head back and forth, looking east and then west. But I knew he would find me. He wasn't stupid—he was cold, calculating, and quick.

I had moments. Only moments.

I jumped into the water.

TWELVE

Blood swirled in the dark waters that surrounded me. *My blood,* I realized. It took me a moment to comprehend what I was seeing. The shock of the warm water after the icy air blowing through the city was disorienting. The clouds of black drifting in front of the shadows of sunken buildings confused me even further.

When I realized it was my blood I immediately began to panic. I wanted to scream out but knew disturbing the waters above would tip Argentum off. My heart hammered, pumping more blood into the water.

I moved my arms upwards, forcing myself deeper, willing my lungs to hold their air. The pressure increased. My lungs burned.

I didn't want to think about the filth that ran down from the nine levels above me and emptied into the Sunk; chemicals, poisons, rat shit, and much worse.

The walkway that ran along this open length of the Sunk had been built on the roof of a long-forgotten building. Sea anemones and barnacles clung to its facade and across the panes of glass that still sat, unbroken, in its window frames. Noises I couldn't comprehend warbled through the water like forlorn music, deep thrums, distant moans, and what sounded like the plaintive out-of-tune cries of a horn that reverberated off the sunken brick.

My lungs ached, and my arms felt weak but I continued to paddle myself downward.

A cephel jetted away, startled by my intrusion while two anur watched with serious expressions as I descended.

A shadowed form approached me, long and lean and cutting across my vision in a flash of motion. At first I took it to be one of the massive eels that I'd heard were common in these waters. As the shape paused in front of me and backpedaled I could see a pair of arms and legs lift from its sides.

I choked on my dwindling supply of air, releasing a torrent of bubbles that rushed upward.

A bok!

I had never seen one in person before. The lizards were loners, didn't congregate in groups, and had a fearsome reputation. Bok, it was said, weren't too far removed from the beasts. It had probably smelled my blood in the water and come for a quick meal. I cursed myself for leaping into such a dangerous place wounded.

An anur shopkeep once told me that most of the other sub-surface races don't cross paths with the large lizards and they were never seen outside of the Sunk. As far as the stories went, they were cold-hearted brutes, uncivilized. Separate from Lovatine society.

The thing studied me, its coal-black eyes deep in the shadows of its long face. I was the intruder. I was the one who didn't belong.

My lungs were past burning now. The moments he stared at me felt like hours.

I was deep enough, I decided. I had to get to the surface. I had to get air but I dared not move. I could see the claws at the end of the bok's webbed hands. Knew that it could do more damage to me with its rows of teeth than Argentum's knife ever could.

But everything inside me burned. The edges of my vision seemed to float and distort. I pointed to my mouth and then motioned to the surface.

More of my blood darkened the shadows around me. I felt lightheaded. The bok shook its head, then pointed to something behind me. It showed its teeth, which might have seemed menacing at any other moment, but wasn't then. I wasn't sure what it meant.

I repeated my gesture, my plea, and then—feeling myself slip toward the edge of consciousness—began kicking towards the surface.

I didn't get very far. A clawed hand wrapped itself around my ankle and jerked me down. I looked down in time to see the bok holding me, and I tried to scream. Brine flooded in, filling my mouth. I inhaled it and gagged violently.

The beast wrapped its arms around me. My eyes wide, I imagined the bok's jagged teeth tearing into my neck. I kicked, longed for the Judge, and then found myself grinning stupidly into the water. What use would it be down here?

It was my last thought.

I woke coughing. Salty brine in my mouth, in my sinuses. In my ears. I sat up in a panic, remembering Argentum. Remembering the large lizard creature and its large claws on my leg. My blood floating around me. The burning of my lungs.

My jeans and hair were still damp but my shirt had been removed and my chest was dry. My suspenders were pulled down around my knees. A thick bandage had been wrapped around my chest and despite my state of undress, I was warm.

I looked around, half-expecting to find myself in the bok's den, with piles of skulls arranged in corners. Instead I was sitting on a narrow cot tucked into a cubby in the side of a wall. A dull gray vine had creeped inside and crawled its way up, draping my little sleeping space with dull green leaves.

Outside of the cubby was a much larger room. Everything was bathed in a pink light that seemed to emanate from nowhere, everywhere. I rose, swinging my legs over the edge of the cot and standing. My right knee throbbed a bit but I wasn't too weak to stand. I stepped out of the sleeping space and into the pink room.

The room itself was cavernous. A mountain of crates was stacked along one wall. The place smelled like a root cellar: earthy, stale, strangely comforting. Whiffs of wet dirt and the faint scent of mildew permeated the place. I could hear a dripping somewhere. A loud *plop* that echoed, suggesting a heavy drop and a long fall.

A strange pink sign grabbed my attention as it crookedly

glowed on one wall, lighting the interior. An animal rendered in neon looked over its shoulder, some sort of tentacle appendage twisting out of its smiling cartoonish face. A set of words were plastered on its side. Some old language, probably pre-Aligning.

Two doors sat in the wall below. The windows in them were blacked out.

"Hello," I said into the room. My words were raspy. My throat raw. My chest ached, from the gash and from inside.

No response.

Where was I? I closed my eyes and rubbed at the ache forming behind them. The last time I had woken up in a place like this I had been underground in one of the ancient half-finished tunnels beneath the city. Removed from Lovat so completely that I couldn't hear the hustle and bustle around me. This did not have the same feeling. In the distance I could still make out Lovat's buzz. The movement of people, the sounds of life.

What time was it? I thought of Hannah, Hagen, and Samantha. They'd be worried.

I padded barefoot across the cold cement floor and began to inspect the crates, hoping they'd give me some insight into my location. Most were sealed shut, but a few had been opened.

Inside one I found stacks and stacks of dry bread. I checked another, and discovered it was filled with onions. I moved on to the sealed crates. Strutten markings on the sides spelled out their contents: beans, coffee, flour, sugar. I stood and blinked. It was a treasure trove! I kept reading: dried corn, dried fish, smoked sausages, potatoes. My stomach rumbled and I reached for some of the food, but then stopped short. I stepped back, stunned, realizing what I was seeing.

Whoever had brought me here was hoarding food. A *lot* of food. I remembered the people storming the jalky cart, the lines at the wharf, the protesters. Sam's story about the riot. Everyone was desperately trying to find something to keep their bellies full in the cold air and someone was hoarding it. Anger flashed inside of me. It was obscene. Perverse. This hoard could feed thousands. But it sat here. In some forgotten warehouse.

Something moved behind me. I snapped out of my thoughts, spinning around, indignation still flowing through me.

The bok. It passed through one of the doors below the neon sign, its smooth scales reflecting the coral light. I could see the creature clearer than I had under the Sunk. It was a deep green in color and would be nearly black in low light. It had a long saurian face, both noble and fearsome, which rose from a pair of hulking shoulders. Dark eyes studied me from under heavy brows. Long arms and legs hung from its thick muscular torso, and a large tail dragged behind it.

I wasn't sure if it was male, female, or something else. It wore clothes. Tight cut-off shorts, and a loose button-up shirt. A patch above its left breast read: "Hank." The name usually skews male, so I supposed he was a he.

The thing was taller than Wensem, and looked stronger than a bufo'anur. My anger subsided, replaced by nervousness. It was no wonder the subsurface Lovatines gave these creatures a wide berth. He looked dangerous.

"Um, hi," I said.

Hank, or what I assumed was Hank, bowed his head.

"Did you patch me up?" I asked, wondering if bok spoke Strutten.

Hank nodded his head slowly.

"Well," I said. "Thanks." I gave him a smile.

Hank looked over his shoulder as a lanky woman stepped into the room. She was all confidence. Her back was straight, her walk sharp and intentional. She took in the room with the same cool regard I had seen in the eyes of trail-hard roaders surveying the route ahead. Her dark hair was pulled into a tight bun that perched on the back of her head. She had sly eyes, a narrow sharp nose, and a wide mouth, the lips of which were turned up at the sides in a wry smile. She reminded me of a fox. She wore a suit of tweed, but in the pink glow of the neon sign it was difficult to tell its color.

"You are starting to get a reputation in my city," she said. Her voice had a low rasp. A slight edge that added authority to her words.

I blinked. I probably looked a sight. Long hair and grizzled. Naked from the waist up, cooling down after finding stacks of food, and now standing opposite a wiry human woman in a suit and a ten-foot lizard-man.

"Uhhh..." I said stupidly.

She laughed a raw hearty laugh and clapped her hands together. Hank's shoulders seemed to shake though he didn't make a sound. Unsure, I waited.

"I see you met Hank."

I nodded. Then remembered how to talk. "Thanks. Um, for the help."

She inclined her head slightly as she crossed the space between us, stopping a few feet away from where I stood. Hank planted himself behind her and a little to the right, folding a pair of scaly arms across his chest.

"It was Hank, really. He saw you hit the water. The blood. He could tell something was up."

"Yeah…" I said, rubbing my neck. I did not exactly want to spill my issues to a stranger. Even with the help.

She held up a hand. "I don't need to know. But I do find it fascinating that Waldo Bell ends up in the Sunk right after an ill-fated visit to Kiver dal Renna's apartments."

I must have looked shocked because her face broke into a broad grin. About a million questions fluttered through my head like a flock of gulls and she anticipated every one.

"It's my business to know what happens in my city. Especially among the elite. Especially right now. When the man who led the Methow refugees to safety shows up at an elevated party it piques my interest. All those rumors about you… The whole Collector Killer escapade." She chuckled. "Funny. Lovat sure is getting a little weird lately, isn't it?"

"We live in strange times," I said.

She studied me for a moment and then clapped her hands together. "Indeed. You thirsty?"

I nodded.

"Come," she said. Then turned and looked up at the neon sign. "As much as I love this thing, the light hurts my eyes after a while."

She motioned for me to follow and we stepped through the doors from the warehouse and into a smaller back room.

A counter ran along one wall broken up by a stove and an icebox. Another pair of doors led elsewhere. Both were closed. At the center of the room, as if lifted from a monochrome serial, sat a rough-hewn table illuminated by a single hooded lamp. A scattering of chairs sat in stationary orbit, a few tucked in. A dimanian with small dark horns lingered in the back. He wore a crisp button-up shirt, the sleeves rolled up, and dark slacks. His long hair was combed back and held in a topknot. He was writing in a small notebook when we entered and looked up as we approached.

"Allard, clear the room."

He nodded and disappeared though a door at the back.

"Have a seat," said the woman. She motioned to a chair on one end of the table. I sat.

Hank moved to the icebox and removed a couple of beers and a pitcher of water. He poured a glass of water and placed it in front of me. Then, using one of his talons, he popped the cap and placed it next to the glass.

He tapped a claw next to the glass of water, then the beer, indicating the order I was to drink. I smiled in comprehension. If he returned any expression I couldn't tell.

"He's a doter," said the woman.

"Not much of a talker," I said. Could bok speak Strutten? He clearly understood it. Maybe they lacked the vocal capability to enunciate the words and had their own language. Similar to the cephel.

"Never has been," the woman said. "We've worked together, what... eight years? Nine?" She looked over at Hank. He shook his head.

"Twelve," he rumbled. His voice was deep and gravelly, like thunder rolling across mountains.

"Well, shit," she laughed.

Hank turned and looked at her. His shoulders shook again with that silent laughter. He set the second beer in front of her and moved to a row of bottles along the counter and poured himself a glass of wine.

"You swallowed a lot of water," said the woman.

"Didn't have much of a choice," I said. I could imagine Argentum's cold fury as he stalked around above the Sunk looking for me.

"Sometimes we don't. You're either incredibly brave or spectacularly foolish."

Samantha's words popped into my mind. "I've been called both."

She grinned. "The world needs both. Though we rarely like to admit it. There's something about a loose cannon that most people can't stomach. But they're often the only ones who can take the right risks at the right time."

The thought of Samantha lingered. I had told my friends I was going to pick up food. It would have taken an hour—max. I had no idea how long I'd been gone. I needed to contact them.

"You have a name?" I asked and took a sip of my water. It stung my throat so I drank slowly. Easing into it.

"I go by Elephant."

"Ele–what?" I asked.

"Elephant," she repeated, enunciating the word. "It's that pink animal on the sign. It was a pre-Aligning critter."

"Elephant," I said around another swallow of water.

She nodded.

"Nice to meet you."

"Likewise."

"Where are we?" I looked around the room again.

Elephant laughed. "Level Two, actually. Above the Sunk, right in the heart of ol' Myrtle."

Myrtle. It was a warren with the reputation of being solid Outfit territory. Things were starting to make sense.

I had never crossed paths with organized crime in Lovat, though it ran rampant. The Outfit operated in the shadows and usually worked hand-in-hand with the corrupt cops and dirty politicians. They had their warrens, and I kept well away for the most part.

Occasionally a name would pop up in the papers. Some hoopla about a crime boss going down, some corruption exposed, but it was rare.

Myrtle wasn't far from King Station. A twenty-minute walk, tops. How quickly do bok swim? Again, she anticipated my question.

"Hank's fast. Even hauling a caravan master. We have a few exits from this building into the Sunk. He was able to slip you inside and perform CPR."

I brought my hand to my mouth and looked at the bok. Hank said nothing, just tipped back his glass of wine.

"I've been wanting to talk to you for a while," she continued.

"Oh, yeah?" I asked, a little surprised.

"Indeed. You a religious man, Waldo?"

I blinked. "Honestly, I'm not sure anymore."

I narrowed my eyes and took another drink. Where was this going?

She smiled. "Well, as my priest would say, I think the guiding hand of Providence brought us together."

"Well, however I got here, I'm grateful. If Hank hadn't saved me, I'm not sure I'd have survived. How can I help you?"

"Tell me about the elevated," she said.

"What about them?"

"Who was killed this time? The papers are being coy."

I studied her expression before answering. Her eyes flashed eagerly.

"Coy?"

"Yes, they indicated that the recent victim was elevated, but they aren't naming names this time. Seems like another glided murder. Is that true?"

I wasn't sure how to answer. Who was this woman? She could be working with the LPD. She could be the killer herself. I did find it strange how interested she was in the deaths.

"It was a human man named Doctor Frank Adderley," I said. I wasn't sure how knowing the victim's name could hurt anything.

Her eyebrows twitched at the name. Her expression wavered a moment. Recognition? Something else? She caught herself and forced a smile.

"So what were you doing all the way up there? Especially an Auseil party. You seem to be good people. Wouldn't expect you to go messing with that crowd."

That crowd? The rich? Or another sort? Maybe the Aklo was not the only place to be looking.

"Small job," I said casually. "I needed the money."

She leaned forward. In the lamplight I could see her eyes were ice blue, the color of the sky on a winter morning. "We all need money. That's why anyone does anything. What I'm wondering, Waldo, is what *you* were doing for Kiver dal Renna. He's not the sort to seek out caravan masters of low breeding. No offense."

I paused and then leaned back.

"Call me Wal," I said, trying to buy time.

The big lizard set down his glass and I worried briefly that he was going to come at me, threaten me in some way. Instead he turned and disappeared from the room, ducking through one of the doors.

Elephant didn't blink, just kept me fixated in her icy stare. "All right, Wal. Level with me. What is going on with Kiver dal Renna?"

I breathed out a long breath. "A kresh servant was found murdered in his apartment."

This was public information. She nodded as if she already knew this.

"He asked me to look into it."

One of her eyebrows rose. "You don't seem the bloodhound type."

I shook my head. "I'm not. I have some experience with some of the questions Kiver has, so he sought me out."

Elephant smiled, white teeth flashing behind her lips. "I assume this… project is how you ended up bleeding out in the Sunk? Why that dauger was chasing you?"

She didn't miss much. I took a deep breath and finished my water, then took a swig of beer. I studied the strange woman across from me and weighed my chances. I didn't know her. But she knew an awful lot already. I wondered if she was an Outfit lieutenant. Everything pointed that way.

I swallowed thickly and decided to keep my doubts about Argentum's legitimacy to myself. "I'm under a collection notice from the Society."

Elephant made a low and long whistle. "Carter's cross."

I nodded and took another swig of beer.

"So you were trying to save your neck."

I nodded.

"So when the LPD showed up and that buffoon Bouchard threw you out…" she let her words trail off.

How did she…? I tried not to let my expression give too much away, but this was a bit much.

"How do you know so much about this? Why have you been tracking me?" I said, my frustration boiling over. Obviously she had a mole in Kiver's organization. Who was she paying to tip her off and why?

"I have my reasons. Business is business."

"Is that business the same reason there's crates of food in that warehouse?" I gestured behind me, my voice rising. "Crates of food hoarded away while the city suffers? While everyone works themselves into a froth?" I tried to keep my emotions in check. Wensem always said I was hotheaded.

She leaned back and drank from her beer. The coat of her jacket opened, revealing a close-fitting shirt with dark stripes.

"It's not personal," she said calmly. "Business is business."

"You sound like one of the Outfit," I said.

Outfit goons generally didn't like being called out. It was chancy, but it seemed like the right thing to say. She seemed as interested in studying me as she was in revealing her own hand.

Elephant smiled but didn't confirm or deny. Hank returned before I could say anything else. He ducked beneath the doorframe and held out a clean white undershirt, a flannel shirt of gray and black, and a thick coat.

"These are for you," said Elephant. "Unfortunately, we don't have a fresh pair of trousers in your size."

I took the undershirt and slipped it over my head, gingerly pulling it over the bandage. The wound was still tender. Then I grabbed the flannel. I left my suspenders loose—no sense adding extra pressure to my chest and shoulders. The coat was wool, thick and black. Nicer than my old jacket. I laid it over the back of my chair.

"Thanks," I said, then turned to face Elephant. Her lips curled into a smile which did not reach her eyes. She was still waiting for more information.

I sat back down and took another pull of my beer.

"Maybe I should have been more upfront. Some of the folks you met at that little Auseil shindig are... friends of mine. Kiver is one, there's a few more. I am concerned for the safety of some of our elevated citizens.

"When I heard that the man who faced a First and won had mingled with my colleagues, I figured I should meet him. It was just dumb luck that Hank found you first. I think we should be willing to trade information. Help each other out. I know things, you know things. We could both benefit."

"Business is business," I said, quoting her words. "It's not personal."

She smiled and spread her hands. "Exactly."

Elephant drained her beer and pulled a pack of pre-rolled cigarettes from a jacket pocket. She withdrew one and stuck it between her lips, lighting it with a silver flip lighter. She offered the pack to me. I waved it away.

Acrid gray smoke drifted above her.

"So what do you know about the recent gilded murders?"

"Very little," I admitted. I didn't read the papers and until recently I hadn't cared much about the happenings on the high levels.

She frowned. "Unfortunate. You know the stories at least?"

"Sure. It's what the scrapes call it when the press pays attention to the deaths of wealthy folk. It's not uncommon," I said flatly, taking a sip. The carbonation burned my throat, but kicked more energy into my limbs.

"Indeed," she inhaled sharply and blew another stream of smoke. "However, they've been happening more frequently. In the last month, there have been fifteen dead. Fifteen. On one hand, the connections seem obvious: they're all wealthy, high-ranking business owners. But the cause of death is different each time. Some look like suicides. Some, accidents. Very few look like murders. But they keep happening."

"So?"

"Curious, isn't it?"

I shifted slightly. "You think they're connected?"

"The constabulary's away on the front and the elevated begin dropping left and right?" she exhaled another cloud of smoke. "Fascinating, don't you think?"

"I guess," I said. I studied her face.

"The upper class are running scared. Leaping at their own shadows, afraid of moving in public. They should be. Someone's hunting them."

"Could be a vigilante," I said. I didn't want to go into details about my own investigation. The two bodies I had looked into were connected by writing, not by social standing. "You know, a defender of the people, a freedom fighter. Why let the rich feast while the poor suffer? That sort of thing. Maybe they're trying to incite riots."

"Forcing mergers and corporate takeovers is an odd way to revolt," Elephant said.

What did she mean by that? I ran a finger through a ring of moisture on the table.

"A defender of the people wouldn't slice open a scrape servant and spend time writing on walls in the victim's blood," she added.

My eyes flicked to hers and a fresh grin broke across her face. I hadn't mentioned the Aklo, or any details about the scenes. How many connections did this woman have?

"Unlike the rush of gilded murders, the case you were looking into was different. There's a consistency. The writing is one, the means of death is another." She took a long drag and then continued. "Freedom fighters smash a face in with a club or a brick. They act out of a wild passion working to stop a perceived injustice. These last two killings were committed ritualistically. That's fueled by a completely different reason."

"And that is?" I asked.

She smiled almost seductively. "Faith."

I blinked. "You think—"

She interrupted. "I believe these two murders, the kresh and the doctor, cannot be assumed to be anything other than what they are. Connected, and for a very specific purpose. The ritualistic death, the writing, it's all for one reason. This is a new pattern.

"The kresh had nothing of value. As far as we know, Adderley was beloved, but he wasn't a shareholder in any major firm. He made most of his money from his standing at Dyer Memorial," she said.

"So, the gilded murders are about power, and the deaths of Adderley and Taaka are about something else?"

She nodded. "It's a convenient time to shake things up. By the time the standoff ends, everyone will have moved on. Meanwhile, if someone needs a body count, the murders could easily be lost in the shuffle." She waved a hand. "This is all speculation, mind you."

It sounded good, but something was missing. There was something else happening behind the scenes, a big hole.

"Why are you telling me this?"

"I'm hoping we can work together. As I said before, a partnership could be very beneficial. I have interests up top. LPD isn't working fast enough. I've lost a few... contracts recently. If we could stop these deaths, I might be able to help you down here."

Help me? I was starting to wonder what strings this woman pulled.

"Help me down here? With what?"

She smiled. "How much do you need for the collectors?"

This woman's intimate knowledge of my life was exhausting. Was she offering to clear my name? I was also starting to wonder if she wasn't more dangerous than Argentum. I said nothing.

"I want to know who is doing this," she said. "I want to know who and why. The deaths of the elevated are hurting business in more ways than one. Recent homicides have got people scared and they're not... working with me the way I prefer. I need to take advantage of this position while I can. Eventually the siege will break and caravans will flood in from the east. The value of that food behind you will drop. I'm not planning on opening a grocery."

Ah, so she was selling food to the elevated. Probably for thousands, maybe millions of lira.

"You help me find out what is happening up there, and I'll wipe that debt of yours clean."

"Seems to me like you know what's happening already."

After a few moments she rubbed out her cigarette and pushed back from the table.

"How much do you owe?"

I studied her. She knew too much. I needed to play this right. Keep her guessing while I sorted out the details.

"Well?" she said, a touch of impatience in her voice.

"Twenty-five thousand lira," I said.

She laughed loudly. "Carter's bloody cross, what did you do?"

"Got into some trouble in Syringa."

"Mhm," she said, her eyes narrowing.

A moment of silence fell between us and we eyed each other across the table. Eventually, she rose, came over to me, and extended a hand. I took it, and gave it a shake. Her palms were soft, the nails well groomed. She hadn't done a hard day's labor in years.

"It was good chatting with you, Wal. Think about the offer. Come back if you're interested. I'm serious about helping end your trouble.

"Hank will show you the exit. Stay safe."

"You too," I said, forcing a smile. She returned it. But hers was a smile that held many secrets.

I let Hank show me the way out. Her words rattled around inside my head. I couldn't help but wonder what the hell I'd stumbled into this time.

THIRTEEN

The doorway to Elephant's warehouse was unassuming and easy to miss. I stood right outside and took in my surroundings. The place was a good enough hiding spot, a narrow door sandwiched between a crematorium and an abandoned automat that had long ago been stripped of any foodstuff. Three dimanian pitch addicts sat at one of the automat's dirty tables rocking back and forth. Forgotten. Abandoned. A dreary tableau of Level Two, where Lovat's lost souls gather to die.

My mind was running through my conversation with Elephant. A partnership? A trade of information? She was willing to free me from the collectors. Words had been spoken but no promises were made. The whole experience left me more confused than anything. Hank was a puzzle of his own. Elevated citizen, another crazed killer, gargoyles, a possible First, and now the Outfit. It was a who's who of Lovat's rich, famous, and strange.

A yawn surfaced and I rubbed my eyes, trying to ignore my headache. I was exhausted. The rush through the city, the near drowning. I might have woken up in the warehouse but I certainly hadn't rested. My throat was raw and sore, my body sluggish and heavy. I had a cut in my side and I was probably covered in bruises.

My friends needed to know what happened to me. I had to contact them—Samantha especially. She already believed me reckless. Disappearing for hours and coming back wounded was not going to help. Heading back to St. Olm wasn't an option, at least not right now. Argentum would probably be haunting the place. I couldn't go to my regular spots, but I needed to get word out.

Hagen had disconnected his telephone and replaced it with a monochrome so that left me the city telegraph system.

I found an office a few blocks down from Elephant's place. It had a dilapidated storefront. The sign above the door flickered, the front window had been boarded over. The interior wasn't much better. A dirty tile floor and standing room for no more than a couple of people. The operator sat behind a glass partition and sipped coffee from a stained paper cup. I shuffled up to the counter and filled out the slip to wire Hagen. Nothing extraneous, just a quick message to set nerves at ease: "Ran into trouble. I'll be by later."

As I stepped out of the telegraph office and back into the cold air I bumped into a pair of kresh. They were arguing right outside, and dressed in shabby clothes. They sported red Breaker armbands similar to what I had seen on the dimanian youth earlier. One of them glared at me.

"Sorry," I said. I noticed one of them was smeared with

green blood across his beak and one of his heart-shaped eyes was swollen shut. He looked like he had been in a brawl. "You all right?"

He shook his head and sneered. "No. Got shoved at the docks. Some bastard maero. I think he might have cracked my skull."

"What's happening at the docks?"

The other kresh turned to me and stuck a boney finger in my face. "Where 'ave you been? There's riots all over the city."

My eyebrows went up, but I wasn't that surprised.

"They started down by the docks. LPD wouldn't let people buy food from the boats."

"Wait, why was LPD not letting people buy food?"

The wounded kresh coughed and the other huffed irritably. "Ah, come on, hume."

"Fine, fine," I said, holding my hands up and ignoring the slur. "Didn't mean to offend."

"Whatever."

I moved on, thinking about the crates of food in Elephant's little warehouse and the tables I had seen at Kiver's Auseil party. No wonder people were rioting. A full belly goes a lot further than vague assurances when you want to placate the masses. Lovat was tired. Tired of the blockade, tired of the cold, tired of the hunger. If the mayor and the LPD didn't act, Lovat could burn.

I walked with my head down, my collar up, and my head pulled as low into my new coat as possible. It was nice, much nicer than the one I lost to Argentum's knife. I was grateful. Cold weather rarely lingers in Lovat—it usually gets cool in the winter, and it's always wet—but we don't see biting cold like this. Not for days and days.

I needed to lay low. Get my bearings. Try to sort this out and reapproach my Society problem. I checked the lamplight. I was nowhere near the edge of the city, so I had to rely on the lights. It had to be about mid-morning, which put me missing for more than twelve hours. I was glad I sent the telegraph off.

I needed sleep and for now there was only one place to find it.

Cedric's was empty when I pushed through the door. There was no one lingering at the bar. No old timers gossiping about the latest jai alai or ausca standings.

"Eggs only!" Cedric shouted from the kitchen in Cephan.

Humans can't speak Cephan—well, not very well. It consists of guttural clacks and grunts easily produced by the cephel's unique beak. It also works well underwater. While humans can't clack and grunt like a cephel we can learn enough to understand.

"Wal!" said a voice from behind the bar and Essie rushed around to throw her arms around me and planted a long kiss on my lips. There was all sorts of emotion in that kiss: concern, kindness, longing. I returned her kiss and enjoyed the warmth that spread across my cheeks and down my neck and chest.

She stepped back, eyes sparkling, and then wrapped her arms around my chest in a tight hug.

"Easy." I winced around a smile. "Easy, Essie."

She pulled back and looked at me, seeming to notice the new coat. I reached a hand up to my chest where the bandage lay.

"You okay?" she asked.

"No," I said. "Ran into some trouble. I need to crash. Lay low for a while. Can I use your place?"

"What's going on?"

"It's nothing," I lied. "I'll explain later. When I can think straight."

"Okay," she said, giving me a long look.

"I'll be okay. I just haven't slept."

She fished a key out from under her apron, pressed it into my hand, and gave me a kiss on the cheek.

"I'm off in a few hours. You get some sleep." She looked at me again. "You sure you're okay?"

"Yeah," I said, flashing a smile. "I'm sure."

Essie woke me from a deep sleep hours later. I had returned to her place careful to check for any prying eyes before I slipped through her building's door and climbed the stairs to her small room. I hadn't wasted time. I threw my coat over a chair, peeled off my new shirt and my jeans, and climbed under the covers. I fell asleep almost immediately. A thick dreamless sleep.

My eyes slowly focused as I looked into Essie's face. She had climbed into bed with me, pulling the covers over herself so only her head peeked out. She smiled and said nothing, and I smiled back.

I turned and looked out the single window. It was getting dark. I had slept most of the day away. The sodium light that hung from the ceiling outside the window had dimmed to twilight levels. A few glittering icicles hung from its bulge, sending shards of cold light through the alley.

I let out a yawn and turned to look down my chest at Essie. She had shed her waitress outfit and I could see the hem of a gray sweater peeking up from under the blankets. Her hair was tousled and pulled back. She smiled and her nose crinkled slightly. I could see the twinges of concern in her dark brown eyes.

"How long was I out?" I asked.

"I got home a few hours ago and you were snoring away. I figured you could use the company and a nap sounded nice."

"Thanks for the bed," I said. "How was work?"

"Quiet. There's riots all over the city. The streets are nearly empty."

"Yeah, I noticed that," I said.

She glanced out the window towards the cold alley. I knew what she was thinking.

"Something's got to break," I said. "Maybe these riots will force the mayor to abandon the Grovedare Span and reopen trade. I know there's a ton of caravans in Syringa poised to rush over here. There was talk that a few had already set out. Were planning to camp right behind the Syringan camp. Add extra pressure."

"Let's hope it works," she said. "Cedric's closing up shop. We were down to eggs only today. No point running a diner without food."

I sighed. If established restaurants were out of luck then the carts and the alley vendors were done. The city was officially starving.

"Okay, enough chitchat," she said, looking me in the eye.

"You want to tell me what's going on?" She reached out and touched the bandage on my chest.

"Oh, this," I said, looking at the white linen. "It's a long story."

She laughed and looked around the room. "I think we have time."

I wasn't so sure we did. I ran a hand through my hair and lay back on a pillow. "Remember me mentioning the Broken Road?"

"You've mentioned it... But I never heard the whole story."

I studied her. Essie was strong. It was one of the things I liked about her. She had tenacity. But did I really want to inflict that tale on her life? It was brutal, gory stuff. It's bad enough people lost their lives with us on that road. I thought about it until something Samantha had said out there, on that road, rang in my ears: *This isn't Wal versus the world.* She was right then, and it was true now. There was no way to do this alone.

So I told her about the Broken Road. Why we left Syringa. Why we went down that path. The disappearances. The forest of the dead. Curwen torturing the people of the town. How he had burned. How Wensem had broken his leg. How we brought what was left of Methow with us. Our return to the city. When I was finished she sat next to me. Silent. Studying my face, her eyes tight around the edges.

"By the Firsts, Wal," she said, her voice near a whisper. "I had no idea it was that bad."

I turned and looked out the window, trying to tamp down the emotions welling up inside of me.

"So...," she huffed out a long breath. "That is a lot to take in."

"Yeah, the papers didn't really cover it. They couldn't."

I had left out the gargoyles, and the part about Curwen being a First. Even the strongest among us still associate that sort of talk with madness. She had enough of the story. Now, to explain why Argentum had come after me.

"So, there's more," I said, interrupting her thoughts. "Shaler's father blames me for Margaret's death."

"Is he in Lovat? Did he do this to you?" She gingerly touched the bandage.

I shook my head. "No, but he's connected... I think. Maybe." To be honest, I was questioning whether Shaler even knew about the contract. "I owe him for the failed delivery but the claim is that I now owe for the death of his daughter. They say I'm in remiss. The Society's involved. I was on my way to a chapterhouse to see about a payment program and..."

I let the word hang, and nodded down at my chest. Her eyes met mine and then went to the bandage. Then she gasped, covered her mouth with her hand, and backed up, edging out from under the blankets.

"Carter's cross," she swore.

"A collector—or at least a dauger pretending to be one, I don't know for sure—Rulon Argentum. He found me first. Didn't like the notion of me going to a chapterhouse..."

"Oh, no. No, no, no, no," Essie stammered. She was shaking her head. "You came here."

"I couldn't go anywhere else," I said, sitting up, ignoring the flare of pain from under my bandages and rising from the bed. "Essie, what is it?" I asked.

She held out an arm and shook her head, her hair

disentangling from the loose bun. I swallowed the lump that had formed in my throat. Her eyes were wild with anger and fear. "You can't stay here. You can't bring them here! You shouldn't have come here." She pointed at the apartment floor.

"Wait, Essie...," I said, stepping close to her.

She backed up into the wall, knocking a framed photo to the floor. Her hand hadn't left her mouth, and she pushed me away with the other. I stepped back.

"Essie."

"No. I mean it, Wal. You're wanted by the Society! You *can't* stay here! He'll... find you here." She nearly whispered the last part.

I was reeling. Didn't she understand what she was to me? Didn't she realize? I looked in her face and saw only fear. My puzzled expression must have triggered something in her. She marched across the apartment and threw open the door.

"Essie, I'm... I'm sorry. I don't—"

"Wal, you need to leave now. You can't stay here," she repeated.

"Essie." I repeated her name. The cold air from the hallway flowed over my toes.

"Now."

FOURTEEN

Looks like the nearest chapterhouse is in Demetrios. Up north. Twenty-Fourth and—"

"Thanks," I said, interrupting the directory agent. He was a small dauger with a plain black-iron mask. He was shivering in the cold. I had wanted to collect the address and let him close his shutters, but he seemed undeterred.

"Don't know why you'd want to go there," he said, his tone conversational. "Them collectors are queer folk with their contracts and their knives. I'm surprised LPD still lets them operate. Barbaric. Tantamount to murder, if you ask me."

"Mhm," I mumbled, slipping him a lira. He tapped the spot on the map for me and I committed it to memory. "Thanks for the info. I'll let you get back to the warmth."

"My pleasure," he said. He closed the huge tome he was referencing and lifted it back into place on one of the shelves that lined the walls of his small booth.

"I meant what I said, son. Steer clear of them butchers." He pulled down the shutter. It clanged loudly and echoed around the empty street. A sign that read: "KNOCK FOR ASSISTANCE" had been pasted crookedly on the outside of the shutter. I smiled, knowing its cockeyed application would have driven Samantha nuts.

The directory agents were a necessity born of desperate need in an ever-changing city. With so many businesses moving in and out all the time it was impossible to keep track of it all and even harder to inform every citizen. Instead of printing compendiums of information, the directory companies opted for agents placed around the city, offering location services for a small fee. It kept printing costs down and made them a hell of a lot of money.

I considered catching a rickshaw to Demetrios but decided a walk would do me good. Clear my head. I was still reeling from Essie kicking me out of her apartment.

Over and over like a skipping record. Then she got quiet and refused to respond. Eventually I quit trying. I just stood there, outside her door, boots and jacket in hand, still bleary from sleep and just stared off at nothing. It had been one of her neighbors who had snapped me out of my daze. Cracking some joke about upsetting the missus. I left.

The temperature had dropped as night set in.

Level Three was quiet. A few people hurriedly walked about, silhouettes against the steam that leaked from pipes and rose from somewhere below. I flipped up the collar of my coat, jammed my hands deep into my warm pockets, and trudged down the street. I could hear the loud rumble of something in the distance. A distant protest maybe? I couldn't be sure. As I rounded a corner I could also hear a wavery radio crackling along as some maero crooner belted out a jazz number I didn't recognize. I felt on edge. I nervously expected a gargoyle to leap out from the shadows, finally make contact with me, but I didn't see one. I was almost disappointed. It took me an hour walking north and then eventually east to get into Demetrios.

Demetrios is a sleepy little warren at the north end of Broadway Island. In ages past, massive housing projects had been constructed here and they now made up the bulk of its lower levels. A portion of the warren's north side had been sheared off along a canal that ran through Level Two. Heavy cranes leaned out from the rears of canneries, export terminals, and warehouses all along the edge. Narrow streets tenaciously crossed the gap between the levels but no buildings dared. The canal was a jagged tear through the core of the city.

Here Level Four was six or seven stories tall and lined with thick brick buildings. They were pressed tightly together leaving no room for alleys. A few enterprising citizens had taken to smashing long toll hallways through a few buildings to provide access between streets. Above, catwalks cut across the street, Auseil branches and banners hanging from their platforms. Decorative Zann hymns were sealed along their railings, the bright wax glowing against tarnished steel.

I found a lift near Twenty-First Avenue and stood next to a small cluster of women waiting for it to arrive. Few people met my eyes and fewer seemed willing to stop. The mood around the warren was tense. Everyone was on a mission.

When the doors to the lift dinged open I let out a long sigh of relief. It was jam-packed. If Argentum found me again it wouldn't be on a crowded public lift.

We boarded the lift and I took position along one of its walls. The ride up was quiet. The people on board all wore similar serious expressions. Their eyes would glance around rapidly, never settling. A few coughed, someone cleared their throat. Conversation was minimal, hushed and conspiratorial.

My stomach growled. Hunger had begun to creep in on the edges but I couldn't dwell on it. Besides, with the way people were behaving about food, it would be impossible to find anything right now.

"We're all hungry, friend," said a maero standing near me. His voice was deep and quiet.

I looked up at him.

"Your stomach, I heard it growl. I know the feeling. We all do." He motioned to the crowd.

"Yeah?" I said. I glanced at the Breakers armband he had around his bicep.

He noticed me looking. "Yeah. I'm with the Breakers. A lot of us are." He glanced around. "We got word that some elevated asshole got the LPD to guard his cannery. Cans and cans of salt fish."

This was the crowd that Wensem had gone off to join. Instead of heading south to break the Purity Movement's blockade these ones were fighting a war within the city itself.

"So, you're going to break in? Steal it?"

He rubbed his eye. "The city's starving."

"And what about the law?"

"Screw the law. There's *kids* starving." He had me there. As much as I wanted to play the law-abiding citizen, his cause was more righteous.

"You should join us."

I considered it, briefly. In a different time I would have joined in. I shook my head. There were other things I had to do first. I wasn't much good to anybody if I didn't clear things up with the Society. Then I could go and find Samantha, Hannah, and Hagen without having to worry about Argentum coming down on me. Then we could start figuring out everything else.

"Level Six!" shouted the conductor and the doors to the lift slid open.

"About damn time," said a thick human in a bowler hat.

The crowd all pushed out of the lift at once, passing me and moving down a street named Roanoke. The same direction I was going.

"It's over here!" said bowler hat, pointing down a street.

"Come on!" said the maero who had tried to recruit me.

The crowd roared in unison and rushed past me, pouring around the corner of Roanoke. People nearby saw them go and moved to join them. I continued to follow, pacing but not drawing too close. It seemed to be only about a hundred people. I could slip past and head down Twenty-Fourth Avenue in a moment.

Shouts echoed from around the corner as I turned.

"I got kids to feed!"

"Let us in!"

"We're hungry!"

"I have a family!"

The cannery was a red building that occupied the majority of the north side of the street. A neon sign of a smiling red fish waved at passersby above white letters that blazed: "Bonheur Seafoods." Most of the building's lower windows had been boarded up from the inside and a set of steps dominated the front and center of the place. As I had suspected it was located on the edge of Level Six and near the cut that allowed the cranes to raise and lower shipments from the barges far below. The whole warren smelled like fish.

Four nervous-looking cops stood outside the door at the top of the stairs. All of them were armed with rifles, their clubs hanging at their hips. It was a surprise to see the LPD carrying guns. They tended to stick to clubs.

"You folks get back! This is private property," said the officer in front, a wiry dimanian with two tusk-like horns extending forward from his cheeks.

I stopped and watched as more people joined the growing crowd. A few of the newcomers sported the red armbands of the Breakers, others looked like curious locals. The shouting increased, drawing in others. The crowd seemed to be doubling in size.

Two officers spoke briefly and one ran off, pushing past the angry crowd and disappearing. Going for backup, most likely.

"Get back!" shouted another officer, this one human.

Everyone was clearly on edge. I needed to get past them. I turned, thinking I could double back and wrap around, avoid the hostile crowd altogether but suddenly, a mass of people was coming my way. They pressed me back and I found myself in the middle of the churning crowd.

"We're hungry!"

"We're *all* hungry," the lead officer yelled back. "Doesn't give you the right to loot people's businesses. Stay back!"

"Let us in!"

"Open the Big Ninety!" someone shouted.

"Let us eat!" screamed another.

"I got kids to feed!"

The officers planted their feet. "Disperse immediately or you'll be arrested."

Fists were raised. I pushed forward, pressing myself between bodies. Moving past angry faces who were sneering up at the three remaining officers on the stairs.

"They're bringing in more police!" someone shouted from behind me, and the crowd turned. A mass of police had appeared down the street, wearing helmets and carrying clubs and small shields. The officer who had left was leading them, his rifle held at the ready.

"Let us in! We're hungry!"

"We're not criminals! We just need food!"

Get out of here, I told myself. *Now.*

I kept pressing forward. I passed Twenty-First Avenue on the right, then Twenty-Second where more and more people were streaming towards the cannery and the standoff with the police. Humans, dauger, maero, kresh, cephel, even a contingent of shadowy umbra were there, demanding to be let into the cannery. The cops cursed at the crowd, shoved back an old man who had approached them, knocking him down.

More shouts echoed from behind me. A few cops began to tussle with the Breakers. I heard the sickening thumps as club met skull.

Someone began to throw trash at the cops on the cannery stairs, which only infuriated them further. I could see the crowd thinning near Twenty-Third Avenue, so I pressed on. Shoving people out of my way, fighting to get to Twenty-Fourth.

But then I saw it.

A brick. Flying.

It sailed past me and struck the tusked police officer. He grunted and then crumpled backwards, a stream of blood drawing an arc in the air as he fell. A hush settled instantly over the crowd. A second of silence. Then the sound of a wet crack as the back of his head smacked against the cement stairs.

Then, as if on cue, the armed cops raised their rifles and began firing wildly. It all went to hell.

It was a stampede. People were knocked over as the crowd was driven backwards by the rifles. Everywhere voices. Shouting and screaming. People collapsing as police struck them down. Gunshots boomed and echoed and the smell of gunpowder was heavy in the narrow street.

A kresh near me went down, moaning. A dauger woman to my left screamed and crumpled next to a dead dauger man with a silvery mask who was missing a portion of chest and stomach. I willed myself to look away.

I pressed on, trying to keep my head low. I was struck in the face by an elbow and kneed in the back. I kept my eyes low, I kept moving. It was hard to know which direction I was heading in. People swarmed around me, pushing, pressing, crushing.

My right knee was knocked once, then twice, by someone trying to crawl his way out. Each knock sent sparks of pain through my leg. My chest felt like it was on fire, and I wondered if the stitches had torn.

More gunshots boomed from behind me and I flinched, and dropped to a crouch.

I saw a maero fall, struck in the shoulder. His blood spattered the ground and he grunted and then growled, pushing himself off of the cement and rushing back into the throng.

It was a massacre. Blood spattered everywhere, it filled the air. More bricks were thrown. A burning bottle crashed next to the advancing wall of police. Smoke began to fill the air, collecting along the ceiling. People began to gag and then choke.

I couldn't believe what I was seeing. These were desperate, hungry people and the cops were now shooting them as they tried to run. People began to fall all around me. Too many. Too many people. Nearby an old anur collapsed, blood welled from his thigh. I slowed, then leaned in and lifted, half-supporting and half-carrying him to the edge of the crowd.

"T–thank you," he rasped. He pressed himself against the brick wall.

"Will you be okay?" I asked, looking over my shoulder at the wounded still writhing in the street.

He nodded, pressing a hand to his leg. I turned to go back for more wounded as people in red armbands rushed the police on the cannery stairs, tackling one of the armed guards and driving him to the ground. They began to kick him and stomp on his chest, his arms and legs.

I stood, shocked and stunned. I felt powerless, helpless. I was one person in a sea of insanity. What could I do? So much carnage. So much death.

The rifle was ripped away and the Breaker who now held it blew away the other cop before succumbing to gunfire herself.

It didn't stop them. Other Breakers joined in and a few began to smash open the cannery doors. Their mouths shouted in joy but they were inaudible under the screams of the wounded and dying.

"You're all under arrest!" boomed a loudspeaker. "Stop what you're doing immediately."

The noise brought me back. I ducked and rushed back into the crowd. Trying to find more wounded.

People around me were noticing that the cannery doors were open and many abandoned fighting to move towards the entrance. Alarm bells were ringing inside the building, adding to the din.

Around me the crowd pressed. People were knocked over, driven beneath the surge. I bent, moved to help another human, but she pushed me off. Her eyes filled with anger. The crowd was beginning to fight with each other, pushing and clawing to get inside. I saw two human women beat one another bloody. I watched an anur stab an old dimanian in the back as she rushed past him, eager to get inside.

I stumbled back, my mouth hanging open.

A dauger in a pair of dirty overalls emerged carrying an armload of cans, and she was pulled down by the crowd. I could hear the muffled slaps and strikes of flesh on flesh mixing with the screams. More gunshots, the sound of shattering bottles, the scent of blood and smoke in the air.

The world was red: burning and bloody.

I retreated, stepped back and away, feeling stunned and numb.

The wall of cops had stopped their advance and instead let the rioters tear each other apart. Men and women so desperate for food that they were fighting and killing one another.

Then I noticed the figure. Standing above the fray on the balcony of a building across from the cannery. Its robes billowed around it as it stood, unmoving, watching with that haunting silence I had observed so many times before. The black-hooded gargoyle turned. It looked directly at me.

FIFTEEN

Just like that, the gargoyle was gone. I blinked. I had seen them pull a similar trick before but never so suddenly. I swallowed and looked again. My eyes weren't lying—the thing was gone.

I stood on my toes, tried to see if I could spot any more of their pointed hoods in the crowd. Nothing. Just the swell of people. Was its presence somehow connected to the riots, or was it merely observing and passing messages?

Police in riot gear were overwhelming the crowd. Arrests were now being made. I could hear the sound of sirens. I moved away from the mass in front of the cannery. My breathing was sharp and a numbness washed over me. I collapsed, my back to a brick wall. I tried to catch my breath. This was madness. First, the march to the cannery, then the assault on the police, and then seeing everyone turn on each other. The hunger madness had spread like a wild fire. All-consuming.

A bloodied dimanian couple came around the corner and collapsed near me. They were wearing heavy coats and gloves. The man had a knit cap with two holes punched through for his sizable, twisting horns. His lips and right eye were bleeding. The woman seemed unscathed.

"Why did they shoot like that? Why?" the man cried. Big tears ran down his face. The woman tried to console him, mumbling words of comfort as they caught their breath.

"Brick," I finally managed to say. "Someone threw a brick."

The man looked up, shook his head. "No. Why? That doesn't make sense."

He was clearly in shock. His hands were shaking.

"We were down on Twenty-Second," said the woman. "We stepped out of the shop to see what was happening and just… got swept up. So many people…"

"Is he shot?" I asked.

She shook her head. "Glass. Someone threw a bottle. He's okay. The cut's shallow."

"The police are going to round up anyone who sticks around," I said, pushing myself off the sidewalk. "You should go home, or find a place to hole-up."

"But we didn't do anything."

"Why did they shoot like that?" the man asked again, dazed. He looked from me to the woman with a confused expression. "I don't understand."

"It doesn't matter," I said to her. I watched as more people emerged from around the corner. Some were bloody, others coughed and stumbled.

I could hear the bullhorn-enhanced voice of an officer shouting orders. A few more gunshots followed and the couple jolted.

"This is a mess. Get out of here if you can."

The woman nodded and helped the man to his feet.

I got moving myself.

The chapterhouse was a small shop with a wide door and no windows. A small neon sign depicting an open hand with a knife resting in its palm glowed green. It was the only thing that delineated this storefront from the other blank doors that lined the street. Had I not known the mark I would have missed the place altogether.

I pushed through the door and entered a small lobby. A reception counter occupied the opposite wall and next to it was a door. If this was on a lower level there would have been a partition separating the counter from the entryway, protecting the receptionist from unsavory visitors. But Level Six wasn't the lower levels. It was the unofficial start of the elevated levels of Lovat, where the poorest of the rich lived.

The place was simple, plain—nothing overtly nice or shabby. It had a well-worn feeling, scuffed and smoothed by time. Very unlike Argentum with his silver mask and finely tailored suits. A lone plant wilted in a corner next to a set of brown leather chairs. The walls were covered with wood panels. A few photos hung in wood frames that blended in with the wall behind them. Men and women of all different species smiled out of them in muted tones of black and white. Small brass plaques had been mounted below them.

"What the hell is going on out there?" said the maero woman peeking out from behind the countertop. She had short black hair and soft features. A pair of big gray eyes flashed concern, looking from me to the door. Standing, she rose to her full height, which wasn't very tall, at least not by maero standards. She was only a head and a half taller than me.

"Some folks rushed the cops guarding the cannery. A cop got hurt. Other cops started shooting. All hell broke loose."

"By the Firsts!" she said, nearly shouting.

I breathed out heavily.

She moved through the door that separated the back office and crossed the lobby in seconds, poking her head outside and craning her neck to look around. She was wearing a pair of dark blue slacks tucked into leather boots with a matching jacket over a white shirt. Standard business fare.

She sniffed the air. "There's smoke. What's on fire?"

I slumped into a leather chair. "People were throwing fire bombs."

First my heartbeat and then my breathing began to slow.

Funny. Here, in a Society chapterhouse, I felt safe. I touched my chest and winced, feeling pain flare up from the wound, reminding me why I was here.

"I wouldn't go outside," I said. "The police are everywhere, arresting everyone."

She closed the door quickly. "Was anyone killed?" I could hear the concern in her voice. Odd for a woman who ran a chapterhouse for an organization that performed legal murders.

"Yes. Don't know how many."

"Carter's cross," she cursed and leaned back against the door. "This is usually such a quiet warren."

A cry came from outside, followed by a bellowing voice through a megaphone: "THIS WARREN IS UNDER POLICE LOCKDOWN. REMAIN INSIDE YOUR HOMES AND BUSINESSES."

The woman pushed off the door then turned and looked at it. She seemed to wonder what was happening behind it.

"How long have the cops been watching over the cannery?" I asked. I wasn't sure how long LPD would be outside.

She moved away from the door, sat in a chair next to mine, and considered my question. "A few days? Maybe a week?"

"Nothing says 'Come inside, we have valuable goods' like armed guards," I said with a chuckle.

She rolled her eyes. "The city is starving, of course people want to get in there. It makes sense they'd want to guard it. Keep looters out. What I don't understand is why public employees were watching over it. The Bonheurs own a security company."

"The Bonheurs own a security company?" I didn't know who the Bonheurs were but it seemed like the right question.

She nodded and leaned close, her voice lowering. "FirstGuard Security."

Now that name I knew. FirstGuard was a mid-level caravan company. They generally worked for financial firms or exporters bringing in expensive cargo loads. It wasn't as big or as well-funded as Frankle or Merck but they did good trade. They were also considered experts in dealing with bandits, something even some of the bigger companies couldn't boast. So why, with the gear and manpower of FirstGuard, would the Bonheurs rely on LPD? She was right, that didn't add up.

"Huh," I said. "That's screwy."

"Yeah," she said. "Honestly, that whole organization was better managed when Aimé was around. One brother's a dolt and the other's a drunk. They can't agree on anything. I've seen them wander past a few times in the last couple of days, heading to or from the cannery. They'll end up running the business into the ground."

"What happened to this Aimé?" I said.

"You didn't hear? It was in the papers. Pretty tragic. Aimé was murdered last week. He was smart, clever. Everyone in the warren was excited for him. He finally got the reins of the family business. It was a bright spot for him after his mother was killed."

"His mother was killed?"

She nodded. "Mhm, found dead a few weeks back." She shuddered. "The papers didn't say much. I wrote it off as another gilded murder. But, you know, I was talking to a friend of mine—he's married to an LPD detective—he told me that there was all this… writing on the walls at the scene. In her own *blood*. Can you believe that? That's no gilded murder, right? It's like something from a horror fil—"

Gunshots rang out. The woman looked toward the door and then at me. She reached out and gripped my arm. "You think they're killing more people?" she whispered.

I was still thinking about what she'd said. Another pair of deaths. Same scene. There was something about the levels…

Mrs. Bonheur on Seven. Taaka on Eight. Adderley on Nine. I was willing to bet that if we looked further back we'd find more ritual murders tracing a grisly vertical line though the city.

"What do you think is happening?" she asked, her fingers digging into my arm, looking over her shoulder toward the door.

I snapped back into reality, filing this new knowledge away. "Er... At this point they're probably just shooting to scare people. Get them in line. They were moving pretty quickly." I thought about the old anur I had helped, I hoped he'd be okay.

She relaxed visibly.

"I'm Wal," I said, offering my hand.

"Patrice," she said. "I guess we're stuck here. You want to get out of the lobby? A bullet could tear through that outer wall. Besides, it's warmer in the back."

She led me through the door and around to the back room.

The space behind the front counter was long and narrow. A faded carpet lay in the center of the floor, sporting the same symbol of the hand and the blade that glowed above the door outside. Four desks were pushed against the walls, leaving an open path to a small kitchenette and a door labeled "Bathroom" at the back.

On the right was a long corkboard with the word "Open" written in Strutten on a large piece of paper and stapled to the top. A few official-looking papers hung below, with typed information and small photographs. On the opposite wall was another board, this one with a sign reading "Filled". More papers hung below this sign. Some way of managing assignments?

I instinctively looked for a contract with my name on it. I doubted they'd have a recent photo of me, one with the long hair and beard.

"I'd offer you coffee but, well. There isn't any. How about tea?"

"Tea would be great," I said. "Thanks."

I watched as she went to the small stove at the back and placed a kettle atop one of the burners.

"So what brought you here today, anyway?" she asked, opening cabinets.

I took a seat in an empty chair and spun around slowly. "Well, the Society has a contract out on me. I was hoping to sort it out."

"Oh," she paused and turned to look at me, the two mugs in her hands dropping slightly. The limp strings that hung over their edges swayed.

"Yeah, apparently I owe twenty-five thousand lira to a guy named Shaler. I was hoping to get a payment system set up. I tried to hit the chapterhouse in New Holly but I got... delayed. The directory agent pointed me here."

Patrice said nothing.

I continued. "See, with the Big Ninety closed I can't work. I'm a caravan master. I've been doing dock work but that dried up, obviously. Tried some consulting but it's looking rocky lately, with the blockade..." I let my voice trail off as the kettle sang. Patrice filled the mugs with hot water, turned, and walked over to me, pressing one of the mugs into my hands. It wasn't cold in the chapterhouse, but I was still chilled from being outside and the walk over. I took it, wrapping my fingers around the warm ceramic.

"Why didn't you work this out with the collector assigned to you?" she asked.

My memory of the lift flashed. Argentum stalking toward me, the blade hanging in his hand. His one long nail reflecting the light. "I... er... I can do that?"

"Well, of course. We're a collection agency. We want to take payments. You realize there's a huge interest payment associated with a Society collection, right?"

"Well, I..."

"Most people don't, I think that's part of the point," she smiled bitterly. I was having trouble figuring out how she felt working here. She was knowledgeable about the collectors' practices but it seemed the less savory aspects of the process bothered her.

"I can look up your contract if you'd like. See what we can do."

"Please," I said eagerly.

She pulled a thick binder with worn corners out from beneath the front counter and flipped it open so it lay in front of her. She looked serene, like a priestess reading from scripture.

"Who's your agent?"

"Rulon Argentum."

"Humm," she said. "I don't know him, but there's a bunch of collection houses. He could be based somewhere else. Argentum, a dauger?"

"Yep," I said, scooting my chair closer to the desk and looking at the contents of the binder. It was filled with contracts, many stamped "Complete". Notes had been written in margins and taped to the pages.

"Argentum. Argentum," she said as she ran her fingers past names. "Humm..."

"What is it?"

"Well..." She looked up at me. "He's not in here."

Patrice closed the book and scooted back from the counter and studied the binder from a distance, thinking. Then she rose and moved to the "Filled" corkboard where she studied the contracts hanging there.

"Hmm," she said absently.

"What?" My heart had started to pound. It was hard to read her. It was all I could do to try and look apathetic as I slouched in my chair.

"Let me check some older records first, one second." She pulled another binder from a drawer beneath one of the other desks and flipped through it, shaking her head. She grunted and then checked another, then another, finally finishing at the last desk. She turned and leaned against it, looking at me. Well, not at me directly—more like through me.

"What's going on?" I asked.

"Argentum isn't in any directories. We have never collected on an Argentum and we have never had a collector named Argentum."

"What?" My voice wavered.

"Let's look at the contract. What's your full name?"

"Waldo Emerson Bell," I said.

"Gotcha." She returned to her chair and began to flip through her binder again and then a second time. She huffed and frowned, lines forming along her cheeks. It was clear she wasn't finding anything.

"You're not pulling a fast one on me, are you?" she asked with a chuckle.

I shook my head.

"Okay, let me send a quick message."

She rolled her chair to the teleprinter next to the counter. It was the size of a sofa. There she hammered out a quick message on its keys and waited, noisily slurping her tea.

I had all but forgotten mine, lost in the search for the contract. Could I be free from the Society? But then who was Argentum? And what the hell did he want with me?

After a few minutes the machine chittered and a message printed out. Patrice read it.

"Well?" I asked.

She slowly turned to look at me. Her gray eyes were wide, her mouth was turned up at the corners. A mocking smile? I couldn't tell.

"Argentum isn't in anyone's records," she said calmly. "Neither is your contract. You're not under contract with the Society, Wal."

I blinked.

"Do you understand? You're not in here. You don't owe us anything."

There was a heavy bang.

Patrice jumped and then laughed. I looked around, and then down. It was me. I'd dropped the mug, spilling tea all over the carpet of the chapterhouse.

I was confused. I was stunned. I tried to talk but just stammered a bit before I closed my mouth.

Patrice smiled what I now understood to be a warm smile. For a moment I felt a weight lift from my shoulders. Then almost as soon as it left, another took its place. Something larger. Heavier. The rules had now changed. I was in a more dangerous position than I had been before. Coming here had only worsened my situation. My hunch had been right. Argentum wasn't a collector, he was an assassin.

Patrice patted my shoulder and got up to get a cloth.

"Don't worry about it," she said over her shoulder. "Happens all the time. Bet you're feeling relieved, huh?"

SIXTEEN

Lovat's smell had changed. The sharp scent of gunpowder and the acrid smell of smoke hung heavy in the air. Hints of smoke wafted in the spaces between the buildings and clung to my clothes. The city was fuming and so was I. A hot anger had flared up inside of me. Argentum. He had lied. He had threatened. He had pushed me around. For what? Twenty-five thousand lira? The bastard. I would kill him. I would tear his mask off and leave him bleeding in a gutter.

The Society clerk had been alarmed when I explained my story. She put out an alert for him. I doubted it would help. But maybe Argentum was on the run now, maybe he was experiencing a little of what he had put me through. The thought made me smile.

The smoke in the air masked the smell of the garbage that had begun to collect on the curbs. Trash cluttered the corners and gathered in the nooks and crannies of alleys. On the lower levels, Two and Three, that sort of buildup wasn't uncommon, but on the upper levels it was strange to see. Crews of sanitation workers usually loaded carts full of trash to drag off to the massive landfill south of the city. Where were they now?

It took me almost three hours to get back to King Station and Saint Olmstead. More riots had broken out over the city. I witnessed a group of Breakers and a pair of police officers go at it in front of a barber shop. Clubs and knives in hand. In another location, cops faced an angry mob demanding food in a small market square. Elsewhere I saw people smash windows and grab what they could, running off down the street.

Most of the city was on lockdown. Barricades had been stretched across roads, guarded by officers with clubs. They blocked the major routes through areas where a riot had taken place. Rickshaws festooned with loudspeakers belted out warnings to empty streets, to the Lovatines who stayed behind closed doors.

One declared, "Any individual wearing a red armband will be arrested on sight and tried for the instigation of riots."

Another thundered, "Groups of six or more wishing to move together in public must now register at the nearest precinct office. Failure to comply will result in arrest."

Normally crowded, Lovat now felt abandoned. People moved around one another nervously. Rushing from street to street and doorway to doorway. No lingering. No talk. Where had the poor gone? The buskers, the beggars, the addicts?

My breath came out in clouds. I half-imagined myself as some angry bull ox pulling at his harness. I was itching for a fight. Every time I saw someone peer through a window I expected to see the glint of Argentum's silver mask. A slammed door, a sudden shout, the wail of a siren, the clamor of a loudspeaker—everything made me jump. Ready to spring.

Instead, I kept to myself. Head down, collar turned up, I burrowed south through the cold. I climbed stairs, descended lifts, and walked down alleyways. I slipped past blockades and closed streets as best I could.

Eventually, I found myself in front of Hagen's door. The lights inside were dim but the door was unlocked. I pushed through with a grunt, glad to feel the warm air on the other side. My anger had subsided. Turning from red fire into seething coals in my belly. I'd have my time. I'd face him again. This time, I'd be ready. I shook my coat and inhaled deeply. The air was fragrant with incense, candle wax, and old wood. Saint Olm had begun to feel a lot like home.

"Wal?" called a voice from behind the shelves.

I navigated the twists and eventually found the counter, a very wide-eyed Samantha standing behind it.

"Thank God!" she yelled and ran around the desk, throwing her arms around my neck. I grunted as she collided into me. "You had us so worried!"

"Easy, easy," I said. "I'm not at a hundred percent."

She released me and stepped back, her eyes narrowing instantly. "What happened?"

I looked around. "Where's Hagen and Hannah?"

"They're out looking for *you*. We've all been looking! Ever since you disappeared. What happened?"

"Didn't you get my telegraph?"

"No?" Samantha moved around to the other side of the counter and shifted through some papers. "There's nothing here."

"I sent one, I swear. I got held up. Then all hell broke loose out there. A massacre. Is there anything to drink? I could use a drink." I moved around the counter to the small space at the rear of the shop. I began poking through the crowded spaces behind the counter, looking for a bottle, any bottle. The tension that had welled up inside me was drifting away. I felt more relaxed, especially next to Samantha.

She watched me for a moment and finally said, "I haven't found anything, Wal. We've been having enough trouble finding food. What happened? What's this about a massacre? Are you talking about the Cannery Massacre?"

"Ah, they gave it a name," I said and nodded.

"It's all over the monochromes. Nine dead, including one officer. The city's on lockdown. The mayor is promising swift action, the Blockade Breakers are being called instigators. It's ugly."

"Yeah, they have sound carts all over the city wailing about it. Arrested on sight and all that."

"They've already tried a few of the Breakers. The mayor is saying he'll seek immediate execution."

"What?" The last comment shook me. "Can they do that?"

Samantha shrugged. I slumped into a wooden chair. Worry reared its ugly face. Wensem had sided with the Breakers. He was helping them at the Purity Movement's blockade in the south. If the LPD was arresting, trying, and *executing* people... Firsts. I hoped he was okay.

Samantha squatted in front of me and reached out to squeeze one of my hands. She read my thoughts. "There's a big difference between the Blockade Breakers here and the group in Destiny. I'm sure he'll be fine."

I looked at her, her dark eyes met mine and she gave me a little smile.

"I hope so," I said and grew silent.

"Okay," she said. "Fill me in. Where have you been? What happened to you? Why were you in Demetrios?"

I took a deep breath. It was time to fess up. I had been keeping secrets, secrets I should never have kept.

"Uh, so... yesterday..." Was it yesterday? Everything had become a blur. "I went on that food run. I was planning on stopping in on a Society chapterhouse."

"A chapterhouse? Why?" Her expression hardened. Subtle lines formed around her mouth and her eyes. The fire that normally flashed in her gaze intensified. Guilt weighed me down. My silence had been what caused trouble between us before. I should never have kept my trouble with Argentum a secret. They had a right to know.

She rubbed her eyes. "What are you involved in now? Wait... when you said you weren't a hundred precent..."

Her eyes narrowed. She studied me, looking for something. I gave an embarrassed chuckle and pulled off my coat, lowered my suspenders, unbuttoned my shirt, and slowly peeled off my new undershirt, exposing my chest and the bandage below.

Samantha gasped and brought her hand up to her mouth. The spurs along her knuckles cast jagged shadows on the back of her hand. The action with the massacre hadn't been kind to my cut. Spots of red had begun to leak through. I would need to change the bandage.

"Did they do this? Did your contract come due? Ugh!" she said with a distressed groan. "Why is it whenever you go traipsing off by yourself you come back banged up?"

I looked down and poked the bandage. "I thought it wouldn't be a big deal and I wouldn't have to involve you guys."

"You always say stupid shit like that." She let out an exasperated sigh and looked at the bandage. "We need to change that."

Samantha moved to the back of the office and returned in moments with a first-aid kit. She began removing the old bandage and gasped when it had come off completely.

"This is ugly."

"Knife," I said. "A nasty one."

She sighed, then looked up at me. A strand of dark hair had fallen across her face, but I could see the concern in her eyes.

"Who stitched you up?" she asked, her voice tender now.

"Not really sure," I said. "Best guess, a bok named Hank."

"A bok? Well, you've already torn some of the stitching."

"Yeah, I figured. I was fighting to get out of the crowd when the bullets started flying. Things got a little, er... hectic after that."

"Wal," she said softly. "If you're wanted by the Society they'll come here, they'll find you and drag you off. Legally we can't do anything, even..." She paused, the words catching for a moment. "...even if we wanted to."

"I'm not wanted by the Society," I said.

She gave me a puzzled expression, but before I could explain further the shop's bell tinkled. I heard an exasperated huff followed by a draft of cold air. Once again, naked from the waist up, I shivered.

"Ugh, not only is it as cold as a First's heart out there but everyone's going crazy," I heard Hannah say as she moved through the shelves. "I saw two cops fight with protesters. A riot outside the market on Horton. A few places on fire in Pergola Square. Nothing on Wal, though, I couldn't find him, checked Cedric's, checked his haunts down by the Sunk. Nothing! Any luck on your—"

Samantha smiled up at me and shook her head again, and dabbed some foul-smelling ointment over the gash. "He's here," she called out, her eyes locked onto mine. I looked away a little sheepishly and was relieved to see Hannah appear around a shelf of statuary. She was out of the fancy dress I had seen her in the day before and had returned to her roader attire: denim, boots, and dark flannel. Over top of it all she wore a thick leather coat, a red keff wrapped around her neck, and a knit cap down over her ears.

I stretched my neck so my head appeared over the counter and gave her a pitiful little wave just as Samantha began repairing some of the stitches with catgut from the first-aid kit.

"Carter's bloody cross!" Hannah spat, her voice raised with heavy levels of irritation. She came around the counter. Samantha finished stitching me up and began to apply fresh bandages. "We've been crawling all over the span! Where the hell did you go? What happened?"

"I sent a telegram," I said.

"One that never came," Samantha said.

Hannah frowned, then walked over and socked me in the left shoulder.

"Easy," I said with a grunt. It was hard not to smile. "I'm wounded." I pointed down at the bandage.

"Wal was just telling me how the last few days have been typical for him. He somehow found himself in the center of the Cannery Massacre, and he has a collector on his ass."

"He's not a collector," I said.

Hannah's eyes widened. "What the shit! Boss? A contract? And you never told us?"

"I just—" I began, but my words disappeared in a yelp as Samantha pulled the bandage tight, squeezing my chest. Her eyes flashed beneath her dark eyelashes, a smile at the corner of her lips.

"And you were at the massacre!" Hannah punched me a second time, same spot. I grunted again.

"You know, usually I only get knocked around by people other than my friends."

She punched me a third time for good measure.

"So?" She took off her coat and pulled herself up onto the counter, her legs dangling. My bandaging finished, Samantha rose and stood next to her, leaning back against the old wood. My stomach took the opportunity to grumble loudly. I smiled, slightly embarrassed.

"So... after we met Kiver I was approached by this dauger who claimed he was a collector. Fancy fella, silver mask, says his name's Argentum. Said he was hired to kill me."

Hannah whistled. "Who hired him? Did he say?"

A lump formed in my throat and I swallowed it down. I had been dreading this moment. Both Samantha and Hannah had been there on the Broken Road. They had seen Shaler and Tin dead, hanging in that forest of bodies around Methow. I knew when I spoke the name it would dredge up terrible memories for them as it did for me.

"William Shaler."

Hannah's expression dropped and she instinctively moved to cover her false hand with her real one. Samantha's eyes grew wide and I could hear her breathing change, it grew shallow and rapid.

"Yeah," I said. I paused for a moment before I continued. "He claimed I owed twenty-five thousand lira for the death of Margaret Shaler. Said I was responsible."

"And you believed him?" Samantha said.

"He knew a lot about what happened out there... Stuff we kept out of the papers. Anyway, once Kiver had paid us I figured I'd go to a chapterhouse, see if I couldn't get on a payment plan and get him off my back. I was going to do that when I stepped out to find food yesterday but Argentum was on the lift. When I told him where I was going he pulled a knife, came at me."

"That's not how collectors operate," said Hannah.

"No kidding," I said. "He gave me this." I pointed to the fresh bandage. "I managed to get away. Later, I decided to check out another chapterhouse and ended up in Demetrios. Which is how I ended up in the middle of the massacre at the cannery.

But here's the kicker. I'm not actually under contract. Argentum isn't a collector at all. It's just a cover or something."

"So what is he?" asked Samantha.

"Opportunist?" suggested Hannah. "Maybe he thought he could squeeze Wal for money."

I stood and twisted, feeling my spine crack. Then I began to dress. I struggled with my undershirt until Samantha took pity on me and moved to help.

"Thanks," I said as the shirt came over my head and around my chest. "I mulled it over on my way back here. It's a good racket, no one is more willing to pony over stacks of lira than someone with a blood debt. He knows too much to be working alone, though."

"What's his full name?"

"Rulon, Rulon Argentum. Though it could be a pseudonym."

"The Argentums are one of the five precious families," Samantha said, holding my shirt out so I could slip it on.

Dauger society goes well beyond their ever-present masks. Each member belongs to a house named after a metal. The five precious families wear masks of precious metals. The Inox wear steel. Brass wear brass, Nickels wear nickel. Iron, iron. And so on. Just like the elements from whence they take their names they are divided into three castes: base, noble, and precious. The upper echelons are rarer and led by families like the Golds, the Platinas, and the Argentums of the South Wold. Wherever the South Wold is. Maybe Rulon Argentum knows.

"So he claims," I said. Maybe it was all an act. Some way for a base dauger to make a lot more money. Could dauger swap masks? I wasn't sure.

"Well, a member of a precious family wouldn't need money," said Hannah. "Especially the Argentums."

"Yeah, that's another weird one," I said. I finished buttoning up my shirt. "So, I ended up getting plucked out of the Sunk by a bok. A guy named Hank."

"The Sunk?" Hannah and Samantha both said in unison.

"What were you doing in the Sunk?" Hannah asked.

I sighed and explained the whole fight, Argentum on the lift, the chase, ending up in the Sunk. They stared at me as I finished.

"So you just leapt in?" Hannah said.

"Yep."

"Just like that?"

"Yep."

"And a bok found you?"

"Yep," I said with a nod.

"Aren't they supposed to be mean? Like near feral?" asked Hannah. "I mean, I've never met one, hell, never even seen one, but..."

"He wasn't. He seemed on the level, even kind. It was his boss who left me spinning."

"His boss?" Samantha asked.

"Yeah. Says her name is Elephant. I woke up on some cot in a warehouse of hers in Myrtle."

"Myrtle? That's Outfit territory."

"Exactly. Get this—the place was filled with food. Fresh vegetables. Canned goods. Potted meats. Crates of it! She strolled in and introduced herself, said she'd heard of me, knew

I was working with Kiver. Said we had mutual goals. She wants to see an end to the gilded murders. Claimed it was affecting her business."

"Her business selling food to the elevated," said Samantha bitterly.

"That'd be my guess as well. She heard I was under contract, too. Was really cagey about it, though she did offer to clear it up if I found out what was happening up top."

"You think she's Outfit?" asked Hannah.

"She didn't correct me when I asked. I don't see why she'd keep it a secret. She let me see the crates."

"Maybe she hired Argentum," said Samantha.

"No, I didn't get that feeling…" I sighed slowly. "So, that's where I am. A dauger trying to kill me in a starved city. And before you even try suggesting it—yes, I could try to go to the LPD but not only do I not trust them, they're stretched too thin and have their hands full. Anyway, they're not too fond of me."

"Still…" said Samantha, though I could tell she didn't believe her own words.

"Yeah," I said.

Samantha looked up at me and realized what I was thinking. "You're going to go after him, aren't you?" It wasn't really a question.

I nodded, feeling that anger surge up inside me again. "I don't exactly have much of a choice. I can't be hunting a First *and* watching my back for this guy." I paused. "I'll need to get the Judge, though. Even the odds a bit."

Samantha frowned.

The doorbell tinkled again. I could hear the door open and

close and then the sound of soft footsteps. I wished there was a line of sight from the counter to the door.

Hagen appeared and stopped when he saw me standing behind the counter. He was wearing a long coat that covered everything above his red leather shoes. He had cut his bowler so his one horn could stick out the front like some jaunty feather. He looked stunned. He blinked a few times as if he was unsure whether I was an illusion.

"Wal! We've been looking everywhere. You okay? Where have you been? You had us scared!"

"I *sent* a telegraph," I said.

"Really?"

"I would have called, but..."

"Yeah, the phone, I know. I should really get that thing replaced."

"So Wal is being hunted by an assassin," Samantha said flatly, cutting right to the point. "He was chased to Level Two, escaped in the Sunk, and got help from some Outfit goon who was interested in Adderley's murder."

Hagen looked from her to me and then back to her. "What? Really?"

Way to ease him into it, Samantha, I thought.

"He was also at the Cannery Massacre. The one all over the monochromes," added Hannah.

He looked between Hannah and me then quickly crossed the floor to the opposite side of the counter. He scowled and pulled off his coat, then took off his hat, careful not to snag it on his horn. Finally he looked at me and adjusted his glasses and said, "What in the bloody Firsts—"

The door clanged again and this time I jumped. Who could

this be? The mood in the city wasn't conducive to antiques shopping. My muscles tensed.

Argentum? Had he followed me here?

I pushed close to the desk, and felt in the cubby beneath for a club I knew Hagen kept there. Ever since we had been attacked in Saint Olm, he kept one there as a precaution.

Quick steps pattered through the shelves, and I felt my fingers wrap around the club's handle.

"Who's there?" asked Hagen, turning to look at the figure who emerged from the shelves. It was a short anur with bulbous gray eyes and a wide mouth. She padded across the floor in the white uniform of a delivery woman.

I relaxed.

"Hagen Dubois?" she said in a small voice, nervously looking at the four people standing by the counter staring at her.

"I'm Hagen," Hagen said. "How can I help you?"

"Telegraph for you, from a Mister Waldo Emerson Bell. Sorry it took so long. Conditions are… not ideal." She pressed the sealed paper into his hand and mumbled, "Thank you for using Lovat Telegraph." Then she turned and disappeared back out the front door.

"See," I said, smiling. "I *sent* a telegraph."

SEVENTEEN

Hagen closed and locked the front door behind the delivery woman and flipped the sign to "Closed". He suggested that everyone stay at Saint Olm for the night. That it'd be safer. We all agreed.

We raided what was left of Hagen's pantry and scraped together a meager meal of boiled beans and dehydrated rice. Afterward we spent some time watching his small monochrome. Another gilded murder opened the news broadcast. It had occurred earlier in the day. The victim was a well-known broker from Level Six. They flashed his picture, a dimanian, round-faced with kind eyes and a pair of heavy horns that drooped off the top of his head.

"Earlier today," began the voice of the lead anchor as it crackled from the monochrome's single speaker. "During a press conference with the Chief of Police, the LPD reiterated that there was no apparent connection between the victims in this string of murders in Lovat's upper levels."

The screen cut to Detective Bouchard and a couple of other high-ranking police officials at a press conference. A white-mustached human in a uniform stated that each case was being looked into as of today, and that so far there was no evidence connecting the deaths. The officers seemed to look at one another awkwardly as reporters hammered them with questions. I could sense Bouchard's fury boiling beneath his professional demeanor. His smile was too tight, his words too clipped.

The lead anchor reappeared, a human with dark skin, pale hair, and a wide smile. He introduced a segment about the protesters. There were recordings of people marching down streets, fires burning in dumpsters, and looters running off with stolen goods. Then a cut to reporters standing outside government buildings, visibly shivering in the cold and recounting stories about the arrests of suspected Breaker leaders and the rush to trial that the mayor's office had demanded.

The camera panned to show Paramount Square in front of City Hall where a crowd of protesters had been camped for days. Starting with a handful, their numbers had swelled to thousands. Angry protesters chanted together and raised signs demanding food, the end to the Grovedare blockade, and the release of the Breakers.

In the back of the crowd, I noticed a suspicious looking but distinctive figure. The same billowing robes I had seen before, the same tall pointed hood. Another gargoyle. I ran my hands through my hair, and let out a puff of breath as I asked, "Did you see that?"

The camera began to pan away. I rose from the couch, pointing at the small screen. Samantha jolted and leaned forward, a small cry escaping her lips.

"See what?" asked Hagen.

"That wasn't..." Samantha said, her words fading off.

The gargoyle was gone, lost beyond the edges of the monochrome. I turned and looked at Samantha. I looked from her to the others and back.

"You saw it?"

Samantha nodded.

"Saw *what*? What did you see?" asked Hannah.

"Well..." I said, rubbing my face. "That makes five, three in the last few days. I saw one shortly after I left here two days ago, then again at the massacre."

"Saw what?" Hannah asked, annoyed.

I took a deep breath. "Gargoyles. I've been seeing them for days."

The room went silent. Hannah's mouth dropped open and she turned to look to Samantha, then back to me. Pain flashed in her bright green eyes, then fear. She gripped her wooden hand with her real one and pushed off the floor and began to pace.

"Here, in the city?" she asked, speaking rapidly.

I nodded. "Yeah. Not sure how many are here, but they're active. Could be they've been here a while. Could be they just arrived. I've seen them four times in person. Once before we met Kiver, once after, twice since I left you guys, now this one on the monochrome. That's five."

"And this is the first time you thought to tell us?" Hannah said on the verge of shouting. "You let us walk into Kiver's flat to look at his Aklo-stained murder scene without letting us know you're seeing gargoyles?"

"I... I wasn't sure what to make of them."

"You should have *told* us, Wal," said Samantha.

"No shit," said Hannah. She glared at me.

"Look, I wasn't sure... I just—"

"But you're sure now?" Hannah asked, her voice venom. She had been the first to spot the creatures. They had been just shadows then, specks along the Broken Road, with their tall pointed hoods and black billowing robes. We had believed them bandits at first, and discovered later that we couldn't have been more wrong.

It was easy to mistake them for cultists. Mystics throughout the scrape dressed in similar garb. However, when you got close, it was clear those were people in a capirote, eyeholes cut out so they could see, fabric sewn together. Gargoyles were different. They were blackness, they drank in the light, blotted it out. They were faceless, they had no eyeholes, their hoods poured over the curves of their blank faces like settled tar. There were no seams in their robes or the fabric that always seemed to billow about them.

"I'm sure," I said. My voice sounded pressed, like I was holding in a deep breath and struggling to talk without letting it go. "You're right. I should have told you." I sighed and ran my hands through my hair again. "I don't know what I was thinking." I looked to her, to Samantha, to Hagen. It was time. I had to do this. I fought past the tightness in my throat as I spoke. "I know this. The last two times I faced a First I tried to go it alone." I looked at Samantha. She stood with her arms folded across her chest. Her lips were set in a severe frown. "I tried to carry it all. Tried to pull the whole damn wainload myself and... well, it's never worked out. I need you all. I need my friends. I should've told you about the gargoyles, and I should've told you about Argentum. I'm sorry. I'm telling you now. I need your help."

I stood, arms hanging at my sides, meeting each of their eyes. There wasn't much more to say.

"It's strange to hear you ask for help," Samantha said with a small laugh. I turned and looked at her. She smiled. It wasn't especially warm, nor was it forgiving, but it was genuine. "But, I'll gladly give it. All you ever need to do is ask, Wal."

I smiled weakly and nodded.

"So," Hannah said after a few moments. She turned to Samantha, avoiding my eyes. "You saw it as well?"

"Just like before. Just like on the Broken Road," Samantha said.

"So, that settles it," said Hagen, his voice cracking the tension. "You said they were basically servants, right? Servants need a master. We're dealing with another First. Aren't we?"

I nodded. "All signs point to yes."

We sat in silence listening to the drone of the monochrome. Each focused inward, realizing what this meant.

Samantha was the first to speak. "I did some research on them."

"Oh?" I said.

"Yeah, I couldn't get them out of my head. There was something strange about them, outside the obvious. They moved so fast, and they were afraid of guns even though bullets didn't hurt them. Remember? They went right through them. So I looked into them."

"What did you find?" I asked.

"Well, there's not much out there, at least about them in their current form. Pre-Aligning texts do account for their role. Alhazred mentions them throughout his work. As do scribes from later centuries. Usually they go by the name *servitors*.

"Some modern cults like to call themselves servitors because they believe they're serving a First. But there's a significant difference between a servitor and a worshipper. Worshippers can come and go, servitors are bound for life. They were created to be slaves. Many are mentioned, and they come in all manner of shapes, but there's no written mention of specific servitors in tall pointed hoods with no faces."

"Maybe they're something else," Hagen said. "There have been cases of devoted members from the outer faiths becoming mindless drones. Mystics often preach about this sort of thing. A true surrendering of the self."

"Ah, but these things aren't mindless drones. They're something else. I spoke with some colleagues at the seminary: Father Olima and Mother Kaewa. Olima has an encyclopedic knowledge of the creatures in the old tomes. When I explained what we saw he suggested they might be shaggs. Well, that's the new word, the original is much too difficult for native Strutten speakers."

She said the name, the sound coming out of the back of her throat. It was like bubbles bursting underwater. I grinned despite the seriousness of the topic. It always made me happy to see Samantha talk about her research, even if I couldn't always keep up. She was good at it. It was amazing watching the way she wielded knowledge.

Somewhere inside I cared for her deeply, I realized. But I had learned. And I wouldn't leave Essie behind. I'd fight for her. She had understood me. I needed to figure out how to see her again, so we could talk things out, see where we stood.

I snapped back to the topic at hand. Samantha was still talking.

"...looked into shaggs and that didn't seem to fit these guys at all. Shaggs seem almost beast-like whereas our gargoyles can think, reason, and act. Shaggs are more like drones. Like worker ants following their instincts. Also, there was no evidence of shaggs changing form and the gargoyles do that."

"So what was the other option?" I said, eyeing Hannah out of the corner of my vision. She had stopped pacing and now sat on the floor next to the couch, staring down at her hands.

"Well, there's no name for the other option yet but it seems closer. This was Mother Kaewa's suggestion. Some call them masses, others call them spawn. They're described as creatures without shape, formless. In a lot of ways it reminds me of Curwen, remember how you said he could change sha—"

"I'm sorry. I can't keep talking about this," Hannah said, rising. "Hagen, I'm going to crash on your bed."

"Okay," Hagen said dumbly.

"It's just, look..." Hannah frowned and shot me a glare, then rubbed her lips. Her hand was shaking. "Look, I'm sorry."

We watched her turn and disappear into the small room near the back of Saint Olm and close the door behind her.

"She going to be okay?" Hagen asked, already knowing the answer.

"She just needs some time alone," Samantha said.

"She'll be okay," I said. I hoped.

Hagen looked over his shoulder towards the bedroom.

Samantha continued. "So the spawn change shape. Most of the time they were described as black masses, beings of pure chaos."

"Mini-Curwens," I said.

"For lack of a better description... yeah. Anyway I found out more. Some old pre-Aligning tome called *Legends of Commoriom*. It talks about the spawn at great length. They lived in these huge bowls within temples as a liquid, then they'd rise up and do their master's bidding."

"Their master being a First."

Samantha nodded, and then seemed to realize what this meant.

I mentally went through what I knew: There were the murders with the messages written in blood. There was the rise in gilded murders. There was Elephant, and her interest in the murders. Her connection wasn't making much sense but she was awfully concerned about Adderley. The gargoyles, potentially these spawn, servitors for some titanic monster. They were no doubt carrying messages to and fro. And finally there was Argentum, the rogue piece in this game. Where did he fit?

I rubbed at my temples. "Ugh, there's so much to this. I don't know where to begin."

Samantha yawned. "We're all tired. We're all hungry. It's hard to think straight. Maybe we get some rest and start fresh in the morning?"

"That," said Hagen, rising from his chair and moving to a closet. "Is a good idea."

He opened the door and pulled out an armful of patchwork

quilts and blankets. Samantha nodded. "I'll crash with Hannah in your room, Hagen. You two fight over the couch."

She rose and stretched and I could hear her spine crack.

I looked at the lumpy couch and then at the carpet on the floor.

"I'll take the floor," I said to Hagen.

"You sure? You're the wounded one."

"Mighty chivalrous of you," I said. "But I learned long ago how to sleep well on hard ground."

"All right. I'm not going to ask twice, if you'll excuse me I need to use the restroom," Hagen said. I watched him turn and disappear behind the door opposite his bedroom.

I laid out a makeshift bedroll on the floor of Hagen's living space. I squatted down, extending my right leg so my knee wouldn't have to bend. Out of the corner of my eye, I caught Samantha watching me.

"What's up?" I asked.

"Your knee still bother you?"

I realized how long it had been since we had seen each other. Up until tonight our encounters had been brief.

I twisted, feeling my back pop. "A little, stairs are still the worst, and the cold hasn't been too fun. But it's not like it used to be. Why?"

"No reason," she said with a slight smile. She turned, walked towards Hagen's room, then stopped and turn to look at me once again. Her long lashes blinked slowly and then she said, "Wal... I'm glad you're okay."

I returned the smile. "Me too."

We stared at the mounds of paper spread out over the counter. Sleep had come quickly and I had spent the night in a restful abyss. In the morning I woke refreshed and alert, though I was ravenous. We'd cleaned out the pantry the night before, and it hadn't been much.

"I could probably get food from Elephant," I said.

"You think?" asked Hannah. She seemed in better spirits this morning, though she still seemed uneasy whenever we mentioned the research.

"We'd need something, information to trade, but I'm sure I could convince her." Returning to her lair wasn't appealing, but we were hungry.

"I don't like it. How can you trust someone who hoards food while people – children – starve?" said Samantha. She began flipping through papers.

"I don't trust her," I said. "But it's an option."

"Let's figure out this puzzle first, then worry about food."

My stomach complained at that, but I settled in, leaning heavily over the countertop. I never had the mind for research—all the books and translations. It made my head hurt. But this was my third crack at it, so I supposed it was time to get used to it.

"Did we translate the Aklo?" I asked, looking at a series of copies Hagen had made sometime over the last few days. He nodded, and took a seat at a barstool.

"I made some progress. I'm nearly done. I hate translating this shit, it always feels like bugs crawling around in my brain."

Samantha agreed. "The legends say Aklo is alive. That each word is a gateway for what it represents—a portal. There's a story, pre-Aligning tale of an old wizard who wrote down a lot of tales in Aklo. As the words flowed through him they left behind remnants. He was slowly driven mad. He took his own life."

Hagen shuddered.

"It's a hideous language, vile to the tongue and the mind. I hate that we see it so often," said Samantha.

"I have my notes as well, er... my sketches at least," said Hannah.

"Let me see those," Samantha said. Hannah handed them over and watched as Samantha flipped through the pages, studying the sketches.

"Adderley's not complete. His body was covering most of it. They match though, right? I'm not crazy?" Hannah asked.

"Oh, they match," said Samantha, almost in awe. She looked up at her brother. "Hey, do you have a copy of Fortier's *Compendium of Geases?* It's pretty recent, post-Aligning. Few hundred years old maybe."

Hagen thought about it and then nodded, slipping his paper and pen away and climbing the spiral staircase to the shelves on the second floor.

"You recognize the mark?"

Samantha nodded. "I just want to be sure."

Hagen returned a few moments later carrying two massive brown tomes bound in leather. Each was about the size of a small suitcase. He grunted as he hefted them on to the counter.

As they banged down puffs of dust dislodged from between the pages and blew out in tiny brown clouds.

"I have two copies, about fifty years apart. Different presses as well. One looks to be Reunified? Wilmarth Press?"

"Yep, that's one of ours. Is it the more recent one?"

Hagen nodded and slid it closer and Samantha pulled it in front of her and began flipping through the pages.

"So I finished getting this Aklo translated," Hagen said after a few moments. "But it's odd. It's nothing at all like what I've seen in books. It's rougher."

"Well, it's written in blood," Hannah said.

"I don't mean like that. I mean it's simple... almost childlike. It's not text taken from a tome or some pagan scripture. This is different. Like reading someone's diary."

Samantha looked up from the copy of the *Compendium* and looked at Hagen's notebook. She blinked and then grew still, her lips parting slightly.

"Wait," said Hannah. "Back up a bit. Where does Aklo even come from? How do we know about that?"

Samantha frowned slightly. "Well, it's kind of hard to believe."

"Try me."

Hagen adjusted his glasses and peered at Hannah. "Well, Aklo is pre-Aligning. You've heard the tales, the Firsts returning to earth and wreaking havoc?"

Hannah let out a sigh. She had been with us on the Broken Road. Curwen had kidnapped her. She was as much a believer as the rest of us.

"Aklo is their language," explained Samantha. "Supposedly.

Any records we have, *real* records, have been lost. All we have are manuscripts copied from manuscripts. For a long time no one believed it existed at all. For decades everyone thought it was a mistranslation. No one took it seriously."

"So what happened?" Hannah asked.

"Well, we found a few full books of Aklo. It was during an expedition outside of the territories. Far to the east, past Leng, in the ruins of an old city on the shore of a dry lakebed. The archeological team had been looking for old technology when they discovered the tomes."

"*The Farnese Manuscripts*," said Hagen, almost reverently.

"It was the first time anyone had seen books like that. The church at the time labeled them blasphemous and they ended up on the forbidden shelf in some library. It wasn't until hundreds of years later that they were found and scholars began to translate them."

"And? What was in them?" asked Hannah.

"It's far less interesting that you'd expect. It was a list of genealogies, nothing relating to the Firsts, but it was the first solid evidence of Aklo as a written language. Since then more and more books have slowly cropped up. Some real, many fake."

Hagen jumped in. "It's easy to spot a fake though. It's a raw language. Nothing like Strutten, Cephan, even Laningal. It's bizarre and twisted, but very blunt. You can usually tell when someone's forced it."

"Can it be spoken?"

Samantha shook her head.

"Not really," explained Hagen. "Not by us, at least. Some have speculated that more bestial races, the bok or the lengish, might be able to, but I've never seen evidence of that. Mostly it's seen as a forgotten piece of history. Well… until recently."

"Until recently," I repeated coldly. My mind was distant. I had seen the language appear three times now. First with Peter Black and The Children of Pan. Then a second time in the den of Curwen, who had terrorized the town of Methow to madness and manipulated flesh to create horrible creatures. Now, once again, in Lovat, at the site of two murders.

I picked up Hannah's sketch again and looked at the twisted shapes of the letters. "So what does it say?"

"It's like an appeal. A sort of… prayer. Whoever wrote it is hoping to earn a place at the side of the master. The victim is a sacrifice for the master, a way to bind them together. Then there's a stanza that looks like lines of a song, over and over, like a chant. At the end there's a plea for mercy, and praises for the greatness of the master."

"What master? Do we have a name?"

"No, no name at either scene. There is a reference to the master as Founder, but that's all."

"Wait, a Founder? I know that term," said Samantha.

"Yeah?" said Hagen.

"Wal, remember that book I had on the Broken Road?"

"Um, vaguely. Written by some crazy lady. The, uh… Mason?"

She smiled. "Close. Keziah Mason. *A Treatise on the Writings of Keziah*. She believed the Firsts talked to her in her sleep. She used the term Founder instead of First."

We all paused, thinking this over.

"So we have two victims," said Samantha. "One, a poor male kresh killed on Level Eight, the other, an elevated male human, killed on Level Nine, or what will eventually be Level Nine."

"That's about as far apart in kind as you can get," said Hannah. "A poor kresh and a hume doctor."

The conversation I had with Patrice in the Society chapterhouse came to mind.

"Three," I blurted.

"What?" they all said in unison.

"There's three murders. When I went to the chapterhouse, the woman who ran it told me about another killing that matches our pattern. The victim was a dimanian woman named Bonheur."

"Bonheur," repeated Hagen softly, his eyes narrowing behind his spectacles as he drummed the spurs along his knuckles on the countertop.

"I don't know much, but Mrs. Bonheur was found dead in her flat on Level Seven." I let that sink in, seeing the reactions on Samantha and Hannah's faces as they realized that was one floor below the kresh. "Her blood was covering the walls. Strange writing. No one could read it."

"She had a son, an Aimé Bonheur," said Hagen.

"Right. You know him?"

"It was all over the monochrome a few weeks ago. Aimé was killed. He was about to start running the family business. He was found with his neck crushed. Still an open case."

"How long ago was Mrs. Bonheur murdered?" asked Hannah.

I scratched my chin. "I don't think it was too recent. Month? Maybe longer?"

"So, before Taaka."

"Level Seven?" Hagan asked.

I nodded.

"Seven, Eight, Nine," said Hagen.

We were close now. I could feel it.

"If I could only see the Aklo at Bonheur's murder. In both Taaka's and Adderley's the Aklo was similar, but the chants were different," Hagen said, he was speaking faster now, flipping pages of notes.

"Could it be different killers?" I wondered aloud.

Hagen shook his head. "No. I think it's the same one, the lines were too similar. Everything had the same pattern. Lots of words being repeated."

"What were the chants?" I asked.

Hagen scratched behind his horn and stared off for a moment before responding. "At the Taaka scene it was sing-songy, like the chorus of a song. Let me find it..."

He pulled out a notepad and tapped some lines of Strutten.

Samantha leaned over and read the first passage. "Take this gift. One more step. One more step. Upwards goes the Founder. Take this gift. One more step." Samantha squinted. "Are you sure it read 'step'? The descenders look off to me."

Hagen squinted at the notes. "My best guess. The lighting wasn't very good and we got interrupted. I was just trying to capture it all before Bouchard kicked us out."

One more step. What did that mean? I wasn't sure what to feel. Fear? I was sure it would come. Exhaustion? That seemed closer. Hannah moved away from the counter and began to walk a slow circle around the living area.

I rubbed my eyes and slumped back in the same wooden chair I had sat in the previous night. I leaned back so my neck arched upwards and stared at the wall behind me, watching Hannah. There was something here. The writing. The song.

The gift mentioned in the little chant was clearly the sacrifices, that was easy. It was the symbolism behind the other lines that was hard.

Upwards goes the Founder. There was something there but what was it? Why did the sacrifices happen where they did? Why did Taaka, Bonheur, or Dr. Adderley matter? What purpose did their deaths serve?

"Wait," said Hagen.

We turned to look at him.

"The chant at Adderley's scene."

"Yeah?" said Hannah.

"It's... well," Hagen cleared his throat and read. "Take your servant. One more step. One more step. Upwards goes the Founder. Take your servant."

Your servant. You wouldn't write that unless...

"Suicide. He killed himself," said Hannah.

"After he killed the others. I think Adderley was our killer," said Hagen. "I think all these deaths, the Aklo, was his doing. His death at Kiver's party was the final ritual—a suicide—the final and ultimate sacrifice to his god."

"But if he's dead," I said. I recalled the news segment from earlier, the broker who had become the latest gilded murder. "...then his murders aren't related to the gilded. Bouchard's wrong. The murders are completely unrelated."

"A doctor," said Hannah. "Who'd have thought..."

I leaned back, remembering my brief encounter with Adderley as the blood rushed to my head. He seemed nervous, but otherwise harmless. Then again, so had Black and so had Curwen.

So how was I supposed to approach this? We had Kiver's killer, but the killer was dead. Any contact he had with the First was lost with him, wasn't it? Should I just waltz up to the Shangdi Tower and say, "Hey, don't fret. That guy we thought was murdered in your new flat, well, he killed himself. You're safe. Sorry about Taaka?"

"By the Firsts, it's a pharos!" Samantha nearly shouted the words. I whipped myself forward snapping into a sharp seated position and looked at her. Awe had crept into her voice. She stabbed a finger at the book with a thick thump.

"What? What's that?"

Samantha looked serious, her eyes flicking at her brother and then back to the paper. "Hannah, you're sure this is right?"

She stopped her pacing and looked at Samantha with an indignant expression.

"Sorry, it's habit," Samantha said. "It's just, they're nearly identical and that means... well... it's an altar. Each altar signals the next. Like a beacon. Ancient Curwenites called them a pharos. Just as their idols change so do their places of worship. They used pharos to guide each other from tabernacle to tabernacle, claiming they could hear the calling in meditation."

"A pharos for what? Guiding another group of killers? Kiver's places are both large but it's not like they're temples," I said. I pushed off from the chair and leaned over the counter to peer down at Hannah's sketches. Dark lines formed the rooms of each murder scene in three dimensions. A symbol was drawn on the floor, two more on walls near the head and the foot of the symbol. It was well done. If only we'd been able to visit the Bonheur murder scenes…

"In some belief systems altars have various uses. These are designed to be channels. Adderley meant them to direct a flow of whatever energy he thinks he's unleashing when he kills." She pointed at the two symbols copied from the walls found near Taaka. "You remember these on the wall, and this one on the floor?"

Hannah nodded and then realized what Samantha was suggesting. She took a deep breath and leaned against the counter to steady herself. "They're entry and exit points."

The pieces all fell into place. I traced a line with my finger from one symbol through the big symbol on the floor where the body had lain and then ended on the wall opposite. It lined up.

"Which direction was Kiver's old place?"

"North-east… roughly," said Hagen with a shrug.

"And where in the room were the entry and exit runes?"

Samantha looked down and studied Hannah's drawings again and then looked back up. Her eyes blinked, her breathing grew more shallow.

"In the new scene, where Adderley died," she said and looked at me, her mouth a sharp line. "Wal… there's no exit."

"He's calling his Founder," said Hagen, his voice soft.

We all paused, letting that sink in.

I leaned forward. "I bet if we traced a line we could draw it through Kiver's old place, to his new place, and down to the Bonheurs'. I bet beyond that we'd find more. More deaths on each level moving down, down to the Sunk if need be. One straight line."

Hannah, Samantha, and Hagen all drew back from the pile of books and documents. They looked at me and then at one another.

"Like a beacon," Hannah said.

"Yeah," I agreed. "But for what?"

EIGHTEEN

Lovat seemed like it was waking up from a bender. The rancid smell of smoke hung heavy in the air and few people were out and about. It was still freezing. My breath came out in thick puffs of white, little clouds that disintegrated as I walked through them.

We saw a pair of dauger in dull masks wearing the bright yellow of city employees. They were taking a break from sweeping up glass and rubble. Gas masks hung around their necks and their jumpsuits were stained a gunmetal gray from the knees down. They shivered in the cold and passed a cigarette between them. They watched us as we passed, heads slowly turning to follow our progress down the street.

"Hey, be careful," called one. "Breakers are out!"

"And LPD," said the other, laughing. "You figure out who to avoid."

Samantha and I glanced at each other, and then plodded on. This city was eating itself. I never liked the police. Had my own reasons for not trusting them, but hearing others speak with such disdain made it seem like we were on the brink of a civil war. Maybe we were already there.

I didn't like being unarmed. Argentum was still out there. The city had strict policies about weapons, but it seemed time to ignore them.

Samantha walked next to me, her back straight, eyes alert. She'd refused to let me venture out alone. Said every time it happened I ended up hurt. I supposed she was right. She had changed into roader boots that laced up mid-calf. They clomped on the cement as we walked, echoed off the brick buildings of King Station.

Hagen and Hannah had gone to the big steel-and-glass library on Level Four. It was an ancient thing, pre-Aligning, stained with rust, many of its glass panels boarded over. It was rarely used but full of information. Lovat Police Department records were public after a year, and we hoped there would be some leads on Adderley's other victims. It was a long shot. People died in this city every day. Thousands of them. If the police hadn't clued in on a serial killer then Hagen and Hannah may not either. Still, the more we were able to find, the closer we would get to the lair of the First. If we could find it, maybe we could kill it. Before it killed anybody else.

"One thing bothers me," said Samantha, stepping over a shattered monochrome. There was glass everywhere and it crunched beneath her boots.

"What's that?"

"If the First is alive, if it's active, why isn't it tearing through the city?"

I looked at her, frowned slightly. It was a good question.

"You know the legends, Wal. When the Aligning happened, they plunged mankind into darkness for thousands of years. We've seen them. They aren't peaceful. They're destroyers."

"You saying this First is killing the elevated?" I said.

Samantha hummed. "No. That doesn't fit. Cybill was ready to destroy, right?"

I nodded.

"Curwen was more surgical but he wanted to terrorize."

"Right," I said. "Maybe it's waiting for something."

She laughed. "When the stars are right and all that? Maybe. It's hard to sort fact from fiction… I think we're missing something."

We moved east, rode an empty lift down a level and walked the rest of the way to my apartment in the Terraces.

It was at the top of a gray brick building on Ament Street. The building stooped on its corner like a tired old man. Its lower half dropped down through the entresol between Levels Three and Two, the basement resting on the back of a bigger building that had its roots somewhere down in the Sunk. The residents ran the gamut of trade but tended to skew poor. Most days, pitch dealers lingered on corners, and a few street gangs laid claim to the warren. The streets here would be considered rough by some standards, but I found they weren't dangerous if you kept your head down.

But I still didn't want to take any chances.

Shivering in the cold, we lingered behind a line of dumpsters and waited to see if anyone was watching the place. I hadn't seen Argentum since the fight on the lift and I did not want to run into him again before I was armed. I'd feel better with the Judge at my side.

We listened. In the distance a baby wailed. A couple fought, a rodent squeaked, and a dog barked. It was quiet. Eerily so.

Samantha had mentioned that there had been a riot here, one of the first, a protest gone bad. You could see signs of it mixed in with the normal trash that cluttered the street. Abandoned banners, scorch marks, shattered glass, and the still-smoldering shell of an overturned police fourgon. The hulk smoked across the street from the entrance to my building, turning the light from the lamps that hung from the ceiling into a gloomy twilight. I guess the riot had gotten a lot closer to my place than Samantha had realized.

"This is where you live?" She sounded taken aback.

"Well, recently," I said, hoping embarrassment wasn't creeping into my voice. I blew into my hands and rubbed them together, realizing it'd been years since I had brought a woman to my apartment. I wondered absently when I'd last cleaned it. "I change places whenever I come back into town."

She nodded.

I scanned the area. "Do you see anyone?"

Samantha craned her neck and looked over the dumpster. The small nubs on her chin stuck out and sharpened her features. "Is Argentum a small elderly anur?"

I laughed. "No, that'd be Mr. Audley. Let's go in."

We made our way up two floors, passing piles of mildewing paper and half-filled garbage bags destined for one of the city's incinerators. I fished the key from its hiding spot behind some molding.

"Very secure," said Samantha.

I put my finger to my lips, turned the handle, and pushed my way inside.

Tensing, I braced myself, but there was nothing. I breathed a sigh of relief. The apartment was empty.

It was also a mess. I had left the bed unmade, a set of yellow sheets were twisted on top of the mattress, the quilt half on the floor. The sink was full of dirty dishes. In one corner the radiator moaned as it quietly fought against the bitter cold. It was warmer in here than in the hall, and warmer in the hall than out on the street. So it was chilly, but not freezing.

Samantha closed the door behind us.

"This is... cozy," she observed.

"Yeah," I said, absently poking around on top of a small chest of drawers. "I haven't had a chance to hang my art collection yet."

I looked over my shoulder and smirked. She rolled her eyes mockingly.

The Judge was where I had left it, in its holster resting in a drawer in the small nightstand by the bed. I pulled it out, tossed it on the bed and fished out a shoulder holster from another drawer. The weapon would have to sit on top of the knife wound Argentum had given me but I didn't have much of a choice. It needed concealing. The cops were already looking for reasons to arrest people, no sense in giving them more.

"Look, I've been meaning to say… thanks," Samantha said.

"For what?"

"For putting your trust in us. In me. For telling us everything," said Samantha. "I know it's not easy for you."

I looked up at her and smiled. "Well, you were right. I can't go at this alone. I need you guys."

She smiled and I could see something else in her expression. Something that could move beyond friendship. It stirred up old feelings.

"Sorry about all the trouble again," I said.

I pulled off my coat, tied my hair into a loose bun, rolled up the sleeves of my shirt, and began to pull on the shoulder holster.

"I'm starting to get used to it," Samantha said. "Trouble finds you."

"Guess that's what comes with being the Guardian," I said.

"Yeah," she said, frowning slightly.

She moved slowly about the room, and I watched her as I buckled the holster in place. Her long fingers traced over the dresser and she frowned a little as they came up dusty.

I went to work cleaning the revolver, letting my hands disassemble it. Feeling the oiled rag play over the chambers and cylinder. I needed it reliable. Who knows what else is out there?

After a few moments Samantha said, "It works."

"I beg pardon?" I looked up. She stood an arm's length away. Her coat was unbuttoned and she had removed her keff.

"This apartment. It feels like you. I can't place what that feeling is."

"Oh?" I said, continuing my work but looking at her.

"Yeah. It's... grounded."

"Huh," I said, dwelling on that. Was that a compliment?

"I just mean... " she laughed. A bright laugh that sent my heart racing. "I'm just surrounded by so much extravagance all the time. But sometimes it's nice to be around someone that shows himself. No hiding... Sure, you keep secrets. You can be brash, but... you're who you say you are."

"And what do I say I am?" I asked, snapping the cylinder into place and giving her a quick smile.

"A dusty caravan master."

She stepped closer.

I was overcome with a different emotion. Was it guilt? I hadn't told her about Essie. What was there to tell? Nothing had ever happened with Samantha. I had been too dumb, too scared. Times were overwhelming. I moved on. But the ice between us had thawed. That much was clear.

She needed to know about Essie. That, too, was clear.

"Look, I..." I started to say.

Samantha looked up at me, tilting her head slightly to one side. Her hair slipped from behind her neck and fell across her shoulders as she waited, a little smile playing across her lips. It would make things a lot easier if she didn't... look like that.

My old man always told me it was better to tear the bandage off rather than draw out the agony. "I'm sort of... seeing someone. We're not together, but... well, I don't know where we stand right now."

Smooth, Wal.

I wasn't sure what I expected as a reaction.

Samantha blinked and her smile disappeared.

"I should have told you earlier. You're a friend. But… I haven't seen you for months." I rubbed my neck.

"I see," said Samantha. She nodded and took a step back. "What do you mean, you don't know where you stand right now?"

I scratched my cheek. "Well, I went to see her after I ran into Elephant. We were talking. I told her a little about the Broken Road. I left off the bits about Curwen being a First, and the gargoyles. I explained about the collector after me and she flipped out. Kicked me out of her place. It left me sort of stunned."

"She sounds great," said Samantha. She had folded her arms across her chest and she was looking out the window to the streets below.

I rubbed the back of my neck and let out a long sigh.

I loaded the Judge and slipped it into the holster. Then I pulled on my wool coat and dropped the remaining box of shells into a pocket.

Samantha hadn't moved, she was still looking outside.

"Look, I am just telling you this. No more secrets."

"You kept secrets from this… Essie. You told her about the Broken Road but left out the First and the gargoyles. Is she someone you care about?"

I nodded.

"Then you need to tell her about all of this. How deep it all goes."

I nodded again. "Look, before we head back to Saint Olm, I want to check in on her. Make sure she's safe. That okay? I'll walk you back to the shop if you—"

"No," she snapped. "I told you, I'm coming with you. You get into too much trouble alone."

I wanted to reach out. Squeeze her arm. Something. But I could see it wasn't the right time.

"Let's head to Cedric's. If it's open, she should be working."

The windows of the diner were dark. The tiled counter and tall-backed booths were shadows behind the glass. The neon sign was off, the tubes dingy and black.

Cedric's clearly wasn't open and the entresol was immersed in shadow. From somewhere deep in that middle space between the levels there came a hacking cough, wet and raw. Closer I could hear the scurry of rats, and the rolling shuffle of centipede feet on the metal floor.

Samantha shuddered next to me. Bits of light caught in her eyes as she hugged her coat close to her chest and looked around.

A sign hung on the door of the diner among the Auseil Zann hymns. Handmade and crude, it read:

TEMPORARILY CLOSED

NO FOOD

"What now?" Samantha asked.

"Come on," I said. "Let's check her place."

We climbed the stairs that led back to street level and walked down the cold blocks turning where necessary to find ourselves in front of Essie's building. I looked around, double and then triple checking to make sure Argentum wasn't lurking nearby.

His words rang in my ears and rattled around inside my skull. *I will always find you, Mister Bell.*

Let him come. I was ready.

A few people milled about. A human and a dauger still sporting red Breakers armbands scuttled down an alleyway and out of sight. A hunched figure completely enveloped in a dirty coat rocked slowly on a bench down the street, steam billowing out from below their collar where they breathed.

I shouldered through the door and led Samantha up the stairs to Essie's apartment.

The door was open when we got there.

I drew my gun and held it pointing upwards. I maneuvered next to the door like they always did on police serials. Samantha moved behind me, and we stood flattened against the plaster wall.

"Essie?" I called out cautiously.

I peered through the crack of the open door. The lights were on. There was no movement from inside.

"Essie?" I said, a little quieter. "You in there?"

I waited and counted to ten. My heart hammered three times as fast.

When I got to ten I pushed my way in, trying to cover the angles. I probably looked ridiculous.

No one in the upper corner.

No one along the back wall.

No one near the bed.

No one was inside. The apartment wasn't big.

I stepped further inside and checked the tiny bathroom, even poking my head behind the shower curtain.

Empty. Sort of.

The place was a mess. Clothes were strewn everywhere. Drawers had been pulled free from their cabinets, the mattress had been flipped. One of Essie's lamps had fallen and shattered on the floor. Bits of blood dotted the ground around the jagged pieces.

Oh no. Oh no, no, no.

"Essie! Essie!" I shouted. I could hear the panic in my voice.

I had a mental image of Argentum shouldering his way into the apartment, tearing it apart as he chased Essie around the room. I imagined him catching her and using the lamp to subdue her. Smacking it across the back of her neck.

"Someone was here," I said. "Look at the lamp. Someone took her."

"Wal, you're leaping pretty quickly to some serious conclusions. Maybe she just… cut herself on the lamp?"

"Argentum was here," I said coldly. I held the Judge at my side, and looked down my arm. The gun felt heavy in my hand. It felt good. A numbness creeped in behind my ears.

"Wal, you don't—"

A knock at the door.

Samantha's eyes went wide. We froze, and heard the sound of feet padding into the room. A voice called, "Hello? Who's there?"

My eyes narrowed. Essie's attacker? I spun, bringing the gun up.

"You son of a—" I shouted.

"Whoa! Whoa! Whoa!"

A large anur stood in the doorway. His already enormous eyes widened further as his many chins quivered and his wide mouth dropped open. His cigar dropped from his mouth to the carpet. He raised his big webbed hands awkwardly.

"Don't shoot! Please don't hurt me."

"Who are you?" I growled.

"I'm the super. You r–robbing the place? Take what you want!" he said. "I'll be no trouble."

"Carter's cross. No, we're not robbers," said Samantha, exasperated. "Wal, put that thing down, you're scaring him to death."

I slipped the Judge back into its holster.

"Sorry," I apologized.

The anur's face screwed up and he glared at me.

"We're looking for Esther Cove. She lives here," I said.

His expression softened. He nervously looked from me to Samantha and back. Finally he cautiously bent down, picked up his cigar and returned it to his wide mouth.

"I'm a friend of hers," I explained. "I'm looking for her."

He eyed me, sized me up, and stuck his hands into the pockets of his cardigan. He began to rock on his heels. "A friend, huh? What kind of friend breaks into an apartment armed with a gun and trashes the place?"

"The door was open when we got here!" Samantha said.

"Hmm. Well, I heard you hollering. I guess thieves don't holler."

"You know where Essie is?" I asked.

"What's it to you?"

"I'm her *friend*."

He has her. Argentum has her. I couldn't stop thinking about it.

"Well, you aren't any longer. She's gone."

"Gone?" I blinked. "What do you mean gone?"

"Gone! Took off. Skipped out on her lease. Handed me a wad of lira and said she was leaving."

I sat back slowly, settling next to the overturned mattress, and looked over at Samantha. The cool expression she had been wearing had given way to concern.

"Did she say where she's going?" I asked, my voice sounding wooden in my ears.

The anur shook his head. "Nope. Even if she did, I wouldn't tell you. Don't know you from Carter."

"Wal, it sounds like she got out. Like she's okay," said Samantha. Her tone had changed, slipping back into priestess mode. Care and concern welling up to overcome any emotions that had been there before.

Had she gotten out? I could only hope she hadn't been captured by Argentum or rounded up by riot police. I hoped she had found passage on a transport or a caravan, someone willing to take her somewhere safe. Some place not eating itself alive. Regardless, the truth rang hollow in my chest: Essie had disappeared.

NINETEEN

Zann hymns tore free from their wax seals and fluttered around our feet as we walked back to Saint Olm. Samantha hadn't said anything since Essie's apartment. I half-expected her to chastise me for sticking the gun in the super's face. She never liked guns and abhorred violence, but I had seen her kill to save and seen her kill to free. This time, no words of chastisement came and so we walked in silence.

A bitter wind cut at us, carrying with it more papers and trash. Copies of the *Lovat Ledger* fluttered about like dead leaves. Headlines reading: "Riot in South Dome!" and "Six Dead in Broadway Hill Demonstration" flicked past like pictures on a monochrome. I put my head down and pushed into the wind.

Essie occupied my thoughts. Why did she leave Lovat? What did I say that had struck a nerve? I went through the scene over and over in my head. Talking about the Broken Road and explaining the rescue of the refugees had been fine. But it was the collectors that had set her off. What had she said? "You can't stay here. You can't bring those people here.

You shouldn't have come here." She had been so angry. What sort of trouble was she in?

I hardly noticed the marching protesters as Samantha guided us past the crowd. The farther we moved away from her apartment, the more I worried. My stomach was in knots wondering what had happened. I tried to remember our conversation from the night we got loaded but it was too hazy. She knew so much about me and I knew so little.

Lovat felt abandoned, but you could see people, watching from windows, poking their heads out from behind doors. The homeless, who usually sat on the streets, now lurked in alleys, ducking behind overflowing dumpsters whenever someone walked past.

Maintenance people worked at some of the damage. Many businesses were closed, their security gates drawn. Some shops had been temporarily boarded up to protect their plate-glass storefronts. A few shopkeeps stood outside doorways and surveyed piles of wreckage.

We were halfway to Saint Olm, in the central business district near Lovat Central, City Hall, and a few other official buildings when the sodium lamps above us went dark.

Ca-chunk!

"What the—" Samantha said.

The lamps above us popped and their filaments quickly cooled. The light faded quickly and left us standing in a well of blackness. It was like watching a sunset happen in seconds instead of minutes.

Everything was silent. Nothing moved. Then came curses and shouts from windows, behind doors, and down the street.

"Argentum," I whispered, hearing the nervousness in my voice. I blinked but everything was black. I couldn't see Samantha, I couldn't see the outlines of buildings. I pulled the Judge from its holster and turned slowly.

It was so dark. A city of levels like Lovat becomes cavernous when the lights go out, the echoes seem more pronounced, and the city feels impossibly dark. I could hear my breath, feel my hands shake.

But nothing came.

"It can't be him. There's no way he could rig a whole warren…" Samantha said from somewhere to my left.

I saw flashes, expected to see his metal face emerge from the murk and feel the sharp pain of his blade as he cut into me.

Still nothing happened.

After a few seconds meager emergency lights kicked on with throaty thrums illuminating portions of the street and parts of buildings. Candles were being lit and they glowed from windows.

Slowly the street transformed from sheer black to forms swimming in the penumbra. Buildings rose around me like obsidian monoliths, a few lights winking against their dark faces, walking figures became silhouettes of ebony against dimly glowing streets.

"Stay alert," I said.

Still something felt wrong. It was like the feeling of being watched, only inverted. I felt a glimpse, but the feeling was... what? It seemed just out of my grasp. My spine tingled with it. Gooseflesh crawled across and up my arms. I shuddered and looked around, still seeing nothing.

"You feel that?" I asked.

Samantha's form turned and even though I couldn't see her features I could tell she was regarding me curiously. "What do you mean?"

"There's something going on, I can just... tell. Maybe not Argentum. But... something..."

It felt familiar, I realized. I'd had similar feelings before though I couldn't place where or when.

People began coming out of their buildings, moving silhouettes backlit from the emergency lamps. Dauger, humans, dimanians, and a few maero all stood around mumbling to one another and staring up at the ceiling.

"Never seen a brownout last this long," someone said.

"I have," said another voice. "Twenty years ago. One of the incinerators went up and took two more with it. Whole city was dark for a day until they got the backups on."

"I heard the plant workers were talking about going on strike."

"I heard that too," said another.

"Can you blame them? Wish I had that kind of leverage."

"What if it doesn't come back on?"

"I bet it's the mayor's doing!" someone shouted. "This is his way of quelling the rioters. Keeping everyone in line!"

Candles and lanterns sprung up around us, adding a meager glow to the titanic space of the warren. There was enough light now, I could see Samantha's face. Beyond her it was difficult to make out details.

I looked up and through the cracks between levels I could see other sections of the city still lit. Others seemed to be experiencing the same darkness we were.

"It's not just us," I said to Samantha. "It looks like Level Six has power, maybe Five. I bet these are rolling outages. I bet the power'll be back soon."

Out of the corner of my eye I caught a glint of something, and my spine shivered. I spun. Argentum?

No. But there was something.

Emerging into a pool of light and then quickly stepping out of it was Janus Gold, the dauger from Kiver's Auseil party. He was moving through the milling crowd, his golden mask catching the occasional glint of light. He was wrapped in a thick billowing cloak, with the heavy hood I'd seen on other elevated during my trip to the Shangdi.

What was he doing down so low? The elevated rarely traipsed below Level Six, and were never seen down here on Four.

"Hey," I whispered and thumbed in the direction of Gold. "Check it out."

Samantha followed my eyes. "Who's that? You know him?"

"Yeah. That's Janus Gold," I said. "Hagen and I met him at that Auseil party."

"Gold, eh? What's he doing down here?" Samantha asked, her eyes following his progress. He dipped past a pair of maero holding candles and moved to an alleyway. One of the small emergency lights blazed above him and caught the sheen of his mask for a second before he disappeared out of its glow.

Then, he stopped, not too far from where Samantha and I

stood. A portion of his left shoulder and his back was illuminated by the small emergency light. No one else on the street seemed to notice the elevated dauger in their presence.

"Good question," I whispered. He was thirty or forty yards away and, judging by his body language, he was engaged in a conversation. I edged closer, slipping into a darkened doorway. Samantha moved in behind me and we were pressed together, careful to remain in the shadows.

"Carter's cross," I said, the words tumbling out of my mouth.

A long narrow head emerged from the gloom. The pointy hood, the blank face, robes curling like living shadow.

A gargoyle.

Samantha gasped. "Wal, that's a gargoyle."

The thing leaned around the corner to look south. Its pointed hood seemed to drink in the light, and its black cloak enveloped Gold. The dauger said something and pointed back the way he had come. The thing nodded, its hood dipping.

Gold stepped back into the light looking almost like an actor in a spotlight. His hands were on his hips and his head tilted in a way that seemed angry. He pointed down at the ground with a forceful gesture. The gargoyle, still half in the shadow and half in the light regarded him, and then acquiesced.

One blink later, it was gone.

Gold didn't move. He stared at the empty space now before him. Finally he sighed and let his head loll forward. His shoulders shook. Laughter? Sorrow? Finally, he turned and looked back the way he had come as if waiting for someone.

"What's he waiting for?" Samantha asked in a hushed whisper.

I squinted in Gold's direction. "No idea."

"You meet this dauger at a party where Adderley kills himself and now we find him down here talking to gargoyles? That's too odd to be a coincidence."

We waited along with him and I wondered who else would show. I expected to see the umbra, Charles Shain, or the obnoxious maero Caleth dal Dunnel appear. But it was the elevated socialite, Cora Dirch, who appeared from behind a building dressed in a similar cloak as Gold. She glided through the blackness. Behind her a second cloaked figure emerged, and then a third. Now four figures stood below the small emergency light.

"Who is that?" Samantha asked.

"Another one of the elevated."

"From the party?"

I nodded. "We should get closer. I want to hear what they're saying."

Samantha didn't protest, so we edged closer. Staying low and keeping to the shadows; grateful that the lights had gone out. We crouched behind a parked fourgon, only a few yards away from the little gathering.

"...he's been getting too impetuous. I doubt we'll be able to manipulate him much longer. It has to be Kiver," said a voice. It sounded like Gold. "Who else could it be?"

"So soon?" It was Dirch.

"It must happen tonight. Our hold is tenuous at best. We need another."

"If we keep going like this there won't *be* any others."

A sigh. "We knew the bargain. For this control to last we must give another."

Dirch looked away in my direction, and I ducked even though I knew she couldn't see me. I could feel Samantha tense.

Gold pressed his point. "You're more powerful than you've ever been, you have more control with the seafood market than anyone else."

"The cost..." Dirch said, letting her voice drift off.

Gold stepped back and looked at the group. "Henry, you were facing bankruptcy before we started this. Melanie, your family has benefited greatly."

"We all appreciate what's been accomplished, but..."

Gold shook his head. "We haven't lifted a knife."

"We wield it just the same," said a man. He wore the same cloak as the others but his face was shadowed beneath a trilby. I assumed he was Henry.

"We beseech. We ask." Gold looked at Dirch. "Cora, the Bonheurs were pushing you out of business. Your children would have been left penniless if that happened."

The Bonheurs. My pulse quickened. My discussion with the woman at the chapterhouse flashed through my memory. What a convenient tragedy for Cora Dirch. After all, she was also in seafood. I remembered Caleth mentioning that at Kiver's party.

"Now your family will lead for generations. This is what we talked about, Cora. You have provided for your children and grandchildren. For generations to come. We've all prospered in ways we couldn't even fathom before."

"Frank didn't like it," said Henry.

"Frank didn't like anything," said Gold.

"He was one of us," Cora said, shaking her head sadly. "One of us, Janus. He stood next to us. He said the words."

"He was a *fool!* He could have been running Dyer if he wanted. Instead he chose devotion." He spat the word. "As if that thing deserves it."

"He said we were making it angry. That it—"

Gold interrupted her. "He never liked the deal to begin with. Carter's cross, Cora, he said it was our duty to *free* the damn thing. Called it the *Herald.* He said he'd do it himself if I didn't go along."

"He still might," she said softly, folding her arms across her chest.

"With what, his scrawls? His sacrifices?" Gold laughed and shook his head. "No, Cora, no. We still control it. *I* still control it." He tapped his chest.

I looked over at Samantha. Her eyes were wide, and her mouth hung open.

"But Kiver?" Dirch didn't look convinced, her mouth was downturned and the shadows that hung from the folds in her skin deepened. "He's a friend."

"What are friends in times like these? We need to move past that. Kiver's the next logical choice. Remember who we're doing this for! Five years ago none of us would have been at a party like that. Now we're kings and queens. We're family. United in a bond that cannot be broken. *Family* is forever."

Dirch stood, staring down at her feet. Her breath came out in small clouds that floated around her head.

"Cora?" asked Gold, his voice kind. He reached out a hand and rubbed her arm. The old woman nodded.

"Come, we must prepare. Caleth will meet us on the way. He's been in contact with the supplier. We'll have what we need."

Gold turned and slipped into the darkness down an alley. The others quickly followed, leaving only an empty pool of light.

"Come on," I said when they were out of earshot.

"Wal, I was wrong. A First *is* doing this. It's killing people. It's killing the elevated."

I nodded and looked down the alley after them.

"Wal, what are we going to do?"

"What do you think?" I said.

Samantha stared into my eyes for a moment, then looked away. "Stop them," she said.

We followed them down the alley, disappearing into the dark.

A few of the lamps had begun to clank back on, but Gold, Dirch, and the others hadn't slowed. They were easy to track in this part of the city and they clearly weren't expecting a tail.

They moved in a column, much like a caravan, twisting and turning through back alleys and down side streets. A few more people joined them, their own cloaks billowing behind them as they moved. One had to be Caleth, but I couldn't tell which. All of them were obscured in shadow.

The newcomers didn't walk with Gold's group. Instead they formed their own trailing party and moved at a slightly slower pace. I guessed that they were trying not to arouse the suspicion of police by moving in a larger group.

I've tailed people before and it wasn't difficult for Samantha and me to stay with them. We followed far enough behind and stuck to the shadows. We carefully lingered when they did, and moved as quietly as we could.

When we neared the warren of Denny Lake both groups stopped at a lift stop and talked quietly among themselves. Then the first group of four entered a stairwell and disappeared.

"Now where are they going…" I wondered quietly.

"We need to know what they're up to," Samantha said. She tilted her head and regarded the next group. "What about them?"

"We could push past them, maybe. But one of them might recognize me." I said, wondering if Caleth was in the group that remained.

So we waited, watching the cloaked party as they loitered outside the stairwell. Whenever someone passed, their leader, the tallest among them, perked up. They seemed to be expecting someone.

Eventually a large maero in a dark wool coat with a bowler hat cocked to one side emerged from the gloom. A bag was thrown over his shoulder, its end clutched in his seven-fingered hand. He stopped in front of the tallest figure, looking him over, and then laughed.

We were too far to hear what they were saying, but brief, heated words were exchanged. I glanced at Samantha.

"Down?" I asked.

"Down," she said, her tone cool and determined.

We moved closer, trying to hear the discussion. The maero in the bowler dropped the bag and gave the tall robed figure a shove. The figure stumbled, regained their footing and held up their hands dismissively.

The guy in the bowler hat laughed. Now Samantha and I were close enough to hear. "You stupid quim. Think you can descend from on high and make your own rules. You're in Outfit territory now. You answer to *us*."

The cloaked figure took something from a pocket and placed it into the hands of the maero. Possibly lira? But in this dark, even only twenty or so yards away, we couldn't tell for sure.

"It's all there," said a voice.

"Yeah? I like to make sure."

The maero in the bowler inspected it, and then, satisfied, he slung the sack from the ground into the outstretched arms of the figure. Then he turned and strolled away whistling to himself as he went.

The three disappeared into the stairwell shortly afterward. Samantha and I followed, waiting only a few seconds before crossing the street and moving in behind. In the enclosed space we could hear them talking, their voices echoing up from below us as they descended the stairwell.

"He is such an asshole, I don't know why we deal with him," said a voice. It sounded familiar.

"Well, they're the only ones able to get the ingredients."

"Yeah, but he doesn't need to be such an ass about it."

Laughter. "He hurt your feelings, Cal?"

"Shut up."

More laughter.

They passed Level Three and continued down. We plodded along in their wake.

They spoke of ausca games and business deals and their plans for the summer. Eventually they left the stairs and moved out onto Level Two.

We emerged after them, catching the last of the three disappearing around a corner. We followed down yet another alley between an abandoned mushroom farm and a building that had once sold live chickens. Two hollow-eyed dimanians watched Samantha from the steps of the farm as we followed the three figures.

The lights down here hadn't gone out like they had on Level Four, but Level Two was never fully lit. Maintenance crews wouldn't come this far down without a police escort and even if they had one, replacing burned out lamps wasn't much of a priority.

The three figures disappeared into the gaping doorway of an old tower that rose out of the Sunk below and up into the streets of Level Two. At one time, this doorway probably served as an exit onto a balcony. Now, it opened up on a narrow alley on Level Two. Here the streets hung between the sunken towers like catwalks, not touching the walls. The Sunk splashed up from between the cracks and barnacles clung to the buildings. The air smelled of equal parts seawater and sewage.

"Here we are," I said, slowing and easing to a stop.

The alley was blanketed by shadows and the open doorway seemed more like a hungry mouth than the entrance to a building.

I drew my gun. Samantha eyed it warily.

"Sorry," I apologized. "Can't take any chances."

"No, I understand," she said. Then her dark eyes raised to meet mine. She was scared, and I couldn't blame her. I was terrified. My heart was pounding in my chest and my stomach had leapt into my throat.

I put my finger to my lips and cocked my head towards the doorway. Samantha nodded.

Steeling myself, I stepped forward and we both disappeared into the maw.

TWENTY

As we stepped through the door the scent of dampness and mildew hit us. It was heavy on the fetid air, hanging above something baser. A pair of torches were mounted on the walls, framing the door behind us. They crackled and popped, casting dim shadows that danced in the flickering light.

We stood on a rickety platform that jutted out over a deep hole that dropped its way through the center of the building. The bones of a crane extended out and over the pit, rotted ropes and rusted chains hung from its arm, covered in a gray moss. There was an opening in the ceiling, a viewport into the floor above. Hooks attached to chains hung down and swayed slightly.

We were alone.

The platform creaked below our feet and I crouched instinctively, trying not to think about the age or condition of the wood.

I pointed towards the edge and Samantha and I carefully moved toward it. We dropped to our bellies and looked over. The platform moaned beneath us.

A deep pit descended down ending at a rough cement floor several hundred feet below. A small group of people were already down there, standing around what looked to be a table near the center. Four figures moved about in torchlight.

This pit *should* have been flooded, but only empty air filled the space between the group below and us above. I studied the walls. Sometime in the past, someone had gone to the trouble of sealing this building off from the Sunk. It was a windowless hole cut into the waters, a portion of the city carved into the sea below.

The second group was moving along a wooden staircase that circled its way down along the walls. Each figure held a torch. I was grateful. Holding a light so close to their faces would make it harder for them to see into the dark.

Occasionally the second group would hit a landing, similar to the one Samantha and I were currently lying upon. Each one was crammed with crates and barrels of varying ages.

Voices rose up from the depths, too far and distorted by echo to understand. The bottom of the hole brightened as more torches were brought in. I scooted forward and looked down, catching a glimpse of someone lighting braziers that sat against the wall directly below us.

"Carter's cross, what is this place?" I whispered.

"Looks like it used to be a warehouse," said Samantha, her voice barely audible. "Someone went to a lot of trouble to build it..."

"Doesn't seem like it's been used for generations," I said. "Some of those crates look real old. Surprised it's not crawling with streetfolk."

She looked over at me and scooted away from the platform's edge. "If they're staying away then there must be a reason."

The second group had now arrived at the bottom and was embracing members of the first group. I could hear laughter mixed with a murmur of conversation.

"Let's get closer. We need to figure out what they're doing," said Samantha.

She rolled to her knees and, keeping low, set off down the stairs. She was careful, moving slowly, back pressed to the cement as she took each step. I followed, ignoring the ache in my knee as we climbed down. My heart raced. We were close to something.

The cement wall that lined the interior of the pit was clammy to the touch. Moss was growing around cracks that had broken the surface. It had begun its slow creep across the face of the interior. The wood beneath our feet flexed with each step, sagging a little too much for comfort. The further we descended, the warmer the air became, and the more rank it grew. I felt like gagging, but fought it down.

When we got to the next platform I saw that the braziers flanked a massive opening several stories tall that had been punched into the wall near the bottom of the hole. It was dark and shadowed. It looked like the entrance to a den…

I pointed and Samantha nodded, mouthing, "First."

Here we were, below Lovat again, moving closer and closer to the lair of a First.

We passed the platform and descended further, keeping to the shadows, careful not to step in the wrong spot.

The figures at the base of the hole were now removing their

cloaks, hoods, and hats and setting them on crates that were scattered against the arching staircase.

There were seven of them. Janus Gold was the easiest to spot, his mask catching the light from the torches and braziers and sending it cascading around the base of the pit. Cora Dirch looked as stately as ever. Her hair was done up in an elegant topknot, and beneath her cloak she wore a sensible business suit of burgundy with a white shirt. Caleth dal Dunnel was dressed the most informally in dark jeans and a collared black shirt. With them were four others I didn't recognize.

There was the man Gold had called Henry, a human. When he removed his trilby his bald head reflected the light. He was handsome and sported a white mustache beneath an aquiline nose. Next to him stood Melanie, a dauger with a simple mask of a blue-white metal. Another member of the precious families, no doubt. Her brown hair had been pulled back into a ponytail.

Two maero had come with Caleth. One was a tall thin woman, the tallest of the group, with severe features and pale eyes that caught the light and made them look ablaze. The other was a thickly built maero with gray hair, square features, and a permanent scowl.

Samantha and I stopped on the last landing. This platform sat opposite from the opening in the wall and about two hundred feet below the platform at the entrance. It was still well above the floor, but close enough to let us see everything, and shadowed enough that we wouldn't risk being spotted. A perfect vantage point.

Samantha and I moved toward some wooden boxes and settled in behind them.

Puddles of water were scattered across the pitted floor, and they dully reflected the light from the torches and braziers. I heard the choking sound of a small engine rumbling in the corner, and could make out a rickety old pump working at an exceptionally deep puddle that had settled around the lattice-work that supported the stairs. Clearly the building wasn't as watertight as I had initially assumed.

"Did we get what we needed?" said one of the maero.

"Aye, we did," said Caleth, upending the bag he had been carrying. The contents fell out on the table. It was an odd collection of items: a torn jacket, a pair of shoes, a stack of papers, and a large vial of something dark. Knowing what I knew so far, I assumed it was blood.

"This is it? *This* is what she gave us?" said Henry.

"By the Firsts, she sent us his old *clothes*," said another, the maero woman, I think.

"It was easier when we had Frank," said Gold with a grumble, his face turned from the table and towards the hole that sat across from them.

Dirch scowled down at the items. "We paid four thousand lira for *this*? Shoes? A jacket? No hair? No nails? No saliva or seminal fluid? Just a vial of blood? Kiver's obsessed with grooming, why didn't they go to his barbers? His doctors?"

She looked from Gold to Caleth and then to the others.

Caleth rocked on his heels. "I didn't check the bag when the goon handed it over. I assumed it'd be like last time."

"We didn't go through the Outfit last time, you idiot! We had Frank then. Did this... goon say anything?"

Caleth scratched his chin with a seven-fingered hand. I wondered if he would talk about the shoving and angry exchange we'd seen. He shook his head.

"No," he said.

"Maybe we could find another doctor? Bring them into the fold?" suggested the maero woman who stood to Dirch's left.

"Perhaps... though after Frank's behavior I'm wary to bring in anyone else. There are seven of us now..." Gold ran his hands through his dark hair and sighed. "It just gets more dangerous for us. The city's turmoil has allowed our plans to thrive. It can't last long."

They all mumbled in agreement and stared at the objects from the bag. Eventually Gold broke them from their malaise. "Come, my friends, we have work to do."

Gold moved to a second crate sitting in the space between the first crate and the large opening. Symbols had been carved around its base and on its top. Jagged writing I didn't recognize. A mortar and pestle sat on top, along with a massive open book. Around the book was an assortment of bric-a-brac: feathers, shells, small cans, and what looked like a jar of small bones. A pile of neatly folded clothes sat near a corner.

"You see that, around that altar-thing? The writing?" I asked in a sharp whisper.

Samantha squinted. "Yeah, I can't make it out. It's not Aklo. Not Strutten either. It's... it doesn't looks familiar."

I didn't press any further. We needed to remain as quiet as possible. Questions could wait.

Gold rolled his sleeve and held up the vial.

"The blood," Gold said, holding it above his head. "May it protect those who call him forth, and mark their sacrifice."

"Protection and sacrifice," the others said in unison.

Gold dropped the vile into the mortar and began working it furiously, glass and all. The glass crunched as he mixed and ground it with the blood. The others moved about him and formed two lines on opposite sides of the makeshift altar. Three on each side, facing one another.

As he worked they began to chant. It was an animal sound, guttural and angry. It bubbled up from deep inside their chests and rolled out from their lips.

"That is not Strutten," I whispered, looking over at Samantha.

She shook her head. "I've never heard it before. It sounds beast-like, those are almost non-words."

Suddenly Gold raised the mortar above his head, holding it there for a few moments while the chanting continued. Then, suddenly, he brought it down with a heavy slam on the wooden crate. The chanting stopped.

"*Xinaián cha hgl mechaus Tsath!*" Gold shouted.

Samantha gasped. She looked at me with wide eyes.

"The book. Bouchard's research," she hissed.

The others echoed Gold and returned to chanting. He went back to work, adding this and that to his mixture; a dab of wine, a drop or two of water, other liquids from other vials. The solution thickened, becoming almost like a batter.

Again he lifted the mortar.

"*Esus N'kai tin rondo. Esus Yoth tin rondo. Esus Tsath tin rondo. Esus tin Lovat!*"

Again he brought it down.

The group echoed his words and returned to chanting.

"Wal, there's something in there. Something..." Samantha said, her words drowned out by the chanting. They repeated the words. Each time he shouted his words. Each time he slammed the mortar on the altar. The chanting intensified, rising in volume until the six were shouting at one another.

Finally, on the eighth slam Gold stepped back. I couldn't see his face. Only his back, his dark hair, the sleeves of his shirt rolled up above his sharp elbows. He put his hands on his hips and regarded the concoction.

"What is he doing?" I asked Samantha.

Samantha shook her head. She continued to stare at the group with rapt attention. Her eyes moved about, catching every movement. She seemed equally horrified and fascinated by it all.

Gold grabbed the big mortar with one hand and moved around the altar, standing between the two rows of followers. The mixture in the bowl slopped about slowly. It was thick and red, and it absorbed the light in the chamber.

He stopped first before Dirch and looked down at the bowl and then back up at her.

"*Dabo tin tur rondo,*" he said, dipping his hand into the bowl. Dirch braced herself. "*Ovartin N'kai, y Yoth, y Tsath, rel choomer.*"

She nodded.

"*Feist!*" Gold said, dragging his hand out of the bowl and slapping a dripping open palm onto Dirch's forehead.

The liquid slowly rolled down her face, dripped off her chin, her eyelashes, the end of her nose. It caught in the wrinkles of her cheeks and settled next to her lips. Gold didn't remove his hand, but left it, touching Dirch's forehead until her eyes rolled back, turning white. She stood stark still.

He held his hand there until a smile broke across her face. Her eyes fluttered back, and she shuddered violently.

"*Feist,*" she said, her tone dark.

She licked at the liquid with a pink tongue.

"For protection," said Gold, reverting to Strutten.

"Protection," Dirch echoed.

They gave one another curt bows and then Gold repeated the rite down the line. Each time he said the same black words. Each time he slapped a bloody hand to the follower's forehead, letting the liquid drip down their faces, and settle onto their clothes.

When all were bloodied they began to chant again. Gold walked slowly to the foot of the rows, stopping between the group and the opening to the cavern. There he laid out the torn jacket and placed the papers on top. He laid the shoes atop those.

"*Esus N'kai, esus Yoth, esus Tsath, esus endar rondo. Esus Lovat!*"

He dipped his hand into the mortar and began to spatter the items with the blood, chanting quietly as he did so.

The voices of those around him rose as he worked, until their growls filled the pit and echoed around us.

I squeezed the grip of the Judge. I had been in situations like this before. I wanted to be ready.

"Wal!" Samantha said, her voice strained under the whisper.

I glanced at her but she wasn't looking at me. She was looking over my right shoulder, toward one of the other platforms above us.

I followed her gaze.

There, on the edge of the platform, was a gargoyle.

I looked back to the group, wondering if they noticed. Two more gargoyles stood near a brazier, and another had appeared near the foot of the stairs. Their robes billowed around them, moving slowly as if there was a breeze.

Their heads were cocked and their blank faces were watching Gold and the group perform their ritual.

"What are they waiting for?" Samantha asked.

"Their master," I said.

Gold had moved to stand before the altar facing the great opening.

"Thus we call," he said in Strutten.

He raised the mortar above his head, and upended it so that the remaining contents poured over his hair, his mask, down his shoulders and back staining his white shirt a deep crimson.

The chanting stopped.

Silence now filled the chamber. The small pump choked and went silent, even the fires in the braziers seemed to stop crackling for a moment.

I heard breathing, and thought it was Samantha at first. But the sound grew louder and I realized it was coming from somewhere else.

Throom.

The sound increased.

Throom.

The breathing grew louder.

Throom.

The platform shook.

It sounded like the bellows of some great furnace working in the darkness beyond the mouth of the cave.

I shuddered. Whispers slithered around in the air. Voices like horrible rushing water. Again I found myself teleported between two realities. I was crouched along the edge of the pit but I also crouched in that horrible, expanse of wasteland. A hot wind licked at my clothing, strange voices crackled across a sky the color of rotting flesh. I could see the pit, but I could see the ruin of the distant city and beyond that a broken sun. I ran my hands through my hair, and gripped it hard. Not now. I couldn't deal with this now!

My skin crawled and I shuddered. Something was coming. Something horrible was coming. There was a dragging sound coming from the cave, flesh against stone.

Throom.

In the wasteland I saw a figure striding toward me. Its several shadows stretched toward me like hungry tentacles. They writhed in the light of the broken sun.

In the pit the seven bloodied figures now all turned toward the opening and raised their arms in a beckoning gesture, like small children begging their parents to lift them.

Madness. This was utter madness.

Then I saw it.

The vision of the wasteland faded. The figure was replaced.

I wanted to scream.

The thing that came forth was the size of a building. Near the top of the cave's opening the shadowed lines of its face appeared, emerging slowly into the light. It was anurish in shape but horrific to look upon. A gray tongue lolled out between rows of uneven stained teeth surrounded by fat pale lips. The tongue dripped a green ooze that mixed with the puddles on the floor.

Narrow eyes, like knife wounds, leered down at the gathered group. They were barely visible under the folds of its brow but they glowed a dim red, like the coal-hot eyes of an umbra.

The thing seemed to lack a nose, but it sniffed at the air with two slashes that seemed to fulfill the purpose.

Its ears had the appearance of bat's wings, and they moved and twitched as it came forward, shuddering in the air.

Its shoulders appeared, then its chest and belly. The creature was covered with matted coarse brown hair. Moss and lichen grew along its stomach, below its wattles, and from its elbows. It hung in thick sheets, swirling in the air.

It stank, and as it emerged into the rusty light of the chamber the room began to smell terrible. The scent of rot extended from it like a fog and my eyes began to water. I covered my nose and mouth with my hand and gagged.

It gripped the sides of the cave with a webbed hand and pulled itself forward. Its girth was immense, its belly dragged along the ground. Its underbelly had been rubbed free of hair and callouses covered its obsidian flesh.

"Damn..." I whispered.

The slithering voices were now muffled cries and screams, wavering and dying out as more and more of the creature became visible.

Stubby legs pushed it forward clawed toes digging furrows into the cement floor until finally it came to rest between the braziers, and before the objects Gold had laid out.

I looked at Samantha and we exchanged a glance. Her eyes were wide. She looked like she was going to be sick. She reached for my hand and I felt her fingers intertwine with my own. She squeezed, her hand tight against mine.

The massive creature regarded the offering, snorted, and looked at Gold.

"He wishes to know what you have brought him," said one of the gargoyles near the braziers in Strutten. The voice was papery, like the rush of wind, or a loud whisper.

"His next meal," said Gold, not taking his eyes off the creature. "As required by our agreement."

The creature pulled back slightly, looking down at the dauger and then at the pile of items before him. Its top lip pulled back, showing its stained upper teeth and an expression of disgust.

"He does not see a meal, only a pair of shoes, some pages, and clothing," said a second gargoyle. This one was near the foot of the stairs.

"His meal is the owner of those items, as before."

"You brought him more before."

"We had a snare."

"A snare?" tittered a gargoyle from far above. The laughter sent shivers down my spine. "Now is not the time for snares."

"It fulfills the requirements, and it is time for another."

"Yes, he supposes it is," said another gargoyle. This one was directly below our platform, between us and Gold. The dauger turned to regard it. Samantha and I ducked low, hoping he hadn't spotted us.

"It is as before. As long as I am alive he must honor the agreement."

The creature frowned and growled a warning. The sound was titanic and filled the space, echoing off the walls.

Gold turned back to the creature and spoke up at it. "You know the rules. I brought you forth. I name myself Gothi. I called you here from black N'kai, through red Yoth, beyond dark Tsath, and into Lovat. I am the one in control. Me! It is my boon!" He tapped his chest.

"He does not like fetching his own sacrifices," said a gargoyle from high above.

"He hates you, little dauger," the voices came from everywhere now. I looked up and saw more gargoyles lining the pit. Hundreds of them. They reminded me of a flock of ravens.

"Your actions offend."

"He will kill you."

"He will kill you all."

"Someday."

"Yes, someday." The voices seemed to come from every corner.

The cultists nervously looked at one another. Gold spun, his face turning from one gargoyle to the other. It was hard to tell his expression with his mask but his movements were all frustration.

"It doesn't matter," he spat. "If it wasn't for me—"

"Watch your words, little one," said another gargoyle.

"You are in the presence of a Mizra."

"You are all but a speck to one like him," said another gargoyle.

"A speck!" another echoed.

"Speck," came a third.

"He will do as you ask, for that is the agreement. He hates it. Hates you."

"He seeks offerings, not commands."

"This will not last."

The whispered words faded. A few of the gargoyles withdrew. Disappeared.

Gold's hands had balled into fists. He stared up at the enormous creature, his posture defiant.

It seemed to regard him with bemusement, an ugly expression playing across its face. Then it began to change. Slowly it shrank, its features shifting. The gashed eyes grew wider, became almond-shaped, the hair grew inward as its skin browned and then lightened. I stretched my neck over the crate, stared and watched as the titan shifted, transforming from monster to man before my eyes. I gripped the Judge tightly in my right hand, my left had lost to Sam's vicelike grip.

Across from Gold, and at the end of the row of cultists, there now stood a naked man. He was clean-shaven with plain features. Pale brown skin, lighter than mine. If it wasn't for the red eyes and slightly too wide mouth he could be human.

The man-creature grinned at Gold. "From the first circle I descended thus," it said. "Down to the second, which, a lesser space. Embracing, so much more of grief contains, provoking bitter moans." He spoke like he was reciting something. His grin widened. "Here Minos stands, grinning with ghastly feature..."

"Ashton," said Gold in a forced greeting.

Ashton looked at his hands. "I hate this form," he said. His voice was deep and warm, and he spoke his Strutten with a light accent I couldn't place.

"You know what needs to be done," Gold said.

"A judgement, perhaps?" said Ashton. "Am I to once again wear the mantle of Lord of the Underworld? Maybe I should grow a tail to really play up the part. Are there souls to examine? Sentences to deal out?" He chuckled. "Or is this just another death for financial gain?"

Gold said nothing.

Ashton continued. "You have the power of the Herald under your control and you use it as an assassination tool. How very... petty."

"You know what needs to be done," Gold said again.

"This isn't over," Ashton said. "You know that, Janus? Rituals cannot protect you. The moment your hold breaks—and it will break—I will tear through this city. I will climb its towers and I will hunt you."

Gold snorted. He folded his arms and stared at the First.

Ashton padded up to Gold and leaned close, sniffing the dauger.

"I hate you dauger most of all," Ashton said. "You're an abomination. He should have known better." He turned and looked at the dauger woman who stood in one of the lines. "The rest of you aren't much better." He reached out and touched the woman's forehead, dabbing the tip of his finger in the blood on her face.

He stared at it for a moment and looked back at Gold. He asked, "Blood of the sacrifice?"

"As always."

"Or should I call it the target?" said Ashton.

"Don't be crass."

Ashton ignored him. "I keep hoping you'll forget the blood."

"I won't," Gold spoke coldly. "We've brought you clothes. They're on the table."

"And when this is done?" Ashton asked.

"Then you return to N'kai, as always."

"Asshole," Ashton growled.

They stood and stared at one another. The First, in its human avatar, regarded the gore-covered dauger with a burning hatred.

"If I had my way, Ashton, you'd still be buried down here."

Ashton laughed and leaned back. "Ah, little dauger. You say that, but you're the one who calls me forth. You're addicted to it. Addicted to control."

He paused, sniffed the air again.

I felt that strange buzzing again.

Ashton whipped his head in our direction, and with those glowing red eyes he looked directly at me.

My heart stopped.

A wicked sneer played across his lips, showing small versions of the stained teeth from its larger form.

"You fool," he growled.

"What?" Gold spun and followed Ashton's gaze up to the platform where we were crouched. He started. Shocked.

"Bell? Waldo Bell? From the party?" stammered Caleth.

"Carter's cross," said Dirch.

I looked over at Samantha and she turned to me, panic in her eyes. I gave her hand a squeeze and released it.

Ashton whipped around and pointed a narrow finger at Gold, "You arrogant cur. You come down here and bind me to your bidding and then you dare lead the Guardian here!"

The gargoyles that stood in the pit now all silently turned to look at us. Hundreds of pointed hoods and blank faces gazed in our direction. The braziers behind Ashton flared up, bathing the hole in a wave of bright light.

Ashton turned and pointed at me.

My stomach dropped. I felt like I was in free fall.

"Get them," he growled.

TWENTY-ONE

I spun, rising to my feet and swinging the Judge with me. My breath had stopped in my chest. I ignored the pain that flared into my body as I leveled the heavy revolver at the nearest gargoyle. The creature balked, then recoiled as I stepped forward, rushing it, driving the Judge up under its chin.

The thing felt weird beneath my hand. Like a gas bag. The barrel didn't connect with bone or soft flesh. No matter. I pulled the trigger.

The thing evaporated before me into a cloud of thick black smoke forcing me to cough. Behind me Samantha pushed herself up and shouldered past a second gargoyle as she moved up the stairwell.

Ashton screamed. "Get them! Get them! Don't let him live!"

His voice had risen an octave. It filled the space, echoed off the walls, and blew through me.

"Bell, get back here!" someone shouted.

I turned and fired over my shoulder down the stairs and into the mass of bodies that were hustling to catch up.

Gargoyles and bloody cultists leapt back, wary of closing in. They paused and looked down at Ashton who sneered up at me.

"What am I, Guardian, that you think a measly firearm could ever harm me?" Ashton shouted. The bastard knew my name.

I focused on following Samantha.

She had become entangled halfway up to the next platform. Two gargoyles had grabbed her jacket, her hair. One had a hand on one of her horns. She elbowed one where a face should have been, and brought her knee up into the stomach of another. One of them stumbled backwards against the cement, while the other slipped and dropped off the stairwell.

We pressed onward. Upward. Higher. Higher!

The stairs beneath our feet quaked and squeaked and cracked. I could see boards shaking loose and portions of the staircase slap against the side of the wall as we moved.

I fired past Samantha at another gargoyle moving down the stairs to stop us, the thing—like others before it—just vanished. Black smoke choked us as we pressed up.

"Keep moving!" I shouted.

"No shit!" Samantha said.

I turned, looking down the stairwell and saw Gold and the others gaining on us. How many shots had I fired? Unsure, I fired the remaining shells from the gun and the group all crouched where they were, cowering for cover.

Below, still standing in the center of the pit was Ashton, slowly getting dressed, a cocky smile splitting his face.

Ashton's voice carried up the stairwell. It rattled around inside my skull. I knew he was now far below, but his voice sounded close, like he was whispering over my shoulder. "You have angered us, Bell. Your name is a curse in our hallowed halls. It echoes down the corridors and enrages the throne. The High Priest will not be pleased! He won't be as considerate as I am!"

Samantha shoved another gargoyle aside and sent it careering off the edge as we passed the third landing. She looked back, checking on me, her face flushed.

"Wal, behind you!" she shouted.

I turned and saw the maero woman lunging. I smacked her across the face with the barrel of the Judge, feeling the cold metal strike bone. She tumbled down.

"Go! I'm right behind you!" I said.

The others slowed and helped the maero to her feet. A trickle of her own blood now mixed with the congealing drips from Gold's earlier concoction.

It was only a moment, but it gave us more time. Put more stairs between us and them.

Higher. Higher!

One step at a time. The journey up felt four times as long as the descent and we had a lot more stairs ahead of us.

A small army of gargoyles blocked our path on the next landing. Samantha slowed slightly, unsure of what to do. I pushed her on the back, urging her forward.

"Go, go, rush 'em! Go!"

She didn't question it. She moved. Her legs pumped and she threw herself at the creatures, the jagged bones that grew from the knuckles of her balled fists catching the light. The gargoyles cried out as the dimanian priestess showed them why her people had been banned from boxing.

Black smoke filled the air, making the murky light even murkier.

The pads of my thumb sizzled as I pressed the shells into the empty cylinder and flipped it back into place. Time seemed to move incredibly slowly.

Gargoyles were slipping and falling off the platform. Their robed bodies disappeared into the space below with howls that vanished before they hit bottom. Samantha lashed out, her jaw set, her breath exploding out in short bursts. Her dark hair flowed around her and beneath it her eyes blazed. She swung her fists, blazing us a trail through the black robes.

I turned, my back to hers.

"I'll handle the others," I shouted over the roars and shouts that filled the air around us.

The others were only half a landing below us. I fired, missing and striking the stairs at their feet.

Henry—the human with the white mustache—was now in the lead and first in line for a full face of wooden shrapnel. It spattered his face, and he slipped. His arms swung around like windmills and someone grabbed for his shirt, missing by inches as he tumbled off the stairwell and towards the pit floor far below. His screams were cut short by a wet thud.

The group stopped, staring over the edge at their fallen companion.

Somewhere below Ashton laughed.

"That's one, Gold," he said cheerily. He still sounded so close.

Samantha threw another two gargoyles over the edge, making a hole through the mass.

I followed, firing the Judge into the faceless head of one of the creatures and pressing on.

We could make it! Henry's death had slowed the cultists and the gargoyles were falling away under Samantha's fists.

I could see the light from Level Two's lamps beyond the pit's entrance at the upper landing.

We took the stairs two, sometimes three at a time. My chest burned. My legs ached. My knee and my side sent waves of pain rippling through my body. I didn't care.

Higher. Higher! Escape. Get out!

As Samantha cleared the top platform, I wanted to shout out my relief. Turn and taunt Ashton, Gold, and the others.

CRACK!

An exasperated wheeze and clatter of cracks echoed through the pit.

Below my feet, the staircase disappeared.

"Wal! *Nooooo!*" Samantha's voice filled my ears. Her words stretched as time around me slowed.

Boards tore loose from the cement wall, some snapped in half. The stair I had been standing on twisted violently to one side. Dust filled the air behind us like a summer storm in Syringa.

Something roared in my ears. My arms scrambled, reaching for anything. There hadn't even been time to jump.

The world rushed around me. It spun... dropped. I looked down and saw only open air below.

Then I hit. My arms slapped against something solid. I felt a snag, a nail, a jagged piece of wood, something puncture my skin. I didn't care. I clambered for purchase as my chest and arms hit the jagged edge of the last platform. My legs dangled.

In times of panic, the mind focuses on strange things. Right then, all I saw was Samantha's boots. Roader boots, beautifully worn in. It was a calming image. Something in this tangled mess was all right.

Strong hands wrapped around my wrists as air returned to my lungs. The boots faded as I was dragged up and forward. The rushing river that had filled my ears subsided and I felt my belly hit a flat surface, then my thighs, then my calves and feet.

Safety.

Salvation.

But only for a moment.

"Come on, Wal," Samantha said. She was already scrambling to her feet. Her face was drawn, her eyes moving towards the door.

Laughter echoed from below.

Ashton.

"We have to get to Kiver," I said.

Samantha nodded.

I pushed myself up, still feeling the rush of adrenaline. Distantly, I could feel new pains in my arms and chest. I had probably torn open my stitches yet again. I didn't care. I was alive.

I looked back to see what ruin lay below.

Only a part of the stairwell had fallen. Now only empty space hung between the second and the upper platforms. Along the ragged edge of the collapse stood the cultists, a few gargoyles mixed in with them. Only five, I realized, where there had been seven. Remaining were Gold, Caleth, the dauger woman, and the two maero. No Dirch. She must have gone over when the staircase collapsed.

As I slipped toward the door I gave them a final look. Ashton was too far below. But I could see the angry expressions on the faces of the maero. The dauger's features were, as ever, inscrutable.

Far, far below Ashton still stood near the altar. From this distance, in his human form, he was nothing more than a dark smudge. Yet I could sense he was looking up at me. And I knew he was smiling.

TWENTY-TWO

The clamor of raised voices reached us before we even saw Paramount Square. Echoes rampaged through Level Eight's towers, carried on the wind. The whole level vibrated from the cacophony and the towers shivered.

When we came upon the square we could see the reason. Hundreds of thousands of people had filled the open space: humans, maero, dauger, umbra, anur, kresh, dimanian, and even cephels. Male and female, young and old, children and broodlings. The crowd stretched out over the plaza, ran down the surrounding streets and wrapped around the looming towers like angry centipedes.

Balled fists, clawed hands, and curled tentacles were raised in unison. Signs rose from the throng with demands spelled out in angry capital letters. City Hall shook in its foundations before them. It looked like a fortress under siege. Its windows had been boarded and cement barriers surrounded it, keeping the throng away from its walls. Armed police with clubs, long rifles, and shotguns lined the roof.

The air simmered with anger. Tension wavered among the throng like a heatwave.

Samantha and I stopped running. My heart thudded in my chest and my lungs ached from the cold. We stood at the fringe of the gathering, buried our hands in our pockets and stuffed our chins into our upturned collars.

Where did all this come from? Lovat itself seemed intent on stopping us from getting to Kiver, from warning him about what was coming. These people didn't realize what walked among them. It wasn't only the rich preying on the rich. It was a creature far more foul. A creature that would stop at nothing to get to its target.

What was one rich maero to this lot? Kiver had eaten dim sum, hosted Auseil parties, and drank wine while these people went hungry. With his silence he had aided a mayor more concerned with control and power than the lives of citizens. No, Kiver would get no sympathy from these folk.

"There's the Shangdi," I said, pointing to the massive tower that rose from Level Eight and punctured the sky. "Kiver's place is near the top, above the Level Nine latticework."

"Look at all these people," Samantha said. I could hear the wonder in her voice. "How are we going to get past them?"

"I'm not quite sure," I said. It'd take hours to press through, and near as long to circumvent the crowd.

"Solve your Society problem yet?" said a familiar voice.

I looked to my left and saw Elephant leaning against a somber statue draped with red fabric. A bowler hat was perched on her head, and tilted so its brim dipped low. Her sly gray eyes flashed from beneath and took us in.

She wore a suit, similar in cut to the one I had seen before, but this one was charcoal gray tweed. Two thick-necked goons loitered nearby. One was the muscled dimanian with stubby jet-black horns I had seen in Elephant's warehouse, the other a paunchy human with a lantern jaw.

"Not yet," I said, trying not to act surprised at her presence. "The collector seems to have disappeared." It was the truth. In our hurry to follow Gold and his cronies Argentum had slipped my mind.

"Little bit of a frenzy, eh?" she said, looking out over the crowd.

"Friends of yours?" I asked, motioning with my chin to the pair of goons that lingered behind her.

"Associates," said Elephant casually. She seemed remarkably calm amid all this chaos. "You've met Allard…" she said, gesturing to the dimanian.

I nodded. "I remember."

"And this is Vaughn." She gestured to the other. "Boys, Waldo Bell. Hank's charity case."

They glanced at me, grunted, and continued to eye the crowd warily.

"Who's the broad?" asked Elephant. She motioned towards Samantha with a tilt of her head.

"Priestess Samantha Dubois," I said. "Samantha, this is Elephant."

"Hi," said Samantha. Her voice lacked warmth.

"Pleasure. Reunified?"

Samantha nodded. "You're the one hoarding all the food," she said.

A few heads snapped in our direction. People studied the

three of us for a moment, realized we didn't have any food and then returned to their protest.

Elephant laughed. "I am a businesswoman, thank you. I just happened to be in the right place at the right time. I prefer to think of myself as an… opportunist."

"It doesn't make it right," said Samantha.

"Moral fluffing bores me," Elephant said, rolling her eyes.

"There are children starving. You're keeping food hidden away—"

A few of the crowd had broken free and were coming closer.

"What's that?" one asked.

"Food?" said another.

"Someone have food?" said a third.

They pressed closer and Elephant cocked her head, motioning her two goons near.

"Back off," drawled Allard, the dimanian. He gave one of the crowd a shove.

A maero next to him moved to leap at him, but Vaughn was next to him in a heartbeat, shaking his head slowly.

"Let's get back to the down-with-the-mayor chants," said Allard with a sly smile. "No need to fight among ourselves. Eh, brothers?"

The hungry Lovatines regarded the two goons and Elephant for a moment before returning to their space in the throng.

"You might want to keep quiet, Mother Dubois."

Samantha stared daggers at the woman.

"Look, we don't have time to argue," I said. "Kiver's in trouble. We need to get to him. Warn him."

Elephant's grin broke and her face grew serious. A threat on

Kiver's life was a threat on her whole business. He was her link to the upper reaches of the city. He needed to remain where he was, for her sake.

"Is he home?" I asked.

"Of course he's home. These days every elevated asshole in the city is home. Cowering. Maybe you haven't noticed but the streets are a bit dangerous, especially for the rich." She waved a hand at the crowd.

"We need to get to him," I said again.

"What's going on?"

"The gilded murders. Kiver's next."

"What?" Elephant nearly shouted. "How do you know this?"

"It's a long story," I said, lifting my voice over the sound of the crowd. She noticed my edge, and looked from me up to the length of the Shangdi. "And if I help you?"

"If you don't, you're out a client."

"Your... supplies will rot," Samantha added.

"Bound to happen soon, anyway. The Breakers were successful in the South. The Purity Movement went running this morning and the caravans are rolling. Some maero broke the blockade and is leading the wagons here. It's all over the papers."

Wensem! It had to be him. If things weren't already chaotic enough I would have beamed. He had done it! He had broken the blockade and was now leading a lifeline back into the city. He'd be hailed as a hero.

Elephant looked at me and then up at the tower. "I can get you there, but I need something in return."

I looked around. Ashton could already be here. Could already be stalking his way through the crowd and towards the tower. I didn't want to find Kiver on the floor of his flat, I didn't want to see his name added to the list of the dead. Ashton had to be stopped. Gold's control over the First had to be severed once and for all.

"I'll owe you," I stammered out.

"Wal!" Samantha said.

"You already owe me, Bell. It was my bonesaw who hauled you out of the Sunk. You'll owe me *double*."

"Wal," said Samantha again, her voice heavy with warning.

I looked from Elephant to Samantha, and then back again. Samantha was right. She generally was. It wasn't wise to owe a debt to someone like Elephant. It'd be even more foolish to owe double.

But time was short, and I had little choice.

"Fine," I said, glancing around and looking for Ashton's wide smile among the crowd. I didn't see him. "Double. But we move *now*."

Elephant spat in her hand and held it out. I repeated the gesture and we clasped hands. Her grip was firm, carrying with it the weight of command and confidence. She smiled. "Great doing business with you."

The entresol between Level Seven and Level Eight was different from the ones in the mids. As Lovat had risen, modern engineers and architects had begun to use the space in various, more efficient ways. Air ducts, pipes, and electrical lines were better grouped and easier to access. The spaces felt more like well-lit and low ceilinged corridors.

Allard and Vaughn had led us down an alley and into a padlocked hatch that was built into the street. One of them had a key and had unlocked the door and hurried us down a steel ladder.

Narrow strips of white neon hummed along the upper edge of the space giving the interior of the entresol an antiseptic feeling. A city worker in a yellow jumpsuit stared at us as we descended, and then held out her hand as Allard approached.

"On assignment from Elephant," Allard said.

"Even in this crowd?" she asked.

He grunted in the affirmative and palmed a few lira into the woman's outstretched rubber glove. The maintenance worker stepped aside and flashed a flat smile.

Allard chuckled, gave her a friendly slap on the shoulder and motioned for Samantha and me to follow.

"We get along with maintenance," he said, moving along the tunnel in a slight jog. We paced him, our boots clanging on the white painted floor.

Small directional signage had been sprayed in blue stencil letters along pipes and tubes that ran along the walls, directing those in the tunnels to various towers. Among them was the word 'Shangdi' next to a little pictogram depicting the tower's dagger shape.

"They see nothing and as a result we move beneath the city unmolested," explained Vaughn from behind us.

"How far is the tower?"

"There's no straight walk in the entresols. It's a twenty-minute walk from the entrance we took. We've got another five minutes or so."

We twisted around another corner and ducked beneath a gurgling sewage line that crossed the small tunnel. The roar from the crowd leaked down through the street above us and shook the white floor beneath our feet.

"Shangdi is this way. Just a few mor—*hurk*."

The dimanian froze midstep and I nearly collided into him.

"Bell," came a low hissing voice. It sent a shiver down my spine.

A gargoyle was standing before Allard, dominating most of the space in the corridor. Its pointed hood was bent back by the low ceiling. Its left hand was embedded in the dimanian's chest up to its forearm. Blood was leaking out around the wound and dripping to the floor in a heavy wet *pat, pat, pat*.

Allard made another noise and then he shuddered violently and went limp.

The gargoyle regarded him, then turned to Samantha and me before turning to Vaughn, who stammered in place.

"W–what the fu—" said Vaughn.

"You son-of-a—" Samantha began.

I drew the Judge.

"You will go no further," said the creature. It slid its hand free from Allard's chest with a slurping sound. His body crumpled to the floor. The gargoyle regarded my gun. "You tried that once on me before," it said. "Near Methow, in the Kadath. Do you… remember?" it asked in an almost gentle tone.

In the Kadath. I remembered. We had first met the gargoyles in that cursed mine. This was one of those? One of the things we faced in that mineshaft? The gun wavered a bit in my hand.

"We're going to the Shangdi," I said.

"Wha—" Another gagging sound. Another wet slurp, followed by a body collapsing to the floor behind me. Vaughn.

The gargoyle laughed.

I looked over my shoulder and saw two more of them in the small space behind us. Vaughn's body lay at their feet. A pool of crimson was forming beneath his corpse. One of their hands glistened with his blood.

"What *are* you?" Samantha demanded with a gasp. In Ashton's lair the gargoyles were nothing more than a nuisance. Here, they'd killed two of Elephant's men.

"We told you once, priestess," said the third.

"We do not like to repeat ourselves," said the first.

I swallowed, and kept my gun trained on the nearest. I saw Samantha's fists clench into balls. Behind me the two gargoyles sounded their eerie laughter. The one in front tilted its head but said nothing. We were running out of time.

"Kiver," I said, looking at Samantha and then at the gargoyle in front of us.

"Gold's sacrifice," said the second gargoyle.

"Ashton will be pleased with him," said the first. "He will do. For now."

I hoped Samantha understood what I wanted her to do.

I flipped the Judge around in my hand and grasped it by the barrel, my brown knuckles paling as I gripped the metal. Then I took a deep breath and lunged.

TWENTY-THREE

My shoulder connected with the creature's chest. I felt something pop and I was driven to the ground alongside the creature. I felt a breeze above me as Samantha sprang over our tangled forms and sprinted down the hallway.

Below me the gargoyle howled. Its curled fingers clawed at my skin. Every time it touched me I could feel its cold leak through my coat, my shirt and into my chest. I pulled myself so I sat astride it and brought the grip of the Judge down on its face like a hammer. The strange black face collapsed inward and then reformed as I repeated the assault again and again, bringing the Judge down. It was like thrashing at water.

In a moment I was lifted and dragged backward. The gargoyles struggled to hold me, but what they lacked in strength they made up for in determination. My feet slipped on the blood that oozed from Elephant's two dead goons, and I dragged wet stains across the white neon-lit floor.

My father always said I was built like a chest of drawers. I think it was a compliment. I'm not tall like Wensem, nor am I thin like Hagen, but I do have a low center of gravity which is handy in a brawl. Especially with opponents like these.

My feet slapped against the floor and I pushed myself up. I lashed out with the Judge, swinging it like a club and catching one of the gargoyles in the belly. It collapsed backwards. As I pushed off I twisted and threw the last gargoyle into a low-hanging pipe. It connected with a throaty clang. I didn't slow. Didn't pause. I grabbed it and slammed it into the pipe again and again. Eventually it evaporated in a cloud of black smoke.

By this time the first gargoyle had scrambled up. Its blank face leveled at me, its back bent forward, and its hands curled like talons.

"My, you're tenacious," I said. My breath wheezed out of my lungs.

"We serve the will of the Mizra. He wants nothing of his uncle's fate."

"So now you're thugs?"

"We are..." began the first.

"...what the Founders will us to be," completed the gargoyle behind me.

"Fair enough."

I flipped the Judge around in my hand and emptied the cylinder into the first gargoyle's face. Its taloned hands clawed at the fabric that covered its face as it scrambled backwards. When the gun clicked empty, I dropped it and spun, dropping low to avoid a blow from the second. The thing had swung at me and missed, its hands hitting only air. Off balance, I pushed upward, my shoulder connecting with its stomach and throwing it backwards.

The second gargoyle cackled as it went sliding through blood, and I turned to see the first recovering. I expected an attack, but the thing just stood there. Five gunshot holes stared at me like eyes from its blank face, small bits of torn fabric floating in the air of the tunnel. "You have the protection but you do not have the touch."

I picked the Judge from the floor and slipped it back into its holster. I wondered if Samantha had made it to the Shangdi. I hoped she was okay. I looked back at the nearest gargoyle. "What happened to your friend?"

"Friend?" the second asked. I could hear it rising behind me.

"You lack the wisdom."

"You are like the last Guardian."

"Yeah? What happened to him?" I asked.

"*Her*," said one of them. They had begun to circle me now, like wolves.

"She went… mad," said one.

"They all go mad eventually," said the other.

One was across from me now, the other behind me. I pushed back, slamming the one behind me into the white wall of the tunnel and pinning it with my body. I reached up and wrapped my hands around two random pipes and jerked down. A stream of steam and a spark of electricity burst from the pipe and pummeled the creature in front of me.

It screamed, a strange blood-curdling sound, and clawed at itself as it disappeared in a whirl of fabric and smoke.

Only one left.

I spun, grabbing it by the throat and slamming it into the wall again and again.

It only laughed.

I only got angrier. Eventually my hands were coming away bloody and I blinked, realizing the thing was gone. It had vanished.

I was alone.

I looked down at my bloody knuckles. I swore I could hear them still, whispering in the distance. Watching, waiting.

Where did that come from? They hadn't been that powerful before. They hadn't been able to stop us on the stairs in Methow. Why now did three of them present such a problem?

I had to catch up with Samantha. I had to warn Kiver. Stop Ashton. I flexed my fingers, and ran down the tunnel, hoping I wasn't too late.

The lobby of the Shangdi was as impressive as when I first visited. Only this time the security forces looked even more on edge. They all stood with their arms folded, their hands in their pockets, or their fingers wrapped around cups of coffee. Occasionally one of them would peek through the narrow slits in the boards that had been hammered up over the exterior windows. They would exchange worried looks at the swelling of the crowd outside. The fervor. The chanting.

"Why doesn't he just capitulate?" asked one.

"He's scared. That crowd will tear them apart."

"LPD is out of control," said another. "Killing people in cold blood? It's no wonder..."

"The mayor will figure it out..."

Murmurs all around.

I stood near the exit of the stairwell, my hands caked with drying blood. My hair tussled. One of my eyes felt like it was swelling shut. I probably looked like I had been trampled. I wasn't the sort of elevated type these guards would normally see.

If they noticed me they didn't seem to care. Their focus was on their nervous conversation or mob outside. They were scared, and rightly so. There were enough people out there to destroy these towers. Any of them could fall, their inhabitants thrown from the windows. Too many angry people and not enough loyal cops in the city. The bloodshed, the hunger, the outrage all boiled together to make one volatile and unsavory stew.

The shouting drowned out my footsteps. It made sneaking past the guards easier than I had expected. I slipped towards the bank of elevators that occupied the center of the building. I wasn't sure how much time I had spent in the tunnel trading punches. I had no idea if Samantha had gotten to Kiver, no idea if Ashton or Gold were up there already, or what I would face in Kiver dal Renna's sun-lit flat.

The elevator dinged and upon entering I thumbed the button for Kiver's floor. The doors closed and the lift began to rise.

During the ascent I reloaded the Judge and tucked it back into its holster. Drew it. Checked it again. Returned it. The noise of the crowd grew more and more distant as the elevator rose.

When the elevator slowed, my breath seemed to stick in my chest. My heart thudded a staccato rhythm against my ribs. My hands felt clammy and I wiped them on my jeans as the doors dinged and then finally opened.

Around me, the building still trembled.

TWENTY-FOUR

The elevator doors opened on the small atrium. This time it was devoid of worried party guests. I saw nothing, but that didn't set me at ease. I held the gun out in front of me, elbow locked, my left hand cradling the right. I moved slowly, taking corners carefully. My breath was tight and controlled.

The heavy door that lead into the flat was ajar. Not a good sign. I moved from the atrium, easing it open gently. Nothing waited beyond but the foyer entrance and beyond that a small hallway. It led down towards another room, where a sliding door allowed me to enter a kitchen. The kitchen was clean and empty, with only one other exit. Through the door I could see a record player sitting along a glass wall. It warbled a tinny instrumental version of that same song that I had heard so many days earlier. My mother's voice once again welled up from my memories, as the lyrics rolled though my head.

...when I die, when I die please bury me,
in my big black wide-brimmed hat.
Put a twenty lira gold piece on my pocket chain.
So the crew'll know I died standing pat...

I wasn't keen on dying. Not today. It was an eerie tune for the occasion.

I continued my progress. I expected every corner to reveal another bloody scene. Another body on the floor. Another wall covered in strange markings.

The song followed me into the next room—a parlor—and I pushed the lyrics out of my head. Each corner revealed only more maero sparseness: square furniture, clean tables lacking adornment, simple cubes that served as stools or chairs. The walls were blank canvases painted a bone gray. Simple and efficient, the maero way. Even the bright Auseil decorations that had been hung all around on my previous visit had disappeared.

A cold sweat dribbled down my forehead and I wiped it with the back of my hand. The sun—visible from Kiver's unobstructed view—had begun to descend behind the Rosalias. It bathed the towers of the elevated levels in a burning red light and turned the interior of Kiver's flat into fire.

Something moved behind me and I spun, the gun tight in my hand. I waved it around, expecting to see Gold, Ashton, or one of the gargoyles. Instead I saw blank walls stained with sunlight.

I let out a deep breath.

I felt the shouts from the throng below in the floor. I looked out the window. Far below, the crowd looked like a sea that flowed towards City Hall.

I pulled myself from the view and continued. As I moved from the parlor to the center of the main room the sound of voices greeted my ear. They were somewhere else in the house and were hurried and hushed, but nearby. Samantha's voice.

Momentum carried me around the next corner revealing more of the empty main room. A table sat along one wall. Papers covered its surface. I recognized this place. This was where Hagen and I had waited at Kiver's party. It was here I had eaten from Kiver's table, the food supplied by Elephant. This was where I had met Janus Gold, Cora Dirch, and the others.

The voices were closer.

Around the next corner I found a large hallway, as wide across as my small apartment in the Terraces. I eased slowly down the hall. Careful not to make any unnecessary noise. The voices continued. My eyes flicked about, expecting to see Ashton, one of the gargoyles, or even Gold coming at me.

It was all I could do not to call out Samantha's name or shout for Kiver—but I stayed silent. If someone other than my friend or employer was here I would lose any advantage in the element of surprise.

Finally, I saw shadows leaking from the doorway of a back room, framed by the sanguine light that filled the rooms along the western edge of the house. I realized what this room was: the room where we found Frank Adderley, his body cut up by his own hand, his words—the pharos he placed for his god—covering the walls in his own blood.

"I don't understand," said a voice. It sounded like Kiver.

"Neither does Wal. Neither did my brother." I was sure that was Samantha. "None of us understood. We had only half the answers. The thing is, this was supposed to happen. I wish I were here when they examined the room. I would've seen it."

I circled, keeping the gun at the ready. They didn't sound distressed. Only scared. It wasn't the sort of conversation you had while facing your enemies. What did Samantha mean when she said, "she would have seen it"? Would have seen what?

The room opened up before me. Adderley's scrawls still stained the walls though in the light of the sunset the marks had become more diffused. The dark stain where Frank Adderley had lain was still centered over the seal he had drawn on the floor. The altar, as Samantha had called it. Police tape still blocked portions of the room, and small numbered placards were scattered near various stains. Remnants of an investigation.

Samantha and Kiver were in the room, some distance apart. Samantha moved about, examining things, her steps harried, her movement rapid. Her eyes were focused on the walls. She pointed.

Kiver didn't move. He stood and watched. From the side he looked tired and haggard. A large glass of brown liquor was clutched in his seven-fingered hand. His sharp features had sharpened even further and the bags had deepened beneath his piercing gray eyes. Scruff decorated his cheeks and his thin hair hung loosely around his face. He was wearing an undershirt, a pair of slacks, and some house shoes. I hadn't seen him for a few days but the guy looked like he hadn't slept in a week.

"Carter's cross, I'm glad you're okay," I said, exasperated.

Both started, and turned to see me.

"Wal!"

"Mister Bell!"

I holstered the Judge, and let out the breath I hadn't realized I was holding. Tension eased from my shoulders.

"Wal, are you okay?" Samantha broke away from Kiver and hurried over to me, her hands playing against my face, gingerly touching around my eyes, my lips. I winced, I had been socked harder than I realized.

"Yeah, yeah. I think so. I'm sure my stitches are torn open again. Hurts like hell."

Samantha frowned and moved to touch my shirt but thought better of it. "What happened to the gargoyles?"

"Gargoyles?" Kiver asked. His voice seemed higher than normal, it cracked and wavered, and I detected a bit of a slur. He was drunk, drunk and scared. "You're not talking about statues, are you?"

I shook my head.

"What are they?" he asked.

I saw Samantha swallow.

"Still trying to figure that one out," I said. "Look, we got to get you out of here. Ashton is on his way. Gold might be close behind. He didn't like being uncovered."

"Ashton? Gold? Janus Gold?"

"Didn't you tell him?" I looked at Samantha.

"Found him back here. Got lost in translation. Wal, there is so much more here. So much more than what Hagen recorded.

"He captured what he recognized, but he missed all of that."

Samantha looked over my shoulder, to the wall behind me. Her dark eyes scanned what was written. When she turned back to me her face was drawn, her lips pressed tight. I could see lines form at their edges, and could hear her nervousness in her sharp exhalations.

"What is it?" I asked, turning and looking at the wall. "What does it say?"

"Adderley knew. He knew what was going on, knew it would all lead here. This was part of the plan."

"What do you mean?" I asked. I stepped into the room and spun. Marveled at the amount of space the dying doctor had been able to cover in the time it took him to bleed out. Bouchard had been along too quickly for us to really take it all in.

"He knew it would come here. He organized it. The trail he left led here for a reason. It was part of the plan."

"I don't understand, Hagen—"

"—didn't get everything. Only a small portion, but this," she motioned to the wall where the doorway sat. "This was Adderley's manifesto. He wasn't just a doctor. He wasn't just a part of Gold's curious little clique. He was something else. Something we'd only heard of. This was him laying it all out, explaining the process. We've been so blind."

"Okay, but how? What'd we miss?"

"It's when you start to link them, that's when the pattern is revealed. Adderley is working for Ashton's freedom. That's the key. He's very specific about that: freedom is the key. As with all of his family, all of the Firsts, he was awakened by the Kindler— by Cybill—and he was empowered by his uncle: Chaos—"

"Curwen," I said.

"Right, with Ashton we have the first step." She pointed to the wall. "The re-Aligning is happening, and it will begin with the Herald's—with Ashton's—release."

I thought the re-Aligning had been stopped with Cybill's destruction. But clearly that had been wrong. Curwen was proof of it. I ran through the numbers in my head, tried to figure out when Curwen had started his siege on Methow. Panic and exhaustion made it difficult.

"The Herald?" I asked.

"Ashton's title."

"Right. And he's bound to Gold."

"For now," Samantha said, her words carrying a tone of finality.

"We need to get out of here," I said.

"What are you two talking about?" asked Kiver.

I took a deep breath and ran my hand through my hair. Kiver had a right to know. "Do you believe in the Firsts?"

He rubbed his stubbled chin with a seven-fingered hand. His eyebrows raised. "Like the monsters of legend?"

"One and the same," I said.

He started to laugh but caught himself as he saw the expressions on our faces.

"They're very real," said Samantha.

"One's after you right now: Ashton. He's being controlled by Janus Gold who has ordered him to come after you."

"Under Gold's command he's been killing the wealthy. It was Ashton who committed all the recent gilded murders… and many others," said Samantha. "Gold and his cronies have been using him to eliminate their competition."

Kiver's expression changed from one of amusement to terror.

"Janus is behind this?"

"Which is why we have to go! We caught him. Samantha and I. He was performing some rite down on Level Two with a group. They marked you as the next target. They won't be far behind us now."

Kiver stared at us blankly. "Assuming I believe you, where would you have me go? Out *there*? Have you seen that crowd? They'll tear me apart!"

"Where's your family?" I asked.

"I sent them away. A week ago. After the Auseil party. They're at our summer home, on the islands."

"Why didn't you go with them?"

"I have business here. In a crisis every business, even one as successful as Renna Monochromes, needs strong leadership." He paused and thought. "This is precisely the time it needs strong leadership."

Outside, Lovat burned. I had just explained how a killer who also happened to be one of the great old ones of legend was gunning for his life. Two people had been found dead in two different apartments owned by him in two different buildings. Yet, he felt the need to preach about the values of strong leadership. Bravery and stupidity are often two sides of the same coin. I should know.

"We can get around the crowd," I said, hoping it was true. I wondered where the gargoyles went. Could we use the pale tunnels of the entresols or would those things show up there as well?

"He is coming here. After you. Gold wants you dead and now you're being hunted. We need to go, the farther we can get from this city, the better."

I considered our options. If the blockade in the South had really been broken the smaller city of Destiny could be an option. Samantha's father lived there and had some sway. If we wanted we could move even farther out into the country. Hide Kiver among the small farming communities scattered between here and the broad flow of the Rediviva.

I will always find you, Mister Bell. Argentum's words sprung up from somewhere inside of me. I hadn't seen my would-be assassin in a while, I wondered where we would face off again. He had told me that I couldn't escape the city. Now I had to try.

"Come on," I said.

"Let me get my—" Kiver began.

"No!" I shouted, spinning to face him. "We don't have time to get anything. We need to go, and we need to go *now!*"

Kiver blinked, and nodded. "Okay."

I turned, feeling the blood surge through me, and drew the Judge again, moving out of Adderley's death chamber and back down the hallway. I was careful and quiet. I studied the way ahead expecting to see an enemy emerge from around every corner.

Kiver and Samantha followed, staying close behind. Careful not to make a sound.

Something felt off, like we were being watched. The hairs on the back of my neck stood on end as we exited the hallway and returned to the main room that stretched along one side of the apartment.

A quick glance in Samantha's direction told me she was also sensing something. Her eyes fixated on mine and then danced around the room as if she expected to see creatures hanging from the corners.

I kept holding my breath, then realized I was doing it and tried to correct myself. The sound of the record player still warbled throughout the flat. I tried to hear anything past it.

Nothing.

I waved with my gun toward the other side of the apartment, beckoning Samantha and Kiver to follow. I continued to move forward. Circling, checking, double-checking, and leading us back towards the elevator.

We stepped from the main room into the parlor where the record player sat. From the parlor we moved into the kitchen, and from there we slipped through the hallway into the atrium where the elevator doors deposited residents and guests. As we approached the gleaming metal doors I felt a bit of relief. One elevator ride down and we'd be in the lobby. There we had the Shangdi's security to help us smuggle Kiver away. I felt better. Like we were going to pull this off.

I reached to press the elevator's call button.

"Did you turn on my record player?" Kiver asked.

Before I tapped the button, the light above the sliding door had clicked on. The glowing plastic circle glared down at me like the judgmental eye of some mythical beast. Its meager light had changed in the setting sun, shifting from a dull yellow into a hateful angry red.

"Wal, the light," Samantha said.

My mouth went dry.

The doors slid open.

In the same instance a metal mask reflected the sunset. The yellow metal caught the light and bent it, causing it to flare hot and bright. I raised a hand to shield my eyes.

The record player skipped. A raspy anur voice filled the apartment. Singing Father Armstrong's old song:

...I want six boneshooters to be pallbearers.
And a chorus girl to sing a song.
Stick a big jazz band on my hearsewain.
Raise hell as I stroll along.

TWENTY-FIVE

The setting sun turned everything red. It poured its light around us, turning our shadows into black pools that stretched across the floor and climbed up the walls.

Two crimson figures, stained with gore, stepped out of the elevator into Kiver's foyer. Janus Gold's mask wore the same placid expression, but the eyes beyond looked panicked. He gripped a hatchet in one hand and his other was balled into a fist. Beside him Caleth stood armed with a thick club and an evil expression that was all furrowed brow and twisted sneer. The bloody handprint Gold had placed on his forehead was now dry, the drips like frozen waterfalls on his face. He breathed in long heavy breaths that inflated his shoulders as much as his chest.

My Judge was raised and leveled at them before either could speak. Everyone froze. Each group trying to get a read off the others.

"B–Bell," stammered Gold. He scratched his dirty hair with his free hand. "This isn't what it seems."

"Yeah? Is that why you look like you just came from a murder scene? And that?" I pointed at the hatchet with the barrel of the Judge. "How are you going to explain that?"

Gold looked down at the weapon and his eyes widened as if noticing it for the first time. He lowered it slightly, clearly unsure of what to do.

"I saw you send that thing after Kiver," I said. I trained the gun back and forth between the two of them. Every time I pointed it at Gold he shied away. Caleth was bolder. He was large and mean and had nearly a foot and a half over me and probably weighed twice my weight. Every time the gun stopped on him his frown deepened, I could hear his teeth grate and see the muscles of his arms tense.

"What is going on? What did you get yourself into, Janus?" asked Kiver. The edge in his voice was clear. "And you, Caleth? This is what I get after all my time, all my investment in you? I expected better."

Caleth pointed his club at the other maero. "You keep quiet, *forsha*."

Kiver gave a guttural growl behind me. I didn't know the meaning but I could recognize Elano, the maero native tongue. It was a language most maero didn't speak anymore. Wensem couldn't speak a lick of it and most folk preferred Strutten. However, it was clear from Caleth's tone and Kiver's reaction that it was offensive.

"He hasn't been here, has he?" The dauger looked from the gun to a space over my shoulder and shook his head. "No... he hasn't. If he'd been here you'd be dead." He looked at me and then at Samantha. "All of you."

"Janus, we've always been competitors but I thought we were also friends. Carter's cross, we went to school together," said Kiver.

Gold scoffed. "It was in school when I learned how *poisoned* you were. As we got older I saw how it spilled into your business. You're a cruel and vindictive maero, Kiver dal Renna. You want to take shame? Imagine what your father would say if he saw how you ran the corporation that bears his name."

"Business is business," said Kiver, his voice a rumble. "It's not personal."

Elephant's words.

"Business is business, eh? Was it business when you fired my brother? Was it business when you forced out the leadership of First Lovat Bank? You know they forced me into default! You move about with no regard. You don't care! You don't think about anything but yourself. So we'll play this your way. We can consider this just an extension of business. A hostile takeover, as it were. It's not *personal*." Gold's voice had a mocking tone. I tensed. How did I end up in the middle of this?

I kept facing Caleth and Gold. I was sure Kiver was livid but I couldn't let my guard down. Both were armed and seemed willing to use their makeshift weapons.

"How'd you get up here?" Samantha asked. "The crowd outside—"

Caleth waved the question away dismissively and gave me a wicked grin.

"And the others?" asked Kiver. "Have you been behind all of those deaths? What did Bonheur do to you? Osmiyum, Styer… old Blake? Were they just other *hostile takeovers*?"

"The ranks of the elevated needed a purge. Too many old families with too much power, stifling those of us with fewer holdings," said Caleth. "You'd be amazed what grieving families are willing to part with for a pittance."

"That's how you ended up on the board of Styer & Sons," said Kiver with a little awe in his voice.

Caleth grinned.

Kiver let out a slow breath.

"You are both a disappointment. Janus, I expected better. Spewing a bunch of trash. You were in default. The managers at First Lovat were corrupt and they needed to be forced out, and yes, I fired your brother but I had suffered his bungling for too long. But I have never killed someone. What would the Precious Families say if they knew you were doing this? What would the Golds say?"

Gold said nothing and Kiver continued. "And you, Caleth. Ever since your father died you've been like a son to me."

"I made my own way," said Caleth.

"You don't understand, do you, Kiver?" said Gold. "You've been so far up your own ass for so long that you don't even see the damage you do." He looked from Kiver to Samantha and then to me. "And you, do you really know the maero you're protecting? Do you understand who it is you strive so hard to defend?"

I met Gold's crazed eyes and steeled myself. There's no use

arguing with crazy.

Caleth sneered. "Let's just kill them. We don't need to waste our breath on a bunch of scrapes."

The maero was faster than I expected. He lifted the club and rushed towards me.

"Caleth, wai—" began Gold, reaching out to grab ahold of the maero's shoulder.

Caleth didn't seem to notice the pull. I could see the knuckles of his hand tighten, his jaw clench. His eyes, narrowed now to slits, glared at me with hatred. The club was a blur.

The motion happened so naturally I barely registered what I was doing. Blood roared in my ears, blocking out all sound. It took fractions of a second to adjust my aim, and even less time to squeeze the trigger.

The first bullet struck him in the chest. I fired again. The second in the shoulder. It put him off balance. The third shot went through his left eye.

Caleth stumbled back, a spray of blood tracing his arc down. He collapsed at my feet, spitting blood, and growled a painful grunt. The three shots had sprayed his blood all over the wall, the doors of the elevator, and Gold.

The dauger looked stunned, he just stared down at Caleth.

I stepped back quickly, pushing Kiver and Samantha back into the kitchen. Caleth was seriously wounded but he wasn't out. He rolled onto his belly and began to crawl forward. He lashed out, trying to catch one of my ankles, but his movements were slow and I stepped out of the way.

I fired again, and his body convulsed. He pushed himself up

onto his hands and knees and crawled towards us. Blood dripped from his lips in long tendrils. His remaining eye stared at me, cold and full of hatred.

I only had one shot left, so I made it count. I took aim and pulled the trigger. The Judge boomed in my hands.

Caleth dal Dunnel collapsed, the top of his head blown in.

Sound began to creep back into my world. A gasp from Gold. A wail from Kiver. The distant shouting from the crowd below. I could smell the scent of gunpowder and blood on the air. My hands started to shake and I willed them to still.

I looked over at Samantha. Caught her eye. She hated guns, and rightfully so. I expected to see a look of disdain, or in the very least pity. Instead her expression was a mix of sadness and something else. Something I couldn't read.

The Judge felt heavy in my hand.

"Y–you killed him," said Gold.

I backed up, waving my hands to Samantha and Kiver and hoping they'd do so as well. The Judge was empty, and I didn't think Gold would give me the chance to reload. He raised his hatchet, leveled his gaze at me and advanced.

"Why did you do that?" His voice had grown distant and he tilted his head when he asked the question. It reminded me of the gargoyles.

"He came after me first," I said. I held the Judge out, hoping it'd be enough to fool him.

"First you kill Cora and now you murder Caleth? Is this the behavior of the Guardian? Aren't you meant to protect?"

We kept up our slow retreat as Gold stalked toward us. We passed through the kitchen, keeping ourselves out of the reach of his hatchet.

"Janus, stop this," said Kiver from over my shoulder.

Gold's eyes were glowing, filled with fire and focused on us, the three of us. His words had grown incoherent and muffled. He chortled a laugh but his eyes never wavered.

"You need to stop this, Janus," said Kiver. His tone was firm.

"Caleth was a good lad," said Gold. "A bit headstrong, but good. Cora was a sweetheart." He kept staring at me, at the Judge. I hoped he wasn't counting the chambers.

"When will that thing arrive?" I said. "Ashton."

The name snapped Gold out of his trance. He looked around almost absently. "He makes his own way, in his own time. I only set him on the course. He chooses how to run it."

We now stood in the central room of the apartment. Samantha stood to one side near the long row of windows. Kiver stood on the other, near the hallway that led to the smaller rooms. Gold stopped and just stood, watching us curiously.

"You're out of bullets," he finally said. "You only have five. You used all of them on poor Caleth."

Damnit.

He stared at me and I lowered the Judge, my charade over. I expected him to leap, swinging the hatchet. Instead he just stood, watching.

There was a movement behind him. A black shadow. A pointed hood. A blank face. The gargoyle leaned around the doorway and then paused.

More appeared outside, and I glanced out the wall of windows.

Below, just one floor down, on the latticework of girders that would eventually form the floor of Level Nine, more gargoyles appeared. Dozens of blank faces stared up.

Gargoyles began to materialize, filling the space behind Gold. Standing out of the way, in corners, near the record player. Any empty space was suddenly filled by them. First one, then two, then three, then ten.

They didn't advance, they didn't move, they just watched, as if waiting for something, or... someone.

I swallowed and looked over at Samantha, who saw them as well. Kiver stammered, clearly struggling to understand these hooded figures. I took deep breaths and tried to calm my nerves.

Samantha's eyes were wide and she instinctively crouched, her hands balled into fists. She looked ready to leap and attack.

I held out a hand. It wasn't time, not yet. She gave me a small nod and mouthed something I couldn't understand. Everything swam around us.

I turned and looked at Gold. The dauger still stood in the same spot, flanked by the robed figures. He now looked past me, the hatchet hanging loosely in his hand. His shoulders slumped and he drooped. Where before he looked crazed, now he seemed strangely defeated.

Just then, a choking sound came from Kiver. Then came a voice that sent sparks running up and down my spine.

"I told you I would always find you, Mister Bell."

TWENTY-SIX

Kiver's body was already dropping by the time I turned around. The elevated maero clutched at a gash in his neck, making a *hurk hurk hurk* sound as blood gurgled out. Janus Gold screamed, but it was obvious that Kiver was not long for this world. The long slash had come from behind and nearly beheaded him and blood was pouring down his shirt and dripping onto his slacks and the floor. Samantha looked at me, her eyes large and wide. In the brief glance I spared I could see the fear, the terror at what she was seeing. I knew that same feeling intimately.

The mask that owned the smooth voice emerged over Kiver's shoulder. Rising above it like a silvery moon. The eyes were the same black slits. In its simplicity the narrow gash of a mouth looked like a mocking smile. I shuddered as Rulon Argentum emerged from behind the falling body of my dying employer.

All around us the choir of gargoyles shouted hushed screams like the crackle of static. Their blank faces were leveled at Argentum, the interloper. If he saw them at all, he didn't show it. The whole of his focus was on me.

"Argentum," I said, my voice carrying with it more terror than I had wanted to show. His head tilted as if he was amused.

"Oh, no," said Gold.

"I warned you, Mister Bell," said Argentum. I could tell he was smiling. The way he tilted his head forward, the way he shifted his shoulders back. He wanted to relish this, he wanted to make it hurt.

A knot had formed in my stomach and I felt cold sweat trickle down my spine. The wound he had torn in my chest flared with pain. I remembered running for my life. Diving into the Sunk as a last resort.

Argentum was still dressed in his dark suit, though his jacket was unbuttoned and the crisp shirt beneath was sweat-stained and rumpled. He was still stylish but more disheveled than I'd seen him before. His right arm was soaked in Kiver's blood up to the elbow. It beaded on the sleeve of his suit jacket and dripped off the end of the wicked knife he held in an outstretched hand. Even the sharp silver nail on the end of his pinky dripped with maero blood.

"You idiot!" shouted Gold, turning and shouting at Argentum. "You stupid silver bastard! You realize what you've done?"

He leapt to his feet and charged across the space between them, hauling his hatchet back for a swing.

The assassin was much faster. He stepped into Gold's swing and grabbed the arm swinging the hatchet. He twisted and wrenched it, spinning the smaller dauger around. With a swift kick he sent Gold sprawling across the floor. He looked at the hatchet in his hand and shook his head and chuckled.

"Let's be a little careful, eh cousin? I'd rather not kill you, as well."

I still held the Judge, though by now I realized we all knew it wasn't loaded. Argentum had been in the apartment. He had watched as I gunned down Caleth. I wondered how he had found Kiver's place. Who had talked? Who else had fallen victim to that blade? A pang of worry for Hagen and Hannah shot through my heart.

I moved for a reload, but Argentum held up his knife and flicked it, making a *tsk* noise.

"Careful."

"You here to kill me?" I said.

"I was always here to kill you, Mister Bell. That's why I was hired." I could hear the smirk in his words.

"Then why the games?" I asked. "Why demand money? Why pretend to be a collector?"

Argentum laughed and shook his head. "So many questions."

"Who hired you?" Samantha asked.

Argentum bowed his head slightly. "Ah, the priestess."

"It wasn't Shaler," I said.

"No, it wasn't Shaler." He took a small step forward. The static sound still wavered from the gargoyles though it had simmered somewhat. Samantha looked all around. Gold hadn't gotten off the floor, he just lay there looking pitiful as Argentum spoke. "I have been scouring this city for you the past three days. Three days you have made me hunt you. Three days of wandering in this muck. I tried that religious trinket store but found it locked, and when I broke in it was empty. I even checked the Sunk. I'll never be able to wash out that smell. Then I did some digging and put it all together. I knew you'd come here... eventually."

I pictured Kiver wandering around his house while Argentum watched from the shadows.

"The bumbling fool had no idea," he said, gesturing towards Kiver's body. "Was so caught up in his business he didn't even hear me put the record on. It's amazing what a man does when he's alone and fears for his life. Shame," he said. Then he stepped towards me.

"Here we are yet again," Argentum said. He scratched the cheek of his mask with his sharp pinky nail. The tinny screech of metal on metal sang through the room.

"So if it wasn't Shaler, then who was it?" I said, backing up.

"The stars are aligning, Bell. You angered some mighty powerful people." Argentum laughed. Then he looked down at the blade in his hand as if pondering it.

Powerful people? Who had the money to send an elevated dauger after me as an assassin?

Together, Samantha and I backed up, pressing our backs to the glass wall. I could feel the cold leeching in, feel the vibrations from the street below.

That feeling returned. The buzz in the back of my skull. Something was happening. The gargoyles' movements seem to indicate as much. Far below the anger of the crowd surged and the floor under my feet vibrated.

Gold had gotten to his feet and was glaring at the other dauger. "You don't realize, do you?" he said. "He was *marked*. He was marked, you dumb bastard."

Gold roared and charged him again. Argentum danced back, gingerly stepping over Kiver's lifeless body. Gold moved like a bear, throwing himself forward. The punch went wide. It took little effort on Argentum's part to flick his knife and catch Gold on the extended arm. The dauger howled and stepped back, his other hand clutching the gash Argentum had made.

The gargoyles' hissing grew louder.

"I heard everything you said, cousin. You don't seem the type to be running with maero, even for protection."

"Who sent you?" Gold demanded.

"The agent of transformation," Argentum said. "The Herald has come. The High Priest approaches."

Gold roared with displeasure. I could see the spittle fly from the mouth-hole of his mask. "NO! You are *dauger*."

Argentum tilted his head, a confused gesture.

"Why work for *them*?" Gold roared in frustration. "You have set plans back thousands of years. Don't you realize? *We* were in control of the Herald. He could do *nothing*. Don't you see? Don't you understand?"

Who was *them*? I looked back and forth between the two masked men. Did Gold mean Ashton? I didn't get any more answers to my questions.

Around us, the gargoyles went silent.

Gold looked around nervously.

The building shook again and the noise from the street below swelled. I used the momentary distraction to reload the Judge from the shells in my pocket. It didn't take long. I gripped the gun tightly in my right hand and felt Samantha take my left. She squeezed it. I squeezed back.

"You've doomed us all," Gold said to Argentum.

Then it happened.

A shockwave—much bigger than the roar of the crowd—shook the Shangdi. I felt the wave roll through the apartment. Heard the sound of rending metal. At first I thought a bomb had gone off, but there was no smoke. No explosion. Samantha and I crouched down. Argentum and Gold—unprepared—were thrown to the floor.

Samantha and I clung to each other, refusing to let go. Not now. Not again.

A second shockwave hit the tower. This one much stronger. A cold wind slammed my chest, it sucked the air from my lungs and I felt like my heart was freezing mid-beat.

"He's here," said Gold.

Behind us, the glass exploded outward.

TWENTY-SEVEN

He came striding down the hallway barefoot, moving like a prince among paupers. I knew where he had come from, knew what had led him to this exact spot: Adderley's pharos. The bloody room where we found his body, the final altar that guided Ashton from the pit in which he lay and into the sun-lit reaches of the upper levels. Somehow the dead doctor had known where this would all go down. He had led his master skyward.

Everything moved in slow motion. The glass that ran externally around the Shangdi Tower fluttered like ice crystals on the air before descending downward. As the world sped back up I could hear the sound of the glass raining down on the level below. Hear the screams of the crowd. Gunshots followed. Smoke began to billow up from below. I heard the distinct sound of sirens wailing to life.

Ashton walked purposefully, still wearing his human visage. He held his arms out at his side, hands forward, like he was moving in for an embrace. That plain face with the slightly too-wide mouth and the bulging eyes carried a relaxed expression. He was dressed simply in slacks and a white button-up shirt. Smoke crawled around his feet, unmindful of the cold and writhing like a mass of snakes.

Ashton the First grinned at us.

We had all been thrown backwards in the blast, but Argentum was the only one of us to have gone out the shattered wall of windows. Somehow he had been able to catch the ledge and with a grunt he hauled his lanky frame back in.

"Dweller," said one of the gargoyles.

"Sleeper," said another.

"Mizra," hissed a third. They bowed their heads low.

Ashton gave a smart little bow and then laughed happily. "Well, well, well..." he said, looking from Samantha and me to Gold and then Argentum. He noticed Kiver's body bleeding out on the floor and snorted. "I have arrived, it seems, just in time for a little fun. So..." He clapped his hands together and rubbed them ferociously. "Let's have at it. Where is the sacrifice? Where is the bonded?"

Gold mumbled something that was hard to hear over the howling wind. Ashton grinned at him. "I didn't catch that, Janus."

"He is there," said Gold, pointing. His voice was weak and thin. Gold cowered, protecting his head with his hands. He was shaking.

Ashton smiled and shook his head. "Yes, I know that. I could smell his blood on the wind as I approached..."

Argentum rose and crossed the open room, lifting his knife from the floor.

"What are we going to do?" whispered Samantha.

"I don't know," I replied, and it was true. I didn't know.

Ashton turned, his back now to us as he squatted and examined Kiver's cooling body.

"This sacrifice is already dead, Janus."

Gold whimpered.

Ashton looked over his shoulder and grinned his too-wide smile.

"Herald," said Argentum. He wiped the blade of his knife on a dirty pant leg and looked at Ashton warily.

Ashton turned and sized him up. "What are you to me, dauger? Another abomination? Another bastard son of the yellow?"

"I'm no Gold," Argentum said.

"Janus, who took my sacrifice?"

Gold pointed at Argentum.

"My target is the Guardian," Argentum said. "He got in the way."

"Did he, now?" Ashton smiled and looked from Argentum to me.

Argentum looked over his shoulder at me. I held the gun out.

Ashton folded his arms across his chest and nodded at him. "Well then. Do as you will."

The tall dauger turned, and I half-expected his unchanging mouth to have split into a grin. He chuckled to himself—a strangely hollow sound—as he began to stalk toward me. His knife, still smeared with Kiver's blood, was held out in front of him.

"Wal," I heard Samantha say. My name was swallowed by a sharp intake of breath.

"You heard the... man," said Argentum. As if the permission mattered to him.

At that moment I no longer cared who had hired Rulon Argentum. I no longer wondered what strings were being pulled. I was going to end him right here.

I breathed deeply and lifted the gun, pointing it directly at him.

Argentum barked a laugh.

That cool metal face with the placid expression didn't change. In the confusion he hadn't seen me reload.

"You're out," said Argentum, moving quickly towards me.

"Am I?" I said coolly.

I wish I could've seen his eyes.

The Judge boomed.

Argentum jerked backward. A hole appeared in his forehead. A single rivulet of blood ran from the hole and down the silver. The knife fell from his hands, and his arms dropped to his sides. Then, slowly, the dauger sank to his knees. He gurgled something unintelligible, then fell forward, landing facedown only inches from my boots. I could see where my bullet had exited the back of his head. The perfect hair was a mess, tangled and bloody. Argentum—the assassin who had chased me through Lovat—was dead.

The buzz grew louder and I could hear whispers pass through the gathered gargoyles.

"You killed him," Samantha said.

I nodded. Looked over my shoulder. She wasn't looking at me, she was looking at Argentum's corpse. Her face drawn, her expression serious, her eyes cold.

From across the room Ashton clapped, and my attention moved from Samantha to him. "I see our Guardian has a bit of a bite."

I looked at the gun in my hands. I didn't like killing. Didn't like killing people. Argentum might have been a bastard, but he was still a person. Yet, he had killed Kiver. He had been willing to kill me. Justice? Of a sort, I supposed. I wondered if I could end Ashton in the same way. Stop him here and now. The gun had been useless against Curwen, but was Ashton the same?

"I wouldn't bother," said Ashton, reading my thoughts. "It'll just piss me off."

I slipped the Judge back into my shoulder holster.

Ashton turned from me and began to walk towards Janus Gold. The small dauger whimpered and began to scoot backwards. He held up his cut arm like some sort of shield. Ashton's smile wavered, and he narrowed his eyes.

"Now, Janus, you and I have some business to attend to."

I could see the look in Ashton's eye. The seething hate and anger.

I had to stop him. But how? The Judge was worthless against a First, which left me with nothing. I looked down at my hands. Held them out pitifully. Samantha reached out and took one, her dark eyes flashing up to meet mine. The vibration at the back of my skull roared with her touch. Around us the gargoyles hissed, a hot white noise.

Ashton stopped and looked at us, saw Samantha gripping my hand. His expression changed. He looked... was that fear? I blinked, and his expression changed. But there had been something. I had seen it dance across his face. His eyes had been focused on my hands. He saw me catch him looking and then he smiled. He turned, moved towards Gold.

My hands? What about my—oh... The scene in the entresol beneath Paramount Square flashed though my mind. The gargoyle hadn't been able to stop me. Unlike Elephant's goons, I had been able to stand against them. I had been able to fight.

Ashton was worried. About *me*.

The vibration now sang. It flowed through me.

"Wal..." Samantha asked, imploring. "What are you going to do?"

"Get yourself away from the ledge," I said.

"No," Samantha said. I looked at her. I could see the stubbornness in her eyes. "I'm staying here. I'm staying with you."

"He'll kill you," I said.

"He'll kill *you*!" she echoed.

"No," I said. "Not like this." I gave Samantha's hand a squeeze and released it as I took a step forward.

I could feel her standing behind me, feet planted. Arms at her sides. She gave me strength.

"Ashton." I spoke his name calmly, my voice sounding stronger than I felt. All around me the gargoyles tittered and warbled in strange noises. Probably calls of Aklo or some other alien language but at that moment I didn't care.

"You need to stop," I said. I had no plan, I had no idea what I was going to do but I knew my duty. I was the Guardian. I was here to protect the people of this world from creatures like Ashton. That protection extended to even the bastards. Even Janus Gold.

"No more death," I said.

"Oh?" Ashton cackled. "Is that for you to decide?"

I said nothing.

"Do you realize how long I have been used by this abomination?" It pointed a lazy finger at Gold. "How long I have been made to serve a creature such as him? My followers beckoned me, called me here, and I was trapped."

"I don't care," I said. I forced the words out.

Ashton's eyes narrowed. "Oh, there will be more death."

"It stops now."

"And what will you do to stop me?" Ashton growled. He took three large steps to the edge of the apartment where Janus Gold lay whimpering. He thrust a finger down at the cowering dauger. His hair whipped around in the wind, gray smoke that circled around his naked feet. "He wanted to kill you! When they saw you had caught them in the ritual they wanted your head."

"So did you," I said.

Ashton snorted. "Technicalities."

He reached down with a human arm and lifted Gold by his collar. The short dauger rocked in the icy breeze. His eyes behind the golden mask were wide, the flesh below his chin quivered, tears rolled down his mask. His facade had broken, and all that was left was a pitiful little dauger, hanging from the hand of the First.

"He seems to want to defend you," said Ashton to Gold. He was between the two of us, his back to the dauger.

"He'll face the consequences of his actions," I said. I balled my hands into fists and stood my ground. The world around me faded. The gargoyles were forgotten. Samantha was a shadow on my periphery. The back of my head buzzed. I breathed deeply in the thin air of the elevated sky.

My teeth clenched and I ground them together as my eyes narrowed. I didn't feel the cold. I hardly felt the breeze. Any pain in my chest or knee was gone. It was just Ashton and me, staring and sizing one another up.

I was going to rush him, I realized. I was going to fight him, challenge him in hand-to-hand combat. My gun might do little harm, but somehow I knew I could hurt this monster. Seconds felt like hours as Ashton and I stared at one another. His smile widened but it didn't meet his narrowing eyes.

"Stop! Police!"

Everyone turned.

A mass of LPD officers clustered on the edge of the common room. In the middle stood a red-faced and sweaty Carl Bouchard, his snub-nose revolver clenched in his thick hand.

Ashton gave them a glance, and then tilted his head at me. He smiled a final languid grin, and then he threw himself out into the open air, carrying a blubbering Janus Gold with him.

TWENTY-EIGHT

Too late I registered that Samantha and Bouchard were shouting my name. I was already dashing forward, their words becoming an unintelligible echo behind me. The drop wasn't far—only a story—but my right knee rang as I hit the steel plating.

The wind howled around me, unrestrained at this height. It pulled at my coat, blew my long hair around my face, and tugged at my beard. My heart pounded, and though I knew that the wind was cold, I didn't feel it. The sharp sensation was numb, a mere annoyance below the buzzing at the back of my skull.

Ashton was moving quickly, already a block away and gaining ground with each moment. He moved gracefully, like he was born to leap across the half-completed framework of Lovat's upper reaches. A hand was wrapped around Gold's neck, and the dauger fought against his grip as he was dragged along. The First bounded across beams and careened around a partially poured concrete floor before disappearing behind another tower.

Recovered, I leaped towards the spot where Ashton had fallen. When he landed, his impact had cratered the cement surface. A much larger impact than a normal-sized human should produce. He might be wearing the form of a human, but he was still the immense thing I had seen in the pit below the city.

Over my shoulder, I saw Samantha standing at the window of Kiver's apartment. She was shouting something. Her hands cupped around her mouth. Her words were stolen by the combination of the howling of the wind and the clamor of the streets below. Next to her appeared Bouchard. The detective looked angry, he was doubled over, his hands on his knees, his back heaving as he sucked in air.

I stepped back, stunned, when I saw what had happened to the Shangdi Tower. It had become a skeleton. The entire facade, all forty stories that extended upward from Level Eight had shed their skin. Its windows had all been blown outward. Smoke billowed a few floors above Samantha and Bouchard, and sparks and fire rippled from others.

Down on Level Eight's streets I could see some of the destruction the Shangdi's shattering had wrought. People lay in the streets, trapped or crushed by fallen debris. The sun reflected on a sea of a million shards of glass. It painted the streets, and from this high up they looked flooded, like channels of blood. Hell, it could have been blood. The glass would have torn through the crowd like hot knives.

Paramount Square was madness. People screamed and shouted, they mobbed the courthouse, barreled past the riot police that had lined its entrance as protection. Smoke burned at the base of a tower on the square opposite the Shangdi. I could feel the vibrations as millions shouted and screamed and rushed City Hall.

This was Ashton's doing. He had wounded these people bleeding in the street below. He had torn through this tower. He had to be stopped. The destruction he could bring to Lovat would be unprecedented. He could bring the city down. Topple its towers and destroy its foundations. He could bring about millions of deaths.

I turned, and felt my coat pull around me. I had to give chase. Protect this city and its people. I looked over my shoulder, back toward the window. I wanted to see Samantha one last time, but she was gone, the hole where she stood was empty.

I took a deep breath, and then I followed. Level Nine was the smallest of Lovat's levels, only the size of King Station, Pergola Square, and part of the Business District combined, and about a quarter of it was still incomplete. I rounded the tower following Ashton's path and came across a wide expanse. A vast plain of steel extended between clusters of buildings. Ashton was nowhere to be seen. He couldn't be that fast? Could he?

A scattering of sheds occupied the wide empty space between the towers. Smoke trailed from a few, their doors closed to the wind. These were the mobile offices for the construction crews that lifted Lovat ever higher.

I rushed past the nearest of the small sheds but slowed to a stop as I passed the third. It was missing its door. I looked around and spotted it, laying a few feet off to one side, tangled in a pile of rebar. Its hinges, still attached, fluttered in the wind. Smoke billowed from the shed's stubby chimney.

My heart drummed heavily, and I held my breath as I stepped inside. I wasn't sure what to expect. A smiling Ashton? A cowering Janus Gold? Instead, I found a fat dimanian foreman with four stubby horns that poked up around his head like a crown, clad in the yellow of a construction worker. He gasped when he saw me and jumped behind a big metal desk.

"Go away!" he shouted. He peeked up over the desk. His eyes were as big as saucers. His hands gripped the edge of the desk, pale around the spurs on his knuckles.

"Did you see a man come through here? Human, about my height. Big eyes, wide mouth. He was dragging a dauger with a gold mask?"

The dimanian whimpered and squeezed his eyes shut.

"He r–ripped off the door. Ripped it off! Like it was nothing."

"Sounds like him." I stepped inside. The small stove in the corner radiated heat and I could feel its warmth through my jeans.

"He came inside. He just looked at me and laughed. Then..." His voice grew silent and his eyes popped open. In a whisper he said, "What *is* he?"

I could hear the fear in his voice, the madness that lurked at the edges. What else had Ashton done in here? Done to him?

When I first saw Cybill I had been nearly driven to insanity myself, and she hadn't even been fully formed. Ashton was at full power...

"Where did he go?"

The foreman stared through me, his eyes focusing on the corrugated metal of the wall. I stepped forward and asked again. The dimanian looked at me, as if seeing me for the first time. He blinked, and said something in a language I couldn't understand.

I shook my head. "Wha—"

"The disciple completed his duty," he said in Strutten. "The Herald has awakened and now all rise. The Aligning has begun."

I left the babbling foreman in his office and stepped out onto the open expanse of Level Nine. In the distance, I could hear the ruckus from Paramount Square. Behind me the Shangdi rose, a tattered ruin among the other high rises.

I continued to move south and east, away from the Shangdi and following the course I thought Ashton would travel. He left no trail and I expected him around every tower. I was unsure of what I would do when we finally met. The Judge was useless, but he had been afraid. Something about me scared him.

As I emerged from between two towers that rose another twenty stories above, I saw him. Standing along the edge of the road in front of a building I recognized: the Arcadia Hotel, its top ten floors rising above Level Nine. It was older than most towers. Built of steel but draped in brick. The top was a small pyramid crested with a radio tower.

Ashton saw me and now I could see panic on his face. His eyes wide, his teeth locked in a grimace. He shook Gold, and the dauger seemed to go limp for a moment. The fear drained from the First's face and was replaced with a grin. Then he punched his way through the outer wall of the hotel. He dragged Gold by the collar. The dauger was shouting and kicking at the air as his fists beat at Ashton's arm.

"Let me be!" The First shouted.

I followed, leaping the space between street and tower where the eventual sidewalk would be constructed. Below me flashed the ten-story drop to Level Eight. I landed inside the Arcadia, stumbling.

Ashton had blown through the next wall, and then the next, tearing a tunnel through the building with his fists as he dragged a choking Gold.

Dust filled the space between us, obscuring my line of sight, but I plowed forward anyway, walls and beams flashing past. I entered living rooms and exited into bedrooms and bathrooms and closets. Sparks danced on the air, they slipped down my collar and scorched my neck. I saw the open-mouthed faces of occupants confused at the destruction, the men appearing in their walls, but I didn't stop. I couldn't stop.

Somewhere ahead Ashton growled. He shouted something— was that Aklo?—and then came another rumble. A gust of cold wind hit me from ahead, blowing my hair back. He had exited the other side of the building.

I careened to a stop, emerging suddenly into the cold air of Level Nine. The crumbling face of the building dropped away, tumbling down to Level Eight below. Level Nine extended away, but there was a five or six-yard gap in between. Jagged spikes of rebar stuck out from the unfinished floor and pointed at me. It was too far to jump though I might be able to clear it with a running leap. There were a few spaces I could land, but if I miscalculated I'd be skewered.

Ashton had stopped and turned to face me. He smiled a languid smile and held up Gold like some trophy he had captured in a game of keep-away. The dauger kicked and spat a curse.

I blinked. The First seemed to shimmer in the wind. He was there, in human form, but he was also there in the shape of the creature I had seen before, and there was something else, something much larger. Looming behind and around him, around all of us, around the city. A titanic form, the size of a mountain. It scraped the sky and regarded me with eyes like small moons.

"You're persistent. I will give you that."

I judged the space between us. It'd be close.

"What do you expect to do? Shoot me?" he asked.

I stepped back and eyed the distance, rocking slightly.

Ashton could see what I was planning.

"Dangerous. Especially with that knee of yours." He sniffed the air. "You're losing blood."

I felt the burning in my chest again, but my wounds were far away, somewhere behind me. Wavering at the edges of my perception.

There, near Ashton's feet. I could land. It'd be close, tight. A jagged piece of rusted rebar just to the left gleamed threateningly.

Ashton frowned. "You fool." He turned and ran, still dragging Gold.

I ran, my legs churning below me, my right knee popping with every curl. The edge of the Arcadia came up fast. My legs pushed me forward.

I leaped. Time slowed around me.

The walls of the Arcadia disappeared and I flew out into open air. I felt the wind catch me and lift me forward. The cement edge of the unfinished Level Nine rushed towards me. The jagged rebar reached out like desperate hands, coming ever closer. Too close.

I had miscalculated. Something in my head screamed.

Panic flooded me.

The edge closed in, I squeezed my eyes shut and readied myself.

My chest slammed into the cement. The air exploded from my lungs, and I gasped at the sky. I opened my eyes. The rebar was just to the side! I hadn't miscalculated! I had made it. I struggled to breathe as I wrapped my hand around the rebar and swung a leg up and over the edge, pulling myself onto Level Nine.

Ashton was more than a hundred yards away now, near the last towers on the southwestern edge of the city. He slowed and stopped, turning to glare at me. "Just go, leave me be!"

I struggled shakily to my feet. The air was returning to my lungs, but I was running out of energy. But I couldn't stop, not now.

This has to end, I thought. For Lovat, for the Territories, for the world. For me.

My legs began to move below me once again. First a walk, then a half-jog. Ashton wanted to flee, but I wouldn't let him. I had to stop him.

He was moving west, over the broken and incomplete form of Level Nine. We passed the last of the towers, their balconies lined with people, elevated citizens staring out, scared. To them we were just two humans in a mad city, one chasing the other.

The floor became more and more unfinished, but Ashton kept going. He was nearing the edge, I realized. I had pushed him to the edge. The jagged western side of the city that loomed out above the sea.

The last few blocks were a loose weaving of steel that jutted out past Level Eight and over the waters of the sound far below. A sign sat near an edge, proclaiming in Strutten: Come See The Level Nine Promenade! Opening Soon! A jaunty-looking couple in embroidered cowls walked along a wide boardwalk arm in arm, examining the glass fronts of high-end fashion boutiques.

A cold wind whipped around me, threatening to throw me off the structure. It brought me to my knees. I saw Ashton, standing on the edge, a shivering Janus Gold kneeling next to him. Ashton's hand was wrapped around his neck. The First sighed and slumped, sitting on a narrow bit of poured cement that ran along the edge, his back to a girder.

"So now you forced me here. To the edge of your city," he said, not turning to look at me. He wiped his mouth with the back of his hand and stared out over the water. I could hear the venom in his voice. "I am not your enemy."

"You sent your servants to kill me."

He considered this, then bowed his head in a gesture of acquiescence and smiled. "We all have parts to play."

"So, what then?" I said. I wanted to keep him talking. Keep his focus on something other than me. A warm blast of air from the south whipped around us. The sky cracked and rumbled with thunder. I looked for a way across to where he was sitting. The beams between us were a spider's web of steel.

"I suppose you wish to fight." He gave a sad chuckle but didn't turn. Gold writhed in his grip. His hands trying to pull the first's long fingers from his neck. "I hate this game. I've always hated this game. I wanted nothing to do with it."

"Yet..." I said, marking a way across the girders to the platform.

"Yet, here we are," Ashton agreed and looked west.

"You killed people," I said.

Ashton grinned. "There are always more."

He looked over his shoulder at me and grinned, his wide white teeth filling an even wider mouth. Beside him, Gold made a weak sound and Ashton gave the little dauger a shove. Gold slid across the narrow platform, coming to rest in the middle. He coughed and rubbed at his neck.

I eased out on an I-beam, crawling towards the future promenade, my hands tight along its edges. I drew closer and closer to Ashton. I didn't want to look down, but I failed. My heart froze as I saw how high up we were. Below me, the tide crashed against the pillars that embedded themselves into the submerged bedrock. Ships the size of caravans looked like small beetles crawling across the shifting water. The caps of the waves were white and pure, a contrast to the fading purple of the sea. The sun was disappearing behind the Rosalias. Around us, streetlights already installed in the unfinished streets began to clank on.

I stepped onto the platform. It was merely the bones, the initial structure that would support the future promenade.

It wasn't very wide and only about fifteen yards long. Ashton crouched along its northernmost edge, me along the southern. Gold lay on his back in the middle.

Ashton laughed and looked around. He spread his arms wide and spun on the end of the platform. "You know you're too late, Bell. It has begun! My grandfather's great works. We don't need to wait for servants to call us forth. I am here. The Founders stir. The High Priest himself comes."

As if on cue, another peel of thunder rumbled.

Gargoyles began to appear around us. They perched on the girders and beams like ravens, their robes fluttering in the ceaseless wind, their blank faces focused on the two of us. Ashton turned and regarded them with a smile. "We have an audience."

"I won't let you continue."

"I have only done what was asked," he gestured to Gold. "It was Adderley who guided me to your upper reaches. I didn't do it myself. I am as much a puppet as anyone." The sky split with thunder again, and Ashton looked up at the clouds. "Grandfather has a dramatic flair, doesn't he? Thunder, lightning, next we'll get rain."

I said nothing. I just slowly rose. Standing, facing this First. This ancient creature that could cause, would cause, so much destruction. Ashton looked at me for a long moment, then at the dauger, and then back at me again.

"What will you do? How will you—a human, *ninth* of creation—stop me? You can't kill me, Bell. Even if you were stronger, even if you were at your full strength you couldn't kill me. Begone."

He waved me away, but I didn't move.

"I've stopped your kind before. I will stop you." I said it with more confidence than I felt.

He *tsked* and then gave a chuckle. "You think you stopped them?"

I narrowed my eyes and regarded him. Lies?

Ashton rose shaking his head; he stood with his hands held out to his sides, fingers twitching. "You can't kill us, Bell. You can only delay. We always come back. That's the cruel trick our place in the universe affords us! We don't die, we are just delayed. Trapped for a time. I thought your kind would have figured it out by now."

Curwen. Cybill. I imagined them somewhere watching us. Hatred in their eyes. Was it true? Could they still be out there somewhere, waiting?

I kept my eyes trained on the First in front of me.

"I ask you one last time. Drop this. There doesn't need to be a fight between us," said Ashton.

"And if I let you go?"

He blinked at me. "Then I go."

In my mind's eye I could see what would happen if I chose to walk away. It was as clear to me as any memory. I saw Ashton in the form of the beast from the pit, tearing through Lovat. I saw Syringa burn, and the world engulfed in flames. It would be a new Aligning, and it would be nothing less than the destruction of the world and the deaths of millions.

The vision. The wasteland. The dead city. I had seen what happens when the Firsts were left unchecked.

"No," I said. I set my shoulders, I felt bones pop. Fear twisted my stomach into a knot. I shook my head. "No," I said again.

Ashton sighed. Behind him lightning flashed. I saw three creatures standing there: the man, the beast, and the titan surrounding the city and waiting to crash into this reality.

The buzzing in the back of my head hardened, it became a thrum, deep and resonating like beckoning war drums.

Ashton looked at me, the cocky smile faded, the soft eyes hardened. His expression grew sour. His smile became a scowl and his gaze was laced with hate. Those too-wide eyes narrowed and his hands curled into claws.

"That's a shame," he said. "You seemed like a smart man."

TWENTY-NINE

Ashton closed the distance between us in a single leap, driving his fist toward me like a battering ram.

I cringed and brought up an arm. I had seen him destroy an entire tower just making an entrance. I steeled myself for the pain, for the sound of my bones snapping.

But it didn't come.

The blow connected with my arm, it rang through me and shook me like a strike from any other person. Nothing broken. Still in one piece. I stumbled back as he swung again, and slapped away the third punch.

He screamed in anger and stepped back, looking down at his fists in confusion. The warm wind whipped around us, the warmest wind I had felt for quite some time. It smelled like the sea, heavy with the scent of salt and seaweed. It energized me, it pulled me forward into the fight. I could hear the gargoyles around us buzzing.

"No, no, no, no," Ashton said. "This didn't need to *happen*!"

I stepped into him, swinging my own fist. The punch went wild, clipping him on the side of the head. The second, a low punch to his midsection, caught him directly. He gasped and then grunted, shoving me back, and I stumbled as he doubled over.

I had hit him. I hurt him!

But how?

I stared at my own fists, dumbstruck. I felt no stronger. Hell, I was wounded and exhausted, yet... I had hurt Ashton. A First.

This shouldn't be happening. I had seen him destroy an entire tower. His shove should have sent me careening off the edge of the platform, but it felt like any old brawl.

Except the stakes were higher.

He came at me again, his fist connecting with my jaw before I could block it. It drove me to the side, and down to one knee. I tasted blood and spat it out.

Ashton kicked me in the side. I wheezed, felt the burning pain in the gash in my chest. I dropped to my shoulder and twisted, feeling more kicks crash against my back.

"Now I understand why my uncle wouldn't face you in this shell. I see why he waited."

I rolled onto my side to avoid another stomp then dragged myself backward across the rough cement to the edge of the platform. Ashton stalked towards me, arms at his sides. His hands were growing larger.

I pulled my feet under me and leapt forward. We crashed together, knocking our heads and dropping into a tangle of punches. I swung wildly, striking him in the stomach, the face, the neck. Gold scrambled out of the way to avoid being pressed over the edge.

Ashton grunted and yelped as my fists made contact. I breathed heavily and punched at his head, feeling my fists come away wet with his shimmering white blood.

He gritted his teeth and shoved me off him. I flew backward. My head slapped against the platform and stars crashed through my vision.

I blinked and rose shakily, stunned by the hit. I shook my head, trying to clear it. Ashton and Gold wavered before me. I could hear the sinister warble of laughter from the audience of gargoyles around us. A trickle of blood dribbled from my nose. I wiped it away with the back of my hand. I could feel bruises forming along my knuckles. We were back where we started, standing opposite one another on the narrow platform at the edge of the city.

"You're cornered," I said. "You can't get away."

Ashton sneered. He wiped his mouth with the heel of a thumb and looked at the milky white fluid that came away. He snorted an annoyed laugh and then glared at me.

He shook his head slowly.

I hurt all over.

Ashton looked down at Gold. The dauger seemed to flinch under his gaze. Where before he had been arrogant, now he cowered. Ashton snorted a laugh.

"You," he said to the dauger. "Get him. Kill Bell."

My vision was clearing. I saw Gold blink. The dauger looked to me and then back to the First.

"It's him or you."

The threat was clear. Gold turned and looked at me, his hands balling into fists.

Ashton egged him on. "Throw him from the platform! We can watch his body burst as it breaks."

Fighting both of these two would be problematic. I held out my hands and hoped I'd be able to convince the dauger otherwise. "Doesn't have to be like this, Janus! He's using you."

Gold regarded me. I could see the look in his eyes soften and seemed to ease.

"I said *kill him!*" Ashton's voice roared with intensity.

The shout sent a jolt of electricity through Gold. He stalked toward me.

Behind him Ashton flopped down to a sitting position and then began to collapse inward. It was like his skeleton had melted. In an instant, I realized what he was doing. Gold was the distraction. He was going to shift. Back into his true form.

"He's shif—" I began to shout.

Gold lunged at me. I ducked, and he dived again. I stepped to the side, sending him careening behind me. I turned as he was coming in for a third lunge. This time he was able to get his arms around my waist.

I was shocked at how strong he was. He lifted me for a moment and then wrestled me to the deck. His hands beat at my chest. I could see his wide eyes through the eyeholes of his mask. Those eyes, so filled with hate and terror. A portion of his mask had been bent and was collapsed on the left side, and blood seeped from the corner of his mouth. He looked wild. Insane.

"You don't have to do this," I said through gritted teeth. I brought up a knee and buried it in his gut. He groaned. I rolled away and rose back to my feet. My head was spinning.

"Yes," Gold wheezed. "I… do. You or me."

Again he lunged at me, tried to shove me towards the edge. I scrambled to keep myself planted. My boots scraped across the cement.

At the opposite edge, Ashton continued his transformation.

I had to stop this. I kneed Gold again, causing him to double over.

Fighting a dauger is a strange thing. Most blows are usually made to the body as their masks protect their faces. However, the backs of their heads are usually unprotected.

I grabbed him by the mask and shoved up and back, driving him backwards. Then I dropped down, slamming him to the ground and smacking his head down on the cement. It made a loud *thwap*. Gold groaned and then lay still. Red blood pooled around his head, staining the cement. He was out cold.

I rose. My shoulders hunched. My back arched. I turned to the creature, now half-changed. He had nearly doubled in size. His belly had become engorged and his face had widened, again resembling a giant anur. The human arms that dangled on either side had begun to elongate, the fingers stretching and turning into wicked claws. He shook and gazed down at me, watching me approach.

In his human form, Ashton had been able to drag Gold around, smash through buildings. Yet when he punched me it felt like he'd had the same strength as Gold? Being punched by Ashton should have felt like being hit by a runaway ox. What would it be like now?

"Stay away," Ashton warned, the cold voice rumbling from behind his thick rolling lips.

I came at him, fists bared. He swiped a half-formed claw at me, raking my coat and causing me to step back, nearly stumbling over the unconscious Gold.

"This is Black's doing. His failure. You shouldn't be alive."

He came towards me, again trying to slash me with his claws. I leapt out of the way, careful not to throw myself over the edge. There wasn't much platform left, and it moaned under our combined weight.

Ashton shook his head, and his human ears became the strange appendages that reminded me of a bat's wings. As his chest expanded the clothes were torn free, ragged cloth hanging about him like tattered flags on the lines of a ship.

His weight was too much too soon. The platform lurched to one side. I slipped, tumbling to the ground, my hands scrambling for a grip.

Gold slid to the edge, but remained motionless. The platform hadn't twisted enough to throw him off—not yet at least. Ashton readjusted his flesh and then pulled himself toward me. His skin rasped as it was dragged against the platform. A deep growl belched from his wide mouth. "To think, I—of all Founders— will do what my aunt and uncle could not."

He threw himself toward me in a leap that looked more like a controlled lurch. His body was now as wide as a cargowain, and I rolled to my belly and let the creature roll over me.

I felt his heavy body drag across my own, pressing down on me. Pushing my breath out of my chest. My ribs moaned under the crushing weight. My face pressed against the rough cement. Then there was the scent of the sea as the warm breeze hit me again and I was out. Behind him.

The platform shook as he came to a stop. Now in the middle of the platform, he turned and lunged again. His proud expression had turned to frustration.

I couldn't react in time. He caught me and drove me back. His claws dug into my flesh. He hooked me in the meat of my thigh and pierced the upper portion of my left arm. I kicked with my free leg, striking an eye, his mouth.

Ashton spun to face southwest again, carrying me with him and slamming me against the platform. The cement scraped the skin from my neck and chin. He released me and loomed above.

I had to get away. Ashton watched me crawl backward until I stopped near Gold's unconscious form.

The creature let out a deep chuckle and settled, returning to his shifting.

"Would that I had the speed of Curwen. I would have shed my weakened fettle in moments and destroyed you."

I took a painful breath, tried to clear my head. I pulled a knee beneath me. Something inside had settled. I was out of time. He was growing, changing, each moment getting stronger. Our fight was evenly matched when he was in his human form, but he was quickly outpacing me. If I acted now I might have an advantage. Maybe I could... yes. It had to be now.

My whole body hurt, but I pushed myself upward.

The First's eyes were narrow and slowly shifting. Seeing him change, seeing portions of him grow and stretch was incomprehensible. It was like watching clay being shaped, but there was no potter to do the shaping.

The dark skin that had held him together in his human form tore apart with a wet ripping sound, revealing a dusky gray flesh beneath that spouted spurts of hair. He was on the edge, his back just above open air. If I could hit him just right…

Behind me, Gold stirred.

Ashton chuckled.

The dauger rose, and I spared a glance to see him stare in horror at Ashton and then settle his gaze on me. He rocked where he stood, head quivering, but his gaze never left mine. There was anger in his eyes.

"This is your fault," he spat. "If you hadn't gotten involved… Kiver would be dead! Everything would be as it should be!"

"Don't you get it?" I shouted. "Adderley *freed* him. You're the reason he's here. If you hadn't called him—"

Gold rushed forward. I knew what he planned. Saw it telegraphed in his run, in the way he held his shoulders, his arms. It was the same plan as my own, just with a different target.

I knew what needed to happen.

The dauger careened toward me. I leaned towards the city, pushing myself out from the platform and towards the floor of Level Nine. Gold hadn't expected that, he tried to correct but stumbled past me. As he went by I threw myself into his back, pushing him forward, using our combined momentum to send him careening into Ashton's chest.

"Wha—" the big creature said as we slammed into him. The two connected with a thump, and Ashton, still shifting, began to slip backwards, hanging out into the open air. The platform gave a long groan and then began to tip. Ashton's claws scrambled for balance, scraping steel and digging into concrete.

"Get off me! Get off!" Ashton yelled. Gold scrambled and made a wet crying sound as he tried to untangle himself from the folds of flesh. His motion had the opposite effect, and the two slid back even farther.

I had to finish it.

I ran forward, allowing the tilt of the platform to aid my speed. Ashton and Gold both saw me coming. Two sets of eyes widened and two mouths cried out as they realized what I had planned. Gold tried to turn, but too late.

I gave them a good, solid kick, and we fell.

THIRTY

Steel squealed with a horrific moan, and the platform broke free below my feet. For a moment I was weightless. As the floor dropped away I half-leapt and half-fell towards a girder that had extended out just beyond the platform, scrambling to keep myself from joining Ashton and Gold on their fall.

Rebar tore at my arms and pierced the sleeve of my coat. Thankfully missing flesh. The girder slammed into my chest, the momentum whipping my head forward. The pain burst through me. I scrambled, feeling my stomach drop.

In a flash I could see my parents, I smelled the scent of tobacco and plum bread. I saw my mother returning home from a day at council, my father bending wood in his shop. I could see trails that I had walked, roaders I had known. I saw that dark tunnel below the city where I had faced Cybill, my first First. The crowded streets of Syringa and the torched remains of Methow. I saw Curwen burn. I saw Wensem laughing as he bounced his son on his knee and Hannah on the trail, hat pulled low, her sharp eyes scanning the horizon. I saw Hagen in his shop curiously inspecting a new arrival. I saw Samantha standing in a shattered window. Her eyes locked with mine. Samantha. Intelligent, fierce, tough-as-nails, beautiful Samantha. She had been next to me this whole time. She had fought at my side. I saw her curls blowing around her face. Saw her dark flashing eyes. The way she set her jaw.

My fingers wrapped around the edge of steel. I clung tight.

Ashton's claw struck out, moving to grab me, trying desperately to pull me down. It met only air, and his face twisted at the realization. His ugly eyes narrowed, and his fleshy mouth opened, the wide features becoming a strange mix of horror and sheer hatred.

"No!" he bellowed as he tumbled backwards, his arms grasping at the air.

Then...

A part of him detached.

The human form seemed to pull from the monster's chest. It leapt from the falling mass of flesh and landed atop a girder above me. He grinned down at me. He was naked now, as he had been in the pit, but it was him. Ashton in his human form. I must have looked puzzled, because he laughed, turning and walking along the length of the girder and onto Level Nine's expansive structure.

I looked back down, not quite believing my eyes. He still fell. Below, the monstrous body tumbled through the air. I watched his arms careening around, the mouth open in a roar. His eyes wide and horrified. Gold had broken free of the creature but fell near him, his screams mixed with that of the First's. But was it the First? I looked back toward Level Nine. The human avatar of Ashton stood, watching me. I blinked. He was still there.

I struggled and pulled myself onto the girder. Dragged myself away from the destruction and towards safety.

I heard a *thwack* and glanced down to see the beast strike the outstretched arm of a crane that extended from Level Five. Across from me the human Ashton groaned and gripped his shoulder. Below, the metal of the crane bent and twisted, the extended cables whipping violently. The crane's arm broke and fell with them, tumbling end over end.

The remnants of the ancient city upon which Lovat had been built rested below the water. Jagged and twisted forms stabbed up below the surface. It threatened any who fell or attempted to dive into the brine. Even boats wouldn't come too close to the city's western edge for fear of tearing open their hulls.

Ashton would be torn apart. Wouldn't he?

I struggled to my feet and moved to face the human form of Ashton. My breathing was heavy. My knee ached. My shirt was soaked with blood. Exhaustion had crept into my legs, my arms. My back hurt. As I straightened it let out a series of pops and the world around me shifted.

I was no longer standing on the edge of Level Nine. I was back in the wasteland, standing among the ruins. Yellow demonic faces peered out from behind the fallen monuments. The same damned vision as before, only this time I wasn't alone. The human Ashton, now clothed in white robes stood across from me. He was bent slightly, and he looked older and he looked broken. One of his eyes was swollen shut and his skin was bruised. Blood trickled from the corner of his mouth. There were scrapes and gashes across his neck and face. He held one of his arms against his stomach. It was twisted strangely along the forearm.

Where we stood was different as well. It was still the wasteland—the flat tableland that extended away in all directions—but this time the city in the distance was much closer. The scent of death that drifted from its ruined levels and shattered towers was heavier. I could see tendrils of smoke the color of sun-bleached bone rise from its lower levels. Around its base I could see the pearly crash of waves as the sea ate at its foundations. And, as always, the monstrosity still moved in the distance. The immense thing, both horrific and indescribable, it moved somewhere beyond the sky.

Ashton followed my gaze and looked over his shoulder at the city.

"Your Lovat."

"No," I said. "Not *my* Lovat. We're still standing in my Lovat." That duality hadn't left me. We might be speaking in the wasteland but we were still on Level Nine. I felt both the hard-packed dirt beneath my feet and the cold cement of the city. The warm dry wind of the desert and the sea-scented wind of the city. I could still hear the noise from the massive crowd, it blended with the howl of the wind across the empty hardpan.

Ashton laughed, but it was weak. Almost sad. It ended in a hacking cough. He looked around. "Are we?"

I looked down. The broken sun of the wasteland cast my shadow before me in two different directions. It was a strange and dizzying realization. Then I realized that there were more shadows cast on the ground.

I looked up, but saw nothing of the creatures that cast these shadows.

Ashton was flanked by four shadows, two on either side. The strange and terrible shadows of two twisted creatures were on his left. The shape on his immediate right was less shadow and more a blackened scorch, like something hot had burned into the earth. A pair of coyotes sat next to it, panting in the sun, looking confused and lost. Past the scorch mark was the fourth and final shadow, the image of a tall man draped in fabric. The shadow of cloth drifted softly in the wind, mimicking Ashton's own garb.

"You've already met mother," said Ashton, gesturing to the shadow closest to him. "You killed her avatar or else she'd be with us here. Her shadow lingers."

I blinked at him, struggling to remember. Cybill? I had watched her get crushed but I had never seen her human form. Had I?

"You know," Ashton continued. "I went to find her. See if I could raise her. I found the collapse. Regretfully, I chose a poor form for aquatic work and Gold's commands always had time limits." He sneered at the dauger's name and walked from Cybill's shadow towards the scorch mark. "And you saw to my uncle as well." One of the coyotes whined.

"How are you doing this?" I said.

"Doing what? Standing here? *You* brought me here, Guardian. Trust me, I'm not exactly enjoying this." He winced, then coughed for punctuation.

"I watched you fall."

"You watched my body fall, but we are much more than that. You should know by now… we can't die. We can only be delayed."

"But I killed you!" I shouted. Around us the wind whipped.

"Yes," agreed Ashton. "Yes, you did. For now…"

Ashton sighed and wiped the blood from his mouth with his good arm. He scowled at his stained fingers.

"I have done my duty. I have said my piece. Let me wander, now, Guardian. I am merely the Herald."

"The Herald for what?"

"You have a lot to learn, Guardian. Your predecessor was much sharper than you. She had known far more, far earlier." Ashton clicked his tongue, turned and hobbled to the nameless shadow on his left. It moved, writhing against the ground like a black puddle stirred by the wind. He gestured to it. "He… is coming. Can't you smell it on the wind?"

I inhaled, but only the scent of death from the city filled my nostrils. The smells from the other world, the other Lovat, were overpowered or blocked.

"And the other one?" I nodded towards the last shadow, the tall man draped in robes.

Ashton looked towards the shadow on the far side of the scorched space.

"A pretender. He is not of our bloodline, though his ambition… is great." He hacked another cough.

I was growing tired of these non-answers. I had fought Ashton on the top of the city. Battled my way through a city on fire. Faced Gold and his cronies in that damned pit. I had even killed a would-be assassin. I was exhausted. I was tired. I couldn't deal with this. Not anymore. My patience was worn out.

"Enough games, Ashton! Enough riddles!" I reached for my gun and felt it in the other Lovat, but not here in the wasteland.

Ashton shook his head and tried to laugh but winced instead. I could see spots of blood beginning to stain the white robes around his chest and belly. "Your weapon is useless here, as are your questions. You want to know about the failed usurper? Ask the dauger. They know far more than they let on." He shook his head and then grimaced. "My job here is done. You've seen to that. But I haven't failed. I have heralded, I have foretold, blah, blah, blah. Now... I am tired."

"And him?" I motioned with my chin to the thing on the horizon.

Ashton looked over his shoulder. "He's the reason for all of this. You see but a shadow, Guardian. But you'll see him soon enough."

"Who is that?"

"He is the first of Firsts." He paused, looked at me. His eyes cold. His expression serious. "My grandfather."

The thing on the horizon writhed and the sky wavered before it. Then it moaned. It was a low sound, organic and wet. It shook the floor of the wasteland. It trumpeted through the sky. I felt it in both worlds, in Lovat and in the wasteland. It was louder, more destructive than Curwen's moans on the Broken Road. The bones of the ruined Lovat swayed.

The first of Firsts. That was what I was hearing. That was the thing that stretched the sky. A shiver traveled along my spine, and I felt my mouth go dry in both realities.

"Enough prattle. Look west, Guardian. The High Priest comes and on his heels… a new Aligning."

He stared at me with his unswollen eye. Where before he had been young, over the course of this conversation he had changed. He had grown old and frail. He was no longer the hearty human man I had seen in the Shangdi. He wasn't the creature that had carried Gold through the upper reaches of the city. He was an old man. An old frail man.

"This isn't over," I said.

"For me, it is. I might be around for a few years still, but…" He waved a hand behind me. When I turned I saw the edge of the city, not the wasteland. The platform was gone, the girder I had climbed upon still twisted. Thick clouds were forming against the gunmetal sky. When I turned back, we were back in the wasteland among the ruins. "I am out of the game," he said. "My part has been played. I'm trapped in your forsaken city, in this form…"

He coughed, spat blood and frowned.

"So I'll be seeing you again?" I narrowed my eyes.

Ashton smiled a pained smile. "Perhaps. Perhaps not."

Two gargoyles materialized beside him, wrapped their arms around his. He leaned into them, a wounded old general being aided by his soldiers at the end of a battle.

I couldn't let him get away.

"No!" I stepped forward, reached out to grab him. I had to stop him.

Ashton smiled weakly.

Then I woke up.

THIRTY-ONE

A cold rain brought me back to consciousness. I lay on my back staring up at black clouds blowing above me. The memories of my discussion with Ashton had already begun to fade as I struggled to comprehend where I was, how I got here, and what I was doing.

"H–hello?" I called out, shocked at how weak my voice sounded.

No one answered.

I half-expected to hear a gargoyle titter or to see a long narrow hood appear, to feel its fist punch through my body like it was soft butter.

But I was alone.

I struggled to rise, pushing myself up from the floor of Level Nine. I stood shakily.

Rain fell around me, drenching me, soaking my shredded winter coat and my long hair and beard. It dripped off me and pooled around my feet. It had warmed somewhat, but the rain made me shiver.

This wasn't a win and I knew it. But it didn't seem to be a clear loss, either. For now Ashton was defeated. But was he out of the picture forever? What had he said? "You should know by now… we can't die. We can only be delayed."

No, it didn't feel like a win. A stalemate… maybe.

I looked around. I saw nothing. Rain-soaked towers and the half-finished foundations of a new level. I was utterly alone.

The distant shouts and cries still floated on the wind from the direction of Paramount Square. An orange glow from the north-east told me the Breakers still fought for control of the city. I hoped they'd win. Lovat needed a civic rebirth. The core had rotted through. A change would do this city good.

I turned and looked westward. Ashton had said look west, and I looked. I saw only the vast stretch of darkening ocean, the water reflecting the Rosalia Mountains and nothing more.

I took a deep breath. I closed my eyes and breathed. Finally, I moved, each step a cascade of pain. Each footfall sending vibrations up my core. I felt each puncture, each gash, and each bruise as I walked. I kept at it, plodding south. Level Nine had lifts—two, actually—one to the north and another in the south. They were gleaming and expensive things, express lifts, inlaid with precious metals and festooned with cushioned seats. Guided by haughty conductors with sharp tailored suits and pencil-thin mustaches.

I pushed the call button and forced the lira into the conductor's hand and ignored her worried glances as the doors slid upward. I was alone in the lift. Warm air from its heaters blew upon me, warming my damp skin and waking me up slightly.

K. M. ALEXANDER

"Where to?" the conductor asked with a sneer. She was human, dark skinned, with pale blue eyes—a rarity among our kind. She looked down her sharp nose at me, her thin lips drawn and bloodless.

"Level Four," I said, and then added a laugh that turned into a cough.

The conductor rolled her eyes and turned her back to me, clearly disgusted by the ruffian who stumbled into her exclusive Level Nine lift.

I slumped into a padded chair and felt my spine pop. I rolled my shoulders and grimaced, realizing the pain I'd be facing over the next few days. I leaned my head forward and watched the blood drip onto the floor of the lift as the conductor punched the button and the lift descended, dropping towards Level Four and into the heart of King Station.

"This is becoming rote," I said to myself.

I looked down, took in my wounds. My jeans were stained with blood above the right knee. My left side felt tender and my left arm was numb with pain. I had been cut, scraped, bashed, stabbed, sliced, and skewered, and yet here I was, still marching on.

I leaned back, staring up at the mirrored ceiling and closed my eyes. The final verse of Pops' old song sprung back to mind:

...I want six boneshooters to be pallbearers.
And a chorus girl to sing a song.
Stick a big jazz band on my hearsewain.
Raise hell as I stroll along.

I sighed. Not today.

THIRTY-TWO

The interior of Cedric's was cozy. The clatter of forks and knives, mixed with the soft murmur of conversation, created a cheery din. Delicious scents wafted from the kitchen, making my stomach growl and my mouth water. I sat down gently next to Hagen and across from Wensem, trying not to wince despite the bright flash of pain from my leg. I was sure Hagen had noticed.

It had been a couple of weeks since all the business with Ashton and the riots. The wounds were healing, but dropping into a wooden booth wasn't exactly comfortable yet.

"See this?" asked Wensem, sliding a copy of the *Lovat Ledger* across the table and tapping the front page. In black letters the headline read: CZANEK OUT. ELECTIONS IN. It had been a long time coming, and with the riot, I was surprised it took this long to finally get him out.

I looked up at Wensem's scowl. My partner's long face looked particularly long today. The lines around his mouth drooped and the bags beneath his gray-blue eyes seemed heavier this morning. Kitasha, his wife, had told me he had slept only fitfully since returning from the blockade, and that he spent most nights tossing and turning. It showed.

"You should be happy," I said.

"I didn't want to lead a revolt," he said. "I just wanted to get this city fed."

"Well, you did. Your brothers and sisters here used your momentum to overthrow the mayor and recall the constabulary. In less than a week trade's opened along the Big Ninety. Everything's different. But most importantly, I get to eat eggs and drink vermouth again."

I gave him a wide smile.

"It's true," said Hagen. "Hannah and I went to Luther Island yesterday. The place is crawling with new folk, supplies. The trade is so thick they're having a difficult time managing the logistics of it all. Never seen so many roaders in one place, not to mention the couriers and rickshaws."

"The caravans were running the short routes in the eastern Territories," said Wensem. "You could tell it was frustrating them. The people out there appreciate caravans but you can only run between Hellgate and Syringa for so long. Lovat runs make up for more than half of most companies' profits. I'm sure when they heard the news they all turned westward."

I nodded and skimmed the story in the paper. The mayor was locked away somewhere in a holding cell in Lovat Central, along with the Chief of Police, the Chief of the Fire Brigade, and two city council members. Elections were planned to take place in a few months, and in the meantime the city was being run by a temporary council. I passed the paper back to my partner.

"You know, I'm surprised they're not begging the Hero of Destiny to run for mayor." I grinned at him, knowing he hated the nickname.

"They did," he said with an annoyed grunt. "I turned them down."

"What?" Hagen laughed. He leaned forward, his eyes wide behind his glasses. "They wanted you to run for mayor and you turned them down?"

"I'm a roader, not a politician," said Wensem. "I hate politics."

"But imagine the changes you could put through! The cabinet you could create! I, for one, would make an excellent Senior City Historian." Hagen leaned back, eyeing the maero from below his brow as he took a noisy slurp from his coffee.

"You're going to have a hard time shaking free of the people," I said. "I mean, you led the final battle against Conrad O'Conner. You helped drive the Purity Movement from the blockade and you led the first wainloads of food into this city. You're a damned hero."

"I didn't do shit," said Wensem sourly. "I just kicked when things needed kicking."

Wensem hadn't been forthright in talking about the fighting at the blockade. All we knew was what we had pieced together from other people's stories and it was tough to believe everything they said. One thing was for certain: it had been bloody. A lot of Blockade Breakers and Purity Movement members had been killed. Some had taken to calling it the Crimson Blockade, and the road south out of Lovat the Crimson Road in honor of those who had fallen.

"The Purity Movement hates you," said Hagen. "It was in the papers, O'Conner was quick to distance himself from those at the blockade. But he's calling for your banishment from the city." Hagen dropped his voice into his best impression of the Purity Movement leader. "No human should ever be assaulted by species born of the loins of Cain—especially the maero. Wensem dal Ibble is not only an affront to the sovereignty of the self but also an affront to God's blessed creation!"

Wensem chuckled at Hagen's impersonation. "That's pretty good."

"O'Conner's saying he's going to run for mayor. Says he has a mandate and he'll easily win."

Wensem chuckled and shook his head.

"A mandate? Not damn likely," I said. "They lost any influence they had with the human population after the blockade. All of Lovat suffered—humans included." I looked across the table at Wensem. "You ever going to tell us what happened down there? It's a pretty rare day when a specific maero's name is dropped in an O'Conner sermon."

"Hero of Destiny!" said Hagen, raising his fork into the air.

"Nice ring to it," I said with a smirk.

Wensem huffed. "Not much to tell. People died. The blockade broke."

"You don't get called a hero if that's all!" said Hagen.

Wensem scoffed. "I'm no hero. Wal's the real hero, facing down another First. Are *you* ever going to tell us what happened up there?"

He parroted my tone. He looked at me across the table and blinked his blue-gray eyes expectantly.

I hadn't been the most forthcoming either. No one had seen the fight on Level Nine, and I wasn't sure how to recount what I really saw. The wasteland. The conversation with Ashton. The fall. It wasn't something I could even easily piece together inside my own head.

Wensem broke the silence. "I'm sorry I wasn't here," he said.

I blinked and refocused on him. The memories of Ashton faded as the sounds of Cedric's eased me back into reality.

"Don't be ridiculous," I said.

A waitress appeared. Essie's replacement was a short dauger with a tin mask that seemed to have a friendly appearance. She wore a similar uniform to Essie's, and was good at her job, but she didn't have quite the same aplomb. I had asked Cedric about Essie, hoping he'd be able to shed light on her disappearance. But he too said there wasn't much to tell. She apologized to him for bailing, told him she was leaving Lovat for good. That she had been here too long. She asked for him to forward her last paycheck to her cousin in Destiny.

"Honestly," Cedric had said, "the place was closed when she broke the news so I didn't realize what a blow it'd be. I sure as hell could have used her when we reopened after the deliveries started coming again. It was a madhouse."

I asked if he thought she was okay, and he had shrugged. It was always an interesting gesture on a cephel, with their eight appendages.

"I hope so," was all he said.

I hoped she had found the simple, quiet life she wanted.

"What'll ya have?" The dauger waitress now asked, setting

down a hot cup of coffee in front me. "Breakfast is all day. We finally got eggs this morning, but we're out of gravy. Only thing still not on the menu is any chicken dish. We do have bacon. Oh, and a nice roasted side pork."

We ordered and the waitress wandered off to tell Cedric. As she did, the bell above the door rang and in walked Hannah. She was wearing a new brown leather jacket and had her hair tied in a bun. A brown leather glove was pulled over her wooden hand. Instead of sliding next to Wensem she pulled a loose chair from a table and sat on it backwards at the end of our booth.

"You need anything, hun?" shouted the waitress from behind the counter.

"Coffee. Black," Hannah said. She turned to me and asked, "How're you holding up?"

"Getting better," I said. "Get my message?"

Hannah grinned and nodded. "I put the word out. Sent a message to Taft, as well. As lovely as this place has gotten lately, it's about damn time we get back on the road. I'm getting bored sitting around."

"A roader's got to eat," I agreed.

"Wal, are you sure?" said Hagen. "You're still banged up. If you want, you're welcome to crash at Saint Olm until you're fully recovered," said Hagen.

I grinned at him. "You sound like your sister."

He chuckled. "Okay, maybe a little. But the offer stands."

"The only place for a roader is the road," said Wensem with a smile.

"I hear that," said Hannah and the two of them pounded on the table.

I had only seen Samantha once since the Shangdi. Apparently she and Bouchard had tried to get out onto Level Nine but a fire had broken out. By the time they got out there and followed our trail I was on my way back to Hagen's. They had seen the streaks of blood on the platform and nothing else. They'd thought I had gone over.

It wasn't until later that she found me. She had burst into the small bonesaw office, wet and exhausted. Water dripped off her horns, and her skin reflected the dull lights. Her clothes were soaked and clung to her. She was shivering.

The concern drained out of her as she saw me, an IV of maero blood being pumped into my arm. The bonesaw, a maero, had smiled at her and disappeared, leaving us alone. Our full conversation escapes me but I had made some joke about her being soaked and cold on my account. She had rebutted with something snarky. I told her what had happened. Everything from Ashton's escape to the fall. When I had finished we looked into the empty air for a long time, sitting in silence. Eventually Samantha smiled, met my eyes for the briefest of instants and then looked away.

"I'm glad you're okay," she had said.

"Me too," I said.

"Wal... I—" she had begun, then stopped herself.

I didn't press. I didn't force the conversation. After a moment I thanked her for her friendship and her help. I told her I couldn't have done it without her. I squeezed her hand and we sat in silence for a while until she excused herself and I watched her walk out of the office. I hadn't seen her since.

"Elephant's looking for you," said Hannah, jarring me from my thoughts. "One of her goons came to talk to me. He seemed nice enough."

"Why you?" I asked.

Hannah gave a little smile. "How should I know? Maybe the Outfit thinks we all operate like they do."

"Possible," said Wensem from behind his coffee. "We tend to think everyone thinks like a roader."

"She give a deadline?" I asked.

"No deadline," said Hannah.

"I don't trust her," said Hagen. "She's been playing a lot of angles."

"Everyone plays an angle," I said.

Hagen *hrumphed* and swallowed some coffee.

"I'm with Hagen," said Hannah. "I don't trust her either. Owing anyone in the Outfit is never a good idea. She'll eventually come to collect."

"She never officially said she was with the Outfit," I pointed out.

"It's been damn well implied," said Hagen.

"Well, if she is, let's hope all she ever needs is a caravan master."

The food arrived. Hagen had the side pork and a pile of fried rice. Wensem a dry piece of toast and plain oatmeal. I couldn't resist Cedric's all-day breakfast and had ordered an omelet as big as my head stuffed with cheese, mushrooms, thick bacon, and spicy peppers. We all began to eat.

We parted ways after our meal, each moving to our corner of the city.

I walked through Lovat, quietly admiring the city that loomed around me, the scent of smoke and cinders still lingering on the air. The sodium lamps burned golden in the roof above. The hum of neon lit the street in flashing greens, blues, whites, reds, and gaudy yellows. Scorched areas could still be seen pockmarking the streets. The vestiges of Auseil decorations littered gutters and alleys.

Unlike the days before, people didn't rush from building to building. Crowds once again filled Lovat's streets. Most carried umbrellas to protect from the downspouts that poured from above. It was cold and damp, not freezing. A true Lovatine winter.

A few hawkers once again braved the corners to sling their goods. Their voices raised over each other, always competing for the attention of customers while buskers played instruments, creating a cacophony of jazz that echoed through the cement canyons.

Scents of grilled and fried foods wavered from pull-trucks and food carts and filled the city streets with a heady aroma. Even as full as I was the smells made my stomach rumble.

I yawned and allowed myself to wander. Like Wensem, my own sleep had been disturbed. I slept fitfully, often waking in a cold sweat. I still saw Ashton, wearing his human skin, being carried away by gargoyles. I wondered if he was still in Lovat. Old, broken, trapped in his human skin. I wondered what a First would do to pass the time.

Gold's body had been recovered. The fall had shattered the

dauger, and apparently it was only the gold mask that allowed authorities to identify him. The papers reported that Kiver was cremated and the ashes scattered in the waters between the city and the Rosalia Mountains. Kiver was well loved. Thousands of Lovatines and employees of Renna Monochromes had come to show their respects at his funeral. I felt bad for his kids.

The papers hadn't mentioned Argentum at all.

I turned a corner, walking past a vendor selling beetles and a dimanian slinging socks, and made my way to the edge of the city, passing beneath a flickering sign that would soon burn out completely. I recognized the spot. I had been here before. This was where Essie had found me, still stunned from my first encounter with Argentum, alone and freezing on the edge of the city. I sat on the same bench and looked out, remembering the cigarette Essie had shared with me and the lights of the boats we had seen in the water far below. A light rain spattered my face, and I breathed deep lungfuls of air as I looked across the archipelago and towards the Rosalias.

We exist in light, we souls of the earth. We can only go on because we don't know what hammers at our door. The darkness that wants to leak in. The insanity that lurks at the edges of perception. But they wait—the Firsts, the elder gods of shadow and terror, the creatures of madness who lurk like ravenous beasts just outside our reality, eager to paw their way inside. Only a certain few are selected to take upon themselves the burden of this knowledge. It is our lot to shoulder through. We may be broken and bent but we must remain steadfast and true. We must stand guard against the darkness. We are the ones chosen, and we must protect this reality no matter how much of our blood spills.

The sun still hung above the horizon, a fading golden disk partially obscured behind a line of broken clouds. Soon it would dip behind the peaks and paint the sky with brilliant purples, bright golden hues, and festive reds. The glass towers above me will reflect the light and glow like beacons visible for miles and miles. Behind those glowing transparent skins the elevated will continue to go about their business. Oblivious of the events that transpired outside their windows.

And still, somewhere beneath us all, below Lovat's red-lit upper reaches, below the lower levels, below even the Sunk, the heartless machinery that powers the fate of the world cranks onward. More pieces are moved into place. More Firsts are waking. When the time comes, I will face those horrors as I faced the creatures before them. But for now I didn't care. I was safe. I was full. And for that moment, it was all my tired soul needed.

ACKNOWLEDGEMENTS

First, I want to thank Kari-Lise, my wife and partner in this crazy life. I cannot think of anyone who has had a bigger impact on my writing. Wal's world would be a much different place without your excitement, encouragement, and boundless understanding.

Thank you to my editor, Lola Landekic. Editing my manuscripts isn't easy. I'm a crazy sloppy writer who needs constant prodding to get this stuff right. Thank you for your patience and guidance in helping make Red Litten World the story it is today. This wouldn't be the same without you.

Again, I extend another huge thanks to Jon Contino, who lent his considerable talents for the lettering that graces the cover. It's the first thing readers see, and it's the perfect connection to Wal's world and had helped set the tone for this series.

Thanks to Steve Leroux and Sarah Steininger Leroux for your encouragement, support, and feedback. It means a lot. Thanks to Steve Toutonghi for your friendship, advice, and for standing with me in all of this. Thanks to Josh Montreuil for spending the time waxing poetic about stories and worlds and monsters. Thanks to Christine Mancuso and Brian Jaramillo for letting me bounce ideas off of them at all hours.

Huge thanks to my crew of beta-roaders who offer insight and impressions as I work through those first—and very rough—drafts: Ben Vanik, J. Rushing, Kelcey Rushing, and Sky Bintliff. You're all amazing. It takes a special kind of talent to suffer through those early manuscripts. I can't thank you enough.

And of course, the biggest thanks goes out to you, my readers. Your excitement and passion for the world of Waldo Bell has continued to push me. This book exists because of you. Thank you for writing your reviews, tweeting your tweets, blogging your blog posts, sending the emails, and drawing the fan art. I hope this book lives up to your expectations. I cannot wait to share more with you.

Finally, of course, B3S. *Magna voce ridere æterna.* Let's keep making the world a better place.

K. M. ALEXANDER is a Pacific Northwest native and novelist living and working in Seattle, Washington with his wife and two dogs. *Red Litten World* is the third book in his urban fantasy series, *The Bell Forging Cycle*. You can follow his exploits at BLOG.KMALEXANDER.COM.

ALSO BY K. M. ALEXANDER

THE BELL FORGING CYCLE, BOOK I
The Stars Were Right
THESTARSWERERIGHT.COM

THE BELL FORGING CYCLE, BOOK II
Old Broken Road
OLDBROKENROAD.COM

The Guardian will return in:

THE BELL FORGING CYCLE, BOOK IV

Gleam Upon The Waves

GLEAMUPONTHEWAVES.COM

The gift of a quality Education

Each year, thanks to generous donations from our members, thousands of underprivileged Lovatine children receive a premium Camalote education at one of our academies all for free with no cost to you, the taxpayer. It's just one small way we endeavor to make Lovat's future a little brighter.

THE CAMALOTE GROUP

Empowering people. Changing lives.

CPSIA information can be obtained
at www.ICGtesting.com
Printed in the USA
LVHW091614011019
632855LV00002B/473/P

9 780989 602266